THE ⅃ ⌐∪⌐

DAVID KAZZIE

GRUB CLUB PUBLISHING

ISBN-10: 1-7331341-8-2

ISBN-13: 978-1-7331341-8-7

✤ Created with Vellum

For my kids

ACKNOWLEDGMENTS

To Scott Weinstein, who was the book's first reader and who made me think that I might have something really good here.

To Dave Buckley, whose comments about the manuscript and insights into life at a big law firm proved invaluable.

To James Mosrie, Matt and Kathy Phillips, Eric and Ericka Snyder, and Wes Walker - your comments on early drafts of the manuscript helped me make this book the best it could be.

And thanks to the Richmond metropolitan area, which kept quiet as I manipulated its geography and landmarks to better serve my story.

1

W hen Julius Wheeler stopped by his cousin Leroy's in time for the late local news, he was worth approximately seventy-five dollars. His assets included eight compact discs, a green plastic picnic table, a broken iPod, and a mattress of questionable repute. He paid two hundred dollars a month for a small apartment in Carrolton Oaks, a crumbling housing project just inside the eastern border of Richmond, Virginia. Twenty hours a week, he cleaned a large downtown law firm as a member of a CleanSweep work crew. He made eight dollars an hour.

"Hey, Julius, you buy a lotto?" Leroy asked.

"Yeah," Julius said, cracking open a beer and taking a seat in the center of the threadbare couch in Leroy's living room. The couch sagged in the middle and was peppered with cigarette burns.

"How many?"

"One."

"Ain't gonna win shit buying one," Leroy said, fanning out his tickets for Julius to see. "I got eight. Gonna make me rich. What numbers you play?"

"Just had the machine pick'em. Like it make a difference. Nobody ever win these things."

"Bullshit," Leroy said. "You think like that, you be stuck in that shitty apartment the rest of your life, and I be living on the beach. You come visit anytime."

"Shouldn't even be playing," Julius said, thinking about his shitty apartment and how much he preferred it to his eight-by-eight cinderblock cell at Red Onion State Prison, where he had once spent three long years. "I ain't working that shitty job so I can piss it away on the lotto. You sure as shit shouldn't be buying eight."

"Shut up, shut up," Leroy said, his attention drawn back to the screen. "They starting. This my night. I can feel it."

Julius shook his head and took a pull from the bottle. There was no arguing with Leroy, his twenty-two-year-old pseudo-cousin and alleged man of the house. Although it was just days before Christmas, no tree adorned this apartment, which was redolent with the aroma of fast-food grease and stale cigarette smoke. Leroy elected not to celebrate the birth of Christ, believing Christmas was a racist holiday, favoring rich white people and making black people poorer. Julius once tried to convince him it was for the kids, but Leroy wouldn't hear it. Racist, he said. Julius suspected that was a convenient cover for Leroy's perpetual poverty and his general inability or unwillingness to provide for his family. Leroy, who last attended school at the age of thirteen, had never held a legal job. He fancied himself a player in the Tree's crack trade, but he smoked far more than he sold. For the most part, he sponged off his girlfriend Rhonda and her part-time gig at Burger King.

From an unseen bedroom, a baby started to wail. As the crying ramped up in intensity, Leroy turned up the volume on the television.

"Jesus, Rhonda!" barked Leroy. "Can't you shut that baby up? I can't hear."

"She your baby, too," Rhonda replied.

"She need a bottle," Leroy said. "Go feed her."

The coffee table was covered with fast-food wrappers, overflowing ashtrays and half-filled bottles of cheap infant formula. Rhonda, who hadn't made it to many parenting classes in her time, had fed the baby from the same bottle all day. She retrieved a lukewarm bottle of likely spoiled formula from the table and disappeared down the hall.

"Our top story tonight," the well-groomed news anchor was saying, "is one that's got people excited all over the Richmond area. SuperLotto fever. Let's go straight to tonight's drawing from SuperLotto headquarters."

"Here we go," Leroy said, scooting forward to the edge of the couch.

SuperLotto, America's first national lottery, was played in all fifty states. Players selected five numbers between one and forty-nine and a sixth number, the mystical SuperBall, between one and fifty-nine. The odds of correctly matching all six numbers were an encouraging one in infinity.

At 11:03 p.m., a pretty SuperLotto employee plucked five numbered Ping-Pong balls from the rotating plastic drum to her left, each delivered via pneumatic tube with a satisfying thwoop. These five white balls shot through the tube like torpedoes: 5, 9, 16, 17, and 43. The sixth Ping-Pong ball, the bright red SuperBall, arrived from its own rotating drum. The SuperBall on this particular night was stamped with the number 24.

Julius checked his ticket.

5. 9. 16. 17. 43.

SuperBall: 24.

His eyes bounced between the numbers posted on the

screen and the ones stamped on the light blue ticket in his hand. Each time he checked, all six numbers on his ticket matched the six winning numbers.

Holy Christ, he thought. It couldn't be.

"The estimated jackpot is four hundred and fifteen million dollars," the SuperLotto spokeswoman said. "Tonight's drawing has been monitored by the accounting firm of Beisswanger & Mosrie. Good luck! Now back to your local news."

Julius had heard people claiming out-of-body experiences and had dismissed them as the ramblings of lunatics. But now, at this moment, he felt something he could only describe as a near-death experience. His heart rate accelerated to nearly a hundred and fifty beats per minute, and his hands started trembling like a window with a freight train rolling by.

"Aww, fuck it," Leroy was saying. "Like you said, J. Nobody ever win these fucking things."

Leroy crumpled up his eight tickets into a tight ball and shot it at the coffee table. Like a BB shot from a gun, it struck a half-full beer can teetering on the edge and toppled it over. Warm, flat beer glugged out onto the floor, but no one made a move to pick up the can.

"Rhonda, get that fuckin' can off the floor."

Rhonda, having just returned from the baby's room, ignored him, instead taking a long drag from her cigarette.

"We have breaking news for you tonight," declared the anchor grimly, which was corroborated by the ominous-looking Breaking News banner striped across the bottom of the screen. You'd have thought the anchor had just gotten word an asteroid was minutes away from colliding with Earth. "SuperLotto officials have confirmed a single ticket matched all six of tonight's winning numbers, and the winning ticket was sold here in Virginia."

"Just my fuckin' luck," Leroy said. "Sold in Virginia."

Julius tried to wrap his head around the news he was hearing. Four hundred and fifteen million dollars. One ticket. How was it even possible? As the magnitude of the situation began to settle in, he became hyper-aware of his surroundings. Everything seemed to be moving in slow motion. He took a long look at the two other people crowded around the television.

At thirty-eight, Julius was basically a town elder and garnered a fair amount of respect. He had no doubt, however, that Leroy would cut Julius' throat and possibly sell his own daughter on eBay to get his hands on the ticket.

"How many you get?" Leroy asked. "Lemme see."

"None," Julius whispered. "Every time, nothing."

"Lemme – Rhonda, I said get that fucking can off the floor!"

Rhonda was twenty-four, but rough, sallow skin drawn tightly across bony cheeks made her look twice that. She had grown up in the Tree, grown up fast, and would almost certainly die here. Years ago, she had shown promise in the classroom, but Rhonda had been more of a follower than a leader, and being a follower meant jumping into sex and drugs with both feet when everyone else did. As they had promised in health class, the sex resulted in a pregnancy, which ended via an abortion. Another pregnancy quickly followed, this one resulting in an underweight baby boy. A year later, a juvenile court terminated her parental rights after finding evidence of extreme neglect.

Rhonda had been with Leroy for about three years, but never for more than a few months at a time. During their courtship, he had taken the time to present her with an assortment of very special gifts – her daughter Angel and a volcanic case of genital herpes. The child was still in her custody because, so far, she had managed not to commit any act that would draw the attention of the city's Department of Social Services. So far.

After a disgusted sigh, she stood up and grabbed a dirty t-shirt that was poking out from under a seat cushion. With a stony glare directed toward her beloved, she began mopping up the beer from the thin carpet. Leroy's interest in housekeeping briefly diverted his attention from Julius' ticket, for which Julius was thankful. He used the interruption to quietly tuck the ticket into his breast pocket.

"You win something, Julius?" Leroy asked, his one-track mind refocusing like a heat-seeking missile.

"No," Julius said.

"Then why you keeping the ticket?"

Julius felt a stab of heat shoot up his back. He was a terrible liar. It was one of the reasons Julius had been unable to talk his way out of any of the police entanglements in which he had found himself during the past twenty years.

"I dunno. Just felt like it."

He forced himself to maintain eye contact with Leroy. That was something he'd learned during police interviews. If you broke eye contact with the interrogator, they smelled blood, and ten minutes later, you were signing a waiver of your *Miranda* rights and a full confession while munching on the fast-food meal the officers were all too happy to provide after you admitted everything. It was just the way these things went down.

"Free ticket," Julius said. He could feel sweat moistening his undershirt, and his voice was shaking. Try as he might, he couldn't maintain eye contact, and his gaze drifted away from Leroy, settling on a half-eaten taco sitting on the table.

"You lying motherfucker." Leroy said. "You won. How much?"

Leroy probably would have made a good detective.

"I swear, it's just a free ticket."

"If it was just a free ticket, you'da said that from the mother-fuckin' get-go."

"The hell with this," Julius said. "I'm going home." He stood up and made his way for the front door.

"Bullshit you are," Leroy said. "Let me see your mother-fuckin' ticket."

Julius was pretty sure he was related to Leroy on his momma's side and had known him for all of his twenty-two years on the planet. Leroy was one of the most dangerous individuals he had ever met. He just had no conscience. For the most part, people in Carrolton Oaks were just well-meaning products of their shitty environment. Crack cocaine was the infected star around which this little corner of the world revolved, and it destroyed everything in its orbit. Leroy, on the other hand, seemed to be missing the part that made him human.

As Julius wrapped his fingers around the doorknob, he glanced over his shoulder and into the gaping barrel of Leroy's nine-millimeter pistol, just a few inches from his face. Just over Leroy's shoulder, Julius saw Rhonda, looking back across the sofa, a cigarette dangling from her lips.

He sighed softly, turning his gaze back toward the door. He felt the barrel press up against the base of his neck. It was not the first time he had had a gun put to his head, and it gave him the opportunity he needed.

"Turn around slow," Leroy said.

Given that many men living in Carrolton Oaks did not

live to see their thirty-fifth birthdays, it was understandable, if not a little short-sighted, that Leroy had pegged Julius as a feeble old man. Moreover, Julius was still vibrant, having avoided meaningful relationships with crack and booze for most of his life. To top it off, he was thick through the chest, and his hands were like bear paws.

Julius followed Leroy's instruction to the letter, but he tossed in one angry and unexpected swipe for good measure, which knocked the gun against the wall. It clattered harmlessly to the floor. Leroy was so startled by Julius' display of self-defense he put up none of his own, other than a muffled *uggh*, when Julius drove him to the floor by his throat. Julius knelt down and drew close to Leroy's face.

"You do that again," Julius said, "I'll kill you."

"Uggh," repeated Leroy.

"Come on, man!" Julius barked at him. "We fuckin' family!"

Julius let go of Leroy and retrieved the gun, his eyes never leaving his would-be robber, not for a second. Although he was deeply disappointed, he wasn't completely surprised by Leroy's attempt to shake him down for the ticket. Truth be told, it was probably to be expected. In his youth, Julius might have been similarly tempted by the shiny promise of a winning lottery ticket. The funny thing was Leroy would never have guessed that not only had Julius won something, he had won all of it. The funnier thing was that it didn't even matter. Leroy would have killed his momma for four hundred dollars. Four hundred million? Shit.

With the gun still trained on Leroy, Julius looked up at Rhonda, who was staring right back at him.

"I don't want no trouble," Julius said.

Rhonda held her ground, still puffing on her cigarette.

Leroy remained on the ground, his head cocked toward Julius, his hands massaging his sore neck.

"Don't you fuckin' hurt him," she barked at him. She said this despite the fact Leroy beat her on a fairly regular basis. True love, Julius thought. The heart wants what it wants.

"I'm gonna leave now," Julius said, his mind whirring. He figured once he exited the apartment, he would have about ten minutes to vacate the Tree before Leroy gathered up his crew and came hunting for him. Didn't matter that Leroy and Rhonda didn't even know how much he'd won. The rumors would start to fly, and for once, rumor would match reality. After all, he did have the winning ticket. And they would come for him.

He had to leave his home tonight. Forever. He could never come back here again.

2

Julius ducked out onto the landing outside Leroy's apartment, the night's chill smacking him hard and good. His hand was stuffed deeply in his pocket, wrapped tightly around the Ticket. Even in his mind, it already deserved a capital T. The freaking thing felt almost alive in his pocket, wriggling and quivering like a newborn.

He bounded down the cracked concrete steps, and after a quick detour to the edge of the complex to deposit Leroy's gun into a storm drain, he continued across the courtyard to Building 349, where he lived in a second-floor unit. But for a guy he knew only as LT walking around in circles, muttering to himself, the courtyard was relatively quiet. While the navy-blue pea coat LT was wearing provided him some protection from the cold, Julius suspected the fact the man was nude from the waist down would limit the coat's warming capabilities. Julius wouldn't miss this part of Carrolton Oaks at all.

"'Night, Mister Julius," LT said.

Julius stopped at his front door and looked back at LT.

"Good night, LT."

He watched for a few more moments before ducking into his apartment, giving himself three minutes to get in and out. Leroy wouldn't come after him immediately. He'd take a few minutes to come up with a strategy to get Julius' ticket, even as he remained blissfully unaware of how much the ticket was actually worth. Part of him questioned the wisdom of returning here, but he had nothing but the clothes on his back, not even a coat, and a lottery ticket that wouldn't be worth much unless he could actually get it to lottery headquarters.

Julius had lived here since his release from Red Onion eight years ago. It wasn't much, really just a single large room with a small bathroom and kitchenette. No artwork or pictures adorned the walls. He slept in the corner on an old mattress, recovered from the apartment next door, which had been vacated when its tenant had himself been shipped out to Red Onion for murder. Still, it was home.

In the apartment's lone closet, Julius found an old duffel bag, in which he had carried home his belongings from Red Onion. He discovered four dollars in the side pocket. From the drawers, he plucked boxer shorts and socks, three pairs of pants and three shirts. Next, he hit the bathroom, grabbing shampoo, soap, a can of shaving cream and a handful of disposable razors. Julius' budget did not allow for the battery-powered razor with the cartridges that ran two dollars a pop. At least his old budget did not.

He hit the kitchen last, where he found a bag of stale Doritos in the pantry and a can of Diet Pepsi in the off-again-on-again refrigerator. Useful. Julius wasn't much of a home cook. Groceries were expensive, so he was better off buying a two-dollar sandwich each night. On a good night, there would be leftovers after one of the many functions at the offices of Willett & Hall, the super-sized law firm that Julius cleaned every evening from five until ten. On those nights, he might bring home a bag of chicken tenders or turkey-and-Swiss-cheese rollups. Sometimes the doggy bags would last two or three nights. Those, indeed, were the salad days.

There was one more item Julius considered taking. It was in the closet, tucked under a loose floorboard, in a shoebox lined with old socks. A black nine-millimeter pistol, which Julius had purchased four years ago from a dealer who did business in the complex. Upon his first conviction for burglary when he was twenty-one, Julius had forever lost his right to legally possess a firearm. But this was Carrolton Oaks, where reality often butted heads with the stated goals of the criminal justice system.

But could he afford to get stopped with a gun? He could just picture getting stopped by an overzealous officer, getting arrested for loitering or trespassing or whatever it was police used to sweep the streets clean of people who looked like him. Then what? His personal effects inventoried? The ticket? He couldn't take the chance, could he?

He pried up the warped slab of pine and flipped the box's flimsy lid aside. The weapon was wrapped in a soft white hand towel. It felt good in his hand, and he instantly felt safer, even when he knew the feeling was illusory, like a puff of breath on a chilly night. With his lips pressed together, he made his decision. He carefully replaced the gun back in the box and under the wood, took one last look at his apartment and ducked out into the cold, clear night.

EVEN ON HIS BETTER DAYS, Leroy Marshall was not a particularly happy or forgiving individual. And today had not been one of his better days. Rhonda had been nagging him all day to find a job, and the baby hadn't stopped howling since dinnertime. To make things worse, cash had been very tight lately, and he still had two grand he needed to kick up to his main supplier, the vig on a loan he took out to get him through a particularly barren stretch. Kids needed so many diapers, he couldn't believe it. That baby went through ten a day.

That and formula. He never did understand why Rhonda hadn't breastfed her, considering that breast milk was free. All he could remember was that she kept saying how tired she was when they came home from the hospital, give her a bottle. Within a week, her milk dried up, and all of a sudden, they needed a hundred a month for formula! Food stamps barely covered the expense, and that didn't leave a whole hell of a lot for Daddy to eat.

The thing was, see, he wasn't even a hundred percent sure Angel was his goddamn kid.

So when he got the sense that Julius had won some cash, and Leroy was all about instinct, he didn't hesitate. Mr. Julius didn't have extra mouths to feed. Mr. Julius had a steady job. He didn't need the money as badly as Leroy did. He wondered how much Julius had won. Five grand? Maybe ten! He had to get his hands on that ticket, and he didn't care what he had to do to get it. Plus, there was the matter of the old man getting the drop on him, and that could not go unpunished.

After Julius left the apartment, Leroy scurried down the hallway to the bedroom, which he occasionally shared with Rhonda and which served as the home to a cache of weapons. On the way, he called his brother Tommy from his cell. Tommy lived in the next building over and was blindly loyal to his brother, like a dependable yellow lab.

"Yo," said Tommy, picking up on the first ring.

"Meet me behind Julius' building," barked Leroy. "Three minutes. Bring the chrome."

"The fuck you say."

"Just do it."

Leroy hung up the phone without another word and stepped into the bedroom. He knew his younger brother wouldn't dare cross him, and that when he got there, Tommy Marshall would be behind the building and loaded for bear.

The bedroom was sparsely furnished, but piles of dirty clothes and empty fast-food bags made it seem even smaller than it really was. The walls were a dingy white and hadn't seen a paint job since the original construction thirty years earlier. A dirty queen-sized mattress, which may or may not have been the site of Angel's conception, lay in the corner. A cheap particle-board chest of drawers against the opposite wall served as home to random urban detritus, including four empty bottles of St. Ides malt liquor, and three half-smoked jumbos, which were marijuana cigarettes gener-ously laced with cocaine. Leroy found his spare nine-millimeter pistol in a grease-stained food bag, and he tucked it into the waistband of his pants.

"Where you goin'?" Rhonda asked when he returned to the living room.

"Out."

"No, you ain't," Rhonda said, climbing up off the couch and intercepting Leroy at the door like a bouncer at a nightclub.

"Bitch, get out my face," said Leroy. The chivalrous drug dealer clamped his hand around Rhonda's small face and shoved her hard against the wall. Her head thumped against the drywall, cracking the cheap plaster, and she crumpled to the floor.

"Fuck you! I hate you!"

Rhonda touched the back of her head, where she felt the warm oiliness of fresh blood.

"Shut the fuck up," Leroy said, "or I bust you up for real next time."

LEROY SLINKED down the stairs to the courtyard, his pistol close to his side. They had to act quickly. Leroy knew there was no one in the apartment complex Julius trusted enough to bunk in with until he could cash the ticket, so he wouldn't be long for the Tree tonight. If he got out with the ticket, they'd never find him in time. It wasn't like he worked for the CIA. Couldn't exactly call in a satellite or some shit like that.

The Tree got dark and shadowy at night, and even long-time residents got nervous when they went out, simply to take out the trash or head out for an overnight shift. You never knew if there would be a stray bullet out there with your name on it. Like roaches, the dealers and the hookers operated in the nooks and crannies of the complex. A healthy drug and sex business flourished in the Tree, drawing customers from the run-down neighborhoods that orbited the apartment complex. Although the cold had drawn many of the usual vendors inside tonight, some hard-core entrepreneurs were starting to filter out into the dark cold. It was important not to disappoint the customer. That's how you got ahead in any business.

This section of the complex was designed in a horseshoe

pattern with three long buildings forming a U around a center courtyard area. Leroy's apartment was in one leg of the U, and Julius' was in the opposite leg. A breezeway cut through each building, allowing for pedestrian ingress and egress from the courtyard. Many residents, the ones who worked hard and came home and locked their doors at night, often asked management to block off the breezeways because of the criminal elements that flowed through them each night like viruses. These requests fell on deaf ears because at the moment, management existed in the form of Devon "Pumpkin" Patch, a wiry thirty-year-old who took a cut of every drug deal that occurred on the property in exchange for looking away and keeping police away.

Leroy slipped across the courtyard and through the breezeway in Julius' building. An old dog searching for his dinner on the far side of the corridor glanced up at Leroy, who kicked the mutt aside with his boot. The dog grunted, unsurprised. It wasn't the first time this human had kicked him. Leroy was not a friend to animals. He found his brother Tommy waiting about twenty yards down the side of the building, in the shadow of a Dumpster, which provided some cover from the biting wind.

"Yo," said Tommy.

"Listen good now," Leroy said. "We go in strong and nobody get hurt."

"Whatever you say."

"You fuckin' listenin' to me?"

"Yeah, yeah," Tommy said. "Whatta we doin', L?"

"Just follow my lead."

The pair eased away from the relative cover of the Dumpster and cut around the end of the building about twenty yards north. Pressing his body against the cold cinderblock, Leroy peeked around back into the courtyard.

The stairwell to Julius' apartment was just a few steps away. They ducked under the stairwell and peered up through the open-air steps.

"Go knock on his door," Leroy whispered. "See if he's home."

"The fuck I do then?"

"Never mind," said Leroy, immediately dismissing the idea. "Lemme think."

While Leroy assessed the situation, the decision was made for him. In the still of the crisp air, he heard a door open softly above him. A moment later, he heard it click shut, just as softly. Footfalls on the concrete steps followed. Leroy's heart started pounding with glee. These were the footsteps of someone wanting to slip away into the night, like a teenage girl sneaking out of the house. They were moments away from getting the ticket. No one would get involved, lest they draw the ire of Leroy Marshall. He leaned over and tapped his brother on the small of his back, where Tommy had tucked away his .38. The men drew their weapons and waited for their prey.

JULIUS HEARD the frantic whispers just as his apartment door clicked shut behind him. Leroy. Probably had his dumbass brother Tommy with him. That did worry Julius a bit, as Tommy was just as likely to accidentally discharge his gun and kill someone as he was to do so intentionally. He thought about the gun under the floorboard, not ten yards away, and wished he had it now. Given their history, he didn't think Leroy would open fire on him. Not right away. First, Leroy would try to strong-arm him into relinquishing the ticket. If that didn't work, then things might get ugly.

Julius paused at the landing, figuring his would-be robbers were waiting under the stairs. It was good and dark here, as the stairwell lighting had burned out years ago, and no one had ever bothered replacing it. He went over the number in his head again. Four hundred and fifteen million. He never even imagined one person could win so much money. Random thoughts spiked through his mind like sparks from a misfiring electrical transformer. Where the hell did they get that much money to pay off a prize so big? Did they give it to him all at once? In one check? In cash? The very idea of the money started to make his head spin, and it occurred to him he had the very pressing matter of staying alive to attend to.

He considered his options. If he continued down the stairs, Julius faced an unpredictable confrontation with a young man who once shot a male friend in the hand for talking to Rhonda at a party without his permission. If he retreated to his apartment, he wasn't sure he could get to his gun in time, and it could very well become his tomb. He thought about the residents of the two other apartments on this floor. The first, the one closest to where he was crouched against the wall, was home to a frighteningly obese woman named Shanique and her three small boys. She was loud and fancied herself the leading socialite among the Tree's single women. Useless.

Across the hall, however, Julius thought he could find some help. Older dude named Monk had lived there since Julius was a teenager. He was on disability, his left leg crippled a few years ago during a drive-by shooting. As fate would have it, Monk had identified Leroy Marshall as the triggerman. It was safe to say that Monk was not fond of Leroy. Crouching low and with his back pressed against the base of the wall, Julius shuffled across the landing and, using his foot, tapped softly on Monk's door.

"Who the fuck is it?" barked Monk.

Julius' heart sank. He'd forgotten how loud Monk was. No time to mess around.

"Open up, it's Julius," he said.

≈

"WHAT IS IT?" asked Tommy, noticing Leroy stiffen visibly.

"Fucker knows we're here," Leroy said. "I think he sneak into Monk's house."

"What we do now?"

"We go in now," Leroy said. "Monk just a little bitch. Won't do nothin'."

≈

MONK OPENED THE DOOR A CRACK, an inky sliver just wide enough to let Julius in the apartment. Julius exhaled slowly, relieved to be in a safe haven, if only temporarily. Monk stepped back and gave Julius a long once over, wiping a hand across his clean-shaven skull. His skin was jet black, the blackest Julius had ever seen, a total absence of color, like a photo negative. His face was layered with thick wrinkles like a relief map, indicative of a life spent in the projects.

"What the fuck do you want?" Monk asked once he had re-closed the door. "Can't you see I'm busy?"

Julius looked around the dimly lit apartment, which was steeped in the unmistakable aroma of marijuana smoke and burning incense. He could not, for the life of him, imagine what exactly Monk was busy with. Based upon prior visits to

Monk's apartment, Julius knew he was in the living room, as it were. Six-foot-high piles of newspaper littered the floor. The shell of a floor console television had been pushed up against the wall. A bizarre squawk erupted from the darkness. It sounded like a pterodactyl.

"Sorry," Julius said. "I got a problem."

"I got my own problems," said the wiry Monk. "I sure as hell don't need yours."

Monk was fifty years old and lived in one of the most dangerous housing projects for a hundred miles in any direction. Indeed, Julius had no doubt that Monk did have his own problems. Not the least of which was that Monk was crazier than shit.

"It's Leroy."

Julius waited for it to sink in. If anyone in the Tree would help him deal with Leroy Marshall, it was Monk.

"What do you need?" he asked.

"They're downstairs," Julius said. "Him and Tommy, I'm guessing. I need to get out the Tree. Tonight."

A knock at the door interrupted them.

"Monk!" It was Leroy. "We know he in there. Just give him up, old man. You don't want no part of this."

"Back bedroom," Monk said to Julius. "Fire escape ladder in the closet. You go out that window."

"Whatcha gonna do?" asked Julius.

"Oh, I got this," said Monk, making his way toward the gutted television chassis. "You get the fuck out of here."

Julius slipped down the short hallway and ducked behind the door. In the dim light, he could just make out Monk's silhouette in the living room. It quickly became clear that he was loading a handgun.

After a second knock at the door, Monk barked again. "Get the fuck outta here!"

Julius suspected Monk's admonition was just as much for him as it was for Leroy and Tommy. Yet he couldn't tear himself away from what appeared to be the fulfillment of Monk's lifelong dream. As he watched, Monk climbed into the skeletal shell of the television and crouched down. Invisible.

"Old man, don't fuck with me tonight," said Leroy. "This don't concern you."

"Rhonda don't concern me neither, but I fucked her anyway," Monk said.

With that, the front door to Monk's apartment blew inward like a roasted turkey leg ripped from its joint. It had, of course, failed under the thrust of Leroy Marshall's size twelve boot. It also represented the final link in a chain of events that had begun years ago.

NEARLY THREE YEARS to the day before he burst into Monk's apartment in his quest for Julius' lottery ticket, Leroy crossed paths with Monk for the first time. Monk's little brother Jimmy owed Leroy two hundred dollars for unpaid crack bills. At the time, a rock went for ten bucks apiece, and Jimmy had racked up a twenty-rock tab. On the night in question, the night that had permanently braided the lives of Leroy Marshall and the man known only as Monk, Jimmy and Monk were smoking weed at the bus stop that served the Tree. Shortly before nine in the evening, Leroy cruised by in his two-door Ford Bronco and sprayed the bus stop with the full clip from a MAC-10 machine gun. Three rounds plowed through Jimmy's skull, killing him instantly; four more peppered Monk's left flank and leg, leaving him with a permanent limp.

Monk unequivocally identified Leroy as the shooter. He memorized the license plate of the Bronco, which indeed was registered to Leroy. There was precious little forensic evidence, but after satisfying itself with his ability to perform on the stand, the prosecution built its case against Leroy around Monk's testimony. They happily charged Leroy with first-degree murder, attempted murder, and two counts of use of a firearm. They prepared the case exquisitely, leaving nothing to chance. Almost nothing.

Given Monk's commitment to the case, his preparation for trial, his obsession with seeing his brother's killer brought to justice, what the prosecutor did not anticipate, what he could never have imagined (or maybe he didn't want to), was that Monk would develop a bad case of nerves on the morning of trial. To soothe those jangled nerves, Monk downed half a bottle of gin and smoked a jumbo about thirty minutes before he was scheduled to testify. And when he got on the witness stand just after lunch on the second day of trial, his nerves indeed had settled. He smiled at the jury, and he laughed at inappropriate moments. He couldn't remember the time or location of the shooting, he identified his brother Jimmy as Jason, and he denied he had been shot during the incident.

Sensing that disaster was at hand, the prosecutor asked for a mistrial, but the judge denied his request, ruling the witness' obvious intoxication was not grounds for mistrial but instead would go to the weight that the jury would award the testimony. The prosecutor was granted permission to treat the witness as hostile, which only served to make Monk even more disposed to the giggles. He didn't grasp that the prosecutor, who had been so nice to him in the four months leading up to trial, was now supremely pissed at him.

Monk's testimony ended immediately after he stated to the prosecutor, "Ooh, you scary!" The jury deliberated for eleven minutes before acquitting Leroy on all counts. The prosecutor, who had to be restrained by the bailiff after taking a swing at Monk, submitted his resignation that afternoon and pursued a career as a carpenter.

After sobering up, Monk was devastated by the acquittal. He blamed himself, which he should have, since the blame belonged squarely at his feet. His family and friends shunned him, as they also laid the blame for the case's outcome squarely at his feet. He retreated to his apartment, living off of the disability check he received as a result of the shooting and only leaving his self-imposed exile to buy groceries and weed.

The only thing keeping him from sticking his head in the oven was the hope that one day he would be able to exact his revenge on the man who murdered his baby brother. It became his obsession, his focus, his reason for being.

JULIUS LEFT the door cracked and backed deeper into the blackness of the bedroom. More strange animal noises greeted him, and he began to question whether he was any safer here than Leroy and Tommy were out there. In the thin light, he could see Monk's front door blow off its hinges like a SWAT team was coming through.

"I told you this don't concern you!" bellowed Leroy, who did not seem to realize that he'd been lured into a trap, much like a fly buzzing around a spider's glistening web. He turned toward the living room, his gun drawn and turned on its side, a maneuver he'd never quite understood but had adopted years ago from his colleagues on the street.

Without saying a word, Monk burst from the cover of the television set like a homicidal jack-in-the-box and opened fire. From a range of three feet, Monk's barrage was inescapable and deadly, his astigmatism and poor night vision not making the least bit of difference. He fired until the clip was empty. With the front door still standing ajar, the gunshots echoed through the stairwell. It sounded like a train had hit the building.

Two bullets caught Leroy, who had entered the apartment first, flush in the chest and hammered him into the ground like a pancake. Each was independently mortal, but Leroy was fortunate in that one was instantly fatal, piercing his heart and shredding it into so much taco meat.

Tommy, who took two rounds in the arm before he'd fully crossed the threshold, was not as lucky. He turned to the sudden and deafening roar of Monk's revenge against his brother in time to catch two more in the stomach. The bullets caused slow-developing but irreversible damage to his intestines, pancreas and liver, and Tommy would spend the next five days in agonizing pain prior to expiring on Christmas Day.

It was over in seconds. Monk eyed his victims, debating whether to put one more in each of their heads, but he figured that might be overdoing it a bit. No need to piss away a perfectly good case of self-defense. Leroy lay still, the machinery of death already at work. Tommy sat spread-eagled against the living room wall, his hands and arms stained with blood, as if he were wearing red evening gloves. He looked up at Monk with a puzzled look on his face, seemingly shocked by the sudden turn of events. Giant pools of blood were soaking the threadbare carpet, and more blood splattered the wall.

"I'm calling 911 now," Monk said. "I'd get moving I were you."

In the darkness of the bedroom, Julius nodded, still stunned by the sudden spasm of violence. It sounded like Monk was talking to him underwater. A shout in the distance galvanized him into action. He scrambled over to the closet, where he found the rescue ladder still in its box. After unpacking it, he pushed on the window, but it held firm. Oh, shit, he thought, his testicles leaping up into his stomach. He tapped the edges of the windowpane firmly and pushed again. After a few anxious moments, the window popped open, and relief flooded through him like a water main had broken. He hung the ladder brace over the windowsill and dropped down the roll-up ladder.

"Yeah, I just shot two guys breakin' in my house!" Monk said loudly. "They dead!"

Julius shook his head in disbelief and shimmied down the ladder. As he slipped into the cold night, he heard a rustling sound behind him. He looked back in time to see the ladder snake its way out of sight, into the maw of Monk's dark bedroom. Good man, he thought. That would have needed some explaining. As it was, he could only hope no one could identify him rappelling down the side of the building.

Not too far away, Julius could hear the first sirens screaming toward the Tree. He jogged up an embankment into a thicket of oak trees on the north side of the complex and disappeared into the cold night.

3

The phone on Samantha Khouri's desk rang insistently, its annoyingly corporate ringtone startling her, even though she had been waiting for it to ring all morning. Immediately, her breathing froze, and her heart seemed to be pounding its way up her throat like a mountain climber. She shoved aside her reading material, a scintillating document known as the AIA General Conditions of the Contract for Construction, and grabbed a legal pad.

She didn't know why she grabbed the pad, given she knew exactly who was on the other end, but she did it anyway. It was her thing, taking nonsensical notes whenever she was on the phone. A day from now, hell, three minutes from now, the notes would be incomprehensible. Still, pen in hand, and after a quick deep breath to clear her head, she punched the hands-free button on her phone.

"This is Samantha," she barked out loudly and quickly, in the way she had been taught during her orientation so many years ago. This method of answering the phone was designed to catch callers off guard and create a psychological advantage. As if to say, *I'm such a busy lawyer, you should be happy I have time to answer my phone.*

"Ms. Khouri," a mousy voice belonging to Karen Bush said on the other end, mousy in the way Karen had been taught during her own orientation so many years ago. "This is Karen Bush."

"Yes?"

She scrawled out the name *Karen Bush.*

"Mr. Smyth would like a moment with you."

Smyth, moment.

Karen was secretary to Hunter Pennington Smyth, III, the managing partner of Willett & Hall, the firm where Samantha had worked for the last eight years.

"I'll be right up," she said, jotting down *Smyth* again.

From her lower right desk drawer, she pulled out a small vanity mirror and took a good look. No eye boogers, no stray nose hairs, no renegade bit of food lodged in her teeth. Her hair was a little shaggier than she liked it, but she hadn't had time to get a decent trim in months. Not with so much at stake. She'd been putting in ninety to a hundred hours a week since the first of the year, and here she was, four days shy of Christmas. Large circles under her eyes were so dark it looked like she'd been hit in the face. A pimple in its embryonic stages was erupting at the base of her chin. Typical. She checked her makeup one last time and set the mirror back in the drawer.

She took a deep breath. At long last, the day had arrived. In a few moments, Hunter Pennington Smyth, III, would tell Samantha Khouri that the firm had voted to make her an equity partner in this most prestigious law firm. Eight long years would finally pay off. Samantha Khouri was just thirty-four years old, and she was going to be making three hundred grand a year! Tack on the yearly bonus, which the associates dreamt and talked about, she'd be pushing four hundred thousand!

As she straightened her suit, she kept that big number bouncing around her head because she didn't want to think about what it had taken to get here. Sleeping in the office two or three nights a week. Two years in therapy. Crushing loneliness. And a little more wine than was probably healthy. OK, a lot more. At least she could afford good wine.

She stepped out of her cramped office on the twenty-ninth floor of the Willett & Hall Building and headed toward the bank of elevators at the end of the hall. The cube farm was hopping now, paralegals and secretaries working hard as they closed in on the Christmas holiday.

At the elevators, she ran into Kimberly Davis, a seventh-year Litigation associate. Kimberly had a fake laugh and dead eyes and Samantha had been leery of the woman since they'd met seven years ago. Kimberly was frightfully skinny, not much more than a bag of skin, bones, and fake boobs. She had once confided in Samantha that vodka and energy bars were her two primary food groups. Samantha often daydreamed about firing Kimberly.

"So where you headed, girl?" Davis asked with a smirk on her face, laughing one of her fake laughs.

"Got a meeting upstairs," Samantha said without elaborating. The elevator doors slid open.

"Upstairs? Wait, is today the day?" Davis asked. "Well, congrats, sweetie, that's super," she said loudly, without waiting for an answer. She chuckled again. Samantha imagined it was what hell sounded like.

Laugh it up, Samantha thought.

Samantha stepped onto the elevator, but Davis lingered behind.

"Going up?" asked Samantha.

"Nope," Davis said, pressing a finger up to her ear. "Hang on a sec."

Samantha waited awkwardly while Kimberly tended to her Bluetooth.

"I gotta run, sweetie," she said. "Well, congrats again!" She laughed. "Text me later, we'll go have appletinis."

Samantha pictured herself enjoying said appletini immediately after letting Kimberly know that while her contributions to the firm had been appreciated, she was so very sorry to have to let her go.

THE THIRTY-STORY WILLETT & Hall Building towered over the relatively modest Richmond, Virginia downtown area, leaving much of it in the firm's shadow. When the firm had outgrown its previous quarters in 1984, the Executive Committee decided it was time to make a stand, architecturally speaking, and overwhelm every other firm within a hundred-mile radius. The Committee's intent was to intimidate the other downtown law firms and scare every company into thinking that if Willett & Hall wasn't its law firm, it was doomed. Sure, there were other law firms, firms with fewer lawyers, fewer resources, fewer Fortune 500 clients. Losers. The firm purchased an entire city block between the James River and Kanawha Canal and demolished it. Up went the building, layering floor after floor like Legos until it was the tallest building in the city.

The firm currently occupied the top six floors of the building, with the remaining floors leased to various highbrow enterprises with which the firm had close dealings. The other tenants included two investment firms, a large branch of First National Bank, an architecture firm, a United States senator and a large medical practice.

The attorneys' offices occupied the perimeter of each floor, ringing the centralized cube farm, which was like a busy anthill. Corner offices, sporting two windows each, provided sweeping views of the city, which on a clear day looked like a painting. Offices were assigned by seniority, and there was no shortage of battles or horse-trading when one of the corners came available. That wasn't to say that the other offices were outhouses. Each was decorated according to the attorney's personal style and preference (subject to Executive Committee approval, naturally), and each was like a self-sufficient legal battle station.

The thirtieth floor was a nauseating display of wealth and power, reserved for the firm's senior-most partners. The walls were soundproofed and the floors were marble. Artwork pilfered for pennies on the dollar from collectors struggling in bankruptcy lined the walls.

Across from the elevators, a five-hundred-gallon saltwater fish tank had been built into the wall. It bubbled soothingly as the brightly colored fish darted among the decorations. The tank was the personal toy of Nathan Marcone, the firm's chairman. Marcone was fifty-one and married to an ex-stripper who was younger than his daughter. He had decided to make fishkeeping his hobby after a snorkeling trip to the Hawaiian island of Kauai several years earlier. Marcone paid a local aquarium merchant a thousand dollars a month to maintain the tank and keep the fish happy and alive.

From the elevator, the corridor on the right led toward the administrative suite containing the partners' offices. On the left was the door to the health club and dining room. Samantha walked slowly, relishing the crisp marble tile clicking under her feet. At the end of the hallway was a circular receptionist's desk made of oak, staffed by a young woman named Susan. She was tall and thin and brown from a life in the sun. Susan's primary job was to look pretty for the twelve male partners who worked on this floor and to serve as a source of gossip for the four female partners.

"Hunter Smyth asked to see me," Samantha said to Susan. She specified Hunter Smyth because there were at least three other partners up here named Hunter.

Susan didn't look up from her magazine, instead pushing a button on the multi-line phone, which was really her only responsibility.

"Your name?"

"Samantha Khouri."

The speaker on her phone crackled.

"Yes?" said the mousy Karen.

"Ms. Khouri is here to see Mr. Smyth," said the bitchy Susan.

"You can send her down."

"Last office down the left hallway," Susan said to Samantha.

Susan's hand drifted over to another button, which unlocked the smoked glass door separating the foyer area from the main hallway leading to the partners' office suites.

Laughter from behind a closed door greeted her, the easy laughter of people who have more money than you. A nervous smile spread across Sam's face. The daughter of Lebanese immigrants, about to take her seat at the big boys' table. If her father could see her now. As she made her way down the hall, Samantha read the names on the doors, a veritable who's who of Richmond's legal elite. These men and women represented Fortune 500 companies, professional sports teams, rock stars, even foreign countries. All made well more than a million dollars a year; some, Samantha had heard, made upwards of $5 million. She thought about the boat she wanted to buy. She wondered what she should name it.

She stopped at Smyth's door and took another deep breath. It was time. She stepped inside the office and smiled broadly, as broadly as she could, at Karen Bush. As she did so, she felt a slight twinge of pain at the back of her throat. Damn. A sore throat. It was the unmistakable harbinger of a cold. On today of all days.

THE OFFICES on this floor were designed on the suite system, with each partner's secretary manning an outer office, which connected to lawyer's private office. It was all very impressive to clients and unnerving for opposing lawyers.

"Mr. Smyth will be with you shortly," Karen said. She looked nervous.

Samantha sat on a leather loveseat, crossed her legs and thought about the money. She ended up spending most of her first bonus in her head before the door to Smyth's office finally opened. As Smyth's round head poked out, she settled on the name Raven for her boat.

"Samantha, come in," he said. He quickly disappeared back into his office, and she followed him in.

Smyth's office was one of the larger ones, about thirty-feet-by-thirty-feet square. One wall was made entirely of thick smoked glass and opened up over the James River to the east. Outside, the day looked gray and bleak, a few flurries dancing a lonely waltz at this elevation. A promised blizzard was moving in, and this was just the northern edge of the storm. Across the metropolitan area, the citizenry was panicking, clearing the local grocery store shelves of milk and bread.

Smyth's all-glass desk sat in the northwest corner. A MacBook was perched on top, but there were no files. Senior partners didn't have to be troubled with files cluttering up their desks. That's what associates and junior partners were for. In the other corner was a small seating area, complete with a loveseat, sofa and recliner, all centered around a flat-screen television mounted on the wall. A full bar completed the picture. And this was in the middle of a recession!

"Drink?" Smyth asked.

"No, thanks," she said.

"Nonsense," he said. "You enjoy red wine?"

"Sure."

"A glass of red, then. I insist."

What the hell, she thought. She'd earned it. She nodded.

He rapped his knuckles on the desk as if to approve her selection.

Smyth waddled over to the bar and poured two glasses of Rioja red. She noticed he poured one of them higher than the other. He handed the larger drink to her and plopped down on the recliner. Smyth was a plump man with red cheeks and a thick mane of black hair. He wore five-thousand-dollar suits and spent money almost as fast as he made it. He lived alone in a big house on River Road, supporting three ex-wives and four children he rarely saw.

"How are you doing?" he asked.

"Fine," she said, taking a sip. Good wine. "Staying busy."

"Good," he said. "Good."

He set his glass down on the table and clapped his hands together.

"I don't know how else to tell you this," Smyth said, "but you didn't make it. You didn't make partner."

She looked at him for a long time. She took another sip of the wine, mainly for the lack of anything else to do.

"The committee voted this morning. It was unanimous. Five to nothing."

She took another sip of the wine, longer this time.

"The thing is, sweetheart, the committee felt you just weren't shareholder material." Smyth made bunny ears around the words 'shareholder material,' a gesture that made Samantha want to rip Smyth's lungs out through his nostrils. For some reason, that bothered her more than Smyth calling her "sweetheart."

"I made this firm a lot of money," Samantha said, immediately hating herself for it. It felt like begging, and she didn't want to beg. She was fighting back tears.

"I know, I know," Smyth said, chuckling. "But you didn't do it for free."

It was the chuckle that set her off.

"You've got to be kidding me!" She was on her feet now, wine sloshing over the lip of the glass, staining the rug.

"Babe, watch the carpet," Smyth said.

She dumped the wine out of her glass. "Fuck you and your carpet!"

He smiled.

"I'll let that one go," he said. "I was thinking about getting new carpet anyway."

"I busted my ass for this firm for eight years."

"Lots of lawyers bust their ass here and don't make partner."

"Yeah, but usually there's a reason."

"There's a reason you didn't either," he said. "I thought I already mentioned that."

"Right. I'm not shareholder material. That's not a reason. That's a load of shit."

"This place isn't for everyone."

More silence followed. Smyth appeared to be out of things to say, and Samantha was trying hard not to pass out.

"I don't believe this," she said. "What the hell am I supposed to do now?"

"You can stay on as of counsel," Smyth said. "You're always welcome here at Willett & Hall. But..."

Samantha knew exactly what was behind the 'but.' A significant cut in pay and permanent exile from the partnership track. She would never again be considered for partner. The fact that Smyth had referred to the firm by name was confirmation she was no longer an integral piece of the puzzle. As if Willett & Hall was a faraway place, and she was on the outside, looking in.

The most devastating ramification of taking an of counsel position would be the immediate and permanent loss of respect, of standing, of clout. She'd be a eunuch, trapped in a netherworld of legal washouts. Other associates would give her a wide berth, lest she contaminate their own futures. Many associates failed to make partner, but only a few decided to stay on as no-counsel, as the joke went. It was the professional equivalent of staying in an abusive relationship because, well, he really loves me.

"Great," she said. "Of counsel. How many people actually take you up on that offer?"

"Not many."

"That's what I thought."

"Take some time to think about your future," Smyth said. "It's a tough economy out there."

One thing Samantha wanted to see in her future was Smyth plummeting down thirty floors to the street below.

"Why wasn't I given some warning?" Samantha asked. "My performance reviews were always good."

"This firm is looking for a very specific type of person to elevate to partner," Smyth said.

Oh, here we go, she thought to herself. She rolled her eyes, making no attempt to hide it. She wasn't much concerned with whether Hunter Pennington Smyth, III, saw her do it. It wasn't like there was much more they could do to her.

"Don't patronize me," she said sharply.

"Well, for one, you lost OmniCare as a client," Smyth said.

OmniCare was a giant health insurance benefits provider serving much of the southeastern United States. During Samantha's first year with the firm, OmniCare retained Willett & Hall to represent it in a lawsuit against HealthSoft, a software company in northern Virginia, for breaching a software contract. The firm agreed to accept a $10,000 flat fee in the hope that OmniCare would join the firm's stable of clients after it successfully handled the HealthSoft matter. That didn't stop Samantha's then-supervising attorney, a decent guy named Damon Evans, from dropping the case on Samantha's lap. Evans left the firm shortly thereafter and became a successful author of children's books.

"That was seven years ago," Samantha said. "And they were a flat-fee client who gave us shitty work, and the only reason they gave us the work was because no one else would do it at that rate. Not even Griffin. And the only reason I was working on OmniCare was because I'd been here for about six months and no one else in the firm wanted to work on it."

"You still lost it."

"Remember why?" Samantha said, wagging her finger at Smyth, almost shouting now. "I filed a response to a counterclaim without running it by their general counsel, and the asshole gets all bent out of shape. Everyone seems to forget OmniCare didn't tell us about the counterclaim until the day before our Answer was due."

"It could've been a big client for us," Smyth said.

"Oh, please just give me the tiniest break, Hunter," Samantha said.

Samantha didn't mention that OmniCare had shipped the case to Griffin & Walker, another local firm, where it ended up paying more than $40,000 in fees and lost the case when the young associate working on the case failed to file answers to Requests for Admission. In Virginia, failing to deny these requests constitutes an admission. Essentially, OmniCare admitted it agreed with all of HealthSoft's allegations. It was sort of like hand-stitching *I you* on the towel before throwing it in to your opponent. She didn't mention it because there was no point.

Because logic and deductive reasoning were not among Smyth's strong suits, the wealthy lawyer clapped his meaty hands together and stood up before Samantha confused him too much about the OmniCare business. The truth was, OmniCare had nothing to do with why Samantha had been passed over for partner, but he could never tell her that.

"Well, I've got to be running along," he said. "You stay and pour another glass of wine. Try and relax."

"So no one made it from Litigation this year," Samantha said.

"I didn't say that," Smyth said quietly. His pace toward the door quickened.

"Who?"

"It doesn't matter," Smyth said.

"You didn't," Samantha said, suddenly remembering the smirk on Kimberly Davis' face when she saw her at the elevator.

"Didn't what?" Smyth asked.

"You made her partner, didn't you?"

"Who are you talking about?"

"You know exactly who I'm talking about."

"Busted," he said with a big fat smile on his face, his palms held out in playful surrender.

"Oh, Jesus H. Christ! She hasn't even put in her eight years yet."

"The Committee decided Kimberly was more in line with firm's image. What we're really looking for as we look to the future."

"What the hell does that mean?" Samantha asked, even as she realized precisely what Smyth meant. Kimberly Ashton Davis was a Richmond native. After attending all the proper private schools, she'd earned her undergraduate degree at the University of Georgia, where she had pledged Kappa. Law school at Washington & Lee University followed. Dubyunell, as the alums were fond of saying. Her father was a judge on the state Court of Appeals, and her mother was heavily involved in the Junior League. This was all very important.

Samantha's parents were Lebanese immigrants who ran an ethnic grocery store in the suburbs. Samantha earned a bachelor's degree from the University of Virginia before moving onto the University of Richmond for law school. She did well there, finishing third in her class and parlaying that performance into a job offer from Willett & Hall. Her career had been workmanlike whereas Davis' had been destiny.

"I'll see you later," Smyth said.

"Go to hell," Samantha said.

Smyth left the room without a word, accepting Samantha's request as acceptable fallout from the bomb he dropped in the young woman's life. As such, Hunter Smyth was not in his office for the remaining fallout, which he likely would not have considered acceptable. Samantha staggered to the bar and poured a second drink. Before she took the first sip, however, she walked over to Smyth's desk and plopped down on his black leather executive chair.

Without comment or ceremony, she poured the entire glass of wine onto the keyboard of his shiny laptop.

4

Whatever bug Sam had contracted exploded like a hurricane over warm waters. By the time the day's weak light started to fade, Samantha was radiating with fever, her head was pounding, and her throat felt like it had been repaved with broken glass. She was stretched out on the floor behind her desk, near the small ceramic heater she used to warm the office, the temperature fluctuations of which tended to be a bit extreme. Even though she was running a temperature, chills rippled across her body like little Samquakes.

All in all, today was screaming its way up Samantha's list of Worst Days of Her Life. In fact, she was having a hard time coming up with another day that matched this one in the breadth and depth of its misery. As she lay on her back, watching a moth flutter about the fluorescent light in her office, she tried to keep her mind clear. She pushed back thoughts of what was next, ready to bust down the walls of her mind like the Kool-Aid man. That was not a discussion she was ready to have just yet. So, she just watched the moth, that brainless wonder, flirting with the light fixture, which would never do anything but be a light fixture. She found herself jealous of the moth.

Her life at the firm spooled out in her mind like a home movie. Willett & Hall was a 2,000-lawyer behemoth with offices in sixteen cities worldwide. They even had an office in Burkina Faso. Burkina Faso! Samantha did not know where Burkina Faso was and had deliberately chosen not to find out. She was secretly afraid that if she knew where it was, the firm would have transferred her there.

For as long as she could remember, she had arrived at the office at eight in the morning, tall cup of Starbucks in hand, and worked until about ten at night. She could probably have been home by nine each night, but she liked to take an hour in the middle of the day to get out of the building for lunch or a workout or even to just clear her head with a quick walk around downtown Richmond. She was confident this daily respite kept her from happily and ritualistically murdering each of her co-workers.

With a grunt and a wave of nausea, she got up off the floor and fished two expired cold/flu tablets from her drawer. Dry-swallowing them was not an appealing option, but finding the strength to go down the hallway to the water cooler was even less appealing. Christ, someone out there might know about her little career hiccup, and she was in no mood to talk about that. She nearly gagged as she swallowed the pills, which, naturally, seemed to get stuck on her swollen glands. Her eyes watered as she got the pills down. With that done, she crumpled into her executive chair. But for the hum of her desktop computer, her office was silent. It felt like a tomb. Jesus, had it always been this small? This had been her home for the better part of a decade. She had spent more time in this room than in any other spot on earth. Quite a legacy, Khouri. Quite a legacy.

Samantha had been with the firm's litigation section since joining Willett & Hall immediately after law school. This was the firm's largest division, made up of more than eight hundred lawyers scattered worldwide like mercenaries, because what good was a law firm if it wasn't litigating across the globe? Currently, the firm had 3,000 active litigation files, fewer than ten of which would ever see trial. The remaining cases were like picnickers on a hot summer day, feeding the insectine lawyers thousands of billable hours of legal research, discovery motions, motions for summary judgment, demurrers, expert depositions, and document reviews.

Her phone rang, breaking her out of her trance. For the briefest of moments, she wondered if it might be Smyth, calling to tell her that the Committee had changed its mind. She didn't even have to look at the caller ID screen to know that was nothing more than a pipe dream. And when her eyes registered the familiar number on the screen, the pit in the center of her stomach just deepened. She took a deep breath and lifted the receiver.

"Hi, Mama," she said.

"Sweetheart, you still coming for dinner, right?"

Samantha bit her lip and exhaled slowly. She had forgotten about dinner.

"I'm coming down with something. I don't know if I'm up for it."

"What? What are you talking about? You too young to be sick. You eat something, you feel better."

Zaina Khouri had never acknowledged the presence of illness in any of her children. It was as if she thought that would be admitting that they were dying.

"I'll try," Samantha said.

"You promised!"

"I have a lot of work to do," Samantha said. The whole career flameout was a discussion for another day.

"That stupid office. Your father will be very disappointed."

"I said I would try. Bye."

"*Yallah.*" An Arabic brush-off, part *Goodbye*, part *Whatever*.

The line clicked dead. Samantha replaced the handset in the cradle, just thankful the conversation was over.

SAMANTHA TAPPED HER COMPUTER MOUSE, which revved up the hard drive and brought the screen back to life. Absently, she clicked on an icon in the corner titled Scoreboard and waited as the firm's billing records popped onscreen. Through the window to her right, she could just make out the James River, a slate grey cord running through the heart of downtown on this cold December afternoon. Just cold, biting misery as far as the eye could see, thought Samantha. She turned her attention back to the screen. She clicked on a link, which brought up the records for the firm's eighth-year associates.

Each Willett & Hall associate was required to bill a minimum of 2,200 hours per year. That meant 2,200 hours of actual work that could be billed to specific clients. What it did not mean was checking non-work-related e-mail, eating lunch, going to the restroom (unless you were particularly discreet in smuggling a file into the john), or calling the dry cleaner after they stained your favorite skirt. If you worked fifty weeks a year, you'd need to average forty-four billable hours per week. And Samantha had long since calculated that it took about ninety minutes of office time to bill one hour. Meaning she was in the office sixty-five hours a week just to reach the minimum.

But 2,200 was just the minimum, and no associate dared clock in the mere minimum if she had any hopes of making partner. The Executive Committee carefully reviewed an associate's billing history when it came time to decide who was making partner. Partnerships, which were offered only after eight years of toil, rarely went to any associate who had averaged less than 2,500 hours per year.

Willett & Hall was a giant factory of law, and its machinery never stopped churning. The firm provided each new associate with an iPhone (never to be turned off), a MacBook Pro equipped with a mobile broadband network card, and a standing order to never let three hours elapse without checking e-mail or voice mail. Each time an associate failed to log on to check his messages within the three-hour window, he or she was docked one billable hour. This requirement ran around the clock, 365 days a year (including holidays, vacations and weekends), because the firm prided itself on customer service for all its clients, foreign and domestic. Two nights a week, Samantha took the hit because she needed a full night's sleep every once in a while. But the price for that was billing an extra hundred hours to make up the deficiency.

Without fail, the feeling of importance that accompanied this technological buffet thrilled every new associate as they started their careers with Willett & Hall. By the end of the first month, though, most of the associates felt like Samantha, who often wondered if there was a way to torture her iPhone and make it suffer. Maybe plug in an incompatible battery charger? Pluck out vital components with tweezers while it was powered up? Take it out in the woods and beat it with a baseball bat, like in the movie *Office Space*?

Associates worked around the clock. Many slept in their offices a couple nights a week in the never-ending quest to bill, bill, bill! On the firm's Intranet, each associate's billable hour total was updated in real time, available for any more senior attorney in the firm to see. The Scoreboard, as it was not so affectionately known, was broken down into eight sections, one for each class of associates, and each associate was ranked, much like college basketball teams. Associates whose hours-to-date left them projected to finish below the minimum saw their names in an embarrassing shade of red. It was like announcing you were infected with the Ebola virus. Immediately, other attorneys began distancing themselves from the Reds, fearing these slackers would somehow infect them as well. Those go-getters who projected to make 2,700 hours (and the rare associate bonus) saw their names shaded in green.

Two consecutive months in red brought an e-mail from the associate's supervising partner, which was half-encouragement, half-warning. Three months brought an in-person visit from the supervising partner. Four months brought a visit from two security officers, who escorted the terminated associate from the building. There was no further discussion about the matter. On any given day, fewer than ten associates' names were in either red or green.

The Committee believed the Scoreboard was an effective motivational tool, especially given that the firm paid twenty percent more than any other large firm on the East Coast. Despite the challenging work conditions, turnover was relatively low at the firm. Everyone was making too much money to complain, so for the most part, associates kept their heads down and billed until they were dry, bitter and wealthy shells of the idealistic law students they had once been. Or until they'd been told they were not going to make partner.

As it usually was, Samantha's name was in green. Since Labor Day, she had billed nearly eight hundred hours, and it had brought her to the precipice of the $10,000 bonus, which awaited those who broke the 2,700-hour mark. She had earned the bonus four years running and was right at the doorstep again this year. And then they had pulled the rug out from under her.

No way it was because of OmniCare. For eight years, she had been a billing dynamo, never finishing outside the top two highest-billing associates. She had snagged a handful of new clients. She wasn't one to dick around gossiping. Internet surfing was not one of her hobbies. What Samantha did, what she was known throughout the firm for, was work. Document review, deposition summaries, legal research, client interviews and brief writing were the bread and butter of her daily life. She felt oddly empty inside, a void she had never felt before. Would that be her legacy after nearly a decade at this desk?

It occurred to her then that in her eight years as a practicing lawyer, she had never tried a case in front of a jury. She had never even seen one for that matter. She had taken a few depositions here and there, tried a few cases in the district courts. Settlement conferences and mediations ruled the day. Insurance companies were not particularly interested in gambling their bottom lines on what they believed were the whims of bored, distracted and uneducated juries. If there was a good chance a case might be lost, the client paid. Otherwise, W&H lawyers pounded the other side with motions and discovery, choking the usually undermanned opposition with bankers' boxes overflowing with documents until it quit. And the cases that did go to trial were handled by partners.

When people asked Samantha what she did for a living, she had once proudly told them that she was a trial lawyer. Sitting here as her career played out the string, like a baseball team eliminated from playoff contention, she felt very silly all of a sudden. She had appeared in court six times in eight years, and never in a court of record. What the hell kind of trial lawyer was she, exactly?

And what was she doing with her life? The questions were coming like machine-gun fire now. Representing giant companies pitted against other giant companies. Or, more accurately and more pathetically, giant insurance companies for giant companies. She thought about the OmniCare case again. OmniCare had sued HealthSoft because it claimed that the proprietary software that it had designed had nearly erased OmniCare's customer database. HealthSoft countersued because countersuing would unnecessarily complicate things, a personal favorite of lawyers.

She could only imagine what a jury would have thought if it saw two extremely large and wealthy corporations fight about a software contract. She suspected that, if they could, the jurors would return a verdict for neither party. Juries were not stupid, despite what big firm attorneys frequently thought.

With that little career retrospective complete, Samantha turned her attention to her personal life. Another highlight reel! Single at the age of thirty-four! No prospects in sight! The love of her life, long since checked out! With her index fingers, she massaged her temples. Her headache was worsening, and this trip down memory lane was not helping. Jesus, she wanted to puke. To top it off, her nose was starting to run, and she caught a big, wet sneeze in a tissue.

She checked the clock in the corner of her computer screen. It was almost 2:30. For the next three hours, the firm would be hopping as the support staff hurried to finish its pre-Christmas work and the attorneys hunkered down in their offices, conducting the important business of the firm. With moist tissue in hand, she staggered to her office door. Cracking it open, she had a view of the cube farm. At a couple of cubicles, partners were barking orders at their secretaries. Rage swelled inside her like helium filling a balloon.

She staggered back to her chair.

5

Unaware of the despair in his soon-to-be-former associate's heart, Carter Livingston Pierce sat in his 5,000-square-foot Windsor Farms home, focusing on his myriad other problems and sipping scotch. Single malt, according to the bottle. Carter didn't have any idea what that meant, but he knew it was important. He didn't normally drink in the afternoon, but what the hell. It had been a long year. And this was expensive scotch.

The house was empty now, his wife Ashley and the twins, Cameron and Madison, out somewhere finishing up the last-minute Christmas shopping that he likely could not afford. Carter was at the dining room table, grimly studying that month's credit card bills like they were bad medical test results. Twenty-six thousand dollars! Finding it difficult to catch his breath, he reached for the top button of his custom-made dress shirt and was surprised to discover it was already undone. He felt like he was choking. Jesus, it was hot in here. He looked up at programmable thermostat on the wall. Seventy degrees. Maybe he was having a heart attack, he thought, more hopefully than he cared to admit.

Carter was forty-five years old and had made partner at Willett & Hall more than a decade ago. He made $1.5 million a year, and yet it was not enough. Money flew out the door like inmates breaking out of jail. He looked around at the opulence before him, and it made him retch a little. The table at which he was now sitting had been custom-made by a well-known local carpenter for the tidy sum of $41,000. In her seemingly constant quest to strip Earth of its usable natural resources, Ashley had requested it cut from a rare tree in the Amazon rainforest. Carter couldn't remember how many times the family had actually eaten at the table, but he didn't think it was more than five.

A matching china cabinet (sixteen grand) stood in the corner, home to a variety of rare plates and silverware that Ashley had collected over the years. Her proudest find was a plate that Princess Diana had eaten from at the Hotel Ritz on the night she died in Paris in 1997. Carter thought it was a bit creepy, but hey, whatever made her happy. That dish alone had sucked $44,000 out of the Pierce bank account. Another $40,000 went to installing new hardwood floors in this room.

At least that crap was paid for. Carter found himself thinking about their monthly and daily expenses, money that drained out of the family's accounts like water from a bathtub. Lunch for the family averaged about a hundred bucks a day, as Ashley and Carter each enjoyed lavish midday meals with friends and associates. For Ashley, lunch was a competitive sport, and she wouldn't dare miss a lunch with the other ladies of the Junior League. The girls refused to pack their lunches, as it would send the massively inappropriate message that they could not afford to buy their lunch. That simply would not do. Not that they ate it. The twins and their friends never ate anything because teenage girls never actually ate lunch. Too many tight clothes to shoehorn themselves into.

Dinner ran at least a hundred bucks a night. Sometimes two hundred. The girls frequently invited friends over for takeout, since Ashley hadn't lifted a finger in the kitchen since they were born. Much of the food ended up in the trash because teenage girls didn't eat dinner either. Carter usually took his dinners in his office, ordering in. Food ran the Pierce family about a thousand bucks a week.

Ashley, who liked driving a new car every year, was currently zipping around in a Mercedes coupe. Carter drove a Hummer that was bright yellow and all but screamed, "I have a small penis!" The girls had received their own SUVs for their sixteenth birthdays in August. Carter had justified them with the latest crash-test data they'd found on the Internet. After all, they needed the girls to be safe. The monthly payments on the vehicles totaled about $3,000.

Madison and Cameron attended St. Genevieve's, the area's most exclusive girls' private school and their mother's alma mater. The Pierces lived inside the city limits, which would've meant sending them to one of the city's wretched public schools. Carter cringed at the idea that the girls would be elbow-to-elbow with the sons and daughters of the crack addicts, the blacks, and God knew what else. So they paid two grand a month to send them to St. Genevieve's.

He tried not to think about the oceanfront cottage that they had bought six years ago. Located right on the beach in Duck, North Carolina, it sported six bedrooms, three stories, wraparound decks on each floor. The mortgage payment was $6,000 a month, much of which, theoretically, could have been recouped by weekly rentals, if Ashley had been willing to let strangers inside her vacation home. Which, of course, she was not. Instead, the house sat empty fifty weeks a year. He didn't want to think about the condominium in Park City either.

Last but not least was Ashley's addiction to Vicodin and Percocet. Five years ago, she had torn her ACL playing tennis, and since the surgery to repair the damage, she had been popping the pills like candy. She got them from Andrew Whitestone, a well-known orthopedic surgeon in the Richmond area. Two grand a month. Plus a monthly blowjob for the good doctor, but Carter didn't know about that. Since that wasn't costing him anything, he probably wouldn't have cared all that much.

Carter Pierce drank more scotch.

AN HOUR LATER, Carter was down in the media room, well into his second scotch of the day and pleasantly buzzed. It was in the basement of the three-story home, and once upon a time, this had been the crown jewel of the house. It was where the family had congregated, ate pizza from Mary Angela's, and enjoyed what little time they had together while Carter had sowed the fields of partnership with the seeds of his soul. Once upon a time, the girls were still little and he was still Daddy and Ashley still planned to return to teaching kindergarten. Once upon a time, they were happy.

When Carter and Ashley bought the house a decade earlier, he had had great plans for this room. He had always wanted a home theater with a theater-like screen, and once his salary reached a point that it could become a reality, he went to work. He shopped long and hard for the right setup. He read magazines, frequented boutique home theater stores, even researched what Hollywood people put in their own homes. Finally, he took his Visa Black card to Speaker City and went to town.

He dropped nearly $100,000 to soundproof the room and retrofit it with an LCD projector (which he upgraded every year or so), a 103-inch screen, Polk audio speakers built into the walls, stadium seating for twelve. A Kegerator stood at the ready, loaded with Heineken, as did a fountain drink station. The walls were painted black to minimize light interference. A functioning popcorn cart completed the room.

For the first year or so, the room was a hit. Time with Madison and Cameron. Time with the wife. As time marched on, Weekly Movie Night turned into Monthly Movie Night, and then they were lucky if they gathered for the rare Night-That-All-Four-Of-Them-Could-Stand-To-Be-In-The-Same-Room Movie Night. Now it sat empty most nights, indicative of the current family dynamic in the way a deserted skyscraper reflected a down economy.

These days, he came here to hide. Madison and Cameron had moved on to their own lives and looked for ways to avoid being home. After all, many of their friends whose parents weren't nearly as weird as theirs had similar entertainment centers in their large homes, so the draw just wasn't there. They didn't understand why Dad had such a hard-on for this room. Ashley herself was busy with the Junior League or tennis or, for all Carter knew, banging her yoga instructor, Malik. Had Carter known Ashley was, in fact, sleeping with her yoga instructor, he would have realized he couldn't judge her too harshly, given that he had been having an affair with his paralegal, Dawn, for the past year. Glass houses and all.

THE CHIMES of the deactivated alarm system roused Carter from his early afternoon stupor. He'd fallen asleep on the leather loveseat, a string of drool arcing from Carter's chin to the throw pillow. His head was pounding and his mouth was dry. Great, he thought. Perfect conditions in which to do battle with the wife. He gave his head a hard shake and made his way upstairs. He was halfway up the stairs when Ashley started calling for him. Jesus, her voice was like broken glass.

"Carter," she called out. "I'm home! You've just got to see what we bought."

Just thinking about it made his heart flutter.

He found Ashley in the living room, surrounded by an army of shopping bags from the mall's ritziest tenants. She sat cross-legged in front of the exquisitely decorated eight-foot Douglas fir that had given its life to become the Pierce Family Christmas tree. It stood majestically in the corner of the living room, strategically placed so it could be seen from the street. Ashley had wanted to have the best-looking house on the street, and so a month ago, she had hired a Christmas consultant to select the tree and decorate the home. Until the moment said consultant showed up at their door, Carter didn't know what a Christmas consultant did or that there even was such a thing, but there was no arguing with Ashley once she'd set her mind to something. He decided that tonight, after everyone was in bed, he would drink more scotch and look at his fantastic-looking tree.

Ashley barely noticed him as he entered the room, intent on the various packages before her. She wore green khakis and a cream-colored turtleneck, filling out the clothes as well as she did ten years ago. Her sandy blond hair caressed her shoulders in soft ringlets. In addition to tennis, yoga and banging Malik, she ran three miles every day and did weights four times a week. If Carter didn't despise her so much, he would've been tempted to take her there on the sectional sofa. He watched her examine a new knife she had purchased from Williams-Sonoma and briefly wondered if she would one day try to kill him with it. It wouldn't surprise him.

"Where are the girls?" he asked as he examined the loot, trying to estimate how much deeper Ashley's latest spasm of spending would bury them.

"Oh, they ran into a couple friends from school and decided to go to lunch. I gave them the credit card in case they wanted to do a little shopping."

"Splendid," he said.

"What's with the tone?"

"Nothing," Carter said. He didn't feel like fighting. His head hurt.

"Good," she said. "Let me show you what I got."

For the next fifteen minutes, she walked him through the spoils of her latest assault on the Short Pump Town Center, the ritzy open-air mall on the west side of town. For a bit of that quarter hour, he wondered how he was going to pay for it all. For the rest, he wondered if Dawn would dress up as Princess Leia the next time they hooked up. It had long been a fantasy of his, and Ashley Matheson Pierce was not one for fulfilling fantasies.

"Are you even listening to me?" Ashley said suddenly, ice in her tone.

"What?"

"You're not listening to me," she said. Each word was shriller than the last.

"So?"

"I want you to listen to me," she said. "This is why we have so many problems."

"It's not because you're spending it faster than I can make it?"

OK, so maybe he was in the mood to scrap a little.

"Screw you," she said, turning her attention back to her packages. "I just want to have a nice Christmas. Don't you ruin it for me."

"Ruin it for you?" Carter said. "I'm subsidizing it for you."

"Leave me alone!"

Well, that was enough of that. Without another word, he turned on his heel and slipped out of the room. Carter decided it was a good thing he was relatively intoxicated, because if he'd been in the mood to really brawl, that scene could have gotten ugly. Whew. Well, time to head to the office. He glanced over his shoulder as he made his way to the garage, suddenly fearful that she might be chasing him down with the new knife.

Traffic was light as Carter made his way east toward downtown, the scotch only marginally affecting his ability to keep the Hummer in his lane. It was just before 4:00. He planned to work until about nine, when he and Dawn would break for a quick dinner and even quicker screw in his office. Hell, maybe there'd be some news about the size of this year's bonus. With any luck, he could undo some of the damage that Ashley had wrought over the past twelve months. Then back home to the harpy.

Merry Christmas!

6

The snow was thickening when Julius Wheeler joined his four-man CleanSweep crew on the twenty-ninth floor of the Willett & Hall Building. He pulled on his coveralls, loaded his cleaning cart, pushed it down the hallway. The ticket (THE TICKET!) was tucked safely in his right shoe, secreted in a zippered plastic baggie to protect it from sweat. He had not slept in more than twenty-four hours. As he silently made his way from office to office, he tried to gather his increasingly fragmented thoughts, which was proving to be about as easy as herding goldfish.

As Julius had fled the Tree the night before, two things had occurred to him. First, he didn't have the first clue what to do with his winning lottery ticket. Second, he had a few bucks in his wallet and no credit card. So, although he was worth nearly half a billion dollars, he had been unable to get a hotel room.

At about three in the morning, he stumbled across the Third Street Diner near downtown, where he sat in a booth and nursed a cup of coffee until sunup. At dawn, he ordered the cheapest breakfast he could and picked at it for another hour. Then he had wandered around downtown until his shift started, freezing his ass off. First thing he was doing was buying a house in Hawaii.

His co-workers were in a festive mood, excited about Christmas, now just four days away. Under normal circumstances, Julius wouldn't have been that excited. Christmas fell on a Tuesday this year, meaning that Monday and Tuesday were both holidays, even at this firm. That meant no work, and no work meant no pay. But these weren't normal circumstances, at least not for him.

He turned his cart down a long corridor of darkened offices, going over his plan once more. Of course, Julius hadn't needed to come to work today, but he did need help.

"J-Dub!"

Julius looked across the cube farm and spotted Luis, another janitor on his crew.

"Merry Christmas!"

Julius nodded. Luis disappeared into the stairwell.

At the next office, he found the lights on and the door slightly ajar. Inside, he heard a sneeze, a loud, wet one. He checked the nameplate on the door, trying to gauge whether this was someone he could trust.

Samantha Khouri.

The olive-skinned young woman, who often worked late into the night, sometimes even after the CleanSweep crew had finished its rounds, was seated with her back to the door, wiping her nose with a tissue. She was slouched low in her chair, staring out the window, her long black hair tied back in a ponytail. She was always nice to him, nicer than most of the attorneys that he came across as he emptied their trashcans.

Well, he had to trust somebody.

Julius Wheeler took a deep breath and knocked on the door.

7

FRIDAY, DECEMBER 21 - 6:40 P.M.

S amantha spun her chair around away from the windows toward the sound of the soft but insistent tapping on her door.

"Yes?"

The door swung open slowly, revealing Julius' presence behind it.

"Yes?" she said.

Sam had been in her chair for a few hours, just staring out at the dark city. She was too tired to move, and she wasn't quite ready to head to her parents' house, where she was expected for dinner shortly.

"Hi," Julius said, rooted in the doorway. Then silence.

Samantha reached for another tissue. After destroying that one, she looked up again a few moments later and with some unease noticed that Julius was still standing in her doorway, eyeing her closely. He hadn't moved. Immediately, and she hated herself for thinking it, she realized that she was effectively cornered by a large black man. She glanced at the clock in the corner of her computer screen. It had been quiet for at least an hour, and it was extremely unlikely that any other W&H employees were still here. Maybe Carter Pierce was still dicking around in his office, but he'd probably hide under his desk if she screamed out for help.

Relax, she told herself. It's just been a few seconds. He's just zoned out.

"Hi," he said again.

"Hello," Samantha thought, wondering if she could get to the pepper spray in her purse in time, if she even had the strength to do so.

"Can you help me?" asked Julius.

Samantha cocked her head.

"Sure," she said, her mind barely registering the question. "I'm sorry?" she said, once she had her bearings. "Help you? Help you with what?"

Julius leaned back, looked up and down the hallway, stepped inside the office. This made Sam's heart race a bit, and her eyes flitted to her phone. She relaxed when he made his way to the empty seat across from her and crumpled into the chair.

"I'm Julius."

"Sam."

"Nice to meet you, ma'am."

He leaned forward and placed his elbows on his knees. Clearly, something was eating away at him. Now Sam really hated herself for thinking that Julius had borne her some ill will or malice. She realized he wasn't much older than she was, but the years had been far less kind to the man who emptied the trashcan than to the woman whose trashcan was emptied.

"I need a lawyer," Julius said. "I think."

Sam was careful not to advise Julius that she was not a criminal defense lawyer, because, well, that would have seemed a bit presumptuous. Racist, too, and she already felt enough like a Klan member.

If she was being honest with herself, and well, it was a pretty good day for honesty, the truth was that she really didn't want to be having this discussion with Julius, regardless of his legal needs. Granted, he didn't know her life was in the toilet, but that didn't mean it wasn't in the toilet. She looked across her desk toward the tired-looking man looking at her hopefully.

Christ, she thought, sighing softly. Isn't that what she liked about being a lawyer in the first place? Helping a guy like Julius?

"Well, OK," Sam said. "What kind of lawyer are you looking for?"

"That's the thing," Julius said. "I don't even know."

"Maybe if you tell me your problem, I can help you figure it out."

He nodded and settled back in his chair. Meanwhile, Sam was at it again, cycling through the names of criminal defense lawyers that she knew. Good heavens, she needed a racial sensitivity class.

"You hear about that lottery last night?" Julius asked after a moment.

"Yeah," Sam said, flipping through her Rolodex. At first, she thought he was simply making conversation. It had been the talk of the firm all week. The secretaries on Sam's floor had pooled their money and purchased a hundred tickets. The only thing they had won was four free tickets for next week's drawing. Samantha herself had bought ten dollars' worth. What a waste.

"That is one lucky duck," she said. "I didn't catch a single number."

"Yup."

A few seconds of silence followed before Sam realized what Julius was telling her, before she realized that he wasn't just making small talk. She looked at him again and saw a man whose wildest dream had split like a mitotic cell into one part joy and one part terror. Julius extracted the plastic baggie from his shoe and set the ticket on her desk, on top of a roll of construction drawings that she had been trying to decipher earlier in the week. They suddenly seemed extremely silly.

"Hang on one second," she said.

Sam pulled up the SuperLotto web page on her computer. The numbers were still posted on the site's main page, gaudy and huge.

5, 9, 16, 17, 43. SuperBall: 24.

The numbers stamped on Julius' ticket screamed at her.

"Oh, my God."

"So you think I need a lawyer?" Julius asked.

She looked across her desk at the tired janitor, make that ex-janitor, deciding that the man had probably emptied his last trash can. Julius was sitting quietly, chewing a piece of dead skin from his thumb.

"Yes, Julius, you need a lawyer," Samantha said. "You need ten lawyers."

"So what do we do now?"

She wanted to tell him that he'd live happily ever after, while she'd be polishing up her resume, but she resisted the urge. Barely.

When Samantha called, Carter was whiling the evening away on the Internet, alt-tabbing between a pornographic website dedicated to clown sex and a gambling site that had not yet been shut down by the government. It was nearly seven o'clock, and he hadn't heard from Dawn the paralegal. He decided that if she stood him up tonight, he would fire her. Legal fallout be damned!

"What?" he asked, as if she had interrupted him while presenting oral argument before the U.S. Supreme Court.

"Do you have a second, Carter?" she said.

He exhaled. He hoped she didn't want to talk about the partnership. God, this was so awkward. He'd been surprised by the decision, but hey, that was above his pay grade. He'd always liked Samantha, thought she was hard-working, but they didn't give partnerships to everyone. Besides, there wasn't anything he could do to help her anyway.

"Uh, yeah," he said. "Sure."

"You know Julius?" Sam asked.

"Who?"

"The man who cleans your office every night?"

"What about him?"

Samantha started talking, but Carter drifted off like a three-year-old drawn to something really shiny. He had discovered online gambling about three years earlier, and despite showing virtually no aptitude for it, he was quite the eager participant. The Redskins were eight-point underdogs against the Giants, whose starting tailback was expected to miss the game after getting arrested that morning for soliciting sex from an undercover police officer. That had to be a lock, right? A ten-thousand gold-star lock! He charged a thousand dollars to his online account and took the points. This was his weekend to make up some losses. Some easy games. And he needed to make up for a recent losing streak. A losing streak that had put him $140,000 in the hole.

It occurred to him that Sam was still on the other line.

"I'm sorry. Were you waiting for me to say something?" he asked.

"Yes, Carter," she said, "I was telling you about your new client, Julius. He's sitting here with me now."

"Who the hell is Julius?"

"The guy who cleans this floor."

"Samantha, what are you talking about?" Carter asked, moving onto the line for the Colts-Chiefs game. "Who's the client?"

"Julius. He's your new client," she said. "Look, forget it. I'll be right down."

She hung up.

Crap.

Well, at least she didn't want to talk about the partnership. He'd listen to anything she had to say, as long as she didn't ask him to try to convince the Executive Committee to change its mind. He thought that would be like trying to convince a cruise missile to change its mind about its target.

When he heard the whispers of conversation outside his doorway, he minimized the PartyClowns.com website and pretended to read some discovery in the Kornheiser medical malpractice case. Samantha entered first, with Julius trailing behind her. She waved him toward one of the guest chairs and closed the door behind him. Carter tried to guess what he'd been charged with. Murder? Shit, that would be kind of exciting, notwithstanding the fact that Carter had not practiced criminal law a day in his life. He hadn't been in court in years!

"This is Julius Wheeler," Sam said. "Julius, this is Carter Pierce. He's a partner with the firm, and he's my boss. He's a fantastic lawyer."

"Pleased to meet you," Julius said, nodding at Carter.

"So you're in some trouble, huh?" Carter asked. "Happens to the best of us."

The three of them sat silently for a few moments, as Carter wondered how the hell Julius was going to pay his legal fees. He carefully eyed Julius, who was checking out the trappings of his office. He loved it when people looked impressed by the office.

"Here's the thing," Samantha said. "Julius won the lottery last night. The big one."

Carter's thick eyebrows rocked upward, like two caterpillars jumping.

"How much?"

"You don't know?" she asked.

"I don't really follow it."

Samantha coughed lightly into her hand and glanced over at Julius, and Carter knew that she was about to blow his mind with her answer.

"Four hundred and fifteen million."

"Four hundred million."

"Four hundred and fifteen million," Samantha corrected him.

"How many people splitting the jackpot?"

Samantha nodded her head.

"He won the whole thing? The whole fucking thing?"

"Yes."

He turned to Julius. "And you came to us."

"I don't know too many lawyers," Julius said.

"I find that hard to believe," Carter said, laughing.

No one else laughed, so Carter decided to keep the conversation moving.

"So where is it?" asked Carter.

"Where's what?" replied Julius.

"The Holy Grail. The hell do you think I'm talking about?"

"Oh. Sorry."

Julius, apparently nonplussed by the outburst, handed the ticket to Carter, who studied it as if it were one of the Dead Sea scrolls.

"Julius, can you give us a moment?" Carter asked.

Julius glanced over at Samantha, who smiled and nodded at him.

"Sure," said Julius. He got up and stepped out into the corridor.

"You've confirmed these are the winning numbers?" Carter asked Samantha when they were alone.

"You really think I didn't check them first?" Samantha snapped.

Carter let her snide comment go. Given the events of the day, he figured she had earned the right toss around a little sass.

"OK, so you've checked," he said. "Do you want a raise?"

"That is hilarious, Carter."

"Oh," he said, feeling a stripe of embarrassment. "Sorry about that. Anyway, he's going to be our client," Carter said, his eyes wide with manic excitement. "I'll call Smyth tonight. Hell, maybe they'll change their minds about you!"

He immediately regretted the comment. Carter would have bet his life on the fact that they would never make Samantha partner now that they'd voted on it. That would be akin to admitting they were wrong, and the Executive Committee of Willett & Hall was never wrong about anything.

"You think they might change their minds?" Sam asked hopefully.

"Sure, absolutely!"

That was a good answer, because he was absolutely sure that he thought that they might change their minds.

"So what do we do for this guy?" asked Carter, changing the subject as quickly as he could.

"What do you mean?" Sam asked.

"I thought you'd already checked on all this," Carter said. "What does he want to do with the money?"

"He just came to me a half-hour ago," she said. "And I have some other things on my mind."

"Jesus Christ," he said. "You still work here, don't you?"

"For now."

"Look, this isn't hard. Just go talk to him, tell him he needs to figure out what to do with the money. Big picture stuff. First, family. Then retirement, charity, that kind of thing. Then his wish list. Thug like that probably has a list a mile long, been dreaming about this his whole pathetic life. Probably wants to start a record label. Once he figures that out, I can start talking about how to help him."

"Fine," she said. "I'll take care of him for now."

Samantha got up and left the room.

FOUR HUNDRED AND fifteen million dollars.

Four hundred and fifteen million dollars.

Four hundred and fifteen million dollars.

The number flashed in Carter's head like a giant electronic sign on the Vegas strip. Julius Wheeler would never know this, but Carter Pierce was as flabbergasted by the figure as Julius was, and Carter was in the top one-tenth of one percent of American wage earners. It had been a punch in the stomach, and it had taken all of his considerable skills as a stone-faced litigator to hide his mind-blowing shock.

Carter would have been less surprised had Julius announced that he was his illegitimate son.

Four hundred and fifteen million dollars, and he had held it in his hands.

He poured a tumbler of scotch and took a long drink, hoping it would calm his jangled nerves. It didn't. In between pulls, the heavy glass simply trembled in his hand. He actually felt a little bit sick to his stomach. Here he was, one of the most successful attorneys in America, and he was falling behind on his bills like some unemployed factory worker.

To make it worse, he was going to have to work for this loser, this junkie who'd beaten the longest of odds, this pathetic nigger – there, he thought, that's what Julius was – who was never going to have to worry about money again and would live a lifestyle that even Carter Livingston Pierce could only dream about. And Carter had no doubt that Julius would never worry about money again. Clearly, he had shown plenty of foresight in seeking counsel rather than cashing in and dumping a hundred million bucks into an interest-free checking account.

A knock at the door startled him, breaking him from the hate-spawned trance that Julius' good fortune had dropped on him like a heavy curtain. He looked up and saw Dawn Robertson standing in the doorway. He chuckled to himself. In the hubbub surrounding the ticket, he'd forgotten all about his planned rendezvous with the saucy young paralegal.

Dawn was twenty-three years old and had been working for Carter for eighteen months. She was tan and brunette and ran marathons and wanted to become an uber-lawyer. As it turned out, he decided Dawn wasn't really that good a paralegal, and he didn't think she showed much potential as an attorney. He didn't really have anyone to blame but himself. He had hired her over a dozen other far more qualified candidates, but she had looked so good in her interview suit, he couldn't remember much about the other candidates. On the plus side, she was extremely adventurous sexually, and that alone warranted her continued employment long after he stopped depending on her work as a paralegal.

Their affair had started one night about six months earlier, while they were preparing the final draft of a brief in support of a motion for summary judgment in a breach of contract lawsuit. The pair had broken for dinner at a sushi bar near the office. He had suggested a little sake with the salmon rolls, just to take the edge off a long day. It was after hours. The rules could be loosened a bit. He remembered her showing some reluctance when the first drinks were poured, but he thought now that had just been part of the act. She had been pursuing him all along.

The first drink had been followed by another, and then another, and then still another. By eight o'clock, they were feeding each other. By nine, they were in a room at the Jefferson Hotel, naked and entwined in a rather complex sexual position that Carter had never even heard of, let alone attempted. She left at eleven, promising him that he had no idea what he was in for. Half of him was terrified of her; the other half told the first half to shut the hell up as this was what he'd had dreamed of since his first hard-on three decades earlier.

And so it had gone on from there. At the office, he was incredibly discreet in his dealings with her. Whenever she was in his office, the door stayed open. They never left the office together. But when they rendezvoused at her apartment two nights a week (never the same two nights, lest someone detect a pattern), all discretion was set aside. He had heard of women with insatiable sexual appetites, but had never actually encountered one. He sure as hell had not married one.

Nothing was off-limits. Porn, toys, food, drugs – they all played significant roles in their sex life. A week ago, he had engaged in his first threesome, when Stacy, Dawn's college roommate, happened to be in town for a conference. That had not been as much fun in reality as it seemed in theory. Two nights ago, she had mentioned something about an orgy with a few friends she met online. Did she expect him to have sex with some dude? He was having nightmares about it. He had to bring her under control.

"You're late," he said, tapping the face of his watch.

She laughed out loud, which sent a spike of heat up Carter's back. He didn't like it when people laughed at something he said if he didn't understand why they were laughing.

"I'm late alright," she said. "I am definitely late."

What the hell was she babbling about? Carter wondered.

"What the hell are you babbling about?" he asked.

"I am late, Carter," Dawn said, her voice turning icy. "I'm late, and I feel nauseous a lot, especially in the morning. Ginger ale? Saltines? Are you getting me?"

He looked at her blankly, and then suddenly, Carter was getting Dawn, he was really getting her, and his insides felt gooey. A Washington & Lee University paperweight on the corner of his desk caught his eye, and he reached out for it while Dawn continued talking. He really couldn't make out much of what she was saying, as if she had instantly transformed into one of the adults from the Peanuts cartoons.

The paperweight felt good and solid in his hand. It was

one of those things you could count on in life. It always did what it was supposed to do. Right now, he wished someone would bash him unconscious with it.

"Carter!"

He snapped back to the present.

"What?"

"I need to know what you think about all this."

"Wait a minute," he said. "You sure I'm the one you should be discussing this with?"

"What's that supposed to mean?"

"I don't see you every night," he said. "We use condoms. I don't know who else you've been with."

"You asshole."

"Hey!" he barked. "I am still your supervisor."

Immediately, he regretted saying it. He pictured himself sitting in her lawyer's office a year from now, giving a deposition in her sexual harassment lawsuit against him and being asked if he had uttered that very line. That short sentence might end up costing him six figures.

"Like I give a shit about that right now," Dawn said. "And you can rest assured that your pen is the only one that's been in my ink for the last six months."

"Fine," he said. "How sure are you?"

"What do you think I've been doing all afternoon?" she said. "I've taken a dozen pregnancy tests. All positive. Jesus, it seemed like some of them were turning positive before I even peed on them."

Silence settled over the conversation. Carter imagined boxes of still-sealed pregnancy tests in the supermarket popping like popcorn as she walked by them.

"Congratulations, Dad," she said. "Jesus, what are we going to do?"

8

J ulius sat in Samantha's office sipping a lukewarm Sprite. His new lawyer had stepped out for a moment, leaving him alone with his thoughts about the money. He really couldn't get his head around it. In his life, Julius had never had more than a few hundred bucks to his name at any one time. He had never owned a car or a house, and he had never had a bank account. He had never filed a tax return. That, he suspected, was about to change.

He wondered if he should finish his shift. On the one hand, he did have some suddenly pressing matters to attend to, and his mind was really not focused on his janitorial duties. On the other hand, if he suddenly quit, Mark Jenks, the need-to-know-everything supervisor of the evening shift, would have a lot of questions that he didn't feel like answering right now. Plus, he was a pain in the ass, and Julius would have liked nothing more than to give him a little heartburn, make him work late. In the end, he decided to bag it. Eff it. Jenks had treated him like dog shit for the last two years. What was Jenks going to do? Fire him?

"How we doing in here?" Samantha asked as she stepped back into the office.

"Okay, I guess," he said. "Little nervous."

"I'm sure you are."

"So what do we do now?" he asked.

"Well, today's Friday. Because of Christmas, the lottery office doesn't open again until Wednesday. That gives you some time to get some stuff in order."

"I got no place to stay," he said.

She looked at him, a puzzled look cutting a fissure in her forehead.

He laughed softly.

"I live in a bad neighborhood," he said. This she would understand. "Carrolton Oaks."

"Ah." A flash of recognition. Naturally, Samantha had seen countless news stories reporting the latest drug bust or drive-by shooting at the Tree.

"Dude I knew found out I won some money last night," he said. "There was some trouble."

"I see," Samantha said in her most professional and lawyerly voice.

"I walked around all night," Julius said. "Didn't even have enough cash for a hotel room. Ain't that a kick in the ass?"

"We'll find you a place for the weekend," Samantha said. "Don't worry about that."

Julius nodded. A weight seemed to have been lifted from his shoulders.

"OK, let's talk numbers," she said. "First of all, you need to understand that the government is going to hit you hard with taxes."

"Oh," Julius said, a cloud settling over him again. The government was going to leave him with nothing. He'd probably owe them money. What a goddamn racket the lottery was. No wonder they called it a tax on poor people.

"Hang on," she said. "I don't want you to get the idea that you're going to be scraping by. If you take the money all at once, rather than in yearly installments, my guess is that you're going to walk away with about a hundred and fifty million dollars, free and clear."

He laughed out loud, a laugh that broke free of him like an escaped jail inmate. There hadn't been a whole lot of shit worth laughing about in Julius' life, and so the fact that he was laughing at all came as a great surprise to him. A shiver rippled through him like an earthquake, and he laughed until tears rolled down his cheeks.

"Yeah," Samantha said. "It's a lot of money. Don't worry. We're going to help you all the way through. You're going to be able to do anything you want. You'll be able to take care of your kids, your kids' kids, your kids – well, you get the idea."

Julius smiled. He felt comfortable with her. Her boss was a jackass, but with each passing minute, he became more confident he'd knocked on the right door earlier this evening.

"Do you have a will, Julius?" she asked.

He laughed. "No."

"You'll need one," she said. "The firm has a trusts and estates section. Do you have a family?"

"No," he said.

"Parents? Siblings?"

"Parents dead," he said. "Brother got killed 'bout ten years ago."

"Cousins?"

"Yeah, a few. Some might even be related to me."

"I'll tell you one thing," she said. "Anyone you've ever met in the last ten years is going to claim to be your cousin."

"Yeah," he said.

Silence followed.

"Actually..." he said.

"What?"

"I do have a son," he said.

"Oh?"

"Jamal."

"How old is he?"

"Fifteen. I think."

"Where does he live?"

"I think with his grandmother. His mama died a while back. I haven't seen them in a long time. I think they live in Ravenwood Court."

Julius tried to act embarrassed because he thought that was what Samantha would expect.

JAMAL WHEELER HAD BEEN the unexpected fruit of a brief and fumbling encounter with a young woman named Alicia. Maybe was it Alison. Alyssa? Julius had never been able to remember. He met her at a party about nine months before Jamal was born. They were both drunk, a keg of beer playing its part as the social lubricant for the evening. Julius had been quite charming, quite debonair, and sometime around three in the morning, Julius and Alicia/Alison/Alyssa consummated their relationship in the breezeway outside the apartment building. Immediately before the forty seconds of intercourse commenced, she inquired whether Julius had a condom. Although Julius did not have one because he didn't like the way they felt, he assured her that he would "pull out in time."

He did not.

When they were done, he zipped up, went home and, before turning in for the night, tossed the girl's telephone number in the trash. Eight weeks later, after two missed periods and unrelenting nausea, the girl took a pregnancy test, which came back positive. The girl, whose name, Julius decided, almost certainly began with the letter A, decided to keep the baby for a number of reasons, primarily because she thought it would convince Julius to hook up with her again.

After steadfastly refusing to take her calls, Julius didn't see her again for about six months, when she approached him while he was playing hoops near the Tree. At first, he didn't even remember who she was. When she reminded him of the romantic moments they had spent in the breeze-way, he was immediately disgusted by the presence of the large belly. He didn't roll with big girls, and he wrote it off to having been pretty drunk that night. It never occurred to him that she was pregnant.

When she told him that not only was she pregnant, but that Julius himself was the baby-daddy, her hope that he would sweep her up into his arms and tell her everything would be OK did not, shockingly enough, come to pass. He certainly did not admit that the baby was his, because seriously, this was the Tree, and young men did not admit paternity in the Tree until a blood test gave them no other choice.

Three months later, the girl gave birth to a healthy baby boy. That the baby was healthy was remarkable, given the fact that his mother spent most of her evenings drinking, smoking and dancing and received no prenatal care until she arrived at the hospital, fully dilated. Julius, of course,

was not present at the birth. Once mother and son arrived
home from the hospital, people quickly noted the strong
resemblance between father and son.

Julius first saw his son when he was two weeks old,
resembling his father more and more with each passing day.
He was on his way home (where he had boxes of condoms
in his night stand), another young lady on his arm, and ran
into Jamal and his mother in the courtyard, where she was
trying to soothe her crying son in the cool night air. The
meeting was, to say the least, awkward. Julius refused the
mother's offer to hold the child. She called him an asshole
and warned the young lady accompanying Julius that she
had contracted herpes from him a month earlier. The girl
left, but Julius didn't even notice. He was so freaked out by
seeing his flesh and blood that he fled to his apartment and
hid for two days.

He didn't see much of them over the next year, avoiding
them when he could. If he saw them in the courtyard, he
went the other way. She called him once asking for child
support, but she might as well have asked him for the identity of the second gunman in Dallas. He laughed at her and
hung up.

When Jamal was about two, he and his mother left the
Tree for good. In the first couple years after they left, Julius
heard rumors about their whereabouts. Another housing
project in Richmond. South Carolina. Texas. Southern Cali-
fornia. Early on, he wondered a lot about little Jamal,
growing up without his real father. Eventually though, he
stopped wondering about Jamal's fatherless existence, and
not long after that, he pretty much stopped wondering
about Jamal at all. After all, Julius was far too occupied
stealing stuff and trying to get laid. God, he'd been such an
idiot back then. More than a decade later, Julius heard from

a cousin that Jamal's mother had died and that Jamal was living in Ravenwood, a housing project on the south side of town.

"I'D LIKE to see Jamal taken care of," Julius said. "Without him knowing about me. No point for him to struggle like me. I wasn't much of a father. Seems the least I could do."

"That's fine," Samantha said, making some notes on a legal pad. "That's something the firm can take care of. Since he's a minor, we can set up a blind trust, appoint a trustee who can deal with him directly and manage the money. We'll set it up so even the trustee won't know the money is coming from you. Is his last name Wheeler?"

"I think so."

"And the mother's last name?"

He shook his head. He saw this concerned her.

"Don't worry. Most kids from the 'hood take their daddy's name. I heard it makes it easier to qualify for benefits. Or something."

"Oh."

"How will they know if it's really Jamal?" he asked.

"They can verify identity through DNA testing," she said. "Take a strand of his hair, compare it to yours."

"Right," Julius said.

"Do you have a recent picture of him?"

"I ain't seen him since he was a baby."

"And you said he lives in Ravenwood?"

"Maybe. I'm not a hundred percent sure."

She made a note of it on her legal pad, enclosing both the name of Julius' son and the name of the complex in a block of blue ink.

"What else?" she asked, mostly of herself. "You can probably afford a place to stay now. Somewhere a little less exciting than Carrolton Oaks. Maybe another city. Even another state."

"Another state? I never lived nowhere else."

Samantha weighed her words carefully.

"Listen," she began, "when you go public, you're going to attract a lot of attention. From family, friends, people who'll tell you they're your friends. People who'll tell you just about anything. People who will get pissed off or worse if you don't help them out because what do you need with all that money?"

In his mind's eye, Julius saw Leroy breaking down Monk's apartment door.

"You really think that it'll be like that?"

"One thing I've learned working here is that money makes people crazy," she said. "Doesn't matter if they're white, black, purple. And you have a shitload of it."

She was right. Had he really thought it would end with Leroy? At first, he had bristled at her words because he figured it was because he was just a black dude from the projects. Hell, it probably was, at least in part, but that didn't make it any less true. He had close to a dozen cousins of varying familial proximity scattered through Richmond's housing projects. He didn't know whether some, none or all of them were even related to him. He could only imagine what they would do when they found out he had a bazillion dollars in the bank.

"No offense, but I'm trying to be honest with you," she said. "Tell you what you need to know."

"No, it's cool," Julius said. "You right. I got enough problems to worry about anyway."

THEY SPENT another thirty minutes making a wish list that Julius could barely wrap his head around. He threw out every wild-haired idea he had ever had, every crazy fantasy he had imagined in prison. Samantha wrote each one down without comment, without acting like it was silly or ridiculous. When they were done, she placed her notes in a folder and set it on her desk. She called Carter and told him they were done.

"Fine," he said. "Just leave it on your desk."

He sounded distracted, which annoyed Samantha almost more than anything else that he had done in the time she had worked for him. She might have cut him a break had she known that he was currently sitting across from his very pregnant paralegal.

"I'm going to take off," she said. "Probably not much reason for me to be working late anymore."

"Fine," he said.

She started to hang up but stopped. She hated to ask, but she couldn't afford to let it go.

"Carter?"

"What?"

"Do you really think this might change the Committee's mind?"

"Yeah, yeah, sure."

"Thanks."

She felt dirty for bringing it up. But shit, it mattered, didn't it? She had to do everything she could, right?

"Fine."

She was silent a moment, feeling like she had mortgaged her soul just by asking.

"What should I do with Julius?" she asked.

"Who?"

"Julius? The client?"

"Right," he said. "Um–"

"Forget it," she said. "I'll set him up in the partners' lounge. He can watch television and have a couple drinks until you're ready to meet with him. I think we should check him into the Marriott on Fifth until Wednesday morning."

"Yeah, good idea. Not sure we have any malt liquor in there though."

Carter laughed hysterically at his own joke and hung up.

"Seems like a nice guy," Julius said.

"He's an ass," she said. "Follow me. The partners' lounge is really nice. Full bar, stocked fridge, widescreen TV. When Carter's done talking to you, he's going to take you to the Marriott. You'll stay there until you can go cash in your ticket."

"Appreciate your help," Julius said.

"Don't worry," she said. "You'll get a bill for every bit of the help."

They took the elevator to the twenty-fifth floor, where they found the partners' lounge dark. Samantha flipped on the light, revealing the opulence that the firm's bottomless pit of income could buy. The north wall was made entirely of three-inch-thick smoked glass. Four leather couches were set up in the southwest corner, surrounding a large LED television. A full bar stood ready against the east wall.

"You hungry?" she asked.

He nodded.

She pointed him to the Viking refrigerator. "Help yourself. The television is pretty easy to use."

"What if someone else shows up?"

"I doubt anyone will, but if they do, just tell them to call Carter Pierce. Everyone's afraid of him."

Julius looked around the room, his breathing rapid and shallow. Samantha watched the man try to pull himself together, and her heart went out to him. This she did not often see in her practice.

"It's gonna be OK," she said, squeezing his shoulder. "Listen, if you need anything tonight, let me give you my cell phone number." She wrote it down on a piece of scrap paper, which Julius tucked into his pocket.

"I'll see you later," she said. "Relax. You're a rich man now."

9

Dawn was pregnant.

This tidbit shoved its way up to the bar in Carter's head, where previously, Julius' lottery ticket had been drinking alone. This new patron was pissed and needed a shot.

He and Dawn had really decided nothing. Nothing other than concluding that they were screwed six ways to Sunday. He poured a glass of scotch and stared out the window. He couldn't believe it – he really was screwed. There was no thought, no consideration of leaving Ashley for Dawn. He certainly did not love her. He wasn't sure he liked her all that much. Stripped down to its core, the relationship was basically a live-action version of what he checked out on his favorite Internet porn sites. And now she was having his child. Dynamite.

Ashley. Christ, what a headache she was going to be.

He thought about the arc of their relationship, which had begun with such promise seventeen years ago. He first met Ashley Matheson on a Thursday night during a fundraiser at the Virginia Museum of Fine Arts. He'd been with the firm a couple of years, and Ashley was a kindergarten teacher. At twenty-seven, she was becoming increasingly antsy about her unmarried status. Nearly all her friends were married, and most already had little ones pitter-pattering around the house.

They were both a little tipsy, happening upon the same impressionistic painting at the same time. He tried to act like he knew what the painting meant, and she acted like she gave a crap. It was a momentous event, the laying of the cornerstone of emotional deceit that would become the foundation of their relationship. Later that night, they had angry (her contribution) and sloppy (his) sex in her apartment. When he woke up the next morning and wasn't overwhelmed with the urge to run screaming into the streets, he decided that there might be a future with this woman.

They jumped into the relationship with both feet. Within a year, they were married. They bought an old Victorian house in the Fan, a historical district just west of downtown, and they started playing house upper-class style. Ashley joined the Junior League. They both joined the Country Club of Virginia, where he played golf every Saturday. He did so despite the fact that he hated playing golf. All his co-workers seemed to like it, so he made himself like it as well. He had never shot under 115.

He worked ninety-hour weeks as the race for partnership kicked into overdrive. Meanwhile, Ashley taught kindergarten at St. Michael's, Carter's own alma mater. Many of the students were children of Carter's co-workers. These were the attorneys who lived inside the city limits of Richmond and wouldn't dare send their kids to a city school. Although they were taxed heavily themselves, they didn't contribute nearly enough to the city's tax base to give rise to decent public schools.

Ashley soured on the marriage within a year, but before she had a chance to nail down an appropriate divorce lawyer, she discovered she was pregnant. An ultrasound revealed twins, which pushed thoughts of ending the marriage to the back burner. Taking center stage were baby registries, endless cravings for Taco Bell, a four-thousand-dollar crib, and other games of upper-class pregnancy. Two of her friends in the Junior League were also pregnant, and suddenly, she was part of a super-exclusive club. Weekends were spent on baby-buying frenzies. Evenings, when she was alone waiting for Carter to come home, she read baby books.

Despite her commitment to prenatal care and advance preparation, the reality of motherhood was much different than the pictures she had painted for herself. Carter took three days off after the twins' birth and then went right back to his hellish work schedule. Ashley's mother came to visit for a week, during which time she witnessed her only daughter display a shocking lack of any maternal instinct.

Ashley never got the hang of breastfeeding, and so she turned to formula relatively quickly. Medically speaking, this would have been fine, except that preparing formula also seemed to be beyond her maternal capabilities. The twins' pediatrician, Terry Murphy, was deeply concerned by Ashley's apparent inability to grasp the fairly simple concept of mixing the powder in tap water. The twins lost an alarming amount of weight between the day they left the hospital and their two-week checkup. The doctor gently urged Ashley to use ready-made formula and had her bring the girls in for weight checks every day for the next week. If they weren't steadily putting on weight, the pediatrician warned her that he'd have to call Social Services. The idea of a child protective services worker in the Pierces' neighborhood galvanized the new parents into action, and Ashley began buying premade infant formula.

The girls did begin putting on weight, and Ashley settled into her role as their distant, inattentive, and relatively disinterested mother. She quit her job as a teacher and began drinking during the girls' naps. Being a stay-at-home mom was more than she could handle, so when the girls were six months old, she enrolled them in a Montessori school. By the time they were three, they'd been expelled from that school and two other daycare centers for a marked refusal to comply with their teachers' instructions.

Madison and Cameron grew into bright, beautiful and out-of-control young women. This stemmed largely from their parents' total unwillingness to impose either discipline or rules from the time they were old enough to have rules and discipline. By the age of twelve, Madison was nipping scotch. By the age of fourteen, Cameron had discovered the joys of marijuana. Both were smart enough to stay in the top ten percent of their high school class, which helped keep the 'rents off their back. It also kept the cell phones, the platinum digital cable package, and the high-speed Internet in service, along with gas in the Jeeps.

The marriage was sacrificed at the twin altars of partnership and wealth. Carter was too busy with work to devote any time to the marriage beyond a fancy dinner and a one-night's stay at the Jefferson Hotel for their anniversary. He began cheating on Ashley about two years into the marriage. His first foray into infidelity involved a fellow associate attorney, a wide-eyed brunette named Amanda Patton. She was interested only in sex, and that was fine with Carter. In its own way, it set the table for his future affairs – sex only, no secret, loving relationship that operated in the dark behind his marriage to Ashley.

There had been half a dozen or so over the years, each involving a woman remarkably similar to the one that had kicked off his adulterous adventures. This had helped avert any risk of feelings getting in the way of a good time. All had been fun, quick-moving, and all had burned out like fire-crackers. He had assumed that was where he had been headed with Dawn, at least until she had told him that she had his proverbial bun in her oven.

His phone rang, and he immediately recognized the number on the caller ID screen. He was afraid to take the call, but he was even more afraid not to.

"Hello?"

"Carter, it's Blinky."

Blinky was Carter's bookie and the man to whom Carter currently owed the $140,000 in gambling losses.

"Hey there you."

"Yeah, Merry Christmas!"

"Same to you."

"So, I'm sitting here, thinking it's almost Christmas, and my kid wants an iPad all of a sudden, one with the 3G connection and all that, and I get to wondering, iPads are not cheap, and I was thinking, 'hey, my good friend Carter Pierce owes me a little bit of scratch,' and I'm wondering when are you gonna have my money?"

"Soon, Blinky. Next week."

"I'm sitting here, Carter, and I hear you say that, and I think, 'Carter said, 'soon, Blinky, next week,' last week, and I'm starting to get a little disappointed in my friend Carter."

"Year-end bonus coming up next week, Blinky. I swear."

"I hope it's been a good year, Carter, because I want it to be a good year too, and if it's not a good year by, say, the time the ball drops in Times Square, I'd bet it's not gonna be a very Happy New Year for one of us in this conversation."

Carter's stomach flipped.

"So enjoy the Christmas and all that and let's make sure things are square by the time baby New Year shows up. Or it won't be a happy new year at all."

The line clicked dead.

Carter recounted the events of what had proven to be a terrible day:

1.His wife pushed him ever closer to the brink of bankruptcy.

2.His mistress announced she was pregnant.

3.His bookie had threatened to kill him.

4.His janitor had won four hundred million bucks.

It was this last nugget that he could not get out of his head. Just thinking about it made his head hurt. Julius or Jerome or whatever his name was – the crack dealer, the pimp, his goddamn janitor – had won the lottery! It seemed a particularly cruel blow for Fate to deliver, in his darkest hour, while he was suffering. As he sat here on one of the last days of the year, he thought it was as good a time as any to take stock of his life.

Didn't he deserve better? He had worked hard. He had gone to a good college, a solid law school. He'd put in the long hours, the sweat, the toil, and what had he gotten in return? A job he had hated for years. A shell of a marriage. A mistress whose ovaries had laughed in the face of contraception. Twin nightmares for daughters. No son to carry on the family name.

Maybe Dawn would have a boy. Maybe he'd take the Pierce name. Wasn't that what they did in the projects? Every goddamn kid, a different last name than the mother. And Dawn could do a lot worse than naming her kid Carter

Livingston Pierce, Jr. Or even Carter Livingston Pierce, II. He'd always liked that, the II hung on the end of a name like marble pillars. Next to the commonplace III, it sounded goddamn regal.

He thought about how it would play out in the firm. Naturally, no one would be told, at least officially, that Dawn was carrying Carter's baby. But it would, of course, get out. It would be like a grassroots campaign, starting with the support staff. Word would trickle up the chain until it was discussed in the executive dining room. No one would say anything to Carter's face. Some attorneys might even feel a twinge of envy. Dawn was considered one of the hottest paralegals at the firm. This was not a matter of opinion, as the male partners kept a Top 25 list in the sauna and updated it monthly to account for boob jobs, new hires and the like.

The partners wouldn't give a shit about the pregnancy, given that half of them had sired children out of wedlock. It was like an NBA team. As long as Carter Pierce kept winning, kept bringing in the business and kept the business in the house, he could take a dump on the floor of his office and no one would say boo.

He wondered if he could keep the news away from Ashley, say forever. You never knew what she might pull when she found out about the pregnancy. The crazy pill-addled cougar might divorce him. Or she might use the child as the ultimate bargaining chip for the rest of his natural life. There was no way to know.

Not telling her scared him even more, because who the hell was he kidding? She would find out. Once word spilled out into the open waters of the firm, it would only be a matter of time before one of his colleagues' backstabbing wives would blab it to Ashley at lunch. Not as a gesture of friendship, but to be the one who got to break the news, because at that moment, the bearer of bad news could rest comfortably in the knowledge that someone else's life was in a bigger shitter than hers.

That his mistress' pregnancy was not even his biggest problem at the moment was really saying something. He thought about Blinky, who, as Carter recalled, had a bit of a temper and claimed he owned a blowtorch. This scared Carter a little – actually it scared him a lot – because despite what he had told the man, Carter would not have the money by New Year's Eve. He thought again about the small, gimpy man's warning that the people he did business with had made people owing far less money disappear. He knew that Blinky had only let Carter ride such a high line of credit because he seemed like a successful man. What Blinky did not know was that Carter was heavily leveraged and cash poor. Carter wondered if he could sign over the title to one of the vacation homes to the guy but dismissed the idea just as quickly. He didn't have six figures in equity in the three homes combined, let alone one of them. And he was pretty sure that the adjustable rate mortgage was about to adjust upward again.

Again, he thought about the lottery ticket, drifting along the track of his mind like a solitary train car. He envisioned himself with the money. He wished he could divorce Ashley and give her ten million bucks on the condition that she never talk to him again. Then again, the money would ease the strain on their marriage. What the hell – maybe they would stick it out. They could move to an island and live on a big plantation. He could set the girls up for life. He could set up Dawn and her baby for life. He could set up future generations for life. He would invest wisely, make the money work for him. Make the Pierce name synonymous with wealth and stature. Like the Kennedys!

The lottery ticket train car kept rolling along the track until it coupled with the other train car in his mind, a boxcar loaded with fear and worry. And then suddenly, it became clear, like a picture in his mind, a snapshot of an event that had yet to pass but most certainly would.

10

T he more Carter thought about it, the more he liked the idea of stealing Julius' ticket and cashing it for himself. The morality of the caper, quite frankly, never entered his cost-benefit analysis. He always believed that a good lawyer never let morality invade the province of law. No, his main problem would be separating man from ticket.

Julius would do anything to protect that ticket. The key would be convincing Julius that he was in a safe place. Earn his trust. Get physical custody of the ticket, ride it out until Wednesday morning, when lottery headquarters would re-open after Christmas. Cash it in, smile big for the camera and disappear from the face of the Earth.

He began sketching out a plan. Julius was counting on Carter to protect him, look out for his interests. That misplaced trust would serve as the foundation for the scheme. He was Julius' lawyer, and Julius would do what Carter told him to do.

Before he could get to all that, though, he had to deal with Samantha, the poster child for bleeding heart lawyers everywhere. That she had been passed over for partner might actually work in his favor. Now that her career with the firm was kaput, she might have a financial incentive to help him. He could throw a few million at her in exchange for her silence, an offer that he thought she might be receptive to. He had seen her harden over the years like concrete, the light in her idealistic eyes slowly flickering out as she learned the realities of the practice of law. And now, all she had left to look at was the wreckage of her career. Yeah, she wouldn't be a problem, but he'd better make it five million. Five million dollars. All the money she would ever need. And for what? Looking the other way? Such a small thing. And if her moral compass quivered, he could always play on her guilt. He knew that she helped her parents' struggling business, that she had relatives in the Middle East she sent money to.

The second issue would, of course, be facilitating the parting of ways between Julius and the ticket. The best and easiest option would be to advise him to store the ticket at the firm to ensure its safety. The problem was that Carter thought it unlikely that Julius would agree to such an arrangement. Julius might have been an uneducated thug from the projects, but he did not appear to have calamari stuffed in between his ears. He wasn't going to let that ticket out of his sight until he handed it over to lottery officials the following Wednesday.

Carter needed to overpower him somehow. The idea scared him more than a bit, because, after all, Julius was a beefy thug from the projects. Carter, a slender but flabby 180 pounds, rode a stationary bicycle three mornings a week while checking his phone. Slowly, a plan began to form in his head. It was going to cost him at least a few million, probably a lot more, but it would be worth it.

He picked up the phone and placed a call. The line picked up after two rings.

"Go," a voice said upon picking up.

"Todd, it's Carter."

"What up?"

TODD MATHESON WAS Ashley Pierce's younger brother, a self-described entrepreneur who had never held any legal job for longer than six months. The working world had never really appealed to Todd, nor did it find him particularly appealing. He discovered at a relatively young age, however, that he had an aptitude for deceit and worked industriously to hone his skills. It was widely known but never discussed at holiday dinners that Todd was a con man.

It wasn't as if Todd Matheson hadn't been granted every opportunity that an upper-middle class upbringing afforded. Like Carter, he had attended St. Michael's, where he first began his criminal enterprise. He didn't join the Key Club or the swim team, focusing his efforts instead on commerce, a true Future Businessman of America. He peddled a range of items, from ecstasy to bootleg Grateful Dead concert tapes to illegally obtained old exams to prescription medication.

His life as a dealer began without much fanfare, just one weekend when he realized he had more weed in his pocket than he could smoke. He sold it to a group of girls home from college for Thanksgiving. When he was dry, he went back to his dealer, a sophomore at James Madison University, and offered to fill the retail need in Richmond's private school market. And there was a need. The dealer agreed, and Todd was off and running, buying wholesale and kicking up twenty percent of his profits.

And by no means was Todd Matheson a one-trick pony. Using a network of spies he enlisted, he blackmailed teachers that were sleeping with students, students who cheated on tests, and administrators who cheated on their spouses. His rackets generated a relatively steady monthly income, one that he used to bankroll a luxurious lifestyle throughout his high school years.

He continued his ways during his four years at Hampden-Sydney College, a small all-male college in south-central Virginia catering to any good man seeking a good education, as long as that man was Southern, wealthy and could trace his lineage back to the Mayflower. As soon as freshman orientation was over, Todd started dealing marijuana and cocaine to these rich, spoiled sons of the Confederacy. Although his venture was relatively profitable, Todd enjoyed living beyond his means. The summer before his sophomore year, he bought a large house on the outskirts of Farmville.

He hosted lavish parties that attracted the horny boozehounds of Hampden-Sydney and husband-hunting co-eds from every small women's college within a fifty-mile radius. He installed a bar in every room, stocking each one with top-shelf liquor. Bowls of cocaine had been scattered through the house like party bowls of peanuts. To his friends, he provided vials of GHB, the date rape drug. He bought three big-screen televisions and drove a Porsche 911.

Todd's proclivity toward excess was surpassed only by his tendency to run his mouth. He was an enthusiastic public relations man. He talked about his dealers, his income, his clients, and his plan to become the biggest dealer in the Southeast. He directed most of this chatter to the young ladies whose pants he was constantly trying to remove. Eventually, he caught the ears of the Farmville Sheriff's Office, and two of its enterprising young sheriff's deputies began surveillance of Todd's activities at the house.

Within a week, they observed patterns consistent with drug trafficking and quickly obtained a search warrant. The strike team found four garbage bags full of marijuana, sixty-eight bricks of cocaine, and twelve binders crammed with sheets of LSD. It was one of the biggest drug busts in the history of southwest Virginia. This attracted the attention of the Drug Enforcement Agency, who wanted to use Todd to blow out the supply pipeline.

Facing fifteen years in a federal prison, Todd quickly became a DEA informant. In exchange for testifying against his suppliers, he was allowed to plead guilty to a state possession charge, and he spent eighteen months in a regional jail. When he got out, his drug supply, not surprisingly, had dried up. He had heard that there was a contract put out on his head. Now saddled with a felony conviction that would follow every job application he'd ever fill out, Todd was less interested than ever in joining the real world.

He turned to conning, which proved to be far easier than the accounting headache of drug dealing. His first scam involved scaring senior citizens into thinking their homes needed expensive repairs. He'd knock on the door of old widows at the beginning of the month, just after they'd received their social security checks. His voice dripping with honey and charm, he'd warn of runaway termite infestations, cracked foundations, or failing roofs, depending on his mood. There was no time to waste! He used fancy words like joists and gables and scared the seniors with statistics as to how much wood termites could eat in twenty-four hours. A small deposit would get Matheson Construction on the job just as soon as an opening cleared on the schedule. Of course, that would be the last time the victims would ever see Todd Matheson. He changed banks frequently, opened numerous accounts, created dozens of shell companies. He ran gambling scams, investment scams, pyramid schemes. He conned bored and lonely house-wives. He conned folks who longed to get rich quick.

He was an equal-opportunity con man.

TODD WALTZED into Carter's office without knocking, even though the door was closed. He carried two bags of Chinese takeout and recommended that they make it a working dinner. Once they got the plates set up, Carter dipped a chunk of battered chicken into the neon-red sweet-and-sour sauce and popped the bite into his mouth. He noticed Todd staring at him, Todd's forkful of sesame chicken suspended midway between his plate and his mouth.

"How'd they make the sauce that color?" asked Todd.

"How am I supposed to know?" replied Carter, his mouth full.

"I mean, look at that shit. It's almost glowing."

"It tastes good," Carter said. "Shut up."

"I mean, that can't be good for you."

"Just leave me alone."

"I'm just saying is all. It looks radioactive."

"Can we get back to work?"

"Right, right," said Todd. He got up from the couch, dumped the remnants of his dinner into Carter's trash can, and lit a cigarette.

"How many times I gotta tell you, that makes my eyes burn," Carter said.

"I could give a witch's fuck." He blew smoke rings into the air.

The smoke made Carter's head throb, and his eyes watered. He had never met anyone like Todd Preston Matheson. The first time they met, Todd asked Carter how he liked "poking Ashley." Todd laughed like a jackal when Carter replied, surprising even himself, that he liked it "fine." Todd had given him a wink and smacked him on his buttocks. It was the most uncomfortable conversation Carter had ever had.

Todd always treated Carter well, which Carter attributed to the fact the he and Ashley had given Todd free use of both the beach cottage and the condo in Park City. As hard as Carter worked, Todd spent more time in each than his brother-in-law.

Carter had not wanted to seek out Todd's help, but the more he thought about what he was doing, the less confident he felt in his abilities to pull it off. He came to this conclusion even though it was going to cost him dearly. He envisioned one scenario after another, all of which ended with Julius blowing his brains out with a Glock or whatever it was these hoodlums used these days, and justifiably so. Oh, Carter fancied himself a fiery litigator, but dealing with a street thug like Julius was as foreign to him as wrestling a cobra. It wasn't like presenting a breach of contract case to a mediator.

Not surprisingly, Todd had been incredibly anxious to assist his Carter in this venture. Carter agreed to cut him in for $50 million in exchange for successfully extracting the ticket from Julius' clutches. Todd told him to relax, that he would take care of everything. Nothing would be left to chance, and no one would get hurt.

"Fine," Carter said, deciding the cigarette wasn't worth arguing about. "I hope you get lung cancer."

"I'm sure as fuck gonna outlive you."

Todd smoked in silence while Carter finished off his sweet-and-sour chicken.

"So, where is this nigger?" he asked, putting out his cigarette on the side of Carter's desk. Racial sensitivity was not Todd Matheson's strong suit.

"He's in the partners' lounge watching television."

"Watching Soul Train?" He laughed at his joke. "And the little hottie?"

"Samantha?"

"Yeah, the Syrian chick."

"She's Lebanese."

"Whatever. She gonna be a problem?"

"I'm cutting her in for a few million," Carter said. "She needs the money."

"A few million? Jesus! Why don't you just give her all of it?" He took a long drag from his cigarette. "Pussy."

"It's gotta be enough to convince her to do it," Carter said. "Keep her quiet."

"Fine."

"You're gonna walk away with more out of this deal than you'll ever need," Carter said. "Stop bitching."

Todd was quiet. Carter was pleased that he'd been able to shut Todd up, even though this sudden burst of silence had nothing to do with Carter's ability to control the man. Carter knew that Todd's imagination had gotten away from him, as it had done a few times since Carter explained what precisely he needed his help for. He was probably thinking of hosting a threesome on his new yacht.

"You still with me?" Carter asked after the silence had gotten uncomfortable.

"I'm gonna get so much ass," Todd said.

Carter noticed a pup tent in Todd's pants, and he looked away, horrified.

"So what's your plan?" Carter asked.

Todd clapped his hands together and scooted forward on the loveseat.

"It's perfect. We tell him I'm firm security," he said. "You and I are going to escort him out to an undisclosed location for his own safety. Keep him there until we – I mean, he – can cash the ticket next week."

Carter nodded.

"How big is this dude?" Todd asked.

"About six feet, I guess. Shorter than you," Carter said. Another thing in their favor was that Todd was a beast of a man. He was six-four and tipped the scales at a robust two-seventy. And Carter knew he wasn't afraid to use it.

"He shouldn't be a problem," Todd said. "You know the shit I learned in the slammer?"

"Yeah, you've mentioned it once or twice."

"Don't get smart with me," Todd said. "I'm the reason you're gonna end up with this ticket."

Carter was careful not to underestimate his new client, but he was confident that together, he and Todd possessed a significant physical advantage over Julius.

"How old?"

"I dunno. Forty?"

"Probably done time," Todd said. "Got to expect a fight."

This made Carter nervous. Anything could go wrong. Money made people do crazy shit. Then he thought about Blinky and his blowtorch. In his mind, he could hear the tongue of flame hissing, angrily looking for something to consume. He wondered where Blinky would start. His eyelids? His toes? Probably something small, leave something to work with later. Carter Pierce pictured his nuts being turned to charcoal, and he felt his stomach turn to liquid.

"I'll be right back," he said suddenly, leaping for the door. "The food didn't sit well."

"I told you. The fucking sauce."

"Fine! It was the sauce!" he said, stomping out in search of the nearest bathroom.

When Carter got back to his office, he found Todd looking at porn on the web. Todd made no attempt to close the web browser, cover his tracks.

"God, I love the Internet," Todd remarked. "Imagine if they'd had this when we were fifteen. I don't know how any teenage boy leaves the house."

"I guess. Are we all set?"

"Yeah," Todd said.

"So what's the plan?"

"We get him to the cabin."

"Yeah, I got that part," Carter said. "It was my idea."

"Then we jump him."

Carter was flabbergasted.

"Jump him? What the hell do you mean, 'jump him'?"

"Relax, baby. It's all taken care of."

Todd lifted up his shirt, revealing the butt of a chrome-plated pistol tucked into his waistband.

"Oh, Jesus," Carter said, stepping back as if Todd had pulled the gun on him.

"He gives us the ticket, and we call the police on him, tell them he was breaking in," he said. He added: "Why does this have to be complicated? It's my house. We'll tell them he was in the office one evening we were talking about my being out of town. Look, if we even mention getting the ticket away from him, he's going to think something's up. Tomorrow, notify his company that you saw him stealing change from people's offices. Have Ashley call and pretend to be your paralegal. Take the family to Cancun for a week. When you get back, we cash in the ticket."

Carter nodded his head. That's right. It didn't need to be complicated. Just pin Julius in a corner he would never get out of, and then destroy his credibility. No one would ever believe his claim to the ticket.

"Where's Samantha?" Todd asked.

"She took off after she met with him about what he wants to do with the money."

"Good," Todd said. "Also, we need to get all the notes she took from her office. Don't let her know what we're doing. Don't let her anywhere near the guy. When the time comes, we'll cut her in."

"What if she doesn't go for it?"

"By then, it will be too late," he said. "When you cash the ticket, no one else will have a legitimate claim to it. If she causes trouble, I don't know, we'll make it look like they were in on it together."

"But they don't even know each other."

"Come on, Carter. You ever heard of a little jungle fever?" Todd said. He stood up and thrust his hips back and forth in a sexually suggestive manner. "She works late, he works late, a few sparks fly, you win the lottery, and they come up with a plan to defraud the legitimate winner of this historic jackpot."

"Looks like we're all set."

"Get our boy in here," Todd said. "Try not to eff it up."

11

S amantha's head was pounding when she pulled up to her parents' house in Glen Allen, an older suburb just north of Richmond. The sky was a sickly orange, the thick cloud cover reflecting the city lights, and the snow was coming down steadily. The driveway was full, so she parked on the grassy strip alongside the drainage culvert that fronted her parents' property. The house sat at the top of a small cul-de-sac, surrounded by seven other almost identical ranchers. Her parents had lived in this small three-bedroom ranch for thirty-five years. It was where Samantha had grown up with her younger sisters, Mariam and Emily, and her brother Ziad. Both sisters were married with kids, even though they were younger than her, her mother liked to remind her roughly once every half hour.

Samantha didn't make it out here often anymore, about two or three times a month. She liked to tell herself (and her parents) that it was because of the heavy sacrifice the firm demanded. The truth was that sitting out in her comfortable Audi, as she often did before going inside, looking at the clapboard structure with the peeling paint made her stomach clench with guilt. Guilt about her parents' sacrifices, guilt about her relationship with them, guilt about her failure to have her own family, guilt about the family she still had in Lebanon, guilt about not feeling guilty enough. And some general non-specific guilt to cover anything she might have missed.

She lit and took a few drags from a cigarette she found in the center console, chasing the smoke with two pieces of gum. When she was confident that her mother would either miss or politely ignore the aromatic residue left behind by Samantha's secret vice, she gave herself a quick once-over in the rearview mirror and got out of the car. As she made her way up the cracked and snow-glazed sidewalk, she glanced over at the driveway, trying to get a sense of who was here tonight. Her sisters and their children, of course, because they never missed Friday dinner at home. They were both married to doctors, both of whom were working tonight. Her sisters were both stay-at-home moms. This, she knew, pleased her mother Zaina, who despite all her pronouncements about the importance of education, seemed to be at peace with the fact that both her younger daughters had graduate degrees and no jobs.

The cherry-red Miata belonged to her maternal uncle Tamir, who owned the all-important title of FAVORITE UNCLE. He was the one who never judged her, never treated her like a child, always supported any decision that she made, and if it backfired on her, never said, "I told you so."

A black Jeep Wrangler announced the presence of her dad's first cousin, Hisham. He owned a struggling Mediterranean restaurant and drank a little too much. She could tell how poorly the restaurant was doing in a given month based on how tipsy he was at the family dinners. When he got really loaded, he became what Samantha liked to call 'grabby' with any female in his crosshairs.

The din was audible from the front porch. Even from here, she could hear Hisham rambling on about something or other. The playful squeals of her three nieces and lone nephew broke up the important grown-up talk that would only get angrier as the evening wore on.

She took a deep breath and stepped inside.

THE AROMA of kibbe baking in her mother's oven filled the house, and even though she felt like dog poo stuck between the treads of a running shoe, Samantha's mouth watered. She hadn't had lunch, and smelling the kibbe now just about made her knees buckle. She loved the traditional Lebanese dish, which consisted of seasoned ground beef layered in a casserole dish and stuffed with sautéed onions, pine nuts and spices.

Samantha found her mother alone in the small kitchen, squeezing two lemons into a giant glass bowl of tabouli, a salad common throughout the Middle East. Like Samantha, Zaina Khouri was a small, slender woman with olive skin. She had lived in the U.S. since she and Omar, Samantha's dad, had immigrated here forty years earlier. The kitchen was not much bigger than a walk-in closet, but it had produced about ninety-five percent of the meals that Samantha had eaten between the time she was born and when she left for college.

"Hi, Mama," Samantha said. She squeezed her mother on the shoulder. "Not too much bulghur in that."

"Don't you worry about that," Zaina said in broken English. "How ya doin', honey? You late."

"I had to work," Samantha said. "And I've got a cold."

"You supposed to be here two hours ago."

"Mama, come on," Samantha said, absently checking her phone. No new messages. She set the mobile phone down on the kitchen counter.

Over the years, Samantha had learned that while the Lebanese possessed a number of stellar attributes, her ancestral people simply did not start anything on time. Dinner guests were invited at six with the full expectation that no one would be there before seven and dinner might hit the table at eight. It was just expected.

"Don't 'Mama, come on' me," Zaina said, wagging an angry finger at her. "You late. We have special company tonight."

"So was everyone else," Samantha said. "What special company are you talking about? Who else is here?"

Zaina ignored her and went back to working on the tabouli. Samantha cracked open the oven door for a peek at the kibbe.

"Get out of there," Zaina said. "It needs another few minutes."

"Then I'm not late for dinner."

"You hush," she said. Zaina placed her hand on the small of Samantha's back and gently pushed her out of the kitchen. "Go say hi to your sisters. Go."

AFTER SAMANTHA SLIPPED OUT of the kitchen, the elderly woman noticed her daughter's mobile phone resting on the counter. A red light was blinking angrily, and the words LOW BATTERY flashed across the screen. She slipped it into her pocket and made a mental note to remind Samantha about the battery at dinner. Part of her wanted to smash the thing into a thousand pieces, but then she'd never hear the end of it from Sam.

SAMANTHA HEADED down the short hallway, where she found her niece Lena playing with two Bratz dolls. Lena, one of Emily's two daughters, was the quietest of her nieces and Samantha's favorite, although she wouldn't admit it to her sisters. The others were loud and spoiled and didn't listen to anyone.

"Hi, Auntie Sam," Lena said. "Do you like my dolls?"

Samantha's heart broke.

"Yes, baby, I like them very much."

Mindful of her developing head cold, Samantha passed on kissing her niece. Instead, she knelt down and pinched Lena's side playfully, which made the little girl squeal with delight, and then continued down the hall.

The hallway opened up on a large family room, where Samantha found the rest of her family in a state of chaos normally reserved for a nuclear power plant control room during a reactor meltdown. Her two other nieces were arguing over a portable Playstation game. Her sisters were sitting on the far edge of the faded sectional couch, prob-ably talking about their older sister behind her back.

Hisham was delivering one of his soliloquies about American politics to her dad and Tamir, who rarely ever got a word in edgewise. A fourth man that Samantha did not recognize was sitting next to her dad. He was younger than the other men, closer to her own age than to theirs. His dark hair and hairy arms, like orangutan hairy, betrayed his Middle Eastern ancestry. She shook her head. This was the 'special company' her mother had mentioned. She should have picked up on it right away. Special company meant that her mother had found yet another single man that she hoped Samantha would just hit it off with. Then she could get married, have babies and make hummus for the rest of her life.

"The American government never gonna want peace," Hisham was saying, pounding his right fist into the palm of his left hand. "War is good for American business. War lets America keep the military in the Middle East, where they keep their eye on what? The oil. All about the oil, this country."

"Hi, everyone," Samantha said.

Her dad, Omar, jumped off the sofa like he'd been fired from a slingshot, happy to see his daughter but also thrilled to get away from his cousin, permanently afflicted with diarrhea of the mouth. Omar bear-hugged his daughter and, despite her warning that she had a cold, planted kisses on each of her cheeks. She hugged him tightly.

"Hi, Papa," she said.

The other men all stood, and she shook hands with each of them. She deliberately took an angle that made it difficult for Hisham to plant one on her, not that he didn't try, even in her condition. Last, she shook hands with Mr. Special Company. He was wearing medical scrubs and he reeked of cologne. Ah. A doctor. Her mother couldn't have hammered home the point any more clearly had she faked a heart attack and awaited Mr. Special Company's delivery of CPR.

"Hi," she said, extending her hand. "Samantha."

"Roger," he said, grasping her hand with his moist, clammy paw. "Good to meet you."

The absence of an accent led Samantha to conclude he was American-born, like she was. Roger was a slightly chubby fellow, and his breath had a certain spoiled-fish bouquet to it. She hoped he worked in intensive care, where his patients would have been too unconscious to care.

"You lucky man," Hisham said, clapping Roger on the shoulder as if he had won Samantha in a carnival game. "She beautiful, no?"

Roger gave her the old eye elevator, up and down, and it gave her the willies.

"Yes. Very."

With some effort, she withdrew her hand and wiped it on the side of her slacks. She stood paralyzed, like a freaked-out gazelle on the African plains, while Roger continued to ogle her. She said a small prayer of thanks when she heard her mother's voice summoning them to dinner.

SAMANTHA HAD BARELY TOUCHED the first toasted pita wedge to the hummus before her mother announced proudly that Roger Bouzein was, in fact, Roger Bouzein, M.D. He was an internist with Richmond Internal Medicine, a highly respected medical practice. She said it with such pride that Roger's own mother would have felt that someone else was muscling in on her proud mama territory.

"Is that right?" Samantha said, turning her attention to the culinary spread before her. They were in the family's tight dining room, around the heavy oak table that her parents had purchased before she was born. On its surface was the ghostly residue of math problems and essays etched into the wood long ago. In the background, the voice of famous Lebanese folk singer Fairuz bubbled from the speakers. Samantha had heard enough Fairuz to last her a lifetime.

"He's Nabila's nephew," Zaina said.

Samantha nodded and smiled, not having the first clue who Nabila was.

"So you're a lawyer," Roger said, turning to face her. Naturally, her mother had seated them side-by-side. He leaned in close, as if this connected them in some way.

Samantha nodded. "Papa, can you please hand me the grape leaves?"

Omar handed the plate to Mariam, who handed it down to Samantha.

"What kind of law do you practice?"

"Corporate."

"What does this entail? I have many lawyers but I am not familiar with the lingo."

"Well," she said, dropping half a dozen stuffed grape leaves onto her plate. "I help really big and rich companies get a little bit bigger and richer. It's very gratifying work."

"I hear this is a lucrative field," he said.

Who the hell used the word lucrative in a sentence?

"It's fine," she said.

"I also do very well," he said. "Internal medicine has been quite good to me."

She smiled and shoved two grape leaves into her mouth. She was starving. Her display of gluttony, however, did not dissuade her intrepid pursuer.

"I live in Stonemill, you know," he said, referring to a fancy subdivision in the western suburbs. "Last year, I bought a boat. I keep it at my house at Smith Mountain Lake. I would love for you to visit me there. I can take you for a ride on the boat."

"You hear that, Sammy," Zaina jumped in. "A boat! How's Nabila, sweetheart?"

"She is well," said Roger. "She sends her regards."

While she continued to ponder who Nabila was, Samantha realized she had never heard anyone speak with such pinpoint accuracy. He was like a grammar ninja.

Within a few minutes, everyone's plates were loaded with food, and the chatter was replaced by the sounds of silverware clinking plates and lips smacking against food. For this, Samantha was thankful. Maybe if she was lucky, she could get out of here without talking to Roger again. Whom, she noted with some dismay, ate like a hyena. He shoveled in hummus and kibbe by the palmful. And he was supposed to be trying to impress her?

"Why don't you two go out for dessert later?" Zaina said, once everyone had started to slow down. As was typical of Lebanese dinners, a mountain of food remained, waiting for deposit into plastic yogurt containers and freezer bags for the kids to take home. "Go enjoy yourselves."

"Mama, I have to get up early," Samantha said. "I have to work."

"Look at you with the 'I have to get up early,'" Zaina said. "This is nonsense. Now Roger, he have to get up early. He's a doctor. I don't see him saying he can't go, he have to get up early. Tomorrow Saturday. Before Christmas. You don't have to work."

"This is a grand idea," Roger said. "I know just the place. Exquisite desserts."

She thought desperately for a change of subject and glanced across the table at her father.

"Papa, how's business?"

His head jerked up, his eyes wide, like that of a schoolboy who had been hoping not to get called upon. He had been happily rolling a chunk of kibbe in some pita bread. She noticed his eyes cut over to her mother, who quickly returned the gaze before looking away.

Her parents operated an ethnic grocery store and deli called Mediterranean Express on West Broad Street, one of the Richmond metropolitan area's main arteries. The store was located in the Tuckernuck Square Shopping Center, a heavily developed commercial area, where it had been since her parents opened it when she was a little girl. The aromatic spices and meat and spinach pies they sold served as the olfactory background of her childhood.

Her first real job had been at the store, starting in junior high school and continuing through summers and college breaks. But as the years slipped by, she started spending less and less time there, even after she moved back to Richmond. She didn't like to shop there because her parents insisted on her giving her all her groceries every week. Forget about Samantha paying for anything.

Once, after her six-figure salary from the firm had started flowing, she had offered to help them catch up on some of their bills. Her father got so angry with her he didn't speak to her for a week. Instead, she funneled some money to an account her mother handled, which Zaina used to pay some of the bills that Omar didn't know about.

"It's fine," Zaina said. "Who wants more tabouli?"

"What?" Samantha asked.

"It's fine," her father said. "Let it go, sweetheart."

He said this almost in jest. She had a pathological inability to let anything go, and she knew her father was goosing her a little. Once her mind locked onto an issue or question, there was no letting go until it had been resolved to her satisfaction. It was what had driven her success through school and through her career. Well, the success up until this morning at least.

Samantha pressed on. She knew that she probably

shouldn't be airing the family's dirty laundry in front of Dr. Roger the Wonder-Doc, but she didn't care.

"Is the store in trouble?"

"It's fine," her father snapped. His voice cracked, ever so slightly, and Samantha knew instantly it had been a very bad year. Jesus, every year since the store opened had been a bad year. This time, though, she could tell that her father was worried that it would be the store's last year.

Tension descended on the room like a heavy curtain. Even her nieces, who normally would be throwing food by this point in the meal, sat as quietly as dolls.

"Things will be fine," Emily said to no one in particular.

"What happened?" asked Samantha.

The table was silent.

"Ziad?" she asked rhetorically. "It's because of Ziad, isn't it? That piece of shit!"

"Samantha!" her mother said. "Don't talk about your brother that way."

"Why didn't you call me?" she barked at her parents. Her anger was rising like good dough. "I could've helped you."

Neither of her parents answered.

"Who wants baklava?" her mother said, after the silence had drifted into the deep space of discomfort like a lost satellite. She must really be worried, Samantha thought. In the mind of Zaina Khouri, food was a ready-made solution to the world's ills. Her mother got up from the table and headed for the kitchen, her two younger daughters trailing behind her. Samantha looked over at her father, who picked absently at a hardening piece of pita bread.

She wanted to go over and hug him, but she knew this would embarrass him in front of the other men at the table, undermine his role as the stalwart head of the family. He was a quiet, thoughtful man, and she knew, as she watched him deconstruct a piece of dry bread into tiny crumbs, that he was thinking about Ziad Khouri, her now-dead brother.

The chirp of her phone ringing broke her from her trance, and she reflexively tapped the pockets of her sweater for the phone. When she felt nothing but fabric, a vise of panic clamped itself around her.

Zaina returned from the kitchen and handed the phone to her.

"You forget it in the kitchen," Zaina said.

Samantha checked the caller ID screen, but she didn't recognize the number. She began to let it ring through to voice mail before she remembered she had given her number to Julius Wheeler just a couple of hours ago.

"Hello?" she said.

"Hey, this Julius."

She cradled the phone against her shoulder, held up a single finger, and ducked out of the living room to take the call. Her father's bombshell was still reverberating inside her head, and she wasn't ready to deal with it yet. What was going to happen? These thoughts ricocheted around her skull like the six Ping-Pong balls that had delivered forth Julius' fortune.

"Hi there," Samantha said when she was alone in the living room. "What's up?"

"I can't talk long," he said in a hushed voice. This made the hairs on the back of her neck stand up.

"What's wrong?"

"I thought you say I going to the Marriott," he said.

"I did."

"We ain't going to the Marriott."

"Where are you?"

"Pay phone just outside a bathroom," he said. "The Exxon at the corner of Parham and Brook Road. I made them stop, told'em I was gonna be sick from being so nervous."

"Them? What them?"

"Some guy from firm security came with us."

"Firm security?"

"Big white guy," said Julius.

"Firm security?" she repeated.

She said it more for herself, as if she couldn't believe it. Something sounded extremely off about this. Why would Carter move him somewhere else? Who was this guy from "firm security"?

"That's what I said," he said. "I got nervous in the car and asked them to stop."

"Which way are you headed?"

"North, I think."

"Julius, did they say where exactly they were going?"

"No."

"See if you can keep them there a while," she said, walking back into the dining room. "Stay in the bathroom as long as you can. Try to make it fifteen minutes. Then tell them you need some crackers or something from inside."

"Got it."

"I'm headed your way now," Samantha said. "I want to see what they're up to."

She hung up the phone. The rest of the family – and Dr. Roger, of course! – watched her carefully.

She started to dial Carter on his cell phone, but she paused over the Send button as a chill rippled through her body. After holding steady for much of the afternoon, her fever felt like it was creeping back up, launching a nighttime offensive against her body. What was the point of calling him? All that would do would tip him off that she suspected something, and that might really screw things up.

"I have to go, Mama."

"Why?"

"Work."

"I'm sick of hearing about your work," Zaina said, the volume of her voice escalating with each word. "I should've thrown that phone out in the snow!" She shook her head and left the room.

"I'll try to be here for Christmas," she said to her father, leaning over to plant a smooch on his stubbly cheek.

"I love you, sweetheart."

She felt her heart crawl up into her throat. Tears welled up in her eyes, but she forced them back in. She didn't want her father to see her cry.

"Good night, everybody," she said, giving the group a single all-encompassing wave.

Roger was up like a shot, suddenly realizing that his promised date was really leaving without experiencing the full range of his charms.

"When can I see you again?" Roger asked, trailing behind her as she made her way to the door.

"I'll call you," she said. "Give me your number."

"You need me to write it down?"

"No, I've got a really good memory," she said, zipping down the front walk. "Look, I really have to be going."

He followed her all the way to the car.

"OK, OK, it's 934-7428."

"Got it," she said, climbing into the driver's seat.

She started up the car and pulled away, leaving Dr. Roger at the edge of her parents' driveway like a jilted prom date.

12

F ive minutes later, the Exxon station's familiar blue sign drew into view as Samantha sped west along Brook Road. At its intersection with Parham Road, she slowed and turned into the gas station. Each of the pumps was occupied. While scanning for an open slot, she recognized Carter's Hummer parked by the curb fronting the filling station's convenience store. She would recognize that thing anywhere; Carter was extremely proud of it. She knew it made him feel very manly. Leaning against the rear bumper was a large man who looked vaguely familiar. Despite the presence of about fifty signs prohibiting smoking, he was smoking a cigarette with the attitude of a man who wanted someone to point out the fact that he was in a No Smoking area. This had to be Mr. Firm Security.

She pulled up to the island farthest from the Hummer and killed her headlights, but she left the engine running. Her Audi's windows were dark enough that she didn't have to worry about anyone recognizing her. She kept her eye on Firm Security, flipping through her mental Rolodex, but was unable to match the man's face with an entry in her head.

Try as she might, his identity remained tucked away in a locked mental filing cabinet.

A few minutes later, Julius and Carter stepped through the market's automatic sliding doors, and the three of them climbed back into the Hummer. She noticed that Julius was holding what appeared to be a package of crackers in his right hand. Nice work, Julius. Nice work. A moment later, the Hummer roared to life, its rear lights flashing briefly as Carter shifted into drive. Carter guided the big gas guzzler out of the parking lot and turned right onto Parham Road, running north away from the lights of the city. Samantha checked her gas gauge, the needle still at F, and followed her boss onto the dark highway. Christmas lights dotted the landscape like runway landing lights.

Thanks to its yellow paint job, the Hummer was easy to track, sort of like an angry and horny rhinoceros. When she could, she kept a car in between hers and Carter's to provide some camouflage. When she couldn't, she dropped back a couple hundred yards. She drew these surveillance tactics from years of watching movies and television, so she had no idea if they really worked or not. For all she knew, Carter had spotted her at the gas station. But the hope was that Carter was so focused on whatever it was he was doing that he wouldn't notice a zippy little coupe trailing behind him. As they edged farther from the metropolitan area, the road grew darker. Small ranch homes dotted the landscape, which increasingly gave way to farmland.

Although she kept a close eye on her quarry, Samantha's mind began to wander. She wished she hadn't had to bail on her parents' dinner. She had long feared that Ziad Khouri, her older brother, would reach out from the grave and stick his dead thumb right up their ass. And it looked like it had finally happened. It sounded like it had been happening slowly since that fateful New Year's Day, almost one year ago. Samantha lit a cigarette and opened her window. The cold rushed in like a tsunami. She didn't care.

ON THAT CHILLY New Year's Day, Ziad Khouri, an energetic but misguided young man, had stepped onto a city bus on the south side of Chicago and blown himself up. With this angry and astonishingly unsuccessful act, Khouri entered the annals of American history as the country's first documented suicide bomber. The college dropout and small-time thief had been planning this attack for about two weeks, rigging together a rather rudimentary explosive involving a plastic two-liter bottle and a witches' brew of ammonia and fertilizer, ignited by a simple homemade trigger. He had discovered the assembly instructions on the Internet.

As evidenced by this unsolicited attempt at martyrdom, however, Khouri was not a terribly skilled bombmaker, and the explosion was limited to the rear half of the 2525 bus, on which he was the only passenger. Walter Guillen, the bus driver, thought he had experienced a backfire, but a peek in his rearview mirror revealed a cloud of black smoke, blood spatter and shattered glass. Guillen, shaken but unscathed, immediately knew that the odd young man he had picked up near U.S. Cellular Field had been the cause of all this mayhem. For years, in some small dark corner of his mind, he had wondered about the prospect of a suicide bomber on one of his buses. After the September 11 terrorist attacks, that dark corner had gotten a little bigger.

A veteran with twenty-six years behind the wheel, Guillen calmly drew the wounded bus to a stop, stepped off the bus and called 911. When he used the word "bomb" in his description of the event, the dispatcher became very serious because the canned script dispatchers used in response to bomb-related incidents was itself very serious. He hadn't been on with the dispatcher but a few seconds beyond that when he heard a bevy of sirens screaming toward him.

A small fire had broken out in the aisle, sending Guillen scrambling before the bus exploded. Checking himself for injuries, Guillen was relieved that no other passengers had been on the bus. This wasn't his normal route, but he was filling in for a younger driver who inevitably had called in sick on New Year's Day. This time of year, when the White Sox were enjoying the offseason, it was a fairly low-volume route with minimal service.

Within a minute of his 911 call, a phalanx of police, fire and rescue vehicles descended on the scene. Five minutes later, the entire block was taped off, and an FBI agent had escorted Walter Guillen to a makeshift command center that had been hastily assembled. Guillen sat on a metal folding chair and sipped on a cup of extraordinarily bad coffee. His formal education had ended with his high school graduation, but he wasn't a stupid man. He knew what had happened. This hadn't been some disgruntled employee with a gun. This was one of America's worst fears realized. Suddenly, the south side of Chicago was downtown Jerusalem, and this incident would lead every newscast around the country for the next week. For all Walter Guillen knew, city buses were exploding all over America.

But weeks passed with no other attacks, and a relieved nation started to relax. News of an embarrassing viral video involving the Speaker of the House quickly dominated the headlines, and so the populace's collective consciousness was drawn to other matters. The buses kept running, and people kept riding them, mainly because the people who rode buses had no choice but to ride them to get to where they were going.

The various three-letter agencies of the federal government fell over both themselves and each other trying to piece together the events leading up to the New Year's Day bombing. Every single item in Khouri's small Chicago apartment a few blocks from the site of the bombing was packed up and inventoried. Millions of e-mails and thousands of hours of intercepted telephone calls were analyzed, scrutinized, cataloged and mostly forgotten. Federal agents poured into Arab communities around the country, interviewing and watching and following and listening. They found nothing. As could be expected, part of the investigation involved a descent upon Ziad Khouri's next of kin – his parents, Omar and Zaina Khouri, small business owners from central Virginia.

Unfortunately for the Khouris, their biological and uncontrollable association with the bomber destroyed business, because no law-abiding American, of Arab descent or otherwise, wanted to be associated with terrorism. They couldn't take the chance that said association would destroy their own businesses, their own reputations. Success for Arab-Americans did not come easily nor did it come cheaply.

Six months after the bombing, a blue-ribbon commission appointed by the President made the following findings regarding the New Year's Day bombing:

1.Ziad Khouri had acted alone.

2.Khouri was a below-average student who dropped out of the University of Illinois-Chicago after one semester.

3.Khouri worked as a pizza delivery driver.

4.He had no contact with any of his relatives in the year leading up to the bombing.

5.Khouri was not nor had he ever been a member of any known terror cell.

6.Khouri was not on the FBI Terrorist Screening Center's watch list nor had he ever been associated with anyone who was on it.

7.Khouri had never been to a mosque.

8.One month before the bombing, an American-born Egyptian woman, with whom Khouri had had one dinner date, told him that she was going back to her old boyfriend, a young man of Anglo-Saxon descent.

9.Khouri's family considered him a thief, a liar, and a cocaine addict.

10.Khouri hated the White Sox.

The commission was unable to identify a single individual of any race, creed, or ethnicity who had counted Khouri as a friend, acquaintance or associate. The commission also determined that Ziad's family in Richmond had no advance knowledge of the attack and cleared Samantha's family of any wrongdoing.

Samantha had known even then, however, that nothing in the final report of the New Year's Day Bombing Commission could undo that damage. She remembered the first local newscast on the NBC affiliate the morning after the attack, breathlessly proclaiming that the bomber was tied to a Richmond family.

The image of her father at dinner tonight, quietly picking at the dry piece of pita bread, haunted her as she sped down the dark highway after Carter Pierce.

A FEW MINUTES out from the gas station, a thought took hold in Samantha's mind like a hearty weed and began to grow.

Carter was planning to steal the ticket.

She supposed she had known this from the moment that Julius had called her from the Exxon bathroom. She suspected that Julius knew this as well. Carter had brought along the big man as muscle, perhaps help to facilitate a peaceful if nonconsensual surrender of the ticket. Or a violent and nonconsensual surrender, if necessary.

Police! She could call the police. Report a kidnapping. Get it on the record that Julius had won the ticket. No matter what happened from here on out, Julius' interest in the ticket would be documented. Still, a twinge of doubt salted her thinking process. Could she be so sure that Carter was planning to steal it? Maybe Carter knew what he was doing. Was it even her problem anymore? And why would he even want to steal the ticket? He made a million bucks a year. He had two vacation homes. What more did he need? Why take such a chance?

Because he was Carter Pierce, that's why.

Time to call the cavalry. Thank God for cell phones.

She picked up the phone and began to dial 911, but the screen was dark. Strange, she thought. Then a spike of fear stabbed her in the stomach as she suddenly realized that she hadn't charged it in days. The battery. She held the power button down, praying for the familiar beep of its power up. Nothing. Now fully seized with panic, she dug around the center console for the car charger. Ahead of her, Carter's Hummer slid into the right lane. Careful not to let him get too much asphalt between them, she pushed down on the gas a bit.

"Damn!" she muttered, her hand finding the console empty. The first time in her life that she had actually needed a cell phone, and the battery was dead. Now she had no choice but to continue her James-Bond-like pursuit of her boss, whom she was now certain was committing a number of felonies, including, but not limited to, the biggest robbery of all time.

As she was making her peace with the useless phone and her boss' felonious proclivities, Samantha noticed the Hummer decelerating. She eased off the gas and dropped back two hundred yards, careful not to risk being spotted. There wasn't much traffic out here at this hour. Another hundred yards up the road, Carter slowed even more and activated his right turn signal.

If she didn't do something soon, Carter was certainly going to notice the car pacing him. Unable to think of a better option, she slammed on the brakes and killed her headlights. Out of sight, out of mind.

Ahead of her, Carter crept along. Just before its taillights winked out of view where the road dropped into a shallow valley, the Hummer made a sharp right turn and disappeared from the road. She hit the gas and kept her eyes pinned on the dirt roads that interlaced with the smooth asphalt like the top of a checkered pie crust.

She nearly passed it when a cloud of dust, illuminated by the red taillights, caught her eye. She drove her foot into the brake pedal, causing the Audi to fishtail on the slick blacktop. The little coupe came to rest in the middle of the two-lane highway.

SAMANTHA PARKED on the side of the road and changed into a pair of running shoes that she had in the trunk. Running shoes that hadn't seen either pavement or a treadmill in more than a year. It was cold, it seemed extra cold away from the buildings and the lights of the city, and she didn't like it. Typically, she loved getting away from the city, but tonight, she felt alone and vulnerable out here. Snowflakes dusted her hair and coat, and a cold wind blew across her face.

Her shoes tied, she started jogging down the dirt path. Within a minute, the sound of two male voices stopped her cold. The voices continued unabated in what sounded like an argument. Quickly, she realized that out here in the boonies, voices carried a long way in the dark, chilly air, and the men's voices had easily drowned out the approaching footfalls of Samantha Khouri, crime fighter. Still, she continued up the side of the path closest to a copse of trees, a little more lightness in her step. She heard a door slam shut, and the voices went silent.

Even in her heavy turtleneck sweater and leather jacket, she was shivering with cold and fear. A substantial part of her was screaming for her to turn around and go back to her car. But she couldn't. Even if Carter wasn't planning on stealing the ticket, she deserved an explanation from Carter, reassurance that Julius would be the one cashing in the ticket on Wednesday. Now that she thought about it, she should have told Julius to ditch Carter at the gas station. She should have told him to just walk away.

Another few seconds up the path brought a lick of artificial light. This was yellow light, like that coming from a porch. A bit farther, and she reached the trail's end. Quickly, she took cover behind a large fir tree. Where it broke through the trees, the path opened up on a circular clearing that fronted the cabin. There was room for several cars, but only Carter's sat here now, the engine still hissing like a snake as it cooled down. Through a window, she could see a figure pacing back and forth. Carter.

She thought about marching right up to the front door and demanding to know what the hell was going on. As long as Willett & Hall employed her, Julius was her client, too, and she would be remiss in her professional duties not to look after her client's interests. If Carter had a better idea about what to do about Julius, fine, but she wanted to know about it. Yet she remained rooted to the spot. It's not like they're going to cash the ticket in the house, she told herself. From here, she could scope things out, get a lay of the land.

This was what she told herself so she wouldn't have to address the fact that she was so scared she was about to go pee-pee in her pants.

Get it together, girl. She took a deep breath, which burned her lungs in a way that was not entirely unpleasant. Throughout the day, her nasal passages had been sealing up with congestion, but the cold, moist air was opening things up a bit. Her nerves bucking like wild mustangs, she tried to think about something else for a minute. Immediately, her thoughts drifted to her parents. Was the store really in trouble? Was it going to go under? How much could she afford to give them? Would it be enough? How much could she help them if she lost her job?

And just like that, she wondered what things would be like if she, rather than Julius, had purchased the winning SuperLotto ticket. The thought broadsided her like a truck running a red light – she had had no time to react. Yeah, she thought again, the truck backing up to T-bone her again, it would've been nice to win that money.

But you didn't, Sam thought. Julius did. And you need to help him. A few more cleansing breaths, and she was ready to, well, she was ready to do something. She just didn't know what.

When she was confident that no one was lurking outside, Samantha scampered across the clearing to the back bumper of the Hummer. Samantha had long thought that the vehicle was an eyesore and the environmental equivalent of a serial killer, but tonight, she decided she had never seen anything so beautiful. It was huge, much bigger up close than she had imagined, and its shadows simply swallowed her up.

She edged along the driver's side to the left front bumper. From there, it was a quick hop to a thick boxwood bush under the large front-facing window. Still tucked away in the shadows, Samantha could see directly into the main room without fear of being spotted. She hoped. Carter and his colleague – who was he? she wondered again – were talking loudly, but the windows muffled their words.

When she saw Julius Wheeler tied up in a chair, a piece of duct tape plastered across his mouth, she decided it was safe to assume that Carter had indeed gone bonkers.

DAMN LAWYERS, Julius thought. He should've known better. After the big fella had tied him to this chair, Pierce had taken the ticket from his shoe and hadn't even had the courtesy to put the shoe back on. Now Julius was stuck like a bug in candle wax, and his right foot was numb with cold.

Four hours ago, he had made what he thought was a smart decision. Hire a lawyer, one of these rich downtown jackasses whose offices he cleaned and never even gave him the time of day. They could have charged him a million bucks in legal fees, and that would have been fine with him.

At least he would know that the money was taken care of. But no, he had found these two idiots, who in all likelihood, were going to kill him before the night was over.

And to make it worse, they had started arguing. Once upon a time, Julius had hoped that his time behind bars had put him square with the house, that his debts with the universe were settled.

Karma was a bitch.

13

S ince they had arrived at the cabin, Carter was becoming increasingly concerned with the way that his brother-in-was looking at him. A couple times, he caught Todd staring at him and looking away quickly when Carter caught his gaze. Todd! For God's sake, he had stood up as a groomsman at Ashley and Carter's wedding!

The bitch of it was that his growing suspicion of Todd was chipping away at his focus on his favorite new game – imagining his new life with the money. All his debts, gone. Blinky, out of his life forever. Ashley set up for life and out of his life. The girls, taken care of, forever. He wouldn't have to worry about paying for college. He wouldn't even have to worry if they went to college.

His ailing parents would get round-the-clock medical care in the best facilities, and he wouldn't have to think about them anymore. Even his grandkids' grandkids would be able to enjoy the wealth. He wondered how much he would make on the interest alone if he just stuck the money in an ordinary checking account. And the most glorious perk of all – he would never have to practice law again. In fact, and he giggled a bit when he thought about it, it was entirely possible that he had billed his last hour, billed his last minute, practiced the last bit of law in his life.

Suddenly, he was overwhelmed with the urge to buy a private jet.

"Hey, fucko," said Todd, interrupting Carter's frolic aboard his new Gulfstream V. There had been two topless flight attendants on Carter's special flight, so he was not terribly pleased with this interruption. "What say you let me hang onto the ticket?"

"Why?"

"I'll make sure that no one will take it from me," he said. "From us, I mean."

"Who's gonna take it?" Carter asked.

"Who the hell knows? You never know these days. That economy is in the shitter," Todd continued, punching a finger into the palm of his hand with each word.

"No one else knows we have the ticket," Carter said. "Why do you need to hold it again?"

"Just let me hang onto it," Todd said. "Look, you've already screwed up once tonight."

"That so?"

"Yeah, I told you to get all the paperwork on this guy out of the chick's office, and you forgot."

Todd's words scraped against Carter's insides like a match, sparking a tiny flame of anger. This was his ticket. This had been his idea. Who the hell did Todd think he was? Todd didn't want to protect it. Todd wanted to steal it from him. Todd wanted to keep it all for himself, hang Carter out to dry.

"No."

"What?"

"You're gonna steal it from me."

"What the hell are you talking about?"

"Oh, I think you know."

Carter glanced around the largest room of the cabin that his brother had called home for the past two years. The walls were wood-paneled, as one might expect to find in a cabin out in the middle of nowhere. A large fireplace was cut into the north wall like a giant cave. On the hearth stood a rack of fireplace tools, a poker, a long-handled pan, and a brush. There was a small kitchenette, but it didn't appear to have been used in some time.

This was why Todd had brought them out here. He was going to kill them both and steal the ticket. Probably stab them to death with the fireplace poker and dump their bodies in the woods for the bears. There were bears out here, weren't there? It was like the Yukon outside the front door. He hated the wilderness.

"Steal it from you?" Todd asked. "Why would I do that?"

"So you can keep it all for yourself!"

"You're insane, Pierce," Todd barked. "That ticket's got you all fucked up. Maybe I really should hold onto it. For your sake, you loon. You give it to me, you just relax. Take it easy. We're gonna be set up for life. Plenty to go around, 'kay, buddy?"

"Oh, no, you stay away from me," Carter said, the fire raging inside him now. "It's my ticket. You keep messing with me, you won't get a dime."

"Whoa, whoa, whoa," Todd said. "A deal is a deal, my friend. You wouldn't even have the goddamn ticket it weren't for me. You try and cut me out, I'll end you."

The fire inside Carter's belly exploded out of control.

～

As she spied on her boss, Samantha wondered what she was doing out here. She should be in bed, slurping down chicken noodle soup and watching reruns of *Cheers* under about ten blankets. She shivered again, but she didn't feel quite as cold anymore, probably because her temperature was on the rise again. Despite the spiking fever, or maybe because of it, a door suddenly opened in her mind, revealing the identity of Carter's colleague. It was his brother-in-law, Todd or Ted or something like that. She recalled a picture on Carter's desk of the pair on a drunken golf outing, both sunburned and glassy-eyed. She had only met him once and had disliked him almost instantly.

This was bad, this was very bad. And the deeper she'd gotten into this mess, the more difficult it had become to extract herself from it. She needed to get back in her car, back to civilization, where she could get the police involved. Let them deal with this. She could vouch for Julius, corroborate his claim to the ticket, if indeed Carter's plan was to steal it. If it worked, great, Julius would be a very wealthy man. If not, she had done what she could. She could live with that. That was that. It was time to go home.

She had made her decision to vamoose, get the hell out of Dodge, when a bloodcurdling howl stopped her cold. It had come from inside the house. Samantha froze and swung her gaze back toward the window, through which she witnessed the ticket claim more human life, not for the first time, and although unbeknownst to Samantha, not yet for the last.

Both Carter and Todd were on their feet now, circling each other like a pair of lions ready to duel for leadership of the pride. Carter edged toward the fireplace, where he grabbed the black steel poker. In the chill of the cabin, each man's breath came in increasingly ragged puffs of vapor. The ticket was clutched in Carter's left hand, dry and numb from the cold.

"Get back," said Carter, waving the lance at Todd.

"I'm really starting to wonder about you," Todd said. He drew the pistol from his waistband. "What, are you Luke Skywalker now?"

"Fuck you," Carter said, his words coated with a thick film of anger.

"Gimme the ticket."

"No."

The word roared from Carter's lips like a shot. Something inside Carter had snapped, he felt it as tangibly as if he'd broken a bone in his hand, and Todd would have to kill him for the ticket. It was that simple. He always suspected there would be a moment in his life where he would have to make a stand, and he realized that the moment had arrived. Sure, maybe once upon a time he thought that moment might come dressed as heroism or leadership in a time of disaster, like maybe during an apocalypse that he'd been strong enough to survive. He always thought he would survive one of those.

Like a sprinter breaking from the blocks, Carter rushed at his brother-in-law, the poker raised like a spear. Almost simultaneously, the three witnesses to Carter's sudden offensive muttered the same exact word.

"Shit."

Julius accepted this latest development with striking poise.

He had been around sudden and terrible bursts of violence before – just last night, actually – and while this was certainly stranger than most, it still came down to money. As most things usually did. For most men of Julius' upbringing and background, death was usually close at hand. Babies dying of neglect, children gunned down in crossfires, mothers beaten by boyfriends armed with baseball bats, young men killed by their contemporaries. Death's constant presence hardened the soul like concrete, to the point that one was no longer afraid of it.

That had to be one of the worst things about the projects.

No one was afraid of death.

Good thing, since death was already in the room, sitting on the sofa and watching the festivities like a drunk Yankees fan.

ACROSS THE ROOM, with Julius equidistant from the combatants, Todd watched, with equal parts terror and shock, his bookish brother-in-law charging him. Carter's eyes revealed a man who seemed to have come unhinged mentally, almost like a zombie from those George Romero movies. In his seventeen-year association with his sister's husband, Todd had never seen this side of Carter Livingston Pierce. Oh, sure, he was a ruthless lawyer and all, but attorneys didn't deal in lead, as the saying went. They dealt in briefs and contracts and arguments and black robes.

Todd fumbled with the pistol, which, while it looked menacing, might as well have been a caulk gun for as much skill as he had with it. Vaguely, he recalled chambering a round when they had arrived. He looked up and saw that

Carter had already covered half the distance, the point of the poker guiding Carter like a divining rod.

Jesus, he thought, his arm feeling like it was encased in quicksand. Come on, come on. The gun came up slowly. When he felt that he had a bead on his brother-in-law-turned-assailant, he pulled back on the trigger. The first shot boomed loudly in the sparsely furnished cabin, and the bullet flew wide left of Carter's head. Carter, insane with bloodlust, ignored the fusillade and continued his rabid assault.

The second battle in the Great SuperLotto War had begun.

OUTSIDE, Samantha watched with horror. At first, she thought she was hallucinating, but her achy joints and sore throat kept her rooted in reality. The scene inside unfolded in rapid and sudden bursts, as if illuminated by a strobe light. For the rest of her life, the image of Carter charging at his brother-in-law would be burned upon her memory banks, as tangibly as a brand sizzling on a cow. She ducked low, her eyes nearly level with the windowsill.

Four more booms crashed the rural stillness before Todd's gun went silent. As the battle raged inside, her mind focused on random yet somewhat interconnected thoughts, perhaps protecting her from the orgy of violence on the other side of the wall. How far would the sound of the gunshots carry? How much attention they would draw, especially in an area where gunfire was not uncommon? Was it deer season? Was it legal to hunt deer this late at night?

Of the five shots that Todd managed to squeeze off, only one found any target.

That lone bullet caught Julius Wheeler, multimillionaire, square in the temple and exited through the left side of his skull. Samantha did not want to believe that the airborne puff of pink was Julius' brain being forcibly ejected from his head. The force of the bullet's impact toppled the chair over, and Julius died a few seconds later. In those last few moments before everything went dark, he had one final, very odd thought.

Samantha's perfume had smelled good.

OBLIVIOUS TO THE wild barrage of lead, Carter never broke stride until he had driven the poker into Todd's chest. The point slid into the flesh between Todd's ribs and pierced his heart. He stumbled forward like a wounded deer, his large frame knocking Carter off balance, and fell flat on his back. With Todd's aorta ruptured, life drained out of his body with frightening rapidity, and he died with his hands wrapped around the instrument of his demise.

Carter, confronted with the image of his very-soon-to-be-late brother-in-law, stumbled backwards. His feet got tangled underneath him, and his momentum sent him sprawling back-first to the hardwood floor. His head struck the rock-hard floor first, slamming his brain against his skull, and Carter Pierce lay still. The lottery ticket, which had come loose from Carter's grip as he tripped, fluttered to the floor.

The battle had lasted less than ten seconds.

SAMANTHA SANK TO THE GROUND, first to her knees and then to her hands. Her stomach rolled and roiled like a ship in rough seas, her dinner threatening to make a re-appearance. She drew in a few deep breaths of the crisp cold air and let each one out slowly. When the world stopped spinning, she willed herself to her feet. Like a baby calf walking for the first time, she staggered to her feet and stumbled across the clearing. Here in the darkness, Carter's Hummer lurked like a prehistoric beast.

She stared at the truck for a moment, trying to comprehend what had just happened. Julius was dead. Todd was dead. Carter was dead. The sensory overload tripped a circuit in her head, and her mind went blank. Just empty. For a full three minutes, she stood numbly in front of the window, barely aware of where she was, or even what she had just seen.

Eventually, though, information began seeping back into her head, and her analytical mind went to work. During law school, she spent a summer with the Henrico County Commonwealth's Attorney's office, which prosecuted crimes in that particular jurisdiction. During her three-month stint with the office, she had been to crime scenes, she had seen murder victims. She knew the police were well-trained, that they were reasonable, and that they would look at the facts.

That was it. She needed to call the police and wait for the cavalry. She had nothing to fear. She was an attorney with no criminal record. She would explain what happened. Quite frankly, it wasn't all that complicated. No conspiracy here. Carter and Todd decided to steal the ticket, they turned on each other, and boom – this triple homicide thing behind her. With that settled, she started jogging back up the path.

Then, just as quickly as she'd started, she stopped.

Hang on there, chiquita. What about this, exactly, was normal? Her boss was dead. His brother-in-law was dead. Her new client was dead. And they were all dead because of a lottery ticket.

What was going to happen to the ticket?

Would Julius' son ever get it?

How would anyone know Julius had been the one who bought the ticket?

Would they even believe her?

She realized that as soon as she called the police, the ticket's fate would be clouded with uncertainty. There was no way to tell who would respond to the scene once she called it in and what moral compass they might be guided by. A patrol officer making thirty-five grand a year. A burned-out homicide detective. An overworked crime scene investigator. Someone would find the ticket and realize what it was. Then what? How would anyone ever prove that it didn't belong to the person who showed up with it at lottery headquarters? Besides her, the only ones who knew who the real owner was were dead. The temptation would be too great to resist.

She knew this because she could feel the ticket's pull on her. Scenes from J.R.R. Tolkien's *Lord of the Rings* trilogy flashed through her mind. She thought about the Ring, about Frodo, about the spell the ring held over its bearer. It was ridiculous to think that she would ever encounter such a quandary. And yet here she was.

Her mind drifted back to Julius, the man who could never escape the violence that surrounded his life like a barbed wire fence. She figured that Julius suspected his life might one day be cut short by gunfire, but she supposed that he never dreamed it would be by two white guys from the suburbs. Now there was a young man out there who had never known and would never know his father.

The ticket was Jamal's.

What the hell was she supposed to do now?

HER TEETH CLENCHED, Samantha turned to face the house. Oh my holy God, she thought. The idea of going in that house was as appealing as being dropped into a swimming pool stocked with crocodiles. Plus, although she was relatively certain that the ticket was in the house – really, they hadn't been killing each other in there over dominoes – the likely reality was that she was going to have to dig through a gigantic bloody mess to get to it.

Did she really want to do this?

First, for all she knew, police cruisers were already on their way, responding to some concerned citizen's 911 call. She held her breath and listened for something, anything, but the night was quiet and still, like a hibernating bear. Nothing moved. The house was on a large lot. She couldn't even see the next house through the thick tree cover. Second, was she really the type of gal who would get herself involved in tampering with a crime scene? But it was the only thing she could think of. If there was another solution, then, heck, she was all ears.

Jesus, why did this have to happen to her? Quite a hand she'd been dealt today, given that waking up with what was likely a good dose of the flu was, by far, the high point of her day. Her head throbbed, as if someone was pushing out on her temples from the inside. Her reserves were fading fast, and the idea of crawling into the house and taking a nap on the couch was becoming increasingly attractive.

She couldn't remember the last time she felt this sick. Quite frankly, if she had been feeling like this when Julius called her from the Exxon, she would've told him that Carter knew what he was doing and wished him luck. Even the thought of walking back to her car was almost too much to process.

In the end, the decision was simple. Which Samantha did she want to look at in the mirror tomorrow morning? The one who had left the ticket's fate to chance? Or the one that had brought justice to Julius Wheeler?

She took a deep breath and let it out slowly. With what little strength she had left, she marched up to the front door, which was still slightly ajar. Thank heavens for small favors. No need to worry about fingerprints. A gentle shove with an elbow sent the door wide open, revealing Julius centered in the doorframe.

"God, if You're up there," she whispered to herself, "if You've got a better idea, I'm all ears."

Getting no response, she stepped into the house. It was just as cold inside as it was outside. She wondered if they had been planning to kill Julius all along. She couldn't imagine Carter being capable of such a decision. Then again, money made people do some crazy shit.

The scene was like one of those torture porn movies that had been all the rage a couple years ago. There was blood everywhere. Although there was no doubt in her mind that Julius was dead, she checked on him first. She knelt by his lifeless body, careful not to touch anything, wondering how much of the crime scene she was compromising just by setting foot in the house.

Indeed, Julius was dead. She deduced this by noting that the bullet had blown out much of the left side of his head. In the chill of the cabin, the blood was already congealing.

Her eyes watered, and a tear from each eye cut an icy trail down her cheeks.

"Sorry, Julius," she whispered. And she was. Sorrier than she had ever been in her life.

She wiped the tears across her sleeve and turned her attention to the two idiot gladiators who had caused all this commotion. Again, her detective skills were in top form when she examined Todd's body. Fine work, Inspector Khouri! Blood had trickled out of his nose and his mouth, and his eyes had rolled back into his head. And then, of course, was the matter of the giant steel pole sticking out of his chest. Well done, Inspector!

Out of the corner of her eye, she noticed the ticket resting on the floor, near Carter's head, his body lying in between her and the ticket. She leaned across his prone figure and plucked it off the ground, still tucked in Julius' plastic baggie. Her breathing became shallow, and her heart began to race. It felt like she was picking up a grenade. The ticket in hand, she knelt back on her haunches and stared at the six imprinted numbers.

5. 9. 16. 17. 43. SuperBall: 24.

Time to skedaddle, she thought. As she turned for the door, she heard a barely audible scrape behind her. The jumpstart to her heart shot her across the room like a cannonball. Quickly, she slipped out the door and down the steps. She snuck around to the side and reassumed her position by the window. From her perch, she watched Carter, still flat on his back, draw a knee up to his chest. He straightened it back out, but he didn't make a move to get up right away. Instead, he grabbed his head with both of his hands and moaned. He didn't seem to be aware of anything going on around him. He was alive, but he had taken a hell of a shot to his head on that ice-cold floor.

Two independent thoughts bubbled to the surface of Samantha's boiling mind.

1.All this activity could not be good for her health.

2.Her career at Willett & Hall was most certainly over.

A minute later, she was back behind the wheel of the Audi and zipping along Mountain Road. The Ticket was tucked snugly in her pocket.

14

"You want me to do what exactly?" the girl asked.

Her website bio identified her as Krista, but her real name was Barbara Ziegler, which just didn't work for a two-grand-an-hour call girl. Krista was five-foot-ten, a redhead, and in extremely high demand. She didn't love her work, but she didn't hate it either, because, quite frankly, the money was effing awesome and the work was easy. Plus, she got to fuck for a living. That wasn't all bad.

She had cracked six figures for the first time three years ago. Twenty-six years old, she had half a million bucks parked in mutual funds and planned to retire by the time she was thirty. Her clients were relatively tame, and the work was usually uneventful. She generally didn't care what even the wilder clients requested of her, because, truth be told, she was a relatively adventurous woman. She was a prostitute, after all. This, though, this took the freaking cake.

They were in the presidential suite at the Ritz-Carlton in downtown Atlanta. She'd been here for an hour or so, and at first, it had started like any other night with a rich, lonely, and slightly overweight white guy in his fifties. They drank scotch, chatted about the Braves, talked about how beautiful she was. Typical stuff.

Then it started to get weird, which had led to her question, clouded with confusion.

Arden McKinley, however, shook his head with extreme disappointment in her query. He was the wealthy, lonely, and slightly overweight client mystifying his escort tonight. For the life of him, he didn't understand what was so hard about this part of the festivities.

"Is it cooled off yet?" he asked.

She shook her head, not in the negative, but in complete disbelief at the discussion she was having. She stepped over to the small oak table wedged in the corner, where she had placed the item that McKinley had requested. Sometimes, clients asked that she bring props, and she frequently complied. Props and toys were easy.

She eyed the casserole dish on the table, filled to the brim with macaroni and cheese, which she had picked up on the way here. When he had booked the date through the service, he had requested homemade macaroni and cheese, but he could kiss her creamy-white Irish ass. She stopped in at a gourmet deli around the corner and paid eleven dollars for it. With a plastic spoon, she took a taste.

"It's room temp," she said.

"Bring it over here," he directed. "Sit in the wingback chair, take off your shoes and set the casserole dish on the floor."

"Want me to get naked, big boy?"

Usually, she teased the clients with a slow-moving strip show, but she was getting tired of this idiot. Something about him was just a bit off, and she didn't feel like putting up with it anymore. Suddenly, a pint of Haagen-Dazs sounded terribly good.

"No, no," he said. "Just the shoes."

Just the shoes. Great.

"What was your name again, sweetie?" she asked as she removed her shoes.

"Louis," he lied. "Louis Friend."

"That your real name?"

"What do you think?" he snapped. "The shoes?"

She did as she was told, whiling away the time with calculations of how much green she was going home with. This macaroni business would take a few minutes, and then, she supposed, he would want to bang her. From the look of him, she guessed that would mean another two minutes. At most. With a little luck, she'd be done in an hour. Nights like this, she was glad she charged a minimum of two hours.

When she was parked in the chair, her bare and freshly pedicured feet straddling the casserole dish, she looked back at the client. He had taken position on the loveseat directly opposite and was watching with unabashed interest. Thankfully, he was still clothed. His gut strained against his shirt, like sausage popping free of its casing, and she saw that he was even chubbier than she thought. They sat silently for a few minutes, and she started to wonder whether she was supposed to know what he wanted her to do, or whether he had already, to put it delicately, physically manifested his satisfaction with the evening's festivities. Then, when she couldn't take it anymore, she asked:

"What do you want me to do?"

He nodded toward the thick casserole.

"With your feet," he said, his breathing getting shallow.

It would be to Krista's disappointment to learn that Arden McKinley was well in control of his faculties and of his body this evening. He had been saving himself for this night for weeks, training his mind and body to draw out the evening's festivities until he reached a zenith of culinary and orgasmic bliss.

With that, Krista dunked her feet into the casserole dish and began mashing the elbow noodles and cheese between her toes. She was surprised by the depth of her revulsion at the act. Quite frankly, it felt like she was running barefoot through a pile of intestines. As noodles squirted between her toes, she felt hesitant to begrudge anyone his sexual fetish, but the allure of wasting perfectly good mac-and-cheese was lost on her.

McKinley watched with rapt interest, unconcerned with the hooker's obvious dismay with his sexual preferences. His surprise at the eroticism of his fetish had been long since addressed in therapy, and besides, who did she think she was? She was just a hooker. And he was Arden McKinley. All he cared about was the fact that her delicate feet were enveloped with warm, moist macaroni and cheese. And what was so weird about this anyway? People loved food. People loved sex. What exactly was the big deal?

"Like this?" she asked.

"A little faster," he said.

Her legs pistoned faster.

"Not that fast."

The ringing of a cell phone interrupted the festivities. Dammit. His staff had strict instructions not to contact him unless it was an emergency. This had better be a goddamn emergency.

"Excuse me," he said, getting up to answer his phone.

"Should I keep my feet in here?" asked Krista.

"Oh, definitely," he said.

Krista, who never again ate macaroni and cheese, leaned back in the chair and exhaled.

Arden checked the caller ID screen. It was Bernard Shelton.

"Yeah?"

"Mr. McKinley, this is Bernard Shelton."

Shelton had worked for McKinley for three years and yet always identified himself in full when he called his boss.

"Yes, I know," McKinley said. "You ever hear of caller ID?"

Shelton said nothing.

"So what is it?" McKinley asked.

"We have a problem."

"Can't it wait until tomorrow?" McKinley pleaded, his eyes darting over to the casserole dish.

"A very big problem."

"What problem?"

Silence on the other end, and it was then that Arden started to get nervous. As if the problem were so big, so catastrophic that Bernard Shelton was having difficulty articulating the scope of the disaster. After what seemed like an hour, Shelton began talking.

McKinley listened carefully and hung up the phone.

Bernard Shelton was right. They did have a problem.

15

"Now appearing on the main stage, Ginger," crowed Mikey the DJ. "Put your hands together for Gingerrrrrr."

When Ginger burst through the curtains and sauntered down the runway, Charles Flagg got up from his table and headed for the restroom. Ginger might have drawn the raucous applause of the mouth-breathers surrounding the stage, but Flagg didn't think she was a worthy specimen. Really, none of the dancers were. As good a time as any to take a leak. He hated using public bathrooms, and if it hadn't been for the fact that his bladder was about take matters into its own hands, he wouldn't be making this particular jaunt. Really, though, what was he expecting at the Eager Beaver, this strip club just south of the Virginia-North Carolina state line?

The Beaver was housed in a former BurgerTown, which was closed by corporate after a massive outbreak of hepatitis B was traced to a shocking disregard for the food safety protocols set forth by the state health department. It sat in a well-heeled strip of motels, gas stations and fast-food joints just off the freeway, way stations for the eternal travelers along Interstate 95.

He found the bathroom at the end of a dark corridor, which led to the Eager Beaver's private dance rooms. The sign posted on the bathroom door did not bode well for his eliminatory future.

WE AIM TO PLEASE. YOU AIM TOO, PLEASE.

After taking a deep breath, Flagg stepped inside and surveyed the restroom, which he found unacceptable. Oh, he did plan on notifying the manager about the bathroom's current state, as the sign pasted to the wall suggested. The black-and-white tile floor was grimy and damp. The paper towel and soap dispensers were both barren. This, Flagg supposed, made it difficult for the men who worked in the club to comply with the posted directive that **ALL EMPLOYEES MUST WASH HANDS BEFORE RETURNING TO WORK**.

Three urinals stood before him like dirty, bacteria-ridden sentinels. In a panic, he patted his pants down and was relieved to find the small plastic dispenser of hand sanitizer tucked into his back pocket. He exhaled. There was one stall, which he preferred to use, but it was missing a door, and the toilet itself was filled to the rim. Thick streams of toilet paper hung out over the sides like dreadlocks from the eighth plane of hell.

Flagg stumbled backwards, fighting the urge to expel his lunch. Jesus, why did he even stop in this stupid club? Sometimes, he let the little head do too much thinking, and really, the little head was just not cut out for advanced thinking. Everyone knew that. He turned his attention back to the urinals. They would have to do.

Abiding by one of the many secret bathroom codes that all men knew, he selected the urinal that was the farthest from the door and stepped up to the porcelain. And waited. And waited. And waited some more. He prayed that things would flow quickly and heavily, but he stood ramrod straight with a bladder that refused to empty. Despite the fact that he was alone in the bathroom, Flagg was overcome with his usual crippling and paralyzing case of stage fright. His heavy bladder was virtually pulsing, and yet he was unable to squeeze out a single drop.

He exhaled slowly as the frustration welled up inside him.

With the club's bass thumping underfoot, he tried every trick he could think of. Deep, slow breaths. Nothing. Thinking about rain. Nothing. Calm down, he thought, calm down.

The door to the bathroom opened behind him, and his heart sank. Might as well close up shop, he thought. He would just have to get a hotel room and piss in privacy. It was then that Flagg witnessed the newcomer. His name was Jimmy Burrell, and he was a big, doughy type, thoroughly filling out his Carolina Panthers jersey, but not in a good way. A patchy beard, which was never going to thicken like the guy hoped, gave him a certain radiation-sickness-chic. And then, to top it all off, he broke one of the Four Rules of the Public Bathroom.

1.If possible, leave one urinal open between you and the next guy.

He stepped up to the urinal next to Flagg and dropped his pants. All the way. This astonished Flagg. The man's pants and boxers were now bunched up at his ankles. His ankles!

Then the guy started began breaking the Rules left and right, almost as if he were enjoying it.

2.Never make eye contact with a stranger in a public bathroom.

He looked right over at Flagg, who had just finished zipping back up.

3.Never speak to a stranger in a public bathroom.

"Tough to take a leak after looking at all that ass, eh, buddy?" the man said. "Dick gets all hard."

With his still-full bladder causing him exquisite misery, this new development was just too much. With the speed of a cobra, Flagg grabbed his new friend's head with his right hand and snapped it down across his left forearm, which he had planted between the man's left shoulder and ear. Upon the sickening snap of his neck, his spinal cord was severed, and Jimmy Burrell died before he could even wonder why this guy was reaching out to touch him.

That, after all, violated the Most Sacred of all the Rules of the Public Bathroom.

4.Never, under any circumstances whatsoever, touch a stranger in a public bathroom.

Flagg gently lowered the man's body to the ground, making it look like he had simply collapsed while taking a whiz. He checked behind him, but luckily, the door remained closed. It wouldn't for long, as sooner or later, some other joker would decide to take a leak. Fortunately, the weather had turned, and there weren't more than twenty men out there, taking in the best of the Eager Beaver's stable of dancers.

FLAGG QUIETLY EXITED the bathroom and, seeing no one in the corridor, sat back down at his table. No one paid too much attention to anyone else in the club (other than, apparently, his now-deceased bathroom buddy), so he wasn't terribly worried about being identified. It wasn't like there was a gaggle of NASA engineers out here. Still, when he saw a young guy disappear down the corridor, he decided it was a good time to make his exit. He left a crumpled dollar tip on the table and headed out the door.

A light freezing rain had been falling since dark, about the time that Flagg stopped in at the Beaver. Already, a thin layer of ice had coated the windshields of Flagg's red station wagon like a good doughnut glaze. The weather forecast called for more frozen precipitation throughout the night, and so Flagg decided to check into a hotel for the night. He could use the sleep. Moreover, he really couldn't afford a fender bender or any situation that would draw police involvement.

He had set out at dawn from Miami, where he had picked up a crate of AR-15 assault rifles that he was selling to a group of gang members in northern Virginia. He told himself that he had stopped by the Eager Beaver when the weather had started to deteriorate earlier this evening, you know, to get off the roads before they got icy. The truth was, and the truth was embarrassing to look at, was that he had wanted to see some boobies. He had to admit to himself that the detour had not been well served.

He checked into a Holiday Inn Express at the foot of the exit ramp and made it into his room just as the freezing rain switched over to a light snow. His overnight bag and crate accompanied him into the room. With a yawn, he dropped his stuff on the spare bed and removed a queen-sized comforter that was tucked into his bag. He gave it a hard shake and spread it across the dingy bedspread, as he couldn't bear to imagine the stories that it, or even more terrifying, the sheets underneath, could tell. Then he took a long and gratifying leak.

Another yawn, and he stretched out on the bed, remote control in hand (after cleaning it down with a sanitizing wipe, of course). Wall-to-wall Christmas specials. The particular special that Flagg had stumbled across involved a man whose wife had died, leaving him to raise his three children. At some point, an angel debating whether to give up her wings got involved.

It was times like these Flagg reminded himself to meditate. It got him back to his baseline, back to normal. He turned off the TV and counted to fifty, carefully regulating his breathing. When he was done, he saw that it was nearly 1:00 a.m., time for the top stories on CNN, and he turned the TV back on.

He began to drift away while the news anchor rolled through one headline after another, each of which simply confirmed his opinion of the world at large. Police in Kansas had arrested a woman when they discovered her nine-year-old daughter was not dying of leukemia and had spent the $31,000 in donations for the girl's medical treatments on spa treatments and a new pickup truck. Another giant chunk of the Arctic ice shelf had collapsed into the North Atlantic. Clearly, mankind was on the back nine. And he was only one man. How much could one man do?

"And our last story before the break," said the newscaster. "Richmond, Virginia is abuzz tonight with talk of last night's SuperLotto drawing," said the newscaster. "Just one ticket matched all six numbers for the $415 million jackpot, and it was purchased in downtown Richmond. Tonight, the town waits to find out who the lucky winner is. Let's go live to Richmond, where our own Amy Morgan is waiting with a live report."

The screen cut to the front of a shady looking convenience store, where a well-bundled reporter was clearly freezing her ass off and wishing that the only time she'd ever been to the convenience store was two days earlier, to buy the winning ticket.

"Kelly," said the half-frozen reporter, "I'm here at Lucky Lou's Chicken Shack, where since yesterday, this little store has been hopping, people just wanting to catch a bit of the lightning that struck here Thursday night."

"Does anyone have any idea who bought the big winner?" asked the anchor.

"No," said the reporter, visibly anxious to end her live report and not forthcoming with many details. Who could blame her? wondered Flagg. Any convenience store called Lucky Lou's Chicken Shack probably wasn't in the safest neighborhood.

"Amy, has anyone been able to talk to the cashier that sold the ticket?" asked Kelly. "Maybe she remembers something from around the time the ticket was purchased."

"Yeah, that would've been nice to get, Kelly," said the reporter. "Reporting live from Richmond, Virginia, this is Amy Morgan, CNN. Back to you in the studio."

"Wait, Amy, I've got a few more questions," said Kelly the anchor.

"I'll have more details as they become available," said Amy, the I've-totally-had-it reporter. "Back to you in the studio." This time with a little more heft in her voice.

"OK," said Kelly the anchor. "Thanks for that enlightening report." She turned back to the main camera and the broadcast cut to commercial.

The story bothered Flagg because it meant someone out there now had more money than they would ever know what to do with. One of these dumb rednecks that would cash in without consulting accountants and lawyers and financial planners. Oh, no, they wanted to get themselves on the Today show and start buying giant pickup trucks equipped with diamond-encrusted gun racks. They'd start buying houses and cars and giving money to desperate relatives addicted to crystal meth.

It gave him a headache just thinking about it.

AFTER EVEN MORE YOGA, the headache subsided, and Flagg got ready for bed. He brushed his teeth, he put on his pajamas, and he plugged in his nightlight. Charles Flagg was not ashamed to admit that he was afraid of the dark. Admit it to himself, at least.

But sleep was hard to come by that night, and so he was wide awake when the phone call came in at three in the morning. He was glad to have the distraction and grabbed the wireless phone from the nightstand. The caller ID screen read Restricted. It was probably a wrong number, but something told him to take the call.

"Flagg."

"Good morning, Mr. Flagg."

"It's three in the morning, and I'm wide awake," Flagg said. "I wouldn't exactly call that good."

"I have a proposition for you," said the caller.

"Who is this?"

"That's not important."

"Then we're done talking," Flagg said.

"Would three million be enough to buy my anonymity?"

Flagg paused. He wasn't an idiot.

"You know who I am?" Flagg asked.

"You came highly recommended."

It always amused Flagg when prospective clients talked like this, as if they were in a James Bond movie.

"Really," Flagg said. "Maybe I should update my list of references."

"Perhaps a good-faith deposit for your services would put you at ease."

More highbrow talk.

"Money's nice."

"Give me an account number, and I'll wire in one hundred thousand dollars right now," the caller said. "All you have to do is listen to my proposal. The money is yours to keep."

"Fair enough."

Flagg gave the caller the number for an empty account in a bank in Grand Cayman. He learned the trick from reading John Grisham books in the early 1990s. Hell if it wasn't a good idea.

"I'll call you back in fifteen minutes," he said. "That should give you enough time to confirm the wire transfer, then move the money into another account."

He hung up.

Flagg was intrigued. It had been a while since his last big payday, as he had been pursuing his life's work for nearly a year without a break. It wasn't the kind of work that paid very well. It was better described as a labor of love. This gun run he was doing tonight was minimum-wage work, labor he equated to illegal aliens working on construction sites, running at the first sight of an Immigration and Customs Enforcement van.

A few minutes later, Flagg confirmed that his account at Grand Cayman Bank had just gotten a hundred grand chubbier, and he bounced the money from there into a Hong Kong bank.

His new employer called back a little later.

"Now do you trust me?"

"I'm listening."

"You're aware of last night's SuperLotto drawing?"

"I am," he said.

"And you know the ticket was purchased in Richmond, Virginia?"

"Just saw it on the news."

"See, the ticket hasn't been cashed yet," the caller said. "At a minimum, it will be out in the wild for at least four more days. Possibly longer, if the ticket-holder goes to a lawyer or financial advisor."

"In the wild?"

"Because of the Christmas holiday," the caller said, "the ticket can't be cashed until Wednesday, which is the next time that SuperLotto's offices will be open."

A tumbler clicked into place.

"You want me to steal the ticket," Flagg said.

"Precisely," the caller said.

"Assuming I accept your offer, what's to stop me to from cashing it for myself?"

"Because I'm hiring you to find it for me."

"If I cash it, I could buy and sell you."

"I hear that you're a man of honor."

"Yeah, but that is a shitload of money."

"So is three million dollars."

"A good point."

"But you're right," the caller said. "I do need an insurance policy. Let me make it simple. If I were you, I wouldn't try to cash the ticket. If you do, you'll get nothing."

Flagg considered the offer. He had no doubt that he'd find the ticket. The real mystery was behind the caller's warning. On the one hand, the guy could be completely full of shit. On the other hand, the man had shown himself to be a legitimate player, what with the good-faith deposit and tracking Flagg down in the first place. It wasn't like Flagg's telephone number was in the phone book. Three million. More than enough to fund his life's work, really for the rest of his life.

"OK," Flagg said. "You've convinced me. What happens after I find the ticket?" The use of the word 'after' instead of 'if' was deliberate. Always good to bolster your employer's confidence in you.

"Payment of three million dollars upon delivery of the ticket. Wired into the bank account of your choice."

"Five million," Flagg said. "And don't bother countering. I don't negotiate. Five million. Take it or leave it."

He could hear the caller pretending to mull things over, clicking his tongue, sniffling, that kind of thing. Flagg knew that the caller was putting on a show because if the opening offer was three million, he was probably prepared to go to six million. But Flagg had built a reputation as a reasonable man.

"Fine," the caller said. "Five million it is."

"How do I contact you?"

The caller gave him the number of a prepaid wireless phone.

"Don't call the number until you've got the ticket in hand and ready to make the delivery," the caller said. "If I see the winner on television with the big oversized check, I'll know you failed."

"You'd make quite the detective," Flagg said. "So dramatic. Anything else, cowboy?"

"Just get it done."

The caller hung up.

16

Carter Livingston Pierce was not dead, but he sort of wished he were. His fingers were stiff with cold, and his teeth were chattering. It was the sound of the chattering that had roused him back to consciousness in the first place. His head throbbed from its collision with the floor. Every blink of his eyelids felt like tiny sledgehammers colliding in his sockets. He'd been out for a while, that much he knew. When his last memory suddenly began replaying in his head, he popped upright, as if awakening from a nightmare.

The nightmare, though, was right in front of him.

When he saw his very deceased and very shish-kabobed brother-in-law staring back at him, nausea rippled through him, and despite his very best efforts to keep it together, his insides rebelled against him. He puked all over the hard-wood floors, turning his head just in time to avoid getting it all over his clothes.

When his insides stopped churning like a washing machine, he rolled over, away from his fresh spew, its ripe smell hanging acidly in the cold air, and onto his stomach. It was then that he saw for the first time what had become of Julius. He hadn't exactly been able to check on his client's well-being while Todd was trying to kill him.

"Oh, shit," he whispered. That probably would not sit well with the Virginia State Bar.

Then it hit him. The whole reason he'd come to this hellhole to start with. The ticket!

Where the hell was the ticket?

Slowly, he staggered to his feet, giving the dizziness a chance to work itself out. The ticket had been in his hand while he defended himself against that dickweed brother-in-law of his. That's what it was, right? Self-defense? Todd was going to kill him all along. There was just too much money at stake to think otherwise. God knew how much money Todd owed to bookies, arms dealers, drug dealers, suppliers, hookers, pimps, loan sharks, terrorists, you name it. Carter hadn't had a choice. He wondered if Ashley would buy it. He wondered if the police would buy it. He wondered if he bought it.

He thought about this while he searched the cabin. He started at Todd's feet and worked his way out in concentric circles. It had to be here somewhere. He remembered very clearly clutching it in his hand as he rushed at Todd with the poker (just because he had charged the man with a fireplace poker didn't mean killing him wasn't self-defense, right?). Nothing.

After two minutes, Carter began to really worry. Feeling lightheaded again, he crumpled against the couch, curling up into a ball. The ticket was gone. Gone.

How could it be gone?

Then it hit him. It hadn't been taken by extraterrestrials.

It hadn't been transported to another dimension. Someone had walked in here and stolen the ticket.

Someone had been here.

No, not someone. Samantha. Samantha had been here. Samantha had stolen the ticket.

Oh, shit.

Another thought gripped him with icy hands.

If she was here, she may have seen everything that had happened. She may have already called the police. They might already be on their way. He massaged his forehead with the palm of his hand. He should've known she would be a problem. He should have kicked her off the case as soon as Julius set foot in his office. Didn't she get it? Couldn't she get it through that thick skull of hers? Julius didn't have any business winning that much money. He wouldn't have been able to shoulder the enormous responsibility that accompanied great wealth. He was black, after all.

Julius had the ticket for one day and had gotten his head blown off. What if he'd actually made it to lottery headquarters and walked away with a couple hundred million bucks? It would've been like sticking a nuclear device in the hands of a terrorist.

His eyes drifted back and forth between the bodies, growing stiffer with death with each passing minute. He needed a plan. He needed to evaluate. In his mind, he ticked off the facts as he knew them to be.

1.Todd and Julius were dead.

2.If the police placed Carter at the scene, he would be the primary suspect in their deaths.

3.Samantha Khouri had the ticket.

4.Samantha knew he had tried to steal the ticket.

5.The police were not here yet.

These five facts served as the premise for his first deduction. Samantha had not yet called the police. Otherwise, they would've been here by now, and he would have been answering a series of extremely uncomfortable questions in some tiny room in Henrico County's Public Safety Building, tackily decorated with Christmas cheer. Upon this foundation, he laid another brick of deduction. Samantha had her own plans for the ticket. Christ, why else would she have taken it? Panic stampeded through his chest like a herd of elephants. Was she going to cash it in? Steal his future? Steal his family's future? No, no, no, he had to stop her.

But how? Come on, Carter, come on! Think! Marshalling the full powers of his average intelligence, he toyed with the idea of calling the police, pinning the deaths on Samantha.

He cleared his throat and practiced his 911 call.

"Please, I just found my brother-in-law dead!"

No, too rehearsed.

"There's been a shooting!"

Too theatrical.

"Yeah! I need an ambulance!"

Too precise.

"Please help!"

OK, not bad.

He tried to visualize the dispatcher's response.

"What's the problem, sir?"

He continued the production.

"It's my brother-in-law. He's been stabbed! I think he's dead!"

"Where are you calling from, sir?" said the imaginary dispatcher.

"Uh, my brother's house. Just off Mountain Road."

Calmer now, appropriately so. Even the brother-in-law/brother discrepancy would make his panic more genuine. The dispatcher would be doing his job, getting the caller calmed down, letting him tell his story. Carter had just been worried about his brother-in-law and came out here to check on him on this Friday night.

"Holy shit, that's the guy that cleans my office!"

"Yeah, I think he and my associate had a little something on the side."

"Her name is Samantha. Samantha Khouri."

"She knew where Todd lived."

"You don't think she had anything to do with this?"

OK, that was a bit much.

He pulled out his phone and started to dial the three familiar digits.

Then he stopped.

Something felt very wrong about this.

Samantha was a shade over five feet tall and weighed about a hundred and ten pounds. Maybe. And he would have the police believe that she had overpowered Julius and tied him to a chair? And skewered Todd to boot? Plus, Todd was his brother-in-law, not Samantha's. Forget teaming them up. It wouldn't take them long to figure out where Julius worked, whose office he cleaned.

What if he untied Julius and knocked him to the ground? He could make it look like a home invasion gone bad. And so what if the police figured out Julius worked for Carter? It wouldn't have been the first time a service person had bitten the hand of those who fed him. Ungrateful bastards.

His brain started to seize up with the complexity of the task. He would have to doctor the scene to make it look like there had only been two people here, and he didn't have the first clue how to do that. He also couldn't calculate the impact of the Samantha Situation, how the ticket played into everything. There were too many variables to consider.

If he called 911 now, he'd be in the same place he would have been had Samantha called the police on him in the first place.

Oh, brother.

17

S amantha spent the night shivering in her recliner, wrapped in a heavy quilt. Sleep came raggedly and in small bursts. The ticket was in her safe, where it would remain until she was ready to deliver it to Jamal. She just needed to rest. The ticket was safe. No one knew she had it. Carter hadn't seen her. The television stayed on all night, a comforting companion, taking her mind off the decidedly unusual events of the previous twelve hours. She watched infomercials and, at about 2:30 in the morning, she ordered a rotisserie oven. She didn't know why she did it, but it seemed to calm her down, and it would be here within three business days. For reasons she could not articulate, this pleased her immensely.

The end of *Animal House* was on the tube now, its familiarity soothing Samantha, although real sleep continued to elude her. A couple of Advil swallowed when she had gotten home had knocked down the fever, but exhaustion had set into her bones like concrete. She could barely muster the energy to change the channel, and the remote was sitting on the armrest, about six inches out of her grasp.

As the credits rolled at movie's end, the entire evening played out in her head again like the back end of a comedy-horror double feature, starting with Julius knocking on her office door. An incident seemingly so minor, so insignificant, yet it had kickstarted a chain of events that had severely and permanently altered the course of her life. This was more than a pebble tossed into Lake Samantha, a few ripples undulating out from center. This was an asteroid that had screamed through the atmosphere and obliterated all life on Planet Samantha.

It didn't seem real. Part of her felt like the images in her head were just the byproduct of reading an account of the incident in the newspaper, maybe catching the story on CNN. That creamy puff of pink behind Julius' head? That was his brain, Sammy! His brain!

And what was she supposed to do now?

She didn't know. She really didn't. She felt adrift, without a tether. During the drive home from the bloodbath at the cabin, she briefly debated stopping at a pay phone and calling the police. But she had felt too sick, too confused, too stunned to make such a decision. They, whoever They were, would trace the call to the pay phone. They would lift her fingerprints from the handset. They would identify her license plates from a surveillance video. They would charge her with murder.

It was too risky. Julius was dead, and there was nothing she could do about that. This was what Julius would want, and given the price he had paid for winning this jackpot, he was probably entitled to have his final wishes carried out. After all, she thought, he had been murdered by his own lawyer. The attorney-client privilege at its finest. When this story got out, it was not going to do much for the image of the legal profession.

At seven, she struggled out of the recliner and staggered into the bathroom, where she took stock of her physical condition. Bad news on all fronts. Her head was pounding. Her muscles still cramped, and her night in the recliner probably hadn't helped that. The sore throat had worsened, and a tickle at the back of her throat portended a hacking cough that would be moving in for the next two weeks. She dry-swallowed two more cold-and-flu tablets and staggered to the kitchen to make coffee.

Rage bubbled up inside her as she considered Carter's behavior.

"Jackass," she whispered as she dumped the ground coffee into the filter.

Wasn't it bad enough that people already thought lawyers were slime? She worked in a profession in which the worse off the clients were, the more their services were needed, and the richer the lawyers got. The better off people were, the more their services were needed, and the richer they got. She recalled a class-action settlement the firm was involved in a few years ago, after which the members of the class ended up with a buy-one-get-one-free coupon for contact lens solution and the firm had used the fees to renovate its partners' lounge. Eighty-one people had gone blind from the contact lens solution that had been contaminated as a result of poor sanitation at the factory. Blind!

As a first-year associate, she worked on a merger of two steel companies that cost nine hundred people their jobs. Very little came of the merger other than the indictment of the newly installed CEO for smuggling steel into North Korea in violation of about two dozen federal laws. She had even received death threats, which Carter advised her were like medals, to be worn proudly.

Carter Pierce made more than a million bucks a year.

That hadn't been enough? He had two vacation homes. Or was it three? She couldn't keep up. That hadn't been enough? And Julius, clearly terrified by his stroke of luck, placed his trust in her and Carter, who might as well have gone pee-pee on Julius' head for all the respect he had showed the man. Moreover, no one besides her would ever know what had really happened in that terrible sixty-second span at the cabin, seeing as how Carter probably wouldn't be in a very truth-telling mood.

As the coffee finished brewing, a sudden and strong urge to check on the ticket washed over her like a wave. She went to the bedroom and knelt before the safe, which was tucked near the back corner of her walk-in closet. Upon making it home from the cabin, she had decided that it was the safest place for the ticket. The key was tied to a piece of dental floss that she had strung around her neck. She slid the key home, unlatched the clasp and swung the lid open. There it was, still safely secured in the plastic baggie. Its feathers had been ruffled a bit in the fight, but it was none worse for the wear.

Four hundred and fifteen million dollars.

Images of a possible future erupted from the depths of her soul like lava. This ticket would sure solve the problem of her parents' struggling business. They could retire. Buy a nice home where they could be comfortable for the rest of their days. Buy a big place for them back in Lebanon, near the family, where they could spend the summers. It could solve the problem of her relatives in Lebanon, struggling to get by in a country that never knew what each sunrise would bring. It would most certainly solve the problem of her dissatisfaction with her chosen profession, a dissatisfaction that she confided in no one. All she had to do was show up at lottery headquarters on Wednesday morning with a big, nervous smile on her face. No one would ever know. The rest would work itself out.

The beep of the coffeemaker jostled her back to reality, and she pushed her plans for the ticket back into a dusty old closet in her mind.

"Go lock it up," she said aloud, as if she needed to order herself to do it.

She hurriedly replaced the ticket in the safe, as if someone might walk in on her. She closed the lid and slid the safe back into its hiding spot. Her heart was racing, and her palms felt clammy.

"Coffee," she said. "You'll feel better after some coffee."

You might even stop talking to yourself, she thought.

After staring at the locked safe for another moment, she got up off the floor and went back to the kitchen. With a steaming mug of coffee in hand, she settled back into the recliner and turned on the morning news. The logo imprinted on the side of the mug caught her eye.

WILLETT & HALL

Your Constant in a Changing World

It was a changing world, alright.

Halfway through her cup of coffee, she decided to check on the ticket again.

Just to be sure it was safe.

SAMANTHA KHOURI first went to work at the Mediterranean Express when she was fourteen. She started by stocking shelves a few hours a week before graduating to the cash register. This was a gigantic thrill for her because handling money made her feel very grown-up. At first, she didn't really notice how little money she was handling, and had she known, she probably wouldn't have cared. During the store's frequent slow times, she did homework or, when her parents weren't looking, read *Tiger Beat* magazine. This was a publication her parents would not have approved of.

After a while, she began to detect some patterns in the life of the store. Rarely did anyone ever wait in line to pay for groceries. Dust collected on many of the canned goods. A good deal of the bread that they bought from a bakery in Fredericksburg often went home with the Khouris just as it started to become stale. This even though they bought the minimum order allowed under their contract with the bakery.

It was how she learned that store never stopped struggling to survive; business was just enough to get by. Sales peaked once a year, just after the Lebanese Food Festival, when people were inspired by the chicken shawarma sandwiches, the baklava and the hummus. The rest of the year, the store catered to the Richmond's supportive but relatively small Arab community, and the Khouris needed every one of them to stay afloat.

Money was a constant worry. Her parents always drove used cars, virtually running them into the ground before buying yet another jalopy already pushing six figures on the odometer. They rarely went out to dinner. Growing up, she recalled an occasional Friday night trip to Red Lobster. She always ordered the popcorn shrimp platter, which was far more than she could eat in one sitting. She didn't care, eating shrimp until her stomach ached because she knew the next night it would be back to tabouli and stuffed grape leaves and stale pita bread.

When she was sixteen, she got her first real sense of just how bad things were. One night shortly before Thanksgiving, she had been unable to sleep and had gotten up for a

172 DAVID KAZZIE

glass of water. Halfway between her room and the kitchen, she saw her father sitting in the dark of the living room, his face in his hands, weeping silently. She knew things had been bad at the store. Business had slowed to a crawl, even during her weekend shifts, and her parents had been sullen and quiet. The phone rang frequently, creditors calling in long past-due accounts. Christmas came a month later, and the space under the tree was a bit more barren than usual.

A month later, while working on a Saturday afternoon, she saw two large men enter her father's office. Loud arguing ensued. She never commented on the bruised eyes and jaw that appeared after they departed. A small inheritance after the death of Samantha's maternal grandfather later that spring floated the store through that crisis, and the store survived. Barely.

By the time she graduated from high school, she had vowed she would never struggle financially. She thought about becoming a doctor, but she was just dreadful at science. She survived her introductory biology class at the University of Virginia with a big fat D, but it was her performance in the two-credit biology lab that really drove home the point that her future did not lie in medicine.

The midterm examination consisted of identifying as many organisms under the microscope as she could in ninety minutes. The easy items were worth three or four points, the more difficult ones worth twice or thrice as much. A score of 180 was worth an A; sixty points was enough to pass. Samantha scored an astonishing fifty-eight. When she asked the professor if she could withdraw from the class, as the drop deadline had long passed, he cautioned her against jumping to any conclusions about her performance.

"How did you do on the midterm?" he had asked kindly.

"I got a 58," Samantha had said, as matter-of-factly as she could. No point in hiding from it.

"Sure, I'll sign your form!"

The professor had agreed to meet Samantha an hour later in the biology building. When she got there, she found him scouring the hallways looking for her, as if he couldn't wait to get her out of the biology program. With his signature inked on her withdrawal form, her medical career ended before it had begun, and she set her sights on law school.

Despite the four-credit D weighing down her GPA, she banged away on the rest of her course work and graduated cum laude from Virginia. After college, she taught English in Japan for a year and then took the LSATs, scoring in the 85th percentile. This earned her admission to University of Richmond's law school, where, from day one, she studied like a fiend, often working late into the night.

After her second year of law school, Samantha accepted a summer clerkship with Willett & Hall, which paid her the princely sum of $2,000 a week. During this twelve-week stint, she participated in a number of important legal events. For example, she took in a Baltimore Orioles game with her fellow summer clerks and sat right behind home plate. Over the July 4 weekend, the clerks traveled to the managing partner's large vacation home at Smith Mountain Lake. Every day, she and her fellow summer clerks were treated to fancy lunches at the city's finest restaurants. She gained ten pounds in twelve weeks. Needless to say, the practice of law was fantastic!

The end of the summer brought an offer from the firm, and she cruised through her final year of law school before buckling down to study for the bar exam. That had been painful for a number of reasons, but she'd gotten through it.

Afterwards, Willett & Hall was waiting with its six-figure offer and, of course, the iPhone. With her law school debt on the very wrong side of six figures, she was ready to start making the big bucks. And the bucks started rolling in.

She would never forget her first paycheck from the firm. After taxes, she had taken home $3,500. Two weeks later, another check. Her bank account grew so quickly it made her head spin. She bought a new Audi coupe and the Tobacco Row condominium. She paid off her law school loans in four years. She splurged on clothes. On her way home from work every night, she dropped forty bucks on a late dinner, confident that she had earned that particular extravagance.

It wasn't long – probably about the time she started dreaming about dousing her iPhone in lighter fluid – before she realized she was nothing more than a profit center to the firm. She smiled at her naïveté; she remembered thinking how nice everyone had been during the summer! She felt so stupid, especially since she'd heard the horrific reports from classmates who graduated earlier than her. She really thought they were exaggerating, and besides, she never took anybody's word on anything. But within a month, the truth lay sprawled out before her like a murder victim.

Just another body to churn out billables. One night, about four years before Julius had walked into her life with half a billion dollars, Samantha had found herself sitting in her office at three in the morning, drinking expensive wine straight from the bottle while she worked on a discovery motion. Tears splashed her arms as she typed. She told herself she should've known this was going to happen. Still, she didn't really think, didn't really believe that they would demand every ounce of her being, every useful part of her. She could still remember how the wine tasted.

She should've known, she should've realized that the firm just didn't care. Odds were, you weren't going to make partner anyway, and if you washed out early, there were twenty more eager beaver law school grads desperate for the opportunity to work a hundred hours a week and develop a substance abuse problem.

Around her, personal lives collapsed in a dank, emotional apocalypse. With each passing year, wedding bands became harder and harder to find on her fellow associates' ring fingers. On her first day at the firm, a dozen of her fellow first-year associates were married. Eight years later, only two of them were, although a number of them were sleeping with each other. Sort of cushioned the blow of divorce. It was like high school, except everyone had oodles of cash and was old enough to drink legally. And, brother, did they drink. Every night, a handful of the younger associates darkened the door of one bar or another, where they drank until the pain went away.

As she sat in her recliner, Samantha wondered what the next ten years held for her. If she went looking for another job after the holidays, was she just going to end up in one of the other big firms? She had long given up on the idea of working as a prosecutor. She just couldn't afford to work for sixty grand a year. She felt she had to keep raking in the big bucks to protect the family.

Curled up in the recliner, thick clouds swirling outside her windows, she couldn't bear to think about going back to the firm. Now that the partnership was gone, how could she ever go back to the office? Of counsel. Give me a break, she thought.

Dammit, Carter, she thought. She couldn't believe the mess he'd made of her life.

She pounded the armrest, which, of course, sent hot

coffee splashing across her arm. This she also blamed on Carter. From now on, she decided, she was going to be blaming everything on that asshole. Who was she kidding, anyway? Yeah, maybe he hadn't seen her up at the house, but he would quickly figure out that she was the one who had stolen the ticket.

Then what? Was he really in a position to hunt her down? Would he hurt her? Didn't he have his own problems to deal with – namely that little double homicide scene out at that cabin? What a mess this was turning out to be. All over a little bit of money. OK, it was a shitload of money, but it was still money.

This scattershot line of thinking brought her back to the ticket again. She'd already checked on it twice in the last hour. She was starting to feel a little frayed at the edges, as if someone had found a loose string poking up from her soul and had started to tug at it. She got out of the chair and drifted back to her closet, where she sat down next to the safe.

A roundtable discussion that Samantha was barely conscious of was underway in her head.

It's Jamal's ticket.

Maybe.

How did Julius know Jamal was his son?

Maybe there were other heirs.

How would she ever find them?

She thought again about her parents, about her father losing the store, losing his life's work. She thought about Ziad Khouri and how that idiot had all but destroyed the family's reputation in the name of an alleged holy war that he was either too stupid or too lazy to understand.

Focus on Jamal, she thought. Jamal.

Try as she might, though, her thoughts kept drifting

back to Lebanon, to her aunts and uncles and cousins, and the years of civil war that they had endured. The bulk of the family lived in tenements in Beirut. Her father had two older brothers, one a butcher, the other, an electrician. Both were dirt poor, living in small concrete dwellings with their families and struggling to get by each day. Her mother had a brother and two sisters, one of whom had died in a car bombing during the war. Money was always tight. The specter of war sat in the nation's core like a cancer in remission.

A thought snuck up on her like a pickpocket in a crowd.

No one would ever know.

No one would ever know.

No one would ever know.

Just disappear until Wednesday and then cash in the ticket. When it came to the lottery, possession was a lot more than nine-tenths of the law, as the saying went. No one could ever question her ownership of the ticket. Anyone who did would be written off as a jealous sideshow freak. It was perfect.

And just like that, Samantha found herself at her line.

Samantha believed that there was a line in every person, a line that once crossed was forever destroyed. Deciding whether to cross it was basically a referendum on the type of person you wanted to be, the type of life you wanted to lead. And here she was. Cross this line and she could make her life easier, make her family's life easier, put an end to their decades-old struggle. The downside, of course, was that she would become one of the greatest thieves in the history of the world.

No, Samantha thought. No. This is wrong.

But so was coming within a whisker of getting her head blown off.

But she'd always be a criminal, she thought.

She could live with that, she decided. It was a small price to pay. If it bothered her too much, she'd get an expensive therapist.

She pulled the quilt tighter around her body as the ticket continued to swirl around her mind. The thing that scared Samantha the most was that she was starting to buy into the argument in favor of keeping the ticket. There was still a part of her that didn't want anything to do with the ticket, let alone keep it, but its voice was getting drowned out by the ever greedier drums of war.

She needed help. She was ready to admit it.

As she sat cross-legged on the closet floor, achy and feverish, she knew she was in no condition to handle this on her own. She crawled across her bedroom floor, yanked her comforter down from the bed and wrapped herself in it. With her strength flagging, she picked up the phone and dialed a number that she had never expected to dial again, but one that she still had committed to memory.

"Yo!" a voice barked out.

"Pasquale, it's Sam," she said. As quickly as she could, before she could change her mind, she added:

"I need your help."

She hung up, crawled into her bed, and fell asleep.

18

The weather deteriorated steadily as Charles Flagg neared the Virginia-North Carolina border, and he debated checking into a motel for the day. The freezing rain was mixing in with snow and caking the roadway with a beautiful but dangerous crust. As he crossed the state line, Flagg decided to keep moving despite the bad weather, as he was only eighty miles from his destination. Visibility was holding steady for now, and there were very few cars on the highway. With any luck, he would be there in the early afternoon.

The cost of waiting would be too high. He would need every minute to track down the ticket, and he couldn't afford to lose another day. It was risky, yes, but natural selection didn't mean you just sat on the sidelines hoping that you didn't get eaten by a hyena. Sometimes, to evolve, one had to take risks. Just in case, though, he decided he needed to hear her voice. Just in case. Using the speed dial function (she was No. 1 on speed dial, she always would be No. 1 on his speed dial, and there was no No. 2), he placed the call.

She picked up on the second ring.

"Hello?"

Oh, that voice, thought Flagg.

"It's me," he said.

A long sigh.

"What do you want, Bobby?"

He would have killed anyone who addressed him by his birth name, long ago discarded in favor of the namesake of the greatest mind in human history. Olivia Kellogg, however, was free to call him whatever she wanted.

"You know that my name is Charles."

"Whatever, Bobby."

"I just wanted to say hi," he said. "Wish you a Merry Christmas."

"I told you not to call me," she said. "You don't even acknowledge Christmas."

"Why did you answer?" he asked. "You have caller ID."

"Oh, don't give me that bullshit! I don't know how you can make the caller ID show that it's someone else calling, but I wish you would stop."

"How are you?"

"Is it time for me to get a court order?"

Olivia brought this up from time to time, but he knew she would never go through with it. Thus, he didn't respond.

"How are you?" he repeated.

"I was fine until you called."

"That hurts."

"It's been six years," she said. "Isn't it about time you moved on?"

"I'm just waiting for you to come to your senses," he said. "I know you will."

"Why don't you just leave me alone?"

"Because I love you."

"I don't love you."

"We're supposed to be together," he said. "It's what nature wants."

"Boy, you're just as crazy as ever."

"They called Galileo crazy. They called Michelangelo crazy."

"Someone's feeling good about himself this morning."

"Can you imagine how perfect our children would be?"

"I try not to think about us procreating," she said. "It hurts my head."

Again, he reminded himself that she was one of the chosen few and therefore exempt from extermination. Plus, she always smelled really good. He wondered if she still wore the same perfume.

"Do you still wear the same perfume?"

"No."

"Why not?"

"Do I really have to explain?"

"What are you wearing now?"

"I'm not telling you."

"Why not?"

"Because I don't want you jerking off while you think about what I'm wearing."

Boy, she was really pushing him today.

"You know I don't do that."

"Right. Your precious seed. Can't afford to spill a single drop."

"It is precious. You're not seeing anyone, right?" he asked.

"None of your business."

"Remember our deal," he said.

"How could I forget?"

Three years ago, Olivia had announced that she was getting engaged to a young accountant she had met at a farmers' market. When Flagg found out, he reassured her that if she went through with the nuptials, he would place a feeding tube down the man's throat and pipe in boiling vegetable oil. She broke off the engagement and had not dated since. She claimed he wasn't being fair, but he didn't want her to dilute her exquisite DNA with genetic garbage from some random idiot. Talk about unfair!

Sometimes, he wished he could just do away with her, but he couldn't go through with it. She was too perfect a specimen. Professor Darwin would not approve.

"Well, keep it in mind."

"Can't you just leave me alone?" she asked. "There are other fish in the sea. Someone as high on the evolutionary ladder as me. I just want to live my life."

"There's no one else!"

He was getting upset now, she had this way of just getting on his last nerve, and he knew that it was because she was his evolutionary equivalent. No one on the lower rungs of the ladder had the ability to press his buttons the way she could. Rationally, to the extent that Charles Flagg was capable of rational thought, he was OK with that, but emotionally, he just wanted to slap her silly.

"Bobby, I'm really nothing special." she said.

"You're so wrong. And I really would prefer it if you called me Charles."

"I'd prefer it if you suffered a massive stroke, but we don't always get what we want, do we?"

"You're upset," he said. "It happens to the best of us. You need time to calm down."

"Please leave me alone."

"I'll call you soon."

"Please don't."

"Merry Christmas."

"Whatever."

She hung up. That she even humored him this long sometimes surprised him, notwithstanding the fact that he promised her he would execute one of her neighbors at random if she refused to take his calls. He supposed that she humored him because she actually believed him. He supposed that she probably should believe him, but really, she was being a bit melodramatic if that was the only reason she indulged him. He wouldn't kill one of her neighbors just because she wouldn't take a particular phone call.

He probably wouldn't.

OK, so maybe he would.

NINETY MINUTES LATER, the high-rises of downtown Richmond drew into view, Flagg's mood darkening with each passing mile. These conversations with Olivia really ate at him. How could she not see that they were meant to be together? Move on, she had suggested on the phone. Might as well suggest moving on without oxygen. Ever since he had first laid eyes on her – on the anniversary of Professor Darwin's birth, no less – he had known she was the one. The only one. There would be no other ones. Anyone else would be inferior to Olivia Kellogg. Her bloodlines were flawless. Her father had been an Olympic swimming champion before becoming a groundbreaking cancer researcher. Her mother, also an Olympic athlete, had been a critically acclaimed novelist until her untimely death at the hands of a drunk driver.

The happy relationship ended on a Tuesday, the day that Flagg confided in the love of his life what had become of the man that had killed her mother. Shortly after hearing the tragic story about the wife and mother cut down in her prime, Flagg paid the drunk driver a visit. When the driver, a divorced welder named Bryan Stewart, got home from work one afternoon, he found Flagg in his single-wide trailer, sitting in his recliner and drinking his last can of Cheerwine.

A week later, police responded to the home after receiving a report of a rancid smell emanating from the trailer, where an officer found Stewart nailed to his bedroom wall. The death of Stewart, who was well-known in the county as a small-time thief and a batterer of women, did not spark an entirely in-depth investigation. His murder remained unsolved.

Much to Flagg's chagrin, Olivia Kellogg did not react favorably to his tale of revenge. Olivia immediately ended her marriage to Flagg, whose only previous hint of strange proclivities was that his copy of *On the Origin of Species* (that he had one at all was a little weird, she later admitted to herself) was dog-eared on every page and heavily high-lighted. She did not react favorably to his statement that his life's mission was to save humanity from itself and, in furtherance of that mission, that he had removed eighty-six people (counting Bryan Stewart) from the gene pool. She was not even swayed by his fervent belief that human evolution was at a crossroads and that something had to be done.

Modern society disgusted Flagg. In just a century, mankind had undone millions years of evolution. Vaccines and antibiotics had been the first dominoes, but they were the first of many that were toppling toward the final domino – one marked EXTINCTION. Beta blockers, chemotherapy drugs, statins, anti-hypertensives, insulin, proton pump inhibitors, steroids – they all served to artificially lengthen life and prevent the timely removal of the weak from the gene pool. Worse, they kept people who otherwise would have been selected out of the herd alive and reproducing, which cycled weak genes through to future generations, further diluting the gene pool. It was a vicious cycle that would undoubtedly end with mankind as a footnote to history.

Virtually no one exercised. People clogged their arteries with saturated fats, inhaling cheeseburgers and French fries like they were running out of cows and potatoes. Modern medicine and surgery kept alive people that shouldn't be alive, and then those same people took absolutely no advantage of the gift they'd been given. It was that simple. Instead of a few hundred million, Mother Earth was carrying seven billion of her children, stumbling through life like mindless zombies, and that was too much. Stories of impending apocalypse always got him excited.

Flagg believed that survival instincts had been bred out of the human race. He had read studies confirming his hypothesis that people simply didn't know how to survive. In one about the September 11 terrorist attacks, Flagg read that after the North Tower of the World Trade Center had been hit, recorded messages broadcast over the public address system directed the office workers in the other tower to remain at their desks. To Flagg's surprise, many heeded the direction, ignoring any instinct to evacuate the building, despite the fact that a jumbo jet had just crashed into the building next door. A jumbo jet! It wasn't like someone had overcooked a bag of microwave popcorn. When the second plane hit the South Tower seventeen minutes later, those same people above the crash zone had become trapped.

Later, Flagg read a dissertation about human reaction to mass shootings, which posited that the average person did not behave in the same manner as any other creature on earth did upon hearing gunfire. Every other species, at the first hint of danger, flees in the opposite direction in a graceful ballet of escape. People, on the other hand, freeze in place, and, in many instances, actually gravitate toward the danger. Toward the gunfire. During post-incident interviews, many of these surviving individuals, when asked why they had not run for their lives, stated that they just wanted to see what was going on.

Olivia had not been impressed by any of this.

Just thinking about the end of the relationship made Flagg's head hurt so badly that he needed to pull over. He eased into the breakdown lane, came to a stop and did his exercises. This was softening his focus on the mission at hand. As it was, finding the ticket was not going to be easy, and the last thing he needed were matters of the heart intruding.

Outside, the snow continued to fall.

FLAGG FOUND Lucky Lou's Chicken Shack at around three in the afternoon. The weak light was fading fast on this, the shortest day of the year. Against the gray backdrop, the store looked as dismal in person as it had looked on television the night before. Located on a side street between Main Street and Cary Street just east of downtown Richmond, it was sandwiched between a dry cleaner and an abandoned storefront, previously home to a beverage place called Hydration Nation. A pathetic-looking banner hung over the convenience store's broken and cracked façade. It read, "We Sold a $415 Million Dollar Winner!" As if that somehow guaranteed that all their tickets would be "$415 Million Dollar Winners!"

With snow piling up on the Saturday before Christmas,

the downtown area was like a ghost town, but Lucky Lou's served the poorer neighborhoods just south and east of downtown, and so it remained open. Flagg, however, didn't see a soul as he made his way up the slippery walk to the front door. With the snow thickening behind him, Flagg stepped inside the store and closed the door behind him. Using his body to shield his hands, he flipped the OPEN sign over to CLOSED.

Other than the clerk behind the counter, the store was empty, which Flagg accepted as a karmic bonus. Fewer people he'd have to kill today. The store was unremarkable in almost every respect, although there was a large deer head mounted on the wall behind the counter, almost staring down at Flagg. Aisles of overpriced and unhealthy groceries, coolers full of cheap beer and malt liquor, cases and cases of cigarettes. Flagg hated these places. They were like way stations on civilization's road trip to extinction.

The clerk, whose name was Carly Madison, was everything Flagg expected – a pale, heavy-set woman in her mid-forties, smoking a Virginia Slim menthol and working a crossword puzzle. Not the New York Times Sunday puzzle, mind you. One of those paperbacks with the simple clues and the three-letter answers. She didn't look up when he came in, and so she didn't notice the madman approaching her counter. He stood at the counter silently until she acknowledged him. He never, ever said, "excuse me." He was the customer!

"Help you?" she asked, not looking up from her still-blank puzzle.

"Who bought the ticket?" he asked.

"What?" Still focused on her puzzle.

"The ticket," Flagg said. "Who bought the winning ticket?"

This seemed to grab her attention.

"Excuse me?" she said, looking up at Flagg.

He grabbed her by the chubby lobe of her left ear and yanked her close, like a miscreant child who wasn't listening.

"You heard me."

"I don't know."

"Yes, you do. You reviewed the security tape when you found out that the ticket had been sold here." He pulled harder.

Carly's eyes went wide with high, thin terror, and Flagg was confident that he finally had her undivided attention. He based this on the fact that she had wet her pants. The aroma of urine filled the air like mustard gas.

"Black dude," she said.

"What's his name?"

"Julius. Julius Wheeler."

"Where's he live?

"I don't know."

He tugged harder on the ear, and when he felt cartilage start to tear, he became confident that she did not know where he lived.

"What else do you know?"

Her ear still in Flagg's death grip, Carly tried to remember everything she knew about the lucky son of a bitch who had bought the ticket. While she did so, she found herself thinking that she probably should have studied a bit harder in high school. That might have sent her down a road that didn't end here, in Lucky Lou's, with her ear being slowly torn off her head.

"Let's make it simple. We'll start with something easy. How do you know him?"

Carly chose her next move carefully, as she strongly

suspected that her life depended on it. Had she known that her life did not depend on her next move, as her fate had been sealed as soon as Flagg had walked in the store, she might have relaxed a bit. Thus, she weighed her options carefully. The truth, she decided, will set you free.

"He works around here," she said, each word coming in between teary gasps.

"Where?"

Carly knew that Julius Wheeler worked at Willett & Hall because one of her co-workers, a young black girl named Tawana who also lived in the Tree, moonlighted on the same CleanSweep crew with Julius.

"Big law firm up the street."

"Which one?"

"Willett & Hall," she said.

"Where is it?"

"Go west on Main," she said. "About half a mile."

Flagg thanked Carly and shot her once in the forehead. He could only imagine the damage she had inflicted upon the local gene pool. For God's sake, she'd been capable of reproducing for at least a quarter century. He just wished he could have found her sooner.

19

"You've got the flu," said Dr. Roger Bouzein, M.D., studying her test results like they were the Dead Sea scrolls. "And strep throat. I'm going to write you a couple prescriptions. An anti-viral, which will help knock back the flu symptoms, and an antibiotic for the strep. You'll feel better in a few days. Really, though, take it easy until Christmas. You overdo it, you'll end up in a hospital. That's a promise."

Samantha looked at him, her puffy eyes spider-webbed with red threads of exhaustion.

"Thank you," she croaked.

"You still look lovely," he said, cutting his eyes quickly to his left.

They were seated in Bouzein's office at Henrico Internal Medicine, tucked in a four-story building on the grounds of Henrico Doctors' Hospital. It was furnished with cheap prefab chairs, accessorized with months-old magazines. A large practice, it was normally buzzing with patients anxious to take advantage of their benefit plans, but today it was a mausoleum. An hour ago, Bouzein had opened the office just for Samantha, even called in a lab technician to work with his favorite patient. The lab technician had been just thrilled to come in on a Saturday.

He was decidedly disappointed when Samantha had appeared with a young man at her side. A few more episodes like this, he was going to start thinking she really wasn't interested in him, which was just a weird thing to contemplate. He was a successful doctor! Chicks dug doctors! Why the hell else did he go to med school? And this friend of hers was really starting to piss him off. Sitting there all superior with his Pac-Man sweatshirt and his baggy jeans. Shaking his head, Bouzein pulled out a small pad from a desk drawer and wrote the prescriptions. He reached across to hand them to Samantha.

"I'll take those," her companion said.

"I'm sorry," Bouzein said, jerking the papers just out of his reach. "Who are you again?"

"Pasquale Paoli. I'm a friend of Samantha's."

"Well, Mr. Paoli," started Bouzein, "I'm afraid I can't give these to you. They're Samantha's. It would be a violation of federal law. Perhaps you've heard of HIPAA? The Health Information Portability and Accountability Act?"

"Right," Pasquale said, his hand still extended to accept the prescriptions. "She invited me in here with her. You really think she has any objection?"

"Roger, it's OK," Samantha said, her voice weak.

"As you wish." He said it with Darth Vader-like verve, even throwing in a head bob for full effect.

Pasquale looked up after he had tucked the prescriptions into his pocket.

"Thanks, Lord Vader," he said.

Sᴀᴍ ᴀɴᴅ PᴀꜱQᴜᴀʟᴇ filled the prescriptions in the hospital pharmacy and stopped at Mary Angela's in Carytown for a quick dinner. Carytown was a bohemian commercial district just west of downtown Richmond where wealthy suburbanites went to feel trendy. It was crammed with sushi bars, overpriced women's boutiques, used bookstores and gift shops that patrons loved to describe as eclectic. Mary Angela's, at the western edge of Carytown, was a Richmond institution, famous for its pizzas and pastas.

Sam and Pasquale took a booth in the corner that looked out onto a snowy Cary Street. A moment later, a young waitress in her early twenties set two glasses of water on the gingham tabletop. Obligatory lemon wedges bobbed like buoys in the glasses.

"Those wedges are crawling with disease," Sam said after the waitress had disappeared. "I saw a story about it on CNN."

Pasquale's glass was nearly at his lips. He paused, considered Sam's warning, and then took a long drink of lemony, disease-infested water.

"Cheers," he said. "Don't forget to take your medicine."

"Don't start with me," she said.

She placed the anti-viral and the antibiotic pills on her tongue and chased them with a swallow from her water glass.

"What about your little plague wedge there?" he asked.

"Honestly, I feel too crappy to care," she said. "Besides, these meds should protect me."

He took another sip.

"This is some good water."

"I'm glad you like it," she said.

"So what are we doing here?"

"What do you mean?"

"I'm a reasonably smart kitty," he said. "You didn't call me for a ride to the doctor's office."

"No, I-..." she started, then quietly: "No."

"I'm kind of at a loss," he said. "I've been here since lunchtime, and all I've done is drive you around from doctor to pharmacy like you were my grandmother. It's not that I don't love seeing you, I do, really. But I didn't think you could stand to be around me anymore, so obviously, you're in some kind of jam, and here we are, and I don't know what it is. So help me help you. What's wrong, tiger?"

She had forgotten how quickly he talked, how he sprayed you with his words like machine-gun fire, as if he had no internal monologue. It was refreshing in that with Pasquale Paoli, what you saw was what you got. It was also terrifying in its own way, in that Pasquale Paoli did not come equipped with any sort of restrictor plate or filter, and once he got going, it was best to stay clear. Pasquale frequently said what he thought, almost immediately. It was one part endearing, two parts horrifying.

Pasquale ordered the linguine with red clam sauce; Samantha went with a single slice of cheese pizza. They decided to split the large antipasto salad. While they waited for their food, Samantha told Pasquale what had happened since Julius had knocked on her door about twenty-four hours earlier. She went into great detail, including her plan to deliver the ticket to its new rightful owner, omitting nothing.

Except for the urge to cash the ticket herself.

She didn't know why she did that.

After all, wasn't that was why she had called Pasquale in the first place?

Wasn't it?

PASQUALE PAOLI WAS ALREADY a bit of a folk hero when Samantha met him during her first year of law school at Richmond. He was two years ahead of her in school, but he was three years older than her. After graduating from Princeton University, he had gone to work for an Internet startup called Leglift.com, which sold pet supplies online. The company never made a penny in profit and paid its employees, in part, in stock options. The founders took the company public after eighteen months. On the first day of trading, the stock opened at $3.25 a share and closed that afternoon at $65.75. Within a month, it was trading at $115. Pasquale, who began to suspect that failing to ever turn a profit was a poor business plan, sold his 40,000 shares and walked away with $4.4 million. Within a few months, the company's venture capital dried up, and the stock price crashed. The founder, the man who hired Pasquale, was last seen working a double shift at a Taco Bell.

His financial future secure, Pasquale decided to go to law school because he thought being a trial lawyer might be fun. After taking the LSATs, he chose to attend Richmond because it was the first school to accept him. The study of law came easily to Pasquale. His mind worked quite logically and was capable of synthesizing a large amount of material and extracting the important threads like wheat. It was an important tool to have in law school, since the study of law was full of reams of useless and unimportant material. Law professors enjoyed spending a large portion of each semester on this useless material before administering a final exam based solely on an obscure point of law buried in a footnote of a case that the professor glossed over on a Friday afternoon. Oh, and the exam was worth 100 percent of the final grade.

From his first day in law school, Pasquale proved true the old adage that a man with nothing to lose was very dangerous indeed. Since he wasn't worried about finding a job or getting good grades, he just didn't give a crap. He argued with professors when principles of law didn't make sense, he drank and played cards every night, he lived in a shitty apartment like everyone else and drove a six-year-old Bronco. Virtually no one knew about his huge wealth, so they just assumed he was crazy. The only hint that he was financially secure was that he did not stick around for the student loan seminar during first-year orientation.

Samantha first met Pasquale Paoli late one night about two weeks into her first semester, just as she was starting to wonder if she could drop out and still get her tuition back. She had been tucked in her study carrel, immersed in the fascinating tale of *Pennoyer v. Neff*, a landmark U.S. Supreme Court case addressing the extremely sexy issue of personal jurisdiction. It was taught to first-year law students nation-wide, nearly all of whom failed to understand the Court's ruling but still managed to remember the name of the case for the rest of their lives.

Samantha had successfully navigated the first four sentences of the court's opinion before her eyes began to droop. Unable to move on to the fifth sentence, she drifted down to the student lounge for a soft drink. Clearly, caffeine was going to become a good friend over the next three years. She couldn't do this alone. The lounge was deserted at that hour but for the stout young man holding each side of the soda machine, his forehead pressed against its glowing façade, as if it were about to topple over. Sporting a shaved head, he was wearing a pair of blue shorts and a t-shirt emblazoned with the phrase: THE INTERNET IS FOREVER.

"Dr Pepper or Cherry Coke?" he asked, after noticing her waiting for the machine.

"Excuse me?" she asked.

"Should I get a Dr Pepper or Cherry Coke?"

"Dr Pepper," she said.

"Fair enough." He slid in three quarters and pressed the corresponding button.

"Why?" he asked. He cracked the can open and took a long swig.

"Because I want Cherry Coke, and I don't want you buying what could be the last one."

He sprayed Dr Pepper across the room.

"You're gonna fit in real good here," he said after he stopped coughing.

They sat at a table and drank their sodas. An hour later, they were at the Sidewalk Cafe, a Fan bar popular with law and medical students, throwing back tequila shots. Two hours after the soda affair, they were in his apartment, where Samantha consciously decided to make what she expected would be a gigantic mistake. Only the strangest thing happened. When she woke up the next morning, wearing nothing but his t-shirt, she didn't feel awkward. He didn't act weird or seem anxious to rush her out the door. Oh, and she had been there before – both as rusher and rushee. He made her scrambled eggs and they watched *Live! With Regis and Kelly*, and it felt like they had been doing it for years.

They kept things under wrap at first, because Samantha found nothing more annoying than young law students in love. There were already two confirmed couplings in her class, one of which involved a pair that obviously had no problem with public displays of affection, often sitting together in a single oversized chair in the student lounge. Samantha found it nauseating, and so she all but ignored Pasquale on campus. He didn't care either way, so he returned the favor.

By the end of the semester, they were virtually living together. Samantha studied hard and earned a 3.6 GPA, which put her near the top of the class. Pasquale, who graduated a semester early, had lined up a job with a small general practice firm, which he started after the New Year. It was then that Samantha first saw whispers of a fundamental change in Pasquale. For him, the practice of law proved far different than the study. It became angry and personal and had little to do with the law.

He represented slum landlords, wife beaters, and companies that violated employment laws. He was called a liar and a crook, and that was by his own clients. The clients rarely, if ever, returned his phone calls, but if he didn't return their calls within a day, they threatened to report him to the state bar. Several actually did. Each of the complaints was dismissed as unfounded, but those clients used the complaint as a convenient excuse to stiff him on the bill.

As Samantha sailed through law school, entrenching herself in the top ten percent of her class, Pasquale slowly unraveled. He worked long hours, becoming obsessed with nothing short of total victory. He lost any interest in solving problems or in negotiating settlements that might benefit both sides. Each case became a war, and he worked tirelessly to destroy his opponents. Each night, he sat in the living room and drank scotch, working while Samantha studied. They ate takeout in silence. As she neared graduation, she begged him to quit, tried to convince him that he didn't need this, that he could retire, that he could volunteer for Legal Aid. He refused to listen.

Pasquale Paoli's legal career ended on a warm Friday afternoon, the day before Samantha graduated from law school. He had been representing Tar Heel Sprinklers, a small company that installed commercial sprinkler systems and had been the subcontractor on a new Walmart distribution center going up in Fairfax County. After the sprinkler system failed to activate during a small warehouse fire, which quickly erupted into a big warehouse fire, inspectors determined that the system had fallen victim to a sprinkler disease called microbiologically induced corrosion. In essence, the system had contracted a sexually transmitted disease. Walmart sued everyone, from the architect who designed the building to Tar Heel Sprinklers. The sprinkler company's insurer retained Pasquale's firm to handle the defense.

On that fateful day, Pasquale traveled to Vienna, Virginia, where he was scheduled to take the deposition of the general contractor's president. He had been up all night, reviewing the project documents and preparing his examination of the witness, and he was just a bit cranky. The attorneys for the other defendants trickled in as the hour drew closer to 9:00 a.m. At 9:00, the shining face of Syd Lehane, the general contractor's attorney, poked into the conference room and announced that he was not producing his client for the deposition, and that everyone could go home.

Police interviews with the ten witnesses and a choppy twelve-second cell phone video revealed that Pasquale responded to this development by pouring a pot of coffee on the large and custom-made conference table. As the steaming coffee trickled over the edges, Pasquale jumped on the table, stripped to his boxers and invited any interested parties to a wrestling match, Greco-Roman style. When no one accepted his offer, he declared himself President of the Republic of Zebulon, jumped off the table and disappeared into the hallway, humming the 1812 Overture. At this point, a secretary had summoned firm security, and three beefy guards tackled Pasquale just outside Syd Lehane's office.

The responding police officers decided to commit him to the psychiatric ward at a Vienna hospital under a temporary detention order. The mental health staff evaluated Pasquale and diagnosed him with extreme exhaustion and clinical depression. After thirty-six hours under mild sedation, the staff discharged him. Samantha took him home, where he lay on the couch and watched old movies. He refused to see a therapist or take his medication. He took his meals alone on the back porch. Samantha watched him drift away as she crammed thousands of rules of law into her brain.

On the last Monday of that July, Samantha drove to Roanoke to sit for the two-day-long Virginia bar examination. When she returned two nights later, Pasquale was gone, his chest of drawers emptied out. He left a note (and she couldn't believe he left a note, she didn't think people really did that) announcing that he still loved her but that he was lost. Devastated, she threw herself into her new job, which, of course, made quite an impression on her employer. She worked sixteen, sometimes eighteen hours a day in an effort to flush Pasquale Paoli from her system.

Four months later, he sent her a postcard from Paraguay, where he'd been living and working on a soybean farm. She cried all night. Four more months went by, and she got a postcard from Kenya, where he'd hooked up as an aid worker. She cried for a couple of hours and then got back to work. Another four months, another postcard, this one from Baden-Baden, Germany, where he'd joined a group of neo-Nazi hunters. That night, she barely cried at all. She felt an ache of nostalgia for the times that they had together, before things went bad. She reminded herself that things had gone bad, and there were bad times, times that she wanted to rip his eyeballs out of his sockets because he'd gotten so good at feeling sorry for himself.

Six months ago, he had called and left her a message, saying he was back in the United States. He told her he still loved her and that he was sorry. He left her his number and told her to call him if she ever needed anything.

SHE WASN'T sure why she felt surprised, lying here, curled up under her comforter. So they had slept together. They had finished dinner about an hour ago and ridden to her apartment in silence. She was starting to feel a bit better, although she figured that was, in part, a psychological byproduct of having started her medication rather than because of the medication itself. And she had been the moving party, all but jumping him as soon as they had gotten in the door. Being a guy, Pasquale, of course, had not thrown up much in the way of resistance, even knowing she had the flu.

What was the big deal? People had sex every day. All over the world, people were having sex right now. Besides, they were always really good at it, and who was she kidding, anyway? It had been a while. One year, three months, and eleven days, to be exact. Not that she was counting, of course. She looked over and saw Pasquale on his side, eyeing her carefully, his head propped up on his hand.

"What?" she asked.

"Nothing," he said.

"This doesn't mean we're getting back together," she said.

"God forbid."

"We're just good at this."

"Right. How are the folks?"

"Trying to set me up with a good Lebanese man."

"Nice to see things haven't changed."

"You're hilarious." She smacked him with a pillow.

"I'm serious," he said. "It's nice to know that there are things in this world that you can count on."

"You're an idiot."

"How's business at the store?" he asked. "Maybe we should swing by tomorrow. You know how long it's been since I've had good grape leaves?"

She rolled back onto her back, her arm cradling the same pillow she'd smacked Pasquale with. She chewed a ragged thumbnail absently. Despite their desire to see her marry Lebanese, her parents had always liked Pasquale. For one, he was Italian, and that made him Mediterranean, which was close enough. For another, he understood the importance of family, also a big part of the Khouri administration's domestic policy. Finally, and not insignificantly, he had charmed their pants off. He was just that kind of guy.

"Okay, let's talk about something else," he said. "How about your little lottery ticket there? A lot of money."

"Indeed it is," she said.

"Aren't you the least bit tempted?" he asked. "Show up at lottery headquarters and say, 'hey! Look what I found!"

"No."

"Then why'd you call me?"

"I needed a friend."

They lay quietly for a few minutes. Samantha was

thirsty, but she didn't feel like getting up. She studied his body, the body that she had once known so well. He was built like a box truck, a solid 170 pounds gripping the small frame. A large scar she'd never seen before twisted around his thick left bicep. A knot the size of an acorn poked out from the center of his right collarbone. She reached out and rubbed her thumb against the calcified bone.

"Where'd you get this?"

"Fell off a pickup truck in the Ivory Coast," he said, flinching slightly at her touch. "Didn't see a doctor for a month. By then it had healed this way. Kinda cool, huh?"

Her throat clenched. There were moments that she desperately missed this man.

"You're sure no one knows you have it?" he asked.

She pictured the two bodies laid out like sportfish at Todd Matheson's cabin. She thought about Carter regaining consciousness, looking stupidly around the room. No need to worry Pasquale any more than she had to.

"I'm sure."

"I'm still glad you called."

"Why?"

"You ever wonder how many maniacs might be out there looking for this thing? It ever got out you had this ticket, we'd have big trouble."

"I hadn't thought about that."

"It's because you don't share my dim view of humanity."

"Right."

"So where does this kid live?"

"Somewhere in Ravenwood Court."

Pasquale showed her a pair of skyward-pointing thumbs. Ravenwood Court wasn't quite as lawless as the Tree, but it was plenty dangerous in its own right.

"Awesome."

"Yeah."

"We'll head over in the morning," he said. "Sam?"

"Yeah?"

"I love you."

"I know."

20

"Where's Julius?" asked Charles Flagg.

Mark Jenks, the subject of this particular interview and Julius' former Clean-Sweep supervisor, was still in shock from having been shoved into a supply closet and hog-tied with fifty yards of dental floss. It was cutting into his wrists like fishing wire. Flagg had found him stealing change and knick-knacks from a lawyer's office. Understandably, the man was paralyzed with fear and appeared unable to comprehend Flagg's question.

"Thought you were alone in here, didn't you?" Flagg asked, changing the subject. He needed to get the guy back to reality. Maybe he was having a psychotic break, a nervous breakdown, whatever. Flagg needed the guy to realize that, yes, this really was happening. "Have your run of the place?"

Jenks nodded his head vigorously.

"Good, very good," Flagg said. "Now we're getting somewhere. Look, we're just going to have a little conversation now, OK?"

Jenks nodded again.

"If you try and call out for help, I'll kill everyone in your family," Flagg promised. "I'll kill all your neighbors. I'll kill everyone you work with. And, of course, I will kill you."

Flagg's sincerity was underscored by the hypodermic needle that he'd plunged into Jenks' left arm. The attached syringe contained five milliliters of electric blue drain cleaner, which, if Flagg elected to depress the plunger, would kill Jenks within a minute.

"Where is he?"

"I don't know."

"When did you see him last?"

"Friday night," Jenks said. "Last night."

"Did he work every night?"

"Weeknights."

Flagg did the math. Julius had come to work the day after the SuperLotto drawing. Two possible reasons for that. Either he didn't know he had won yet, or he knew he had won, and he didn't know what else to do.

"Notice anything out of the ordinary?"

"No," Jenks said. "Wait! Yeah! I did notice! He didn't finish cleaning his floor!" He said it with the verve of a man who'd cracked the Nazi code machine at the peak of the war.

"What are you talking about?"

"He's got the twenty-ninth floor," he said. "Thirty-some offices. At the end of the night, I do a quick sweep of each floor and I noticed that he had left six, seven offices untouched. It was weird. He always starts with the office near the stairwell and finishes at the elevators. "

"Did you see him before he left?"

"No."

"Why do you think he did that?"

"I don't know," Jenks said. "I've had guys quit during a

shift. This ain't brain surgery. If he didn't quit, I'm firing his ass after Christmas."

Flagg pondered this for a moment. Something had stopped Julius. Had it occurred to him after a couple dozen offices that he didn't need to empty out trash cans anymore? That seemed a little odd. Why almost finish the shift and then bail out? Another thought bloomed. Maybe it wasn't that something had stopped him. Maybe someone had stopped him. Big law firm. A lot of important downtown lawyers, working late. Maybe Julius had hired one of these lawyers to help him with his newfound fortune.

"Which was the first office he skipped?"

"I don't remember," Jenks said.

Flagg reached over to the plunger.

"OK, OK! It was the sixth one down from the elevators."

"You sure?"

"Yes! I'm sure, I swear to God."

"How can you be so sure?"

"Because the chick works in that office is a piece of ass."

Flagg shook his head again.

"Have you ever even heard of evolution?" he asked.

"What?"

Flagg depressed the plunger. The drain cleaner scorched through Jenks' veins like a comet, and he was dead sixty miserable seconds later.

FLAGG TOOK the steps two at a time to the twenty-ninth floor, where he found an identical cube farm, ringed by the little lawyer fiefdoms. It was late, and the floor was devoid of any sound other than the low hum of electricity. Emergency track lighting illuminated the corridors but left much of the floor in shadow. Every office on the floor was dark. Quickly, Flagg zigzagged through the cube maze toward the elevators and counted off six offices. He checked the nameplate affixed to the door of office number six: SAMANTHA KHOURI.

The door was slightly ajar, but like the other offices on the floor, it was dark. He checked behind the door, his gun drawn. He hated to admit even to himself that the cloak-and-dagger shit still gave him a thrill.

Satisfied that the office was empty, he started his search on her desk. The thin laptop computer perched in the corner was in a low-power mode, a three-dimensional clock spinning wildly across the black void of the screen. Samantha Khouri kept her desk immaculate, every piece of paper stacked precisely and at ninety-degree angles. Using a small flashlight, he scanned each pile of pages, coming to rest on a manila folder on the center of the desk. In it was a stack of papers. He leaned in closer for a look.

Across the top of the first page in the stack, the author had scratched out: *Mtg w/J. Wheeler (12/21)*.

Underneath that was what appeared to be a laundry list of someone's financial wet dream. Cars, houses, boats, trips. At the bottom, Samantha had written: *CLP, JW to Marriott until Wednesday*. Underneath that, she had imprisoned the word *Ravenwood* in a solid box of ink.

The initials JW were easy enough to figure out, but who was CLP? Another attorney, maybe? He removed a small notepad from his pocket and copied all the useful information from Samantha's memo. Samantha's phone caught his eye, and it gave him an idea. He picked up the receiver and pressed REDIAL. A few moments later, he heard the low, soothing electronic ring of a corporate phone elsewhere on the floor. On the phone's information screen, he saw the extension he had dialed, 4676, and the name the extension belonged to: PIERCE, CARTER L.

CLP.

Next he scrolled through the phone's list of Dialed Numbers and noted that Samantha had made the call at 6:55 p.m. Friday.

Damn, he felt like an FBI agent!

Those idiots who had kicked him out of the FBI Academy a decade ago would be sorry now. He had actually begun the Bureau's sixteen-week academy at Quantico but was expelled when he displayed certain attributes that led the FBI psychiatrists to conclude that he was unfit for duty. The FBI determined that he was so mentally unstable that it placed him on a watch list, which would have been problematic for his present line of work had he continued to use his real name. In fact, he remained a bit of a pet project of one of his FBI instructors, Alan Nichols, who had nightmares about Flagg for weeks after he was expelled from the Academy. Flagg would have been amused to know that Nichols, now the Special Agent in Charge of the New York City field office, kept Flagg's academy orientation photograph tucked into a corner of his bathroom mirror, wondering daily what had become of his former student.

Carter's voice mail picked up.

"You've reached Carter Pierce. Please leave me a message, and I will return your call within twenty-four hours. If you need immediate assistance, please dial zero for my professional assistant, Althea."

Flagg replaced the phone in its cradle while he pondered the idea of a professional assistant. He tried to conjure up a fancier turn-of-phrase for the word secretary, and he decided he couldn't. Leave it to these bigwig lawyers. After a few more minutes of searching, he concluded that he'd gotten all he was going to get out of Samantha's office, and he set his sights on Pierce's.

He slipped back out into the hallway, contemplating a lawyer's place on the evolutionary food chain. Flagg had to hand it to them. They had made themselves virtually indispensable in society. You couldn't do anything without a lawyer these days. Like latter-day viruses, they had set up shop in every cell of the modern world. They had backstage passes to the worlds of business, technology, science, crime, family, even entertainment. They could make or break companies. They could put people in prison. They could put people on death row. Impressive.

Pierce's office was three doors down from Samantha's, in the batch that Wheeler had failed to clean. The aroma of bad Chinese food hung in the air like smog. Flagg swept the room quickly for threats before getting down to the business at hand. The desktop was clear, which Flagg interpreted as a sign that this man doled out the work to the underlings but took all the credit for himself. Kind of a conundrum there. Was Carter Pierce a man who'd gotten fat and lazy, or a man who was truly king of his jungle?

There was just no way to know.

Nothing on the desk caught his eye.

He checked the notes he took in Samantha's office. The Marriott? That made sense. Julius, janitor-turned-bazillionaire, comes to the lawyers he knows best for help. They slap each other on the back with glee and stash the client in a nice hotel until he can cash in the ticket and they can take their $600 an hour for the rest of this guy's natural life. Could it really be that easy? Was Julius cooling his heels down at the Marriott? He couldn't remember exactly where it was, but he knew it was downtown somewhere. A mile or two from where he now stood. He wondered where the lawyers were right now. Probably on their leather couches in front of a fire, cozy under an afghan, sipping cognac, satisfied that their client was safe. Morons.

There was a phone book in Carter's lower right-hand drawer, its spine never creased. Flagg suspected that Carter Pierce had not looked up a phone number in many years. He found a listing for the Marriott and called the front desk.

"Good evening," said a pleasant voice, dusted with a sprinkle of an Irish accent. "Thank you for calling the Marriott on Fifth."

"Julius Wheeler, please."

Tapping of a keyboard.

"I'm sorry, sir, we don't have anyone by that name."

"Carter Pierce?"

More tapping.

"No, sir," he said. "No one by that name with us, either."

He inhaled deeply, feeling the frustration bubble up inside him.

"Samantha Khouri?"

A pause this time, virtually dripping with suspicion, and then more tapping. The sound reminded Flagg of horses clocking across pavement.

"I'm sorry, sir."

"Aw, shit, they must be at a different hotel!"

"Yes, sir," she said.

He set the phone back in its cradle and wandered over to the window. Thousands of Christmas lights shimmered against the snow on the downtown skyline. From this height, the city appeared still, but he knew that carousing of all kinds was underway in the bars and clubs below. Somewhere down there, right now, some poor girl was hours away from being raped by a nice guy she'd just met. A guy was dancing with a girl who would, later tonight, after he'd consumed a few too many Alabama slammers, infect him with HIV. Yet another would drive home drunk and kill a migrant worker riding a bicycle. It was like this every night in every city in the world. It never ceased to amaze him. Natural selection never stopped.

As he drove the deserted streets of Richmond in Ashley's car, Carter Pierce found himself thinking about Amy Cuddyer. He also found himself sexually aroused, and this just annoyed him, because he had grown to associate Amy Cuddyer with the destruction of his parents' marriage.

He wasn't sure what she was doing up there, running through his mind like it was some sort of cranial meadow. He hadn't thought about her in years. He thought again about his father, Dr. Wesley Pierce, and his mother, Mrs. Wesley Pierce. That was how she always identified herself, even today. Mrs. Wesley Pierce. Carter didn't even know her name was Janice until he was about eight years old.

Carter Pierce was twelve years old when he first observed his father being unfaithful to Dr. Mrs. Wesley Pierce. He had stolen a pack of cigarettes from his mother earlier that afternoon and was intent on torching his way through all twenty smokes by the pool while his parents were out. His mother was around the corner playing bridge with Mrs. Fletcher, because that's what doctors' wives did when their husbands were at the hospital, sticking their hands inside people's chests and saving lives. Thus, Carter thought he had the house to himself when he slinked down the stairs and onto the back deck on that warm summer evening thirty-two years earlier.

Amy Cuddyer was twenty-one years old and had just

graduated from Sweetbriar College. Her parents lived across the street from the Pierces. She had a boyfriend, a chap that she had grown up with and fully intended to marry and whom she later did marry. But none of that mattered on that particular night.

For the first twelve years of his life, Carter Pierce had had virtually no relationship with his father. The man was a gifted heart surgeon, a pioneer in the field, which, unfortunately for Carter, did not leave many opportunities for father-son bonding. On the day Carter was born, Dr. Pierce had just started a seventy-two-hour shift. Despite several chances, he didn't see his son until he stumbled home, reeling with exhaustion, three days later. Janice Pierce had been the stalwart parent, Carter's rock. It was thus with much horror that Carter found his father and an extremely naked Amy Cuddyer smooching by the pool.

Things progressed far beyond smooching that night, and Carter Pierce watched the whole thing from behind the grove of boxwoods guarding the pool, too terrified to move, too fascinated by Amy Cuddyer's splendidly bare jugs to do anything but remain crouched behind the bushes. He watched them until her orgasm burst forth, loud and reckless and startling in its intensity. At first, he thought his father was hurting her, a thought quickly dismissed upon hearing her cries for "more, more!" It was under this cover of cacophony that Carter retreated from the bushes and back into the house. His mother found the cigarettes in his room the next day and gave him the beating of his life.

He never told her about what he had seen.

He drove on, the thing that needed to be done laid out before him like an old photograph.

21

S am bolted upright from the dream, afraid she had screamed aloud. Pasquale, however, remained sound asleep next to her. The room was quiet. Gently, she lowered herself back down against the sheets, which were damp with perspiration. Gross, she thought. She had woken up in an honest-to-goodness cold sweat. She thought that only happened in the movies. She peeked over at Pasquale again. He was on his back, his chest rising and falling rhythmically.

A wistful smile crossed her face as she remembered their relationship, before the dark times. There was no middle ground with him. If he fell asleep, he slept like the dead; if something was eating at him, bothering him, he didn't sleep a wink until he had resolved whatever it was chewing away at his insides. Once, he had gone four days without sleeping. She, on the other hand, was a perpetually light sleeper, her slumber punctuated with bad dreams that she rarely remembered but left her feeling uneasy all day.

This dream, while she did remember it, was already starting to fade, the fine details dissolving like the outer edges of a sandcastle. The core of it remained though. She was back in law school, in one of the large lecture halls, standing at the podium. The classroom was full, standing room only, like it was the beginning of the semester when students are trying to figure out whether to stay or drop the class. An overhead projector was on her right, beaming an image up against the wall. The image, however, was obscured because the drop-down screen was still hidden in the ceiling panels.

Samantha scanned the crowd. After a moment, she realized that they were her relatives. Every single one of them. Her parents and sisters. Twenty-seven first cousins. A dozen aunts and uncles. All four grandparents, even though three were deceased. Still other blood relatives scattered about. They were chattering quietly, the way students do just before class starts. Sam noticed a small remote device in her hand, about the size of a deck of cards. In the center was a red button, which she pushed. Immediately, a motor started whirring loudly, and the screen descended from the ceiling. As the screen completed its trip downward, its smooth, reflective surface caught the previously amorphous image spit out by the overhead projector. It was the Ticket, splashed up against the projector screen, the winning numbers highlighted as if they proved some elemental point Samantha was trying to make.

When Samantha turned back to face the audience, something had changed. They were all wearing Julius Wheeler masks. She blinked twice, hard, and the scene changed again. She was on her grandfather's porch in Lebanon, drinking warm lemonade. Her grandfather, who had been dead since 1975, was next to her, rocking back and forth in his chair. He touched her shoulder and, with a bony, frail hand, gestured down to the street. Six dusty olive-green tanks rolled by, groaning on their tracks, smoke billowing from their turrets. Something about the tanks caught her eye. She couldn't quite put her finger on it – then, it hit her. The side of each tank was stamped with a number: 5, 9, 16, 17, 24, 43.

That was when she woke up.

She touched her forehead again. It was cool to the touch, and her fever seemed to have broken. With the dream still reverberating like a mental echo, she slid out of bed and threw on a pair of jeans and a sweatshirt. Quietly, she backed into the closet and knelt down by the safe. She slid the key home and turned it as slowly as she could. Still, the metal screeched.

She flipped up the lid. There it was.

Her career was over. Her soul was battered from years of hundred-hour weeks. An interesting government job had never been an option; there were too many people to take care of. She hadn't saved a dime for retirement. Her parents' debts were vast. Her family back in the old country lived in ramshackle homes and struggled to make ends meet, constantly wondering whether the political crisis du jour would bubble over like an unattended soup pot into yet another civil war.

With one fell swoop, she could end all their suffering and take care of her family forever. She could give every aunt, uncle and first cousin a million bucks each and have $100 million to spare. Her brain began crafting rationalizations. There was no guarantee that Jamal Wheeler was in Virginia, let alone in Richmond. Hell, Wheeler might not even be his last name. Jamal might not even be Julius' son. Jamal might be dead. There may never even have been a Jamal!

Her hand hovering over the ticket, Samantha's mind

wandered into the past like a lost traveler. She drifted in and out of scenes of her parents arguing about money, of her cousin trying to borrow a little bit, of being pulled out of private school because they couldn't afford the tuition. She thought about her family trips to Lebanon as a kid, about family too poor to ever think about visiting the U.S., even if they could get entry visas, which was never a sure bet these days.

She stopped and closed the lid.

She knew it was wrong.

She found herself not really caring.

It was a tough old world out there.

She opened the lid, plucked out the ticket and shoved it into the pocket of her jeans.

"What are you doing up?" a sleepy voice asked from behind. Her back was to him, so he couldn't see what she was doing. He yawned loudly, and she heard him stretch. "Man, I was sleeping like a rock."

She wanted to hate him for sleeping well. She was afraid it meant that he didn't think about her anymore.

"Nothing," she said. "Go back to bed."

Silence enveloped the dark room.

"What time is it?"

"It's late."

"Yes, I gathered that."

"I need to go out for a bit."

"With the ticket?" he asked. "Does it need to take a piss?"

"Shut up."

"Hey, take it easy."

She popped out of her crouch and brushed past Pasquale on her way out of the room. Pasquale followed behind, but not too closely.

"I told you to go back to bed," she said.

"I'm hungry. Got any cereal?"

"Check the pantry."

She stopped at the closet and grabbed a navy blue pea coat. As she put it on, Pasquale fixed himself a bowl of Golden Grahams. They were his favorite, and for reasons that remained unclear to her, Sam always kept a box of it in her pantry. She stopped and watched him root through the refrigerator for milk. He found it and poured it over the cereal.

"Jesus, I love this stuff," he said with a mouthful of flakes.

She paused and chewed on a fingernail.

"I know."

"You're gonna keep that ticket, aren't you?"

"So what if I am?"

"Hey, you called me."

"You don't know what I've seen tonight."

"I do. You told me."

"You know what I mean."

"Still, I'm fuzzy on how that entitles you to the ticket."

"Like you're the world's preeminent expert on doing the right thing."

"What does that mean?"

"You know exactly what it means."

"No, I don't." He kept eating his cereal. As he neared the bottom of the bowl, he tipped it up to his lips and slurped down the milk.

"Charming."

"Is this because I left?"

She was silent.

"I had to get away."

"No matter what happened to me," she said.

"It wasn't about you."

"Really? The 'it wasn't you, it was me' speech? A little late for that, isn't it?"

"I never meant to hurt you."

"Well, I guess that lets you off the hook then."

"I am sorry."

"Sorry doesn't get me back those years," she said. "Not the leaving so much. The damage was done by then. What really pissed me off, what really hurt me was that you never even tried to get better. You just started downhill and that was it for you. You never gave a shit about anyone but yourself."

"What about you?" he snapped back. "When I was having a hard time, you quit on me."

"Oh, what a bunch of bullshit!"

"Listen to you," he said. "You were running around like the goddamn law student of the year while I was dying inside."

"I had to hate it because you did?"

"Yeah, like law school really shows you what practicing law is like," he said. He dumped the ceramic cereal bowl into the sink with a loud clatter.

"Careful with that," she said. "I can't afford to buy any replacements."

"Jesus Christ," he went on, ignoring her. "You just got shown the door after eight miserable years!"

"They didn't show me the door," she said quietly.

"What, did they give you the 'of counsel' speech? Because that's what you put in all the ninety-hour weeks for. Of counsel. No profit sharing. No equity share. What a bunch of bullshit."

"Then maybe I should fucking steal it!"

Samantha was shouting now, her insides boiling with anger. With his independent wealth, Pasquale had had the luxury of stepping off of the hellish merry-go-round that was the practice of law, whereas the impoverished schmucks like her had to think about their futures, mortgages and student loans and families with struggling businesses.

"For you," she continued, "law was like a thing for you to try, like scuba lessons or pottery. You didn't like it, you could've checked out any time. But instead of putting us first, you chose to become one of these assholes that thought the goddamn fate of civilization depended on the outcome of some landlord-tenant dispute."

"I wasn't allowed to get into my work just because I had money?" he asked.

"That's not what I meant," she said softly.

"Sure it is."

"No-"

"Yes, it is. I never cared about the money. I didn't like who it made me. I wanted to work for a living. I didn't want to sit around all day watching *Golden Girls* reruns. And here's the thing. I liked the idea of being a lawyer. I liked the stuff that's in the brochure. I still like it."

"Well, then, you're an even bigger idiot than-" she said.

"Let me finish," he said, cutting her off and ignoring her latest fusillade of insults. "When I got into the muck of practicing law, I was crushed. Do you know that the first time I took a deposition and I asked the witness his name, his lawyer actually objected to form? I still don't even know what that means!

"Objected to form," Pasquale repeated softly, as if he still couldn't believe it.

"So why did you stick with it?"

"Because I thought if I did things the right way, it wouldn't matter what others did."

"Boy, you were naïve."

He chuckled. Her comment defused the escalating situation like a hostage negotiator acceding to a terrorist's first demand.

"Then, when that didn't work, I decided that the only thing to do was win every goddamn case that I could. Maybe I could humiliate them into changing their ways. I forgot something, though."

"What was that?"

"Your average lawyer has no shame," he said. "You can't shame someone who feels no shame."

Samantha thought about Carter Pierce. Talk about no shame.

"What about us?" she asked. "Are we any better?"

"I don't know," he said. "When I was still practicing, I did things I'm not proud of. Maybe not bad enough to draw the attention of the bar, but when you're trying to decide whether something is ethical, you're probably better off not doing it in the first place."

"And where has being ethical ever gotten anyone?" she asked. "My parents' business is dead because of that dipshit brother of mine. My career is in the toilet because I'm not in the boys' club, despite the fact that I've billed about twelve billion hours in the last eight years. What do you say about that?"

"All I can say is that you're better than that," said Pasquale.

"Screw that," Sam said. "Enjoy your cereal."

With that, she buttoned up her coat and slipped out the door.

A fter their fight, Samantha got in her car and drove aimlessly around the city. The Downtown Expressway was deserted this morning, and the little coupe felt good underneath her despite the treacherous road conditions. Deciding to forgo the heat, she rolled down the windows and felt the cold, tight air close in around her like a cocoon. She didn't care about getting a ticket. She didn't want to hear any more of Pasquale Paoli's Platitudes. She didn't want to hear about what was right and what was wrong.

When you got right down to it, the truth was this: the ticket had made its way into her pocket. It was hers. Call it karma. Destiny. Whatever. The firm had driven a stake into the heart of her career. It would take her months to find another job, and any work she did find would pay far less than she made now. She would no longer be able to bail out her parents. She was thirty-four and alone, and the thought of practicing law for one more second made her want to drive her little Audi over a cliff. The ticket had to be a sign.

Maybe a warning. Maybe even a warning from the universe. How could she ignore the universe? How?

A few miles north of downtown, she took the Broad Street exit, which looped around and dumped her into the middle of an aging industrial and commercial corridor on the fringes of the city limits. At the end of the ramp, she saw two men engaged in what appeared to be an illegitimate business transaction. They looked over at her as she paused at the stop sign and quickly returned to their contribution to the local economy.

Keep it up, fellas, she thought, turning south toward Broad Street. A month from now, she'd be far away from this, living in Fiji or Tahiti.

At Broad, she turned left and headed east back toward the city. She caught another red light at Boulevard, one of the city's major crossroads. Boulevard continued north past the Diamond, the city's aging minor-league baseball stadium, and toward the gentrified area known as Northside. Ahead of her on Broad, the lanes were empty but for a pickup truck meandering between the left and center lanes. Samantha kept her distance.

The stoplights turned her way for a mile or so, and she cruised through half a dozen greens before her luck ran out at Harrison Street. The light had switched over to red despite the absence of any traffic crossing on Harrison. This phenomenon never ceased to amaze her. As she continued to idle at the light, she felt the anger start to well inside her. Samantha Khouri could put up with a lot. Traffic lights, though. They drove her crazy. A minute went by, then another. The light stayed red. She started drumming her fingers on the steering wheel. Didn't work. She craned her neck to look at the cross light, which, inexplicably, continued to shine green.

"Oh, you've gotta be kidding me," she yelled to no one.

She peeked in her sideview mirrors, and then checked the oncoming lanes for any stray police cruisers. The cross streets remained free of any traffic. Satisfied the coast was clear, she eased off the brake. When she heard the soft groan of a large vehicle behind her, she pushed down on the brake again. Her heart was racing, as if she'd been caught with her hand in the cookie jar. She checked her rearview mirror and saw a city bus ease in next to her in the right lane, shuddering as it came to a stop. In the early-morning gloom, she could see the bus was empty. The driver, a middle-aged white guy with a bushy mustache, sipped on a large cup of coffee.

The light finally changed to green, and Samantha watched as the bus grumbled into gear and pulled away from the light. As the bus continued east on Broad Street, Samantha found herself thinking about Ziad Khouri, who died with martyrdom in his heart and shit in his brains. Everything about that terrible day seemed so clear now, even though the day had begun in such a fog.

ON THE NIGHT before Ziad's attack on the bus, perhaps as he was conducting his final, pathetic walkthrough (she wondered if he'd actually done a walkthrough, she wondered if he'd even given any thought to what he was doing at all), Samantha had been at the firm's annual New Year's Eve party at the Jefferson Hotel. A thousand people of varying levels of social and professional importance were in attendance, guzzling free booze and slurping down one heavy tray of shrimp cocktail after another. Samantha herself drank cosmopolitans long after Ryan Seacrest had rung in the New Year. Her ability to put away cocktail after cocktail and feel none worse for the wear left her feeling young and vibrant. She even ordered a pizza after stumbling home at three in the morning.

The next morning, however, proved to be the proverbial credit card bill to the previous night's shopping spree. She woke up on the couch, still wearing her little black dress, along with two slices of pizza stuck to the dress. Classy, she remembered thinking. Her head felt like it had been dipped in hot lava, and her lips were stuck together. Her memory of the evening was mostly intact, and, other than a midnight kiss with a guy from Real Estate that may have lasted a bit too long, it had been a relatively uneventful evening.

After a gingerly walk to the bedroom and a methodical change into sweats, she took position under a blanket on the sofa while her liver metabolized the last of the alcohol like a lonely factory worker. At noon, she flipped over to CNN, where she was greeted with its Breaking News graphic striped across the bottom of the screen. A sucker for breaking news, Samantha lingered there.

The on-screen headline screamed for attention: **SUICIDE BOMBER STRIKES IN CHICAGO.** She sat up suddenly, the vertigo from her hangover almost inducing a major upchuck. The details on the bombing were sketchy: a bus had exploded on the city's south side two hours ago, the bomber was dead, but no one else had perished. She watched, mouth agape, as the nation's terror alert level was kicked up to a really scary color. There were special news bulletins and press conferences all day long. Buses, planes, trains, subways, even taxicabs ground to a halt.

When word slipped out that the bomber was of Arab descent, the media, along with the public, went predictably wild. A rash of hate crimes against folks with olive skin, regardless of actual ethnic descent, erupted overnight. In Phoenix, Arizona, a Pakistani convenience store owner was shot dead by assailants who didn't even bother stealing anything. In Ogunquit, Maine, three teenage boys burned down a bed-and-breakfast owned by a Jordanian couple. A CNN/USA Today poll taken the day after the attack found that 89 percent of Americans supported immediate military action, even though they weren't sure who to take this military action against.

Samantha clawed her way out of her hangover like millions of other Americans did that New Year's afternoon, glued to television coverage of the attack. Everything changed, however, when two young FBI agents knocked on her door that evening. She remembered the agents well, one white and serious, the other black and serious, both named Smith. That was what really stuck out for her on that surreal night, when the black one introduced himself as Agent Smith, and then nodded toward the other and identified him as Agent Smith as well.

They asked her to accompany them to the FBI's Richmond field office, where she spent much of that night fielding questions that she didn't have the answers to. The agents insisted that she was free to leave at any time (even though she didn't have her car), and so technically, she wasn't entitled to have her *Miranda* rights read to her. A clever little ruse that law-enforcement types liked to use. If they had, Samantha knew better than to remain silent or to ask for an attorney. Even first-year law students knew that was akin to admitting you were guilty. Most of the time she spent explaining that she had no relationship with her loser of a brother. She spent the rest worrying about her parents, whom she suspected were in a very similar interview room.

Agent Smith, the white one, drove them all back to her

parents' house around four in the morning and told them to stay in town for the immediate future. After getting out of the black Chevy Suburban, Zaina Khouri told Smith to "fuck yourself" and slammed the door. Her father apologized for his wife's outburst, claiming that the lack of sleep had made her a bit crazy. Samantha said nothing and took in a few restless hours of shuteye in her old bedroom.

At seven, her dad drove her to her car, and she drove into the office, where she shut her door and buried herself in work. Later, she met with Carter and Hunter Pennington Smyth, III, who wanted to make extra sure that she was not a member of al-Qaeda, Hezbollah, or Islam. She assured them that she was not but dismissed the idea of telling him that Islam was a religion, not a terrorist organization. Satisfied that one of their lucrative profit centers probably wouldn't come to work with dynamite strapped to her chest, they quickly sent her back to her desk to start billing again. Suicide bombing or not, it was, after all, a new year.

But things were different after that meeting, she had to admit to herself, now, in the bright shining light of her wrecked career. Not hugely different. Subtle. A few weeks later, they sent her on a document review trip, a mindless task she hadn't done in three years. Her performance evaluation had just a shade of negativity, the first less-than-stellar review she'd received during her time at the firm. She started working harder and longer, but her once-promising shine had dulled like an old penny.

SHE WAS CRYING NOW, her car still idling at the stoplight where she had seen the city bus.

Jesus, how could she have been so stupid? How could

she not have seen that her brother had destroyed more than an empty city bus? Ziad had infected the Khouri family tree with his hate and his anger and his poison. It remained to be seen whether the tree would survive. It remained to be seen whether the other branches of the tree could inject the roots with enough life, enough vitality to make the tree strong again. She thought about her sisters, doing their best to raise children, who, whether they liked it or not, were charged with bridging the gap between the old country and the new world that was America. She thought about her parents, who had sacrificed their entire lives to provide for their children. Most of all, she thought about the empty chair at each Khouri family gathering.

And what about Samantha herself? She was a bright young attorney who could do anything she wanted. So this firm, this bottomless pit where souls went to die, didn't want her? The hell with them! She could do better than making rich, giant companies a little bit richer and more giant. She'd read stories about lawyers who worked for a pittance and slept the sleep of the righteous. Why not her? For years, the only thing she had liked about her law practice was that the firm encouraged the associates to take on *pro bono* work, which was encouraged largely because it looked good in the firm's press releases.

Her thoughts drifted back to the ticket, tucked safely into her pocket. How could she ever think about stealing it? If she stole it, she would be no better than Ziad Khouri. She would be the suicide bomber to Jamal Wheeler's future. She would be another Ziad Khouri, only she would be alive to know the damage that she had inflicted – even if Jamal, or whoever the rightful owner of the ticket was, never did. Her parents, already devastated by their only son's legacy, would really be proud of her.

OK, she thought to herself. It was over. Just a little crisis of conscience, as her eighth-grade English teacher had referred to episodes like these as. She would protect the ticket until she could find Julius Wheeler's rightful heir, whether it was a son, a daughter or the man in the moon. It was her burden, her cross to bear, especially since it was now clear that W&H probably didn't have the best interests of their late client in mind. She reached for her phone to call Pasquale but remembered that she had left it on the kitchen counter when she stormed out earlier.

As the snow intensified, Samantha turned her Audi south for a handful of blocks before heading east onto Cary Street toward home. Not surprisingly, the streets were deserted on this Sunday morning, the blizzard still packing a punch. She parked her car and took the elevator to her floor. She was starting to feel like herself again. The weight of the ticket didn't seem quite so crushing anymore.

She realized something was wrong as soon as the elevator doors whooshed open. The elevator opened onto a long corridor, flanked on each side by two apartments. From her vantage point in the corridor, she could see her front door was ajar. Pasquale would not have left the door open. She froze, too afraid to even take a breath. Ohmigod, she thought. Pasquale had been right. Someone had come looking for the ticket.

In the dead silence of the corridor, she listened for any sound, any indication that would give her a sense of what had happened. Behind her, the whoosh of the elevator doors sliding closed again startled her, causing yet another near-miss bladder incident like the one back at the cabin.

She debated retreating back to her car, but the idea of going down the elevator or the stairwell alone now terrified her. Forget it. She had visions of being strangled in the empty darkness of the building's foyer. At least there was light in the hallway. And what if Pasquale needed her in there? She couldn't just abandon him. Pressing her back to the wall, she edged down the hallway toward her apartment, her ears primed for any sound. Nothing. The Christmas lights blinking in the hallway seemed to flash a warning for Samantha to run while she still could.

Oh, Jesus, what the hell are you doing, Samantha?

That was when she saw it. An envelope with her named scrawled across it, perched on the threshold between the corridor and her home. She knelt down and picked it up; it was an ordinary business envelope, sealed shut. She opened it and found a note inside, etched upon a piece of her personalized stationery that she kept in her desk. The message was short and made her veins ice over.

You left your cell phone on the kitchen counter. If you want to see Pasquale alive again, I recommend you leave it on and wait for my call.

Without much regard for whether anyone was lurking in her apartment, Samantha made a beeline for her guest bathroom, where she threw up in the toilet. After finishing her peristaltic backflush, she discovered that the apartment was empty.

Pasquale was gone.

23

When Pasquale regained consciousness, he initially thought he had died and discovered that the afterlife smelled like old rags and spare tires. It was pitch black, the void broken up by a constant thrum surrounding him, punctuated by intermittent thumps. Slowly, it dawned on him, the smells and sounds clicking into place. He was in the trunk of a moving car. Broken shards of the events that brought him here lay scattered before him like a jigsaw puzzle missing a few pieces. He remembered Samantha storming out of the apartment. He decided to have a second bowl of cereal. He heard a rustle behind him, thinking Samantha had come back to the apartment. He wasn't sure if he'd seen who was behind him and just couldn't remember, or if he hadn't turned around in time before the world had gone dark.

His hands were tied behind his back, and a piece of duct tape was affixed to his mouth. While simultaneously trying to wrestle his terror to the ground, he took stock of the present situation. He took solace in the fact that he was still alive, which suggested to him that his life had some value to his captor. He knew that it didn't necessarily mean his life would continue to have value, but it was better than, say, having already been shot in the head and dumped in the river. He primed his ears and listened to the ambient noise, wondering if he could get a sense of where they were. After a minute, he gave up. It had been years since he'd lived in Richmond, and besides, they could've been driving down the street he grew up on, and he would never know.

In retrospect, he was glad that Samantha had stormed out of the apartment earlier. Obviously, his new friend up in the driver's seat was after the ticket, and had she been there, Pasquale and Samantha might both be dead by now. He hadn't been kidding her earlier. There were many, many people who would, without the slightest hint of remorse, kill anyone for the little ticket in Samantha's pocket. Pasquale had met the type in the days since he left the practice of law and the love of his life behind.

Pasquale knew that he was now being held for ransom, to the tune of $415 million. He almost smiled at the thought of it. His father had once told him that if you were going to be something, be the best at it. Don't mess around. Well, it sure seemed like he was being held for the largest ransom in the history of kidnapping. Maybe he would make the cover of *Kidnapping Weekly*. His father would have been proud of him.

Pasquale wondered whether the guy had checked if Pasquale himself had the ticket. He supposed that the man could've searched his pockets and the apartment while Pasquale was unconscious. Yeah, that was possible. But he'd come directly to Samantha's apartment. So he knew that she had it, he knew that much. How would he know?

As the vehicle continued bouncing down the road, Pasquale went over what he knew. A janitor in Samantha's building had bought the winning ticket and gone to her for help. Her boss and his brother-in-law had come up with a scheme to steal the ticket from the janitor, and all three had wound up dead. Pasquale thought about this for a moment. Samantha had assumed they were all dead. Maybe someone had survived and come hunting for the ticket. He dismissed the janitor outright – Samantha mentioned him taking a bullet to the head. She last saw the brother-in-law with a fireplace poker sticking out of his chest, so he was an unlikely candidate.

Carter Pierce, though. Pasquale wondered about Carter Pierce. Samantha claimed that he had taken a bullet as he charged after Matheson. Pasquale had met him a few times, during Christmas parties and firm barbecues. Thought he was a gigantic prick. Who else would know where Samantha lived? Who else would know that she would even end up with the ticket, given the fact that she had not been the one who purchased it? What if he wasn't dead at all?

He was careful not to dismiss the possibility that some unknown third party had entered the equation, someone who had tracked down the ticket like a phantom blood-hound. This prospect terrified him more than anything. Anyone who had managed to hunt them down in the span of just a couple days was a formidable opponent indeed. Sort of like a Terminator sent from the future to destroy mankind. Yeah, sort of like that. He wondered if it was a sign of insanity to analyze his current situation through the prism of a science-fiction movie.

He had to get out of here. He couldn't take a chance that whoever was driving would get close to Samantha. No way would he let them live. Quite frankly, Pasquale was surprised that he was still alive. Why hadn't the guy just killed him and waited in the apartment for Samantha?

Possibly because the apartment was an uncontrolled environment. No way to tell who might be coming and going, who had access to the apartment. Someone might notice something amiss, call the police. Plus, there was the possibility that she was never coming back.

The important thing was that whatever value his life had was already sluicing away like sand through an hourglass, regardless of who was sitting behind the wheel. Carter Pierce already had his hands bloody with two murders, and there was no reason to think he would stop there to save himself. Moreover, Carter might not have been the one who snatched him. Pasquale decided it would be prudent to assume Mr. Mystery Guest, if there was one, posed just as much of a threat as Carter Pierce. Possibly more.

SAMANTHA FOUND a pack of cigarettes in a kitchen drawer and was lighting her fifth one of the morning. Her ears were stopped up with fluid now, which made for an interesting sensation as she dragged in the carcinogenic smoke. The nicotine seemed to perk her up, despite her medical situation. If she had just been here, she thought, blowing out the match, she could have given up the ticket and it would have been over. Images of Pasquale being tortured and killed or a psychopath wiping out her whole family in a never-ending quest for the fortune of a lifetime ran roughshod through her mind.

After plugging her phone into the wall to charge, she had wandered aimlessly from room to room, like a refugee after a storm. The loft, which had always seemed empty and lifeless, seemed especially so since she'd found Pasquale missing. She couldn't deny that his return had electrified her, a feeling she wanted desperately to deny. It wasn't that she couldn't make it in this dog-eat-dog world without a man to lead the way. That version of her had never existed. She'd spent her whole life proving that a woman didn't need a man. She'd seen enough of the traditional Lebanese culture to know, deep down, what her family expected of her.

Yes, yes, it's all fine and dandy to get an education and a job and all that. But when you find the right fella, Samantha, or, if need be because you're thirty-five and single, when we find him for you, it'll be time to jump in the stirrups and start pushing out babies.

Her mother had done it, she'd watched her sisters do it, and she'd be damned if she was going to do it before she was ready. That had been the beauty of Pasquale. He didn't push her. He always expected her to be an equal partner in the relationship. He told her once that if they ever had kids and she wanted to keep working, he'd stay home with them. To this day, she didn't even know if he'd been serious, or more importantly, if she could actually go through such a circus. She had wondered then how that would have gone over with the folks in the old country.

Oh, he stays home?

She works?

This is not a man Samantha has married.

The old-timers would have mocked him. She saw the bitterness in her mother's eyes, brewing acidity from a lifetime of sitting on the sidelines while her father directed the family's future. She knew her father was a difficult man who loved his family on his own rigid terms.

Had it been this singular focus that had driven Pasquale away in his hour of need? She wasn't going to let herself believe that it was her desire to be independent that had led to the destruction of their relationship. After all, he'd been the one who'd stripped down to his boxers during a deposition, right? But then she recalled her reaction when she found out about the incident late that morning.

Was this going to ruin graduation?

At a time he had needed her most, she had turned her back on him. That didn't have anything to do with being a good woman, whether Lebanese, American or Martian. That was just simple manners. No wonder he had left.

The scent of burnt paper snapped her back to reality. The cigarette in her hand had burned down to the filter, leaving a cylinder of ash perching precariously on the precipice. Carefully, she deposited the ash into an empty water glass on the table and dropped the cigarette into the dribble of water at the bottom. It died an unceremonious death with a sizzle.

She couldn't sit in the apartment anymore. Left alone with her thoughts, she felt panic morphing into insanity. The ticket, which was still tucked in her pocket, seemed radioactive, poisoning her from the inside out. She couldn't believe only a couple of days had elapsed since she'd gotten the call from Smyth's secretary. Her mind continued to examine the fallout from her taking custody of the ticket. Her family. She wanted to be near her family. She didn't know what was going to happen when the call came. She didn't know if she would live or die. She didn't know if her family was in danger. All she knew was that in one spasm of greed, she had jeopardized all she had held dear. There was only one way to make this right.

Quickly, she packed an overnight bag and left the apartment, this time remembering her fully charged cell phone.

24

F lagg clicked his tongue while he searched Samantha's empty apartment, deeply disappointed with this turn of events. The whole Olivia affair had really unsettled him. He was more than ready to recover the ticket, do away with these lawyers and go down and have Christmas dinner with Olivia, whether she liked it or not. Instead, he found an empty apartment and no toothbrush in the bathroom. That was just going to extend the assignment, and he was really in the middle of a personal crisis here. His frustration bubbled over, and he fired two bullets into the couch.

He turned toward the front door when something on the floor by the kitchen bar caught his eye. It was more like a discoloration on the shiny hardwood floors. He knelt down for a closer look. It looked like blood, not flake dry, but well on its way. Flagg had seen enough blood spilled to recognize that this little bit of biohazard had been circulating through its owner's veins no more than a few hours ago.

He imagined some kind of struggle had erupted here over the ticket. Perhaps between the two lawyers. Briefly, he again marveled at Professor Darwin's work. Natural selection was at work here. Only the strong would survive. Only the strong could adapt to the inherent dangers the ticket presented. Certainly, the ticket would draw out its hunters, the way young zebras attracted lions on the safari. Natural selection, however, would shake out the weaker hunters, leaving them hungry. It would not surprise Flagg to learn that the ticket had already led to the death of four people, not counting the ones that had he had dispatched.

Whoever had walked away from this battle with the ticket was not coming back. He thought about what the average person would do in this situation. Both Pierce and Khouri had family in the area; the ticketholder might try to find safe haven with loved ones while waiting to cash the ticket. He was careful not to underestimate either one, but he thought the odds favored Pierce in having recovered the ticket. Like it or not, it was still a macho world out there. It always would be. Maybe Samantha Khouri was a black belt in jujitsu, and maybe she had kicked Carter Pierce's ass all over this apartment. If so, he would adjust accordingly. But he had to play the odds. He had to start somewhere.

He would start with Carter.

25

There was no way that Ashley Matheson Pierce was going to let this happen. No fucking way. For tits' sake, she was a Matheson! She still held the NCAA record in the 200-meter individual medley! And now, her legacy would be as the jilted wife of a tiny-dicked lawyer who had managed to knock up some teenage whore? No, sir. There was going to be a different ending to the story, one that Ashley was going to write herself. Actually, it was a story that Ashley already had written.

They were in the formal living room, which was just off the foyer. It was a beautiful room, furnished with antiques and uncomfortable high-backed sofas. Ashley paced back and forth at the threshold of the room. Carter found himself seated on one of these sofas with nowhere to go. He had nowhere to go because Ashley was pointing a .38-caliber revolver at his head.

An hour earlier, Ashley had received a telephone call from Dawn the paralegal, who Ashley knew had been moonlighting as her husband's sperm Dumpster. For some reason, Dawn had been overwhelmed with the urge to confess her sins. Ashley laughed at her and told her she knew, but she stopped laughing upon hearing the news that Dawn was pregnant. She hung up the phone and wandered around the empty house in shock.

With the twins spending the night at a friend's house, there was no buffer to soften the blow of the news. The funny part was that she was surprised she was so surprised. She knew that Carter had been cheating on her for years; the idea that he would impregnate someone was not all that far-fetched. Lousy as he was in bed, he was capable of reproduction. She had become pregnant with the girls the minute she had stopped taking her birth control pills.

When he pulled into the driveway fifteen minutes ago with a very special package in the trunk, she'd been waiting in the foyer with a well-worn bottle of scotch and his gun.

"So, you planning on running away with her?" she asked. "Was that it?"

Carter didn't answer, focusing instead on the second gun that had ever been pointed at him. Given the events of the last forty-eight hours, he'd concluded that the framers of the Constitution had not written the Second Amendment to create a private right to own a gun. The tiny 'o' of the barrel mouth seemed to express the same surprise he had felt since she had first cornered him with it ten minutes ago.

"You're the biggest pussy I've ever met," she said. "And you suck in bed. Not one orgasm, our entire marriage. You believe that? How could you be so bad at it?"

Carter remained silent, concerned that the wrong thing out of his mouth would result in his immediate execution. So far, he was keeping quiet and he was still alive. Maybe one didn't have anything to do with the other, but you never knew. He also decided that now would not be a good time to tell her about her brother's untimely demise out at the cabin. He was no psychiatrist, but he suspected that might push her over the edge.

He really didn't know if Ashley was capable of pulling the trigger, but it wasn't the sort of thing he was ready to gamble his life on. Maybe this flurry of insults would take the wind out of her sails, and she would just kick him out. That would be OK with him. He was pretty much tired of women anyway. Man, this was turning out to be an especially shitty Christmas. He thought about the ticket again, which motivated him to focus on the crisis at hand. All he had to do was find Samantha, and he had what he needed to accomplish that. Well, first, he had to get away from his homicidal and presumably soon-to-be-ex-wife. Then he could find Samantha.

SADLY FOR CARTER, Ashley had no intention of letting Carter walk away from his indiscretion unscathed. She shuddered at the thought of the news getting out that this para-whore was carrying her husband's baby. Assumptions about her ability to satisfy her husband would be made. Junior League meetings would be awkward. She would always wonder whether her doubles tennis partner was talking about her behind her back. And, of course, she would be.

No, she had to take care of this on her own terms. She had it all planned out. She had her story ready. It was a hard thing to admit, but she'd been planning this day for years. Tonight, when she had hung up the phone after her enlightening discussion with Dawn, the story had rotated around to the forefront of her subconscious, the way a forgotten

DVD in a multi-disc changer spun into play after you had forgotten it was there.

She had built a paper trail like a contractor poured a foundation. Over the past two years, she had called 911 on six separate occasions to report a domestic dispute. She was appropriately weepy and breathy with the 911 operator, who would follow standard procedure and quickly dispatch a police cruiser to the home. When officers arrived, she met them at the door with a cigarette dangling from her lips and eyes puffy from crying. She reported that she'd gotten into a terrible argument with her husband, and she was afraid he was going to do something crazy.

Did he hit you, ma'am?

No, not really, she would say. *Maybe a little shoving. I can't remember.*

Equivocation was the name of the game. Draw enough attention to establish a history, but never in a way that would have them look into the matter any further. The incident would be memorialized in an Incident & Crime Report, tucked away in Criminal Records and called upon if ever needed.

Carter didn't know about these little late night visits from police because he had never been there for one. He had never even been present for any of the supposed domestic disputes that his wife had called in. When asked about his whereabouts, she always told the police that he had stormed out so he could cool down. Each time, the officer would say, "that was probably a good idea, ma'am." She wondered if they taught them that line at the police academy. They would always ask if she wanted to swear out a warrant against him, and each time she would thank them politely and decline.

All these calls would serve to prove that she had been a

battered woman, once protecting her abusive husband but unable to take it anymore. And when the time came to blow his brains out, her story of self-defense would be rock solid. She had the story memorized. The key was never, ever wavering from her statement. That was how criminals got into trouble. She watched *Law & Order*. It wasn't rocket science.

She had been very careful not to run ridiculous Internet searches like "how to kill your husband." She didn't change her spending habits. She didn't make strange telephone calls. There were no trips to the Caribbean booked. And finally, she had started tonight's festivities with a bit of screaming and yelling. She hoped someone next door would hear them. A bit of verisimilitude tossed in to tie everything together, which would come in handy when police started questioning the neighbors.

The piece de resistance would be the bullet to her foot, safely removed from any major arteries. This second gunshot would occur immediately after she had shot Carter in the chest, nice and messy and very self-defense-like. Maybe she would break a bone, maybe she would suffer a little nerve damage, but police would definitely arrive to find a terrified housewife, covered in blood, thankful that she was alive. That was how it was going to break down. It was perfect.

The day had finally arrived.

"JESUS, YOU'RE SUCH AN ASSHOLE!" she said, pushing the gas down on the volume.

Why was she yelling? he wondered. Carter was really starting to worry. He'd never seen her go off the rails like this. Maybe he should tell her about the ticket. They could split up, go their separate ways, never see each other again. Then she did something that made him realize that he really needed to tell her about the money. She cocked the gun.

"Wait, wait, wait!" he squealed, rolling off the couch onto the floor. She fired once, but the bullet flew wide and buried itself in the back of the couch. Very much like a scorned wife who's made up her mind to take care of her little problem, she moved in for a better shot.

"I won the lottery!" he yelled.

It broke his heart to tell her, but with the scent of gunpowder hanging in the air, wondering whether she actually planned to kill him now seemed more of an academic discussion. He figured his life was worth the $80 million or so it was going to cost him to save it.

This caught her off guard, and she stopped.

"What?"

"The big one!" he said. "I won it all."

"What the hell are you talking about?"

"I won a bunch of money! I mean, a lot of money! The lottery the other night!"

Ashley lifted the gun again, and then she lowered it. Carter was on his knees, his hands clasped together at his chest as if in prayer. Which they kind of were.

"Start talking," she said.

"See, I bought this SuperLotto ticket Thursday night," he started. "I was working late, and I just felt like doing it. I went down to that convenience store on 20th Street. You know the one?"

"I guess."

"Yeah, so I buy this ticket, and I'm watching the drawing in my office. I'm sitting there as the little balls come up. The numbers came up out of order, so I didn't realize it at first. But then they re-arranged them and I realized I'd won. Can you believe that, sweetheart?"

"That's amazing," she whispered.

"Yeah, so I've just been wandering around for the last day or so, just in shock," he said.

"That's amazing that you actually think I believe that load of bullshit," Ashley said. "You've been planning your little getaway with whatever-her-name-is."

Her finger slid back to the trigger and began applying the requisite pressure when a strange noise, the sound of exploding metal, behind her drew her attention. She looked back over her shoulder toward the foyer, where she saw a man she did not know standing with a gun pointed at her. The front door swung open behind him, smoking from where the doorknob had been shot off.

"Good evening," the man said. "I'm Charles Flagg."

TEN MINUTES LATER, Flagg finished tying each of them to a pair of Ashley's exquisite dining room chairs, which he had set back to back. Apparently grasping the gravity of their situation, the Pierces laced their fingers together. It was the first time they had held hands in years. Behind them, the magnificent Pierce family Christmas tree blinked uninterestedly.

"Well, this is just pathetic," Flagg said. "You disgust me, both of you. You'd made it. Don't you see that? Top of the food chain. Yet it wasn't enough. You just had to dip your toes back into the pool. You ever see any other creature behave like us? It's shocking, really."

He motioned to a picture of the twins on an end table. "It's a good thing your daughters aren't here."

"You lay a hand on them and I'll-" Carter started to say.

Flagg leaned in and slapped Carter lightly on the cheek.

"You'll what, tough guy?" Flagg said. "Relax. They have done nothing to warrant their termination. Yet. Quite the contrary, they're beautiful young women who have a lot to add to the gene pool. What I meant was that they'd be embarrassed by the example their parents have set for them. Just shameful."

"I really have no idea what you're talking about," Carter said. "You've got us confused with someone else."

"Do I?" Flagg said. "I guess you don't know anything about Julius and his little lottery ticket, then, do you?"

"Christ," Ashley said. "The one goddamn time you're honest with me."

This shocked Carter into silence.

Sensing an opportunity, Ashley sprung to her own defense.

"Then you don't really have any beef with me," she said. "This is between you guys. Please let me go."

"Really, Ms. Pierce," Flagg said. "I watched you take a shot at your husband here. Ever heard of transference?"

She shook her head.

"Never took a psych class in college?" he asked, stepping forward and kneeling in front of her. "Basic human behavior? Never wanted to nail that down?"

She was wide-eyed with terror now.

"Never mind," he said. "It's when you project feelings you actually have about one person or about yourself toward a third party."

She shook her head again.

"Come now, Ms. Pierce," Flagg said. "You're not planning

a little rendezvous with some nice accountant or something like that once you get out of this terrible, abusive marriage you've been in?"

Now it was Ashley's turn to sit quietly.

"Was that your plan?" asked Carter.

"What do you want me to say?" she said. "Sorry? Or did you forget you're the one who's got a baby on the way?"

"Oh, bravo," Flagg said, looking back at Carter. "Just super. Knocked up some genetically inferior whore just so you could get your jollies."

"She is not genetically inferior," Carter said.

"Oh, now you're defending her?" she said. "You make me sick."

She looked back at Flagg.

"I wish you would shoot him," she said.

"Hey, I'm not the one who needs a narcotic supplement to make it through each day of this supposedly terrible life."

"Yeah, but I am the one who has to be married to a pompous ass like you. Every day I have to find a new reason not to smother you with your pillow."

"I never held a gun to your head to stay," he yelled. "You never complain about the new car every year or the condo at Park City, oh, no, you never seem to have any problem with that."

"Go to hell," she said.

"Shut up! Both of you!" Flagg bellowed.

Flagg's head was starting to throb. He had never encountered shallower or more self-centered individuals, or at least spent enough time with anyone to discover such depths of their inanity. It was as unnerving as having made contact with extraterrestrials.

"Mr. Pierce, I'm going to ask you only once," Flagg said,

grabbing Carter by the nape of his neck. "Where is the ticket?"

Carter cut his eyes away.

"I don't know."

"Where's Samantha Khouri?"

"I don't know."

Flagg placed the silenced barrel of his gun against Ashley's temple and pulled the trigger. It was as if Flagg's gun whispered a terrible secret into her ear. Ashley was dead before she even realized Flagg had turned the gun on her, and her body listed to its side.

"Are you ready to talk?"

Carter vigorously nodded his head.

"Where is the ticket?" Flagg asked again.

With his late wife's blood and brain spattered against his neck and arm, Carter suddenly found himself seized with the desire to be very cooperative with Charles Flagg. It did not occur to him to grieve for his late wife. If he had had time to consider it, he would have been surprised to learn that the impact of her sudden death was heavily outweighed by the fear for his own life.

"Samantha Khouri has it," he said. "She'd just gotten fired."

"How did she end up with the ticket?"

"She stole it from Julius and took off."

"You sure you didn't have anything to do with all this?"

"I was trying to help Julius!"

"How, exactly, were you doing that?" Flagg asked. "I would really like to know."

"He wanted to help his family out," Carter said, making up every word as he went along. "See, Julius was from the projects, so it wasn't entirely clear who his family was."

"Are you suggesting that people from the projects don't know who their families are?"

"I was just saying—"

"You were just saying. I see."

"Right," Carter said, nodding his head like a windup toy monkey.

"By the way, where is Julius?" Flagg asked.

Carter took a chance that perhaps his visitor had missed the carnage at Todd's cabin.

"I don't know."

"You don't know."

"No."

"You're not a very good liar, Mr. Pierce."

Carter took serious umbrage at this, given that he fancied himself an exceptional liar.

"You expect me to believe that you don't know where your star client is?"

"I really don't know! Maybe Samantha killed him!"

"Well, my friend, once again, Professor Darwin was right."

Flagg shot Carter Livingston Pierce in the forehead, and Carter no longer had to worry about Dawn the paralegal, the mortgage on the Park City condo, the money he owed his bookie, or the Kornheiser trial. Later, the first police officer on the scene of the Pierce murders would be struck by the look on Carter's face. It almost looked like he was smiling.

Flagg found Carter's cell phone in a small wicker basket on a table in the foyer. He scrolled through the extensive contact list and found the number he wanted. Without missing a beat, he pressed the SEND button and waited for his destiny.

ACROSS THE STREET and two doors down from the Pierce home, Samantha's Audi eased to a stop in front another behemoth house. She ducked low in the driver's seat, most of her face hidden by the door. She could see the front walk of the Pierce home and three vehicles parked in the driveway. She recognized Carter's Hummer and Ashley's car, but the other, a 1970s-style station wagon, was a mystery to her. It was painted fire-engine red and sported shiny whitewalls. She wasn't sure what she'd find in coming here, but she felt better taking action. Like she was helping Pasquale.

She wondered, not for the first time, when or even if this nightmare would ever end. Already, she had forgotten what her life was like before Julius knocked on her door Friday night. A thin film of nervous sweat seemed to be permanently glazed on her body. Her heart had been racing for days. And if she somehow crawled off of this shitheap, she would find herself on another one, this one called Unemployment. Why was she giving up this ticket again?

Her iPhone rang, startling her. Before answering it, she checked the caller ID. Carter Pierce. Her heart leapt into her throat like a high jumper. Well, she thought. The time had arrived.

"Hello?" she answered as casually as she could.

"Your boss is dead," Flagg said.

The words cemented Samantha into silence. Snipping out her tongue would not have had as disabling effect on her power of speech.

"He was a gigantic pain in the ass," Flagg said. "Trust me, I've done evolution a huge favor. Huge."

"Carter's dead?"

"I see that I've got your attention," Flagg said. "I just want the ticket. If you agree to surrender it to me, I will leave you alone."

Samantha knew that this was, of course, an absolute and total lie. He'd confessed to killing Carter the way a man might announce he's taken out the garbage. She suspected he was simply giving her a chance to surrender it in a way that was a lot easier than having to hunt her down, break into her apartment and deal with all that. No one liked hassle.

"You think if you just hang on until Wednesday, you can cash it in and that will be that?"

His question was met with the soft hiss of the open telephone line.

Sam sat stone still, stunned by the news of Carter's death. For reasons that were unclear to her, she was having a hard time processing the news about her now-very-former supervisor. That struck her as odd, given that she thought that she'd seen him die two nights ago and had actually prayed for his death many times while in his employ.

Something about this telephone call unnerved her to her very core, as if she were on a conference call with the boogeyman.

Pasquale. She had to save Pasquale.

"You can have it," she said. "Just let him go."

"Let him go? I already told you that he was dead."

His words scraped against her heart like fingernails on brick. Her mouth opened, but then closed again without making a sound. The man's last sentence seemed pregnant with meaning, but she struggled to process it.

I already told you that he was dead.

He was calling from Carter's phone.

I already told you that he was dead.

Then it hit her. He already told her that Carter was dead.

He didn't mention anyone else. Was it possible that he didn't know about Pasquale? Was Pasquale still safe somewhere? She debated pressing the matter further, perhaps trying to set him up with a fake name. But if he bit on it, she wouldn't necessarily know for certain whether he had Pasquale or not. Plus, he would've mentioned the fact that he had another chip to play. She decided on another approach.

"Yeah, I guess you're right. Well, you'll never find me then."

"I'm watching you right now."

Her body rippled with fear. Was he inside the Pierces' house? Was he peering out at her through the blinds? Were all the Pierces dead? Was that his weird-looking station wagon in the driveway? Faaaan-tastic.

"Gotcha!" he said. "Trust me, if I could see you, you'd already be dead."

At precisely that moment, Samantha realized Carter's killer was in the house. That was his station wagon over there. Calm down, she told herself, calm down. She took stock of her situation. Her Audi was parked right behind a Ford Excursion, which was like a mouse using a skyscraper for cover. Even if he was looking out the blinds, there was no way he could see her. Time to get moving.

As she reached up to start the car, a slight flicker caught her eye. At first, she thought she imagined it, but as she turned her gaze toward it, in the Pierces' driveway, the flicker became more pronounced. She blinked twice, but it was still there. In the gloom of the evening, she realized what it was.

Ashley's car was rockin'.

Don't come a-knockin'.

26

For two full minutes, Samantha kept her hand on the door handle, fully intending to open it and check Ashley's car. The fear was like glue, however, keeping her pasted to her seat. Was it possible that Carter had been the one who kidnapped Pasquale? It made sense. This other nutjob that had called her didn't seem to know anything about him. And Pasquale was right there, thirty yards away.

She wondered how long he had been in the trunk, if that's indeed what she was seeing. It was pretty cold out here, she knew that, and while the Mercedes was a nice car, she didn't think they came with heated trunks yet. The idea of him trapped in there like an animal made her sick to her stomach, but she told herself that if he was frisky enough to thrash around, then he was probably in good physical health.

OK, she was ready to do this. But as she started to tug on the door handle, she saw the Pierces' front door swing open. Gasping, she let go of the handle and slid down the seat, angling her head near the back edge of the driver's door to keep an eye on this new development. Flagg bounded down the steps of the Pierces' porch steps like a man on his way to work. To get to the red station wagon, he would have to make his way down the serpentine brick walk, out onto the asphalt driveway and past the Pierces' two vehicles. Right past the Mercedes.

Oh, please, please, don't let him see the car shaking. Oh, dammit, Pasquale, stop flopping around in there.

Flagg stopped.

Right at the bumper.

Sam looked around the neighborhood quickly, hoping to see someone who would notice that there were strange goings-on afoot, but there was nothing. Didn't these people ever leave their houses? Wasn't anyone out doing a little last-minute Christmas shopping?

Flagg paused and placed a hand on the trunk. When the car started rocking again, he pulled away, as if he had touched a hot stove. He checked the doors, which were locked, and quickly retreated back into the house. Samantha suspected he was going for the car keys. Before she could even form another thought, he was back outside. He pointed the key fob at the car, and the car's lights blinked twice. He repeated the gesture, and the trunk unlatched, swinging open slowly.

Even from here, she could see Pasquale sitting up for a look around, like a groundhog poking his head out to look for his shadow. Flagg came around the back bumper, his gun drawn, sending Pasquale back down into the trunk. Flagg made a circular motion with his free hand, apparently directing Pasquale out of the trunk. Pasquale climbed out slowly, swinging one leg at a time over the edge, his eyes never leaving the gun. Samantha could see that his hands were bound together, and his mouth was covered with tape.

Quickly, Flagg sliced through the wrist bindings, and Pasquale pulled the tape off his mouth, wincing as he did so. Flagg directed Pasquale to his own vehicle and into the driver's seat. He was going to make Pasquale drive.

The police. She needed to call the police. They could come and rescue Pasquale, and whatever happened, happened. Her phone was charged; it was right there in her hand. She needed to save Pasquale. Nothing else mattered. Not the ticket, not Jamal Wheeler, not the untimely demise of Carter Pierce.

She pressed the 9, which beeped loudly.

Could the police save him?

She pressed the 1.

Who was this guy?

She pressed the 1 again.

She prayed this was the right move.

"911, what is your emergency?" answered a tired-sounding woman.

"I need to report a kidnapping," she whispered.

"Where are you, ma'am?"

"On Crestwood Circle. 681 Crestwood Circle. They're in a red station wagon. Please hurry."

"Can you give me any more information?"

"What else do you need? I gave you the address! Please, send a car now!"

"Ma'am, I've already dispatched officers to the scene. I'm just trying to gather some information. The license plates?"

"Okay, okay. The snow is too thick. I can't make out the plates."

"Do you see any weapons?"

"Yes, there's a gun."

"Do you know who the victim is?"

"Yes. His name is Pasquale Paoli."

"Where are you?"

"I'm visiting across the street for Christmas," she said. "I was just looking out the window."

"What's your name, ma'am?"

"I'd rather not say."

"And you're calling from 513-2617?"

They had her cell phone number. How long before they tied her number to the dead guy in the house?

"Yes, that's right."

The red station wagon rumbled to life just as Samantha heard the first hint of sirens in the distance. White rear tail-lights glowed in the darkness as Pasquale shifted into reverse, and the wagon eased back out onto Crestwood Circle. He straightened the wheels and headed north. Thirty seconds from now, they'd be out of the subdivision, and they would disappear.

The sirens continued to wail, but they didn't seem to be getting any closer. Samantha started to call 911 again, but she stopped at the second digit. She remembered the man's voice on the phone. It gave her the chills, and she started to wonder whether police could save Pasquale now. She had far less confidence in his safety now that they were on the run. She did believe very strongly that Pasquale's captor would kill him if he sensed even the slightest threat.

After a deep breath, she pulled out from behind the Ford Expedition and zoomed down Crestwood after the red station wagon. She saw the wagon turn northwest onto the main road, which wound through a quiet neighborhood of big houses and spoiled children. Outside, the snow continued to fall.

PASQUALE TOOK his second kidnapping of the night and third of his life in stride. On the one hand, he was terrified beyond what he thought was humanly possible, and he would gladly have given up his left arm to be a thousand miles away from this psychopath. On the other hand, there wasn't much he could do about his situation right now. Once again, he concentrated on gathering information. So far, he knew the man called himself Charles Flagg. Pasquale hadn't had to talk much, considering that this guy literally would not shut up. At the moment, he was wrapping up a soliloquy on climate change.

"Earth's got a tipping point, you understand. We get to a certain level of greenhouse gases or drop below a certain amount of Arctic ice, and that will be it. Every human being on Earth could stop burning fossil fuels the very next day, and it won't matter. Sort of like a smoker with lung cancer who doesn't need to bother with quitting. We've already lost the bees. The bees!"

"Colony collapse disorder," Pasquale said. "I read about it."

"Good man," Flagg said. "Good man. Not every day I find someone worthy of some rousing discourse."

Discourse away, buddy, discourse away.

"So tell me," he said, clearing his throat. "What were you doing in the trunk? That fellow in the apartment get the drop on you?"

"The last thing I remember was standing in the kitchen, eating cereal."

"I have to say I'm disappointed in you," Flagg said. "That guy was a total loser. I can't believe he cold-cocked you like that."

"Yeah." It was the least objectionable thing he could think of to say.

"Go south. Across the river," Flagg said. He seemed to be done with the subject of disappointment.

Pasquale continued away from the city, passing a sliver of a shopping district that was home to a trendy Asian restaurant and an overpriced women's clothing boutique.

"Just another suburban nightmare," Flagg said, shaking his head. "Humans are such sheep. Earth should do herself a favor and just slough us off. The weak ones, at least."

Pasquale nodded as he curled south toward the bridge. Putting aside for the moment the disturbing realization that he actually agreed with the guy about climate change, silent acquiescence seemed to be the best approach to dealing with this maniac. Pasquale didn't have to wonder what Flagg meant by "the weak ones." This was an ominous development, given that Flagg obviously didn't view him as one of the "strong ones." Not good.

"So, do you know this Samantha?" Flagg asked.

Upon hearing the question, Pasquale's shoulders tightened ever so slightly.

"Don't bother lying," Flagg said. "Obviously, you know her. What, she your girlfriend or something?"

"No."

"But she was, right? Right? A long time ago, is that the deal?"

"Yeah," Pasquale said. "She was."

"So where is she now?"

"I honestly don't know." Pasquale had never been so happy to truthfully answer a question in his life.

"She ran off with the ticket?"

"She took off, yes."

"Can't say I blame her," he said. "That little ticket is worth a lot of money. In this world, to the victors go the spoils."

This statement bothered Pasquale on a number of levels. It was as if this man viewed Samantha as some worthy opponent and was planning a duel with her. He had to keep him away from her.

"Where are we going?" Pasquale asked, taking a chance.

"Aren't we Mr. Curious!"

"Sorry."

"That's the difference between me and you," said Flagg. "You have to ask where we're going. You say 'sorry' like a teenage girl. Pathetic. Professor Darwin would not be happy with you. Fulfilling his mission is why I was put here."

That was about the time Pasquale realized that Flagg was going to kill him, no matter what he did or said. Clearly, Flagg viewed him as a substandard entry in the human race, although he seemed to be impressed by Samantha. Pasquale had come across a few whackos, but this guy really took the cake. There would be no point in trying to talk his way out of his own extermination. He needed to escape, and he needed to do it soon.

A MOMENT LATER, the Huguenot Bridge, which connected the city of Richmond to Chesterfield County to the south, came into view. It was an old two-lane bridge, long since targeted for replacement. Pasquale executed his plan the moment they were on the bridge. He was afraid that if he waited even an extra second, he would lose his nerve. As the roar of the tires underneath them morphed to a high-pitched hum once they left *terra firma*, Pasquale turned the wheel sharply to the left and back to the right. The old wagon, which would have made her manufacturers proud, gripped the road hard and shimmied across the empty lane of the bridge. As Flagg lost his balance, Pasquale reached across and slapped the gun out of Flagg's left hand. It hit the center console with a clap and clattered to Flagg's feet.

"Shit!" Flagg barked.

Pasquale repeated the move, this time bringing the large wagon right up against the left bridge railing. Metal screamed against concrete, sending an arc of sparks shooting against the snowflakes still blanketing the city. He pulled the wheel hard to the right again, which, bless the engineers of the Ford Motor Company, was more than the car could handle.

The driver's side window shattered on this second impact with the bridge railing, and cold air rushed in like Spartans overrunning Troy. The wagon's grill hit the railing hard, causing the rear bumper to flip up and over the threshold of the railing. The car somersaulted once and dropped much like one would expect a 3,000-pound hunk of metal to drop. Pasquale's stomach flipped as the car went airborne. In the two-second drop to the icy depths of the James, Pasquale sketched together an escape plan. As much as one could sketch out a plan together in two seconds.

He clenched his teeth and waited for impact.

This was going to suck.

27

A t first, Samantha thought Pasquale had lost control of the car in the snow and was just fishtailing a bit. She didn't react at first, thinking that certainly, he would regain control of the car, and they would continue their trip to nowhere. That was the way it was when you first saw things going to shit. You don't actually think that the really crappy thing is going to happen. That was the wall Samantha's mind had built up for her. A moment later, the car veered wildly a second time, and she came to the horrific realization that it was deliberate. She slammed on the brakes, which sent her Audi fishtailing before she was able to bring it to a stop. As she did so, she saw the wagon break free of the laws of gravity, if only for a moment.

~

THE WAGON HIT the water nosefirst like a cluster bomb. It pierced the surface of the water, black and rippling like mink fur, and zoomed toward the bottom before the water's buoyancy caught the vehicle in a soft, icy embrace. Thousands of gallons of water rushed into each nook and cranny of the vehicle, desperate to fill every available space. The car's momentary seaworthiness abandoned it within seconds, and it began sinking front end first.

As he wasn't wearing a seatbelt, Pasquale slammed against the roof of the car upon impact, breaking two of his ribs, and collapsed in a heap against his passenger. His whole body lit up with pain, and for a moment, he felt his window on the world narrow to a dark tunnel. He grunted hard, forcing himself to stay conscious. For the moment, Flagg was not moving. For this, Pasquale was eternally grateful. At this point, the water had risen halfway up the passenger compartment, and the car was leaning hard to the left. With one hand, he grabbed the gearshift and used it to brace himself against the onrushing water. Once he had steadied himself, he pushed off the seats hard through the window. As he did so, he smacked his head against the doorframe on the way out, slicing a long but superficial gash against his temple and filling his already blurred field of vision with white light.

Once he was in the water, he kicked as hard as he could to get away from the suction created by the sinking wagon's descent to the riverbed. Instinctively, he knew he was upside down in the inky blackness of the water. He righted himself and started kicking for the surface. Holy shit, it was cold. Temperature in the low forties. He knew he had less than five minutes to get out of the water before disabling hypothermia set in. If that happened, he would have been better off with Flagg putting his gun to his head and pulling the trigger.

He knifed through the water toward the surface, careful not to gasp from the cold, lest he breathe in a liter of river water, which would likely mean the end of Pasquale. Fortunately, breathing was really not an attractive option because of the pain in his ribs, cutting into him like tiny knives. His head broke the surface a moment later, and despite the cracked ribs, he sucked in giant gobs of fresh, icy air. Never in his life had anything tasted so sweet, and he doubted anything would again. Slowly, his eyes adjusted to the darkness, and he treaded water until he picked up lights along the riverbank.

Fortunately, the James River was only about an eighth of a mile wide at this point, and they had gone into the water near the north bank. Behind him, a giant bubble rippled to the surface as the car sank out of sight. He kicked hard for the shore.

OHSHIT-OHSHIT-OHSHIT! Samantha thought as she watched the wagon vanish into the darkness. An instant later, she heard the boom of the car hitting the water, even though her windows were rolled up. The spray leapt high enough for her to see over the edge of the railing. She jumped out of the car, narrowly avoiding a minivan zipping along the bridge. She was still wearing her running shoes, which she took full advantage of now.

On the south side of the bridge, Samantha jumped over the railing and onto a rocky embankment that dropped down to the river's edge. With a coating of ice forming on them, the rocks were like smooth glass. Two-thirds of the way down, she lost her balance and pinballed the rest of the way to level ground. As she reached bottom, her left ankle started to roll over, sending a searing pain through her foot, but she regained her balance before all her weight crashed down on the ankle.

"Dammit," she muttered through gritted teeth. She walked gingerly in small circles, testing the ankle. It was sore, but it was stable.

"Pasquale!" she shrieked. "Pasquale!"

Nothing.

Her eyes desperately scanned the water, looking for any movement, seeing none.

"Pasquale! You son of a bitch!"

She took one step toward the water, tears filling her eyes. There was no way she could swim out there and survive. No way. She fell to her knees, pushing her frozen hair out of her eyes, willing herself to dive in after him.

That was when she saw it. The outline of a head bobbed to the surface off to her left, coughing and grunting like a seal. All she could hope was that it was Pasquale and not the other dude. A minute later, Pasquale Paoli staggered to the shore twenty yards west of Samantha. She limped down the bank and found him shivering, his teeth chattering like machine-gun fire. He collapsed to the ground, oblivious to Samantha's presence.

"Pasquale! It's me!" She slapped him gently on the cheeks, earning a soft moan for her efforts. "Come on, we need to get you out of here."

She wrenched off his sweatshirt, which was like trying to peel a frozen banana, and wrapped her own coat around his shoulders. It was too small for him, but it would have to do for now.

"My car is up on the bridge," she said. "Can you make it?"

He nodded, then shivered violently.

"I think so," he said. "Jesus, it's cold out here. I can't

believe anyone's ever been this cold. It's like I swallowed one of the polar ice caps."

"Shhh," she said. "Let's just concentrate on getting out of here."

THE PAIR STUMBLED down the bank and up the embankment like a pair of drunken revelers. For Pasquale, two steps forward meant one step back. His legs were stiff from the cold and deadened from the swim. Still, he didn't stop. He hadn't survived that goddamn crash (and how many nights would he spend dreaming about that little plunge?) just so he could freeze to death underneath the Huguenot Bridge. On his hands and knees, he crawled up the embankment like a slow turtle. Samantha stayed by his side, keeping her hand on his back for encouragement. There wasn't much more she could do; he outweighed her by seventy pounds. After fifteen agonizing minutes, they made it back to the roadway.

Her car was still idling on the bridge. With the snow still piling up, the roads were virtually deserted, and the few people out and about paid little attention to anyone but themselves. A snowplow roared by them, shoving salt and ice and snow to the edges of the roadway, but it did little good. This was the biggest storm to hit central Virginia in a quarter century, and the localities did not have the trucks, salt or chemicals to keep up with a storm of this magnitude.

Pasquale poured himself into the front passenger seat, where he began stripping off his clothes, heavy with icy water. Every move hurt like hell, and his numb fingers weren't helping much. After climbing into the driver's seat, Samantha cranked up the heat, helped him out of the wet clothes and covered him with her coat. She'd found an old sweatshirt and pair of running shorts in the trunk, which he was just able to squeeze into. They weren't much, but at least they were dry.

"You OK?" she asked.

"I'll live," he said, shivering. "I need more clothes. And coffee."

She shifted the car into gear and eased back onto the highway.

"What were you thinking?" she said. "You should be dead right now."

"That nutjob was going to kill us both," he said. "I had to do something."

"You don't know that," she said. "I was going to give him the ticket. He would've left us alone."

Pasquale laughed.

"He was going to kill us both and possibly have a cup of hot chocolate before bed tonight."

"We need to get you to a doctor," she said, turning onto Huguenot Road and heading south into Chesterfield County.

"No," he said. "They'll start asking a bunch of questions, and they'll get suspicious."

She was silent.

"What do we do now?" asked Pasquale.

"We find Jamal."

"What about your parents?"

"What about them?"

"They're not safe."

"They won't be safe while I have this ticket."

"Maybe you can tell them to bunk in a hotel for a couple nights."

"Yeah, because that really sounds like something my dad would do."

"He might listen to me!"

"Are you out of your effing mind?" said Samantha. "What do you think my father's going to say when his daughter tells him he needs to abandon his home and hide?"

Pasquale shivered violently.

"I guess you're right," he said.

"You really think he was dead?" she asked hopefully.

"Honestly, I don't know," he said. "I doubt we were that lucky. That guy probably practices getting out of submerged cars."

At Huguenot Road's intersection with Route 60, Samantha turned west toward a heavily developed commercial area along the county's main business corridor. The land was dotted with fast-food joints and car dealerships.

"Up there," Pasquale said, pointing to the right. "Hit that Walmart. I can get some clothes."

She pulled into the parking lot and eased up to the gaudily lit entrance area. As he started to get out of the car, she grabbed him by the elbow.

"You want me to go in?" she asked.

"No. Why?"

"You look a little weird in my shorts," she said.

"You have been in one of these places before, right? I don't think anyone's going to notice."

"Right. Here's my debit card," she said, handing it to him. "The PIN number is your birthday."

"Thanks."

"I'm glad you're OK," she said.

He nodded and then disappeared into the bright store. She took a deep breath and let it out slowly. If there was one thing you could count on in this world, it was that Walmart was open. It actually calmed her down a bit. No matter who was out there trying to kill you, there would always be a place to pick up your mouthwash, a pair of sweatpants and a can of fish food. Or a camping tent, a box of cereal, and a trash can. The exercise calmed her down, and she began thinking of groups of three items that she could find at Walmart. A pacifier, charcoal and a monster truck DVD. This was fun!

Fifteen minutes later, Pasquale was back in the car, munching on a hot dog. He was wearing a pair of jeans, a Washington Redskins sweatshirt and a Chicago Blackhawks winter cap.

"Nice hat," she said.

"Most of your body heat is lost through your head," he said.

"That so?"

"Yes," he said, polishing off the rest of the hot dog.

"That's not all that's lost through your head."

"You're hilarious. I'm still hungry. Wanna buy me some dinner?"

"I guess it's the least I can do."

"I could go for a steak."

"Maybe we better stick to a drive-through for now."

"You owe me a steak."

"I promise to get you a steak the size of your head," Samantha said. "If we live through this."

28

D r. Roger Bouzein was pissed off, sighing loudly as he pulled on his scrubs in the doctors' locker room of Henrico Doctors' Hospital. No one was there to hear him sigh, all exasperated-like, but it made him feel better just the same. Before stuffing his belongings into his locker, he sighed once more for good measure. Typically, it made him feel very doctor-like to be starting a shift at five in the morning. It always gave him a chance to tell people what he did for a living.

Gotta be up early. Oh, I'm a doctor.

Since he had hospital privileges here, he'd agreed to cover the 36-hour Christmas shift for a friend. But two nights ago, still bitter about Samantha Khouri's rebuff, he had met this little biscuit, a senior at the University of Richmond, who invited him to her parents' house on Amelia Island for the next two days. She was alone, as her parents were in Europe, and she had promised him that he would never forget this Christmas or Chanukah or Kwanzaa.

He was in the middle of packing for his trip the night before when he remembered that he had to work. He had tried switching with someone else, even offering any takers a thousand bucks, but no one was biting. The others all were married or had kids. So here he sat on Christmas Eve morning, and Suzanne Foster was all by herself in that big beach house, doing God knew what to herself. *Oy vay!*

So it was in a relatively foul mood that he had reported for his shift and approached the nurses' station for the morning's charts. As he grabbed the first clipboard of the day, he noted two police officers parked outside Room 476, which as luck would have it, was his first chart for the day.

"What's with the cops?" he asked the charge nurse, who was sipping what smelled like hot chocolate from an Oceanic Airlines coffee mug.

"That guy's a suspect in a double murder," she said, all breathy-like. "They pulled him out of the James River. He's alive, but barely."

"Really?" he said, not giving the smallest shit.

"Apparently, he killed this couple out in Windsor Farms," said the nurse. "Right in their living room! He lost control on the Huguenot Bridge, ended up in the water. He's in bad shape."

"Wow," he said softly. Someone having a worse night than he was. That actually made him feel a little better. Not that he reveled in the misfortune of his patients. What, was it some sin that he went home every night thankful he didn't have whatever ailment or injury he had treated that day? Death really didn't bother him too much. Oh, he would do the dance and operate and medicate, but he was a firm believer that when someone's time was up, it was up, and there wasn't a whole hell of a lot he could do about it, no matter how many medical journal articles he read.

As the charge nurse had explained to him, Room 476's current occupant was a John Doe who'd been found along the south bank of the James River about four hours ago. A city cop at the end of his shift noticed some fresh damage to the bridge railing and although all he wanted to do was get home and drink a little Bailey's and coffee, he pulled over and examined the scene a little more closely. When he got down to the river with his portable spotlight, he was amazed to discover a man lying on the bank, still alive. He called for an ambulance, and two paramedics slopped through the slushy mud to load him onto a stretcher. The man's body temperature was eighty-three degrees, and his pulse had slowed to twenty beats per minute.

Because there wasn't much else to do once they hooked up the tubes and monitors, the two EMTs treating him bet on whether the man would die on the way to the hospital. He didn't. Now the police were waiting to talk to him about how, exactly, he had ended up on the south bank of the James River.

Time-lapse surveillance video from the bridge revealed the crash in all its grainy, herky-jerky glory, and a recovery effort was now underway. The video also showed Samantha stopping and assisting Pasquale back up the riverbank, but the combination of the snow and the poor video quality made it impossible for the police to identify them or their vehicle's tags. State Police divers reported that there was no one else still in the doomed car, now resting comfortably at the bottom of the river, and were concentrating efforts to find anyone else who might have been ejected from the vehicle. A crash investigation team was also at work, trying to reconstruct the accident. In these terrible weather conditions, it wasn't difficult to fathom someone losing control on the glassy surface of the bridge. Although it was clear that at least two people had gone in the river, none of the area hospitals reported seeing a patient that matched the description of the second John Doe who'd left the scene with the passing motorist.

Things got very interesting around 2:30 in the morning, when police linked the red station wagon found at the bottom of the James River to the one Samantha had reported in her 911 call. The patrol officers who'd responded to Samantha's call discovered the doorknob had been shot off. The two excitedly drew their weapons, each for the first time in their careers, and entered the house. For the life of them, neither could remember if they were supposed to go in first or call for backup first, but they figured that if there was an intruder in the house, they better get in there and do some saving while there was saving to be done. That was how you got promoted! Of course, they hadn't had to look far, and there hadn't been any saving to do. The bodies of Mr. and Mrs. Carter Livingston Pierce were exactly where Flagg had left them and posed no real threat.

Now Richmond Police had a deadly home invasion on their hands in a pretty damn nice neighborhood, and there were going to be a lot of pissed-off and rich white people if they didn't have some answers by the time Santa Claus dropped his fat ass down the chimney tonight. The Chief of Police and the Commonwealth's Attorney both got telephone calls, and the homicide detective, a ten-year veteran named Douglas Byrd, was very happy to tell them both that RPD had a suspect in the hospital.

All Dr. Bouzein knew was that it was slowing everything down. He was thinking about all this when he stepped into the room and discovered, much to his amazement, that the patient's bed was empty. For a brief moment, he thought his wish for the man's death had come true and all these officers could get the hell out of his hospital. It was about that moment he sensed movement behind him, a pair of hands grabbing his head like a vise. Flagg wrenched Dr. Bouzein's head counterclockwise like he was opening a tough jar, severing the spinal cord. His body went limp, and Flagg gently lowered him to the bed. Quickly, Flagg stripped Bouzein down to his boxers, dressed him in his hospital gown and pulled the blanket up near the doctor's chin.

As he pulled on Bouzein's scrubs and lab coat, Flagg thought about his next move. He had noted the police presence about two hours ago and suspected there were a pair of officers guarding his door. By now, they would know the Pierces were dead and probably had pegged him as a spree killer. A smart detective might even have started connecting the trail of bodies he had left behind tonight. Fortunately for Flagg, the good doctor's build was relatively similar to his own.

Even he knew that luck sometimes played a role in evolution.

With his nose buried in his own medical chart, Flagg stepped out in the hall and around the two officers sleepily guarding the door. They never looked up, losing interest as soon as they saw the aquamarine scrubs slipping by. Of far greater interest to the cops was the saucy blonde at the nurses' station. Flagg strutted down the long hallway, relatively quiet at this hour, keeping his eyes planted firmly on the chart. No one bothered a doctor reviewing a medical chart.

Bright red exit signs mounted at the top of the wall greeted him at the end of the hallway. Flagg ducked into the stairwell, a giant 4 painted on the wall next to the door, preferring its openness to the claustrophobic nature of the elevator. He passed a tired-looking doctor on the steps, drawing a look of puzzlement but no more. A minute later, he was zipping through the emergency department and out the sliding double doors. As he did so, he heard the call over the loudspeaker, "Dr. Black, 4 West." He had once heard that a Code Black was an alert of a non-medical threat to human life in a hospital, and that to avoid panic, the code calls were disguised as doctors' names. He figured they had found the little gift that he had left in Room 476 and hurried out into the frigid dawn.

DETECTIVE DOUGLAS BYRD pressed his lips together and blew out a noisy sigh. He was in Room 476, looking at the remains of Dr. Roger Bouzein, M.D. His hands were cupped firmly on his hips while the two patrol officers that had been guarding the door stood behind him with their hats literally in their hands. Neither spoke. Byrd knew they were expecting him to tear them a new one, but he just didn't have the energy.

The hospital's chief of medicine, Anne Kelso, stood at the foot of the bed, checking the final readings from the various machines to which the suspect had been connected. Thirty minutes ago, she had been sleeping soundly on her couch, tucked under a quilt, a small blaze still crackling in the fireplace. Her husband, an Oceanic Airlines pilot, was due home later that morning and would be off the rest of the year. It was going to be a goddamn Merry Christmas at the Kelso household.

So when the telephone rang and broke her out of her slumber, she was prepared to start yelling at whoever was calling. That was one of the perks of being chief. Until she heard the news about Bouzein. Pompous jackass that he was, the idea that a doctor had been murdered in a patient's room – by a patient, no less – had pretty much freaked her out. She kept looking at the machines, wondering when she would be able to get out of this room. Her gaze kept drifting to Bouzein's lifeless face, his eyes empty and glassy.

"I thought you all said this guy was at death's door," said Byrd. "That's what I heard. That he would be lucky to live through the night."

"What can I say?" Dr. Kelso said. "He was critical when he got here. With a body temperature in the mid-eighties, he had a fighting chance to recover, but you never know with these kinds of cases. We followed standard protocol for extreme hypothermia. He was intubated, and we administered warmed oxygen and a heated IV saline drip. His pulse was steady but extremely slow. Not much we could do other than wait for him to either get better or die."

"So how is it possible that he overpowered and killed a doctor, exchanged clothes with him and then slipped past these two ninjas back here?"

One of the officers, Raburn, took a deep breath and let it out slowly.

She sighed. "I don't know," she said. "Let's just say the average person would not have been capable. Severe hypothermia is a very debilitating condition."

"What do you mean?" asked Byrd.

"You say this guy killed two people?"

"Three, counting your colleague here," Byrd said, nodding toward Bouzein's body. "Maybe more."

"This guy pulled out his breathing tube, his IV and still had the strength to go on this rampage," she said. "What I mean is that this is one crazy bastard you've got on your hands."

∾

BYRD BOUGHT a bottle of Mountain Dew from the vending machine in the ER's waiting room and sat down in front of the television mounted on the wall. It was tuned to the NBC affiliate, which was in its last half-hour of local news before the Today show. The top story was the Pierce double murder. A tall, thin reporter was stationed at the edge of the Pierces' yard, blue lights oscillating behind him. He couldn't report much more than the fact that there were two very dead people in the house, although he did keep one hand pressed to the radio in his ear, which made it seem as if he was privy to all kinds of juicy details about the slayings.

The story really hadn't picked up much steam yet, because although this was a Monday morning, it was Christmas Eve, a holiday, and most people were likely still asleep. It would quickly mushroom, though, when word got out there was a homicidal lunatic on the loose. That may not have been an accurate profile of the suspect, but that's what would be making the rounds this holiday season. The media getting involved, yeah, that was always Byrd's favorite part of these investigations.

His cell phone rang, the ring tone set to Christmas music. Douglas Byrd loved himself some Christmas; he let it ring a bit before reaching in his pocket to answer it. The number on the caller ID was familiar, but he couldn't place it.

"Detective Byrd."

"Hey, this is Paul Ruiz." Ruiz was a homicide detective with the Henrico Police Department.

"Merry Christmas."

"Same to you," he said. "Hey, you still at the hospital?"

"Yeah."

"I heard the suspect jumped a doctor or something?"

"Killed him."

"Christ," he said. "Look, we got another mess on our hands. I got two more bodies out here off Mountain Road. One tied up and shot in the head. The other's got a goddamn fireplace poker in his chest."

"Wow. Don't see that every day."

"There's more," Ruiz said. "You might be interested in this guy."

"How so?"

"Con named Todd Matheson. Appears to be the brother of the Pierce woman you've got down at Windsor Farms. He's the one got shish-kabobed."

"Awesome. Any idea what happened?"

"We think there was someone else here. Unless he stabbed himself with the fireplace poker."

"How long since they died?"

"Oh, a while, I'm guessing," Ruiz said. "M.E.'s not here yet."

"You gonna wait for her?"

"Unless I can find someone to wait in my place," Ruiz said. "I've got a shitload of relatives back at the house, and I'm supposed to start cooking Christmas Eve dinner in a few hours."

"You cook?"

"I'm a liberated man."

"Learn something new every day."

"Eat your heart out. Later."

"See ya."

Byrd snapped his phone closed and slipped it into his jacket pocket. He could almost hear it causing cancer. He sipped his soda and continued to watch the news.

29

MONDAY, DECEMBER 24 - 7:38 A.M.

P asquale woke up shivering, his throat dry and raw. His head felt heavy and tight, thanks to the pops he'd taken in the apartment and against the door-frame in the river. His quads and calves burned from the desperate swim to shore after he'd escaped the car. The ribs, however, were the star of the pain show. Every breath was painful, like he was drawing each one against a blade. The six ibuprofen tablets before bed had taken a little of the edge off, but just a little. And that many pills really couldn't have been good for his liver, so he made a note not to take anymore until tonight. This was assuming, of course, he and Samantha lived that long.

Samantha was already awake, sitting on the edge of the bed and watching the news. They were in a Comfort Inn on West Broad Street, a few miles from downtown, having made their way back north across the river the night before. A sliver of grey light seeped in from between the curtains. The sun was up, but it didn't seem like there was much point in its having risen today.

"Time to get moving," she said when she saw him rustling.

She disappeared into the bathroom. A moment later, Pasquale heard the groan of the pipes and the hiss of the shower. While Samantha showered, Pasquale took in the local news, which led with the story on the Pierce murders.

"There's a story about your boss," he said when she emerged from the bathroom a few minutes later.

"What else did they say?"

"His wife's dead, too."

Samantha's chin dropped.

"What about their daughters?" she asked.

"The reporter said they weren't home when it happened and they were staying with friends."

"That's good," she said. "I guess it's something. This goddamn ticket."

"Where did you say the kid lived?"

"Ravenwood Court," she said. "Remember it?"

"Sure," he said. "Don't know where it is, though."

"Me either," she said. She got dressed, her mind focused on the task at hand

"How do we live here for so long and not know where it is?" asked Sam.

"It's not exactly Disneyland," Pasquale said, tracing a finger along the map. They had picked it up in the lobby of the hotel after checking in.

"Shouldn't I know?" she asked.

"What, your knowing where it is will make things better in the projects? Spare me the 'I feel guilty' speech. The place is what it is. I'm not a sociologist. It just is."

Samantha bristled as Pasquale's oral floodgates opened.

"You've got nothing to feel guilty about," he went on, never looking up from the map. "You're the picture of the goddamn American dream. Nobody gave your parents shit when they got here. They did it themselves, opened all the doors in the world for you, and you walked through them. Then that brother of yours did what he did, and you've been paying for it ever since. You've got enough shit to worry about. Let's get this thing out of our lives."

"I'm sorry I never called you back, by the way," she said.

A day after the bombing, Pasquale called her parents' house from London. Two hours later, he was interviewed by a pair of British intelligence agents.

He lowered his head and turned his attention back to the task at hand.

"Here it is," he said, poking the map hard with his index finger.

THEY RODE IN SILENCE, listening to the local news on the radio, as Samantha carefully picked her way east toward the city proper. The streets were quiet under the gray blanket of clouds on this Christmas Eve, barely passable in certain spots. The snow had tapered off considerably in the last hour, but it was still coming down like sprinkles on top of an already thick layer of icing. Reports indicated it had been the biggest storm in a generation, dropping nearly two feet of snow on the region, and more was on the way. Another low-pressure system was screaming up from the Gulf of Mexico and was on a collision course with the extremely cold air that had been parked over the mid-Atlantic for the past week.

They motored through an industrial section of town, past the Sauers vanilla plant, its famous marquee blinking against the gray backdrop. Further east, abandoned storefronts looked particularly blight-ridden on a morning like this. Pictures like this were what ended careers on city council. It looked like nuclear winter.

A few moments later, Samantha turned right onto Allen Avenue, which was dotted with brownstone apartment buildings and antebellum-style homes. A few neighborhood kids were out and about, firing snowballs, and generally exposing each others' parents to gigantic tort liability. A modern-day winter wonderland. Still, there weren't that many kids, a testament to how big a storm this had been.

At the corner of Allen and Claiborne, south of the I-195 bypass, the Audi slid against the curb and into a snowdrift it couldn't overcome. Pasquale got out to push while Samantha revved the engine, but the wheels spun as if they weren't even touching the ground. Sam took a quick look around and walked around to the passenger side window.

"We need some kitty litter," she said.

"Fresh out," Pasquale said.

"Looks like we're walking," she said. "It's not much farther. How're you feeling?"

"I'm fine," he said. "Should we knock on someone's door and ask for help?"

Sam chewed on her lower lip while she considered the question. The street looked familiar, and it suddenly hit her why. During her internship with the prosecutor's office, she had come to this neighborhood in search of a witness to an aggravated assault. It was a warm summer night, and the neighborhood was bustling with people, some proud, some scared, some beaten, some desperate to get out, and some up to no good. Sam had never been in a neighborhood like this before, and she had been scared shitless.

She knocked on several doors, looking for a teenage girl who allegedly had witnessed the beating. Nearly everyone denied knowing her, and those that did claimed they didn't know where she was. After an hour, a pair of young thugs began harassing her, and she gave up looking for the witness, her deodorant in total failure. She ran back to her car, her legal pad tucked underneath her arm. She drove home, quiet tears streaming down her cheeks.

"Let's just not draw any more attention to ourselves than we need to."

Samantha zipped up her parka, popped the hood over her head and joined Pasquale on the street. A push of the button on her key fob locked her car doors with a *boop*, leaving them alone on the street. Nervously, she pulled the drawstrings of the hood tight. Her last prep was to tuck the ticket into a waterproof pocket inside her jacket.

"Ravenwood is a few blocks south of here," she said.

"Let's get on with it," he said.

Samantha turned on her heel headed south, crunching her way through the snowpack. It was slow going, calling for high-stepping through the snow. Luckily, the snow was relatively dry powder, so their pants stayed relatively dry as well. They were, however, freezing their behinds off.

THE SMALLER BUT wiser older brother to Carrolton Oaks, Ravenwood was also a Richmond Redevelopment & Housing Authority project. Built in 1963, it was located at the corner of Allen and Kemper and bracketed to the east by Lombardy Street. Four stories high and occupying two city blocks, it had long been riddled with drugs and prostitution, pockmarked with violence. It had eight hundred units and was home to nearly 1,200 people.

Recently, the complex had come under the control of a

new drug lord, who, while young, was nevertheless intelligent, charismatic and ruthless. He had consolidated power and had helped reduce violence by bringing together the various dealers that had fought like rival religious factions. Richmond Police, aware of the shift in the balance of power and the relative peace that had descended on the area, had backed off patrols and focused their attention on more lawless areas of the city. This was not something they admitted in the press releases.

The complex itself was shaped like the letter "H" closed off at the ends, with an extra slash across the middle, leaving three large open courtyards, connected by corridors. The smaller apartments ringed the perimeter of the complex, opening up onto the courtyard. Larger units filled the center of the complex, like the middle of a jelly doughnut. Samantha and Pasquale approached from the west side and entered through the breezeway leading to the outer courtyard. The snow was deep and pure at this end and looked lovely, even though it was going to turn these courtyards into slop as soon as it melted. They could hear kids squealing in one of the other courtyards, but this one remained unspoiled for now.

"Let's just knock on a few doors," she said. "Someone's bound to know him."

"You're optimistic in the morning," replied Pasquale.

"Hope springs eternal, what can I say?"

The sound of a door screeching open behind them caught their attention, and they both turned to look. A woman donning ski pants, a heavy jacket and a thick hood came roaring out with a snow shovel, going to work on the drifts that had piled up in front of her apartment. The courtyard was quiet except for the *scritch-scritch* of the shovel scraping against the sidewalk.

"Excuse me," Samantha said, taking a few high steps toward the woman.

The woman didn't respond.

"We're looking for a boy named Jamal Wheeler," she said. "Do you know him?"

"You police?"

"No."

She continued shoveling snow.

"Young kid," Sam said, "maybe sixteen years old?"

"Don't know him," the woman said. "Now get out of here. I'm busy."

"Sorry to bother you, ma'am," Samantha said.

The woman continued to chew away at the snow with her shovel, slowly reclaiming the sidewalk in front of her apartment. Samantha retreated back toward Pasquale.

"That went well, don't you think?" Pasquale said.

"Shut up," she said. "My legs are freezing."

"I can't believe how helpful she was."

She whipped her head around and gave him a look she rarely gave anyone. It was the sort of look that suggested she might hold his head down in the snow until he stopped struggling.

"Sorry," he said.

"We are getting this goddamn ticket to Jamal."

"Right," he said. "Right. I know. We will."

Knocks on three more doors drew no answer, but people were starting to take notice of their presence. Blinds covering darkened living rooms rippled around the complex like waves. The kids playing in the next courtyard snapped into silence, like they were waiting for a tee shot on the eighteenth hole at Augusta National.

As they neared the fourth door of the morning, two young men strode intently toward them, approaching from the opposite side of the courtyard. Both were tall and thin. The older one, whose skin was black like cooled lava, wore a Washington Redskins jacket and cap. His name was Ricky, and he was twenty-six. His colleague, Leon, was twenty-three, lighter skinned, and dead-eyed.

"The fuck y'all doing up in here?" asked Leon.

"You know Jamal Wheeler?" asked Samantha. No point in beating around the bush.

"Who wants to know?"

"That's between me and Jamal," Samantha said.

"Listen to this shit," said Leon, looking over at Ricky. Ricky looked nervous and didn't reply. He was just hungry and wanted to go get some breakfast from his aunt's house across the way. He hated getting in fights and attributed his survival so far to this aversion. Two of his brothers had been killed before they made it to twenty-six. He wasn't ready to see them at the crossroads just yet.

"Don't talk to her that way," Pasquale said quietly.

"The fuck you say to me?" Leon said.

"You heard me."

Oh, shit, Samantha thought. We're dead.

Slowly, Leon's hand slid behind his back. As it did, Pasquale was already on the move. The gun had barely come level before Pasquale grabbed it by the barrel and wrenched Leon's wrist counterclockwise until it snapped with a soft, sickening crack. In the same motion, he yanked Leon toward him, side-stepped him and drove his elbow into the nape of his neck. The boy dropped to his knees, and Pasquale dropped the butt of the gun on his head with a satisfying crack. Leon fell face forward into the snow. The icy shock of the snow revived him almost instantly, and he was back up on his knees, moaning in pain.

"What'd you do to him?" wailed Ricky.

Samantha became dully aware of a presence behind her. She looked over her shoulder just in time for a right cross against her cheek. She crumpled to her knees, hearing an "ooph" that sounded very Pasquale-like behind her.

AFTER TEN HAZY MINUTES, clarity and focus started seeping back in like the outer edges of a Polaroid picture. Sam was in a soft chair, her hands tied behind her back. In front of her, there was a low-slung table, on which several basketball and football magazines were splayed out like a fan. Beyond that, a large flat-screen television was tuned to ESPN. It helped orient her. She was in someone's living room. She had a wicked headache, and her cheek felt numb where it had taken the blow.

She could hear the outlines of conversation in the room, but she was still too woozy to make out the words. As her vision improved, she saw Pasquale laid out on a sofa like a freshly caught fish. His chest rose and fell rhythmically. He appeared to be unconscious but otherwise OK. A light-skinned teenager stood by the door. Another sat next to Pasquale.

The ticket! Her thoughts immediately went to the ticket. She was still in her parka, and while she couldn't tell if the ticket was still in her pocket, her jacket seemed undisturbed. She didn't think anyone had tried to take it off since she had gotten her ass kicked ten minutes ago. She had never been in a fight before; she supposed that was still true, as getting flattened with one punch didn't really constitute a fight.

"You awake?" a voice called out.

She turned toward the voice, belonging to a young black man sporting a Cleveland Indians baseball cap, the brim pulled low. He wore low-ride jeans and a black hooded sweatshirt. He was a big guy, well over six feet tall and built like a cinderblock. Despite the baggy clothes, the chiseled face left no doubt about the powerfully built man underneath.

"Now who the hell are you?" he asked, his voice tinged with more exasperation than anger.

"Samantha. Samantha Khouri."

"What are you doin' down here? You know you white, right?"

"What's your point?"

"Could be dangerous for a young lady."

"I'm a big girl," she said, stunned by the level of her sassiness.

He took a sip of his coffee.

"Is he OK?" she asked, nodding toward Pasquale.

"Yeah, fine," he asked, dismissing her with a wave of the hand. "Let's get back to my question."

"I'm looking for someone."

"Who?"

"Jamal Wheeler."

"Jamal Wheeler," he said.

"You know him?"

"I didn't say that," he asked.

"So you don't know him," she said.

"I didn't say that either."

Silence filled the room like carbon monoxide, invisible and potentially deadly if not dealt with immediately. Samantha worried that if she didn't do something soon, they'd both be dead.

"Let's say I know Jamal Wheeler," he said finally. "What do you want with him?"

"I have something for him."

"What?"

"That's between me and Jamal."

"What is it? Why you gotta be all mysterious about it?"

Samantha took a deep breath and exhaled slowly. "Something from his father."

The man's head rocked backward slightly, just barely, but just enough for Samantha to notice. He whispered to himself softly, too softly for Samantha to hear. Immediately, though, his tone hardened, like quick-dry concrete.

"The fuck you want with Jamal's father?"

He peeled off his baseball cap and dropped it on the coffee table, ran his fingers across the shiny dome of his pristine scalp. When he looked back up at Samantha, she saw it. There was no questioning it. The nose bore the same crook, and the chin jutted out at the same angle. The thing that sealed it, though, was the eyes. They were identical.

"Jamal?"

30

Samantha took two ibuprofen that Jamal offered her and washed it down with a few sips of coffee. It was the best coffee she'd had in a long time. They sat back down in the living room.

"So, you're not fifteen," Samantha said, taking a sip of the hot coffee.

"What made you think I was fifteen?"

"Your father said you were about fifteen."

"That stupid old man," he said. "He ain't seen me in twenty years. I'm twenty-three. How you know him, anyway? You in book club together?"

"I didn't know him long," she said. "I just met him a few days ago. Look, Jamal, I have some bad news," Samantha said.

"What?"

She took a deep breath and let it out slowly.

"Your father's dead."

"So?"

"I'm sorry," she said.

"Don't be," he said. "The fuck do I care if he's dead?"

Samantha didn't know what to say to this. On one hand, she supposed she shouldn't be surprised. Julius never claimed to be father of the year. On the other hand ... well, there was no other hand. Why should Jamal care if Julius was dead? The man had been dead to Jamal all his life. That he was now actually dead really didn't make a whole hell of a lot of difference.

"Well, I've got something for you," she said.

A groan interrupted them. Samantha looked over and saw Pasquale stirring on the couch. He rolled up into a sitting position, moaning, his hand pressed against the back of his head. Samantha's heart crumbled. The last eighteen hours had not been particularly kind to Pasquale Paoli.

"You OK, little man?" he asked.

"You the one that clocked me?" Pasquale asked softly.

"No," said Jamal. "One of my boys. They saw you kick Leon's ass, they got worried. Good thing you're white."

"Why?"

"Why, he asks. Why? Because if you looked like me," he said, tapping a finger against his chest, "they'da popped a cap in you. Seriously."

Pasquale slowly leaned back against the sofa and closed his eyes. Jamal turned his attention back to Samantha.

"So what is it you've come all this way to show me?"

She chewed on her lower lip. Was she so sure this was Jamal Wheeler?

"You got some kind of ID?"

He leaned forward in his seat, propping his elbows on his knees. His eyes narrowed to slits, and then he started laughing. It started as a few chuckles, like light rain showers, before exploding into a thunderstorm of laughter. His compadres, sensing that it was OK to laugh, joined in, guffawing as well, never as loud as Jamal, but not much softer either. Like, yeah, boss, this is some funny shit, and we're right there with you.

By the time the laughter began to die down, Jamal was wiping tears away from his face.

"Yeah," he said. "Yeah, I got some ID."

Still laughing, he got up and slipped down a dark corridor to Samantha's left. His two foot soldiers stayed behind.

"ID?" Pasquale asked. "What are you, a bartender?"

"Look, I gotta be sure."

"Better safe than sorry, I guess."

"Let me make this right and we can get the hell out of here," Samantha said.

Jamal returned a moment later and handed her his driver's license. Samantha looked at it for a moment, which was more than enough time to convince her that this young man was who he said he was. She handed it back to him.

"That good enough, Officer?" he asked.

"Yeah," she said. "It's fine."

"Glad to hear it."

"Can we talk in private?" Samantha asked.

"These are my boys," Jamal said harshly. "What you say to me, you can say to them."

Wonder if you'll still think that when I show you what I've got, she thought.

"Alright," she said. "I'm a lawyer. I work downtown. Your father was a janitor in my building. Four nights ago, he came to my office looking for some legal advice."

"So you a criminal lawyer," Jamal said.

"Not exactly," she said, thinking about her own reaction to Julius' statement in her office that he needed a lawyer. "Anyway, Julius needed some legal advice because he'd come into a bit of money."

"Really?" Jamal asked, his mood brightening a bit. The other men in the room shifted as their interest in the proceedings ramped up.

"Look, I really think we need to talk in private."

"Don't start with that shit again," Jamal said with a flash of anger. "I'll decide when we need to talk in private."

"Fine," she said. "Your call. Here's the deal. Your father won the lottery the other night."

One of his men whistled softly.

"How much?" asked Jamal.

Samantha sat quietly, glancing around the room at the other men. She wondered if they were armed. She wondered if Jamal was armed. She wondered if she should be armed.

Jamal seemed to be getting the picture. He waved his hand behind his head brusquely. "Y'all bust outta here. I got this."

The pair obediently stepped outside the apartment, leaving Samantha and Pasquale alone with Jamal.

"How much?" Jamal asked.

"Four hundred and fifteen million," she said. "Before taxes."

Jamal stared at her blankly for a full minute. Then his head spun around toward Pasquale, as if to look for help, confirmation, advice, something. Pasquale nodded his head.

"How much after?"

"If you take it all at once, about a hundred and fifty million. Give or take."

Jamal looked at Pasquale again. "Is she serious?"

Pasquale nodded again.

Another long silence filled the room. Jamal lit a cigarette and smoked half of it before speaking again.

"So what is it you're here to give me?"

"The ticket."

"The ticket? You mean the actual ticket?"

"You're the only known heir to Julius Wheeler's estate," she said. "He told me that he did not have a will. Under Virginia law, everything in his estate passes to you. I got the impression there wasn't a whole lot else to the estate besides the ticket. And he wanted you to have it."

"You mean you have the ticket with you? Like right now?"

She nodded.

"Shit, you fucking crazy."

She remained quiet, contemplating whether to share the fact that there was another player in this little game, and he had sort of cornered the market on "fucking crazy."

"I didn't have any choice but to keep it with me."

"Why didn't you keep it for yourself? No one would ever have known."

She chuckled softly. "Long story short. It wasn't mine to keep."

Jamal looked at her closely.

Samantha nodded.

"What happened to Julius?" Jamal asked.

"Some men tried to steal the ticket from him," she said.

"What men?"

"One of them was my boss."

"The fuck kinda lawyer are you?"

"Not a very good one, I guess."

"What happened to your boss?"

Samantha laughed loudly, and then tears started streaming down her face. "He's dead, too."

"So this ticket ain't been very lucky yet," Jamal said.

"No," she said. "Not yet."

"But y'all are still alive," he said.

"For now," she said. "Look, we need to get you out of here, hide you until you can cash the ticket."

"I ain't going anywhere."

"Jamal," she said, "it might not be safe for you."

"I ain't gonna tell anyone about it," he said. "Are you?"

"No. But my boss wasn't the only one trying to get his hands on the ticket," Samantha said.

"Explain."

"WHAT ARE THEY TALKING ABOUT?" asked Piggy. He was the teenage boy that had been leaning against the doorjamb in the kitchen. Eighteen years old, he was a newcomer to Jamal's crew. He was not particularly bright, but he was unquestionably loyal to Jamal.

Scotty Mitchell shook his head. "Can't hear shit with you asking me every two seconds. Shut the fuck up."

Scotty was older, twenty-five, and Jamal's top lieutenant. He oversaw the gambling operations in Ravenwood and surrounding neighborhoods. He had been in prison for most of his adult life, but this was a lull in his time behind bars, like planet Earth between ice ages. The world had been and would again be covered in ice, and sure as day followed night, Scotty would be in prison again.

The day's events had been odd, to be sure. Scotty wondered what his boss was up to, what these two strangers wanted from him. Clearly, something about them had intrigued Jamal, which surprised Scotty. Time was, Jamal would have popped them because he didn't like to take any chances. Maybe Jamal was getting soft. Or maybe he was getting wise. Who knew? Maybe he just had a little Christmas spirit bubbling underneath.

A sound to his left snapped him out of his thoughts. A man he had never seen before was trudging through the snow like Bigfoot. Even though he was wearing his heaviest parka, gooseflesh popped up all over Scotty's arms, and instinctively, his hands slipped into his waistband for his nine-millimeter pistol. Although his instincts had served him well, he was far too late in executing his response. Behind him, Piggy was just now picking up on the threat. Useless, Scotty thought.

Flagg was on them like a puma.

"Motherfucker!" hissed Scotty.

Flagg fired two shots into Piggy, who collapsed into the snow and died. A third shot caught Scotty in the shin, staggering but not dropping him. Flagg came up behind him and pressed the barrel into his back.

"The next one's in your head unless you do what I say."

JAMAL WHEELER WAS the first and only child of Alicia Ray, born via a cesarean section that became medically necessary when it was discovered that she'd taken two hits off a crack pipe while she was in labor. As fate would have it, on that very day, the on-call obstetrician, Dr. Mark Bernard, reached the end of his moral rope when it came to young, unwed, and drug-addled mothers. When confronted with Alicia Ray, he went a bit haywire and performed an unnecessary hysterectomy on her. Dr. Bernard advised Alicia's mother that he had discovered a cancerous tumor on Alicia's uterus, warranting the drastic procedure. This was, of course, a complete and total fabrication, but Dr. Bernard had no desire to deliver six more of Alicia's children. Two months later, Bernard shot himself in the bathroom of a Las Vegas McDonald's.

When Jamal was two, he and Alicia moved to Raven-wood, where mother and son shared an apartment with Alicia's thirty-five-year-old mother, Shawna Jackson. Shawna, who worked the day shift deboning chicken at a Tyson plant, became a *de facto* mommy to Jamal, as Alicia was a big fan of the nightlife and romantic rendezvous with men whom she did not know. Shawna fed him, changed him, toilet-trained him, and got him to bed. Some nights, Alicia came home. Often, she did not. Sometimes Jamal asked where his Mommy was. Most nights, he did not.

Several years later, Alicia made the acquaintance of a man she knew as Smiley, a man whom she would only know as Smiley. They met in the courtyard, and two nights later, the platonic phase of their relationship came to an end. Within a week, he had moved in with Alicia, Shawna and Jamal. Shortly thereafter, the happy couple concocted a scheme to rob a Bank of America, a plan that they believed would solve their myriad financial issues.

The robbery happened on a rainy Monday morning. Smiley led the way with a shotgun, directing the few customers and bank employees toward the floor. Alicia trailed behind with a .22-caliber pistol, which Smiley had taught her to use on the way to the bank. One of the customers that morning was an off-duty police officer who had stopped in to cash a check. Shortly after taking over the bank, Smiley and Alicia forgot about the hostages and turned their attention toward the teller filling a bank bag with cash. Now in their defense, they were as high as kites, having shared a doobie on the way to the bank. With one exception, the hostages lay quietly on the floor behind the bank robbers, each hoping that, like a bad sexual encounter, this would be over soon.

The officer, Thomas Coventry, leapt to his feet and loudly demanded that the robbers drop their weapons and get on the floor. Much to Coventry's delight, both robbers turned to face him, without first complying with his request to disarm themselves. Coventry was a long-suffering patrol officer, desperate to make detective, and he thought that this chance occurrence would kick open the door to his shield.

As both Smiley and Alicia raised their weapons, Coventry began firing, emptying his clip into the would-be robbers. Smiley took two in the chest, which killed him instantly. While two bullets plowed into Alicia's stomach, she sprayed her pistol wildly, an act that ended Officer Coventry's quest to make detective. A single bullet caught him in the throat, mortally wounding him. Although he died before earning his shield, he did earn a hero's funeral.

Alicia died in surgery two hours later. The day after the funeral, Shawna Jackson filed a petition for relief of custody of Jamal in the Richmond Juvenile and Domestic Relations District Court, which was granted with little fanfare. Nine-year-old Jamal went to live with foster parents Butch and Nancy Cox, who were far more interested in collecting the monthly stipend check from the Department of Social Services than parenting Jamal and his two foster brothers.

With no moral compass to guide him, Jamal quickly found himself in situations frowned upon by his foster care worker, and shortly thereafter, his probation officer. For the next nine years, Jamal bounced between Richmond's juvenile detention center, therapeutic foster care, and the Department of Juvenile Justice, which was basically juvenile detention for really naughty kids.

At the age of eighteen, Jamal was six feet, two inches tall, weighed 230 pounds, and had become the bane of the Richmond Department of Social Services. Every placement had failed, every attempt to set the boy on the right path had gone down in flames. He dealt drugs, he assaulted teachers, he spread STDs. On the day he turned eighteen, a juvenile court judge signed an order dismissing Jamal from foster care. That night, Jamal's exhausted social worker, a twenty-five-year veteran of the Department, gleefully drank three Bombay Sapphire martinis and passed out in a heap. The next day, she retired and moved to Maui.

Once he was out of foster care, Jamal really came into his own. First things first. He moved home to Ravenwood. He fell in with a gang called the Black Diamonds and quickly rose through the ranks. The Diamonds had cornered Ravenwood's open-air drug market and had spread their tentacles into prostitution and gambling. Like an eager intern with a Fortune 500 company, Jamal enthusiastically performed the Diamonds' dirty work. He carried drugs as a mule, he slapped around girls who got out of line, and he made sure people paid their unpaid balances.

Within a year of Jamal's joining, however, the Diamonds found themselves with a problem. Multiple problems, actually. Another gang, the Little Rascals, had started horning in on some of the business at Ravenwood and in the surrounding neighborhoods, long considered Diamond territory. Second, the Diamonds' titular heads were not exactly suited for executive positions. They had a poor understanding of price points and never quite grasped the neighborhood's geopolitical dynamic. They ordered hits on low-level Rascals, thugs whose passing would barely be noticed. They flooded the market with low-quality drugs, overcapitalizing as they did so.

In short, they were all broke and dying like flies.

On his twenty-first birthday, Jamal decided that he had seen enough. He recruited his two brothers from his first foster home, and on a chilly Halloween night, he solved all of the Diamonds' problems in one fell swoop. He shot and killed four top-level Rascals himself, ordered hits on two more that were carried out before the sun rose the next day. For good measure, he executed two Black Diamond bigwigs that had been particularly cruel to the younger Diamonds. By nightfall, he had commandeered all of the Diamonds' books, accounts, passwords and lists of suppliers and customers. The other Diamonds, thrilled to have someone step forward and take over, fell in line almost immediately, as did a number of the surviving Rascals. As a final wagon-circling maneuver, Jamal implemented a no-snitching policy in Ravenwood, to which both Diamonds and civilians adhered, lest they be found on the bank of the James River with two in the back of the head.

After taking power, he realized that he needed dependable cash streams, and so he had turned his focus on the wealthy western and northern suburbs. He built inroads into the community, which was quite the market for high-end cocaine and marijuana. He did not know it, but the late Ashley Pierce herself had been a loyal customer of the Black Diamonds. Rich high school kids and bored housewives had provided a never-ending gravy train down here. Things were good.

Then the mortgage crisis hit, and the banks got into trouble, and the automakers got into trouble, and jobs started disappearing, and then retail took a hit, and before you knew it, the rich suburbanites stopped coming down here, and business started to fall apart. Jamal followed the market, so he knew what was going on. The mid-level guys were getting nervous, asking him questions to which he did not have the answers. He was up nights, eating little, losing weight.

So when he had heard about two strangers poking around the Wood that morning, he thought it might be a sign.

JAMAL HEARD Scotty Mitchell's expletive just as Samantha reached into her inside pocket for the ticket. It was still pinched between her fingers when he drew his nine-millimeter pistol from his waistband. Something wasn't right; he could feel it in his bones. He pressed a single index finger to his lips, signaling the others to keep quiet, and dropped into a crouch. With the barrel of the gun, he waved Samantha and Pasquale into the kitchen, where a back door to the alley provided a means of escape. His guests skittered quietly into the dingy kitchen like frightened mice.

White people, he thought, watching them slip away. They always struck him as weak. Never had to face the shit he did. Soft. Pampered. All thanks to the color of their skin. It never ceased to amaze him. These two, though... The girl, she had risked life and limb to deliver the ticket to him. That had to be worth something. Least he could do was get her out of here with her head intact.

Plus, no one was getting this ticket from him. The news was still settling in, and the deeper it settled, the better it felt. All his prayers had been answered. Things in Raven-wood were going bad, and they were going bad fast. The Diamonds were going to run out of money soon; as it was, he had barely made payroll this week. And now this shining angel had strolled into his life and shown him the way out.

He slid backward against the wall, which the door would

swing inward against. It would give him a clear shot at anyone trying to break into the apartment. His Glock pistol was upright, the barrel tapping at his lips. Fear rippled through him, as it always did when he felt violence was at the doorstep. He never understood people who claimed to not be afraid in moments like this. Shit, there might be someone out there with a gun! With real bullets! His breath came in ragged gasps.

The door opened.

Jamal opened fire.

PASQUALE HURRIED Samantha through the narrow kitchen, out the back door and into the alley behind Jamal's building. The snowpack was deep out here, as high as three feet in some places where the wind had caught hold of it.

"We need to help him," Samantha said when they were on the back stoop. The alley was deserted. She turned back toward the door.

"Forget it," Pasquale said. "I am not letting anything happen to you."

"You're sweet," she said. "Get out of my way."

She drove her shoulder into his side, trying to squeeze in by the door, but he held firm like a statue.

"Sam," he said, "I'm a lot heavier than you. It's not happening."

"Come on! We can't just leave him there."

"The hell we can't!" he snapped at her. "I don't know what circle of hell we've walked into, or what we did to deserve it, but if we do not get out of here right now, we are going to end up dead."

"This is his ticket."

"Then leave it under his goddamn welcome mat," he said. "I'm not going to let you die here. I was all into this idea yesterday. But things have changed."

"Please," she begged. Tears streamed down her ice-crusted cheeks, creating the very odd image of steam misting off her face.

He looked back over his shoulder toward the door.

"We go around the front," he said. "Double back behind whoever was coming in. You stay behind me."

Pasquale jumped off the stoop and into a foot of snow, with Samantha trailing close behind him. They stayed close to the wall of the building, where the snow wasn't as deep and which gave them a bit of cover. At the corner of the building, he peered around toward the building's façade, where he saw the body of the late Piggy lying in the snow. The snow was tinged bright red, a biohazardous snow cone.

"Body at the front door," he whispered back to Samantha. "Can't see who it is."

Samantha sighed softly. She had seen more death today than she thought she would see in her lifetime. She couldn't even remember how many people had died today as a result of this stupid ticket, maybe not burning a hole through her pocket anymore, but most definitely burning one through her world. She tapped Pasquale on the shoulder.

"OK," she said. "You win. Let's get out of here."

"Good idea," Pasquale replied.

"That is a good idea!" a voice said behind her.

The pair turned to find Charles Flagg looking at them. He looked cold and pissed.

31

"**M**y goodness," Flagg said, pointing his gun at Samantha. "You two have been running me ragged. I am just exhausted. Hand it over. I've got places to be."

"Hand what over?" Samantha asked. She was desperate to extend things a bit, knowing that Carter's fate surely awaited them.

Flagg sighed. "Trying to drag things out a bit? Look, you can just give me the ticket now, and I kill you quick. But you're already burning what little goodwill you may have accumulated. Continue to give me a hard time, and I'll shoot you both in the stomach. I can assure you, it's a painful way to die."

"What if I don't have it on me?" she asked. "If you kill me, then you'll never find it."

"Oh, you've got it," he said. "If you're as smart as I think you are."

"Look, we give it to you, and we go our separate ways," Samantha said, terror coursing through her veins. "Why can't we do that? Why does it have to be like this?"

"I'm going to count to three," he said.

So this was it, she thought. Giving up the ticket now would be pointless. He could just shoot her and search her pockets for it. Death was at hand here. She was going to die in the alley of a housing project at thirty-four, her life a complete and total failure.

"One.

"Two.

As Flagg's tongue tightened up between his teeth to enunciate "three," the back door to Jamal's apartment blew open like a bomb had gone off. Flagg's head turned just a notch, one click of the dial. It gave Samantha and Pasquale the opening they needed.

Samantha rushed at his legs, while Pasquale launched himself at Flagg's midsection, swiping at the man's gun for the second time in their brief relationship. The still-warm gun dropped silently into the snow and sank into the drift like an anchor. Flagg stumbled backward against the sudden onslaught, but he kept his balance. Back on the stoop, two gunshots shattered the Christmas Eve silence. Sam's survival instinct kicked into overdrive; she grabbed Pasquale's right hand and staggered forward, away from the gunfire and toward the building.

Had he not been focused on the stinging, searing pain shooting up his thigh, Flagg would have been impressed by this display of self-preservation. A second bullet sliced through his shoulder. He grunted, wondering how he could have been so stupid. As he ducked for cover, he reflected back on the scene in Jamal's apartment.

Using Mitchell as a human shield, he had breached

Jamal's apartment like a battering ram. Jamal opened fire immediately, inadvertently shredding his bodyguard into ground beef. Flagg dropped Mitchell's body, its mission accomplished, and spun around the door. He found Jamal crouched in the corner and emptied three bullets into his torso before he could fire back. While Flagg paused to reload, Jamal kicked his legs out, toppling Flagg to the ground, and scampered down the dark hallway, trailing blood behind him. The corridor was pitch black, more so than Flagg was comfortable with. He willed himself to follow Jamal down the hallway, but he couldn't bring himself to do it. After emptying his clip into the blackness, he turned and followed Sam and Pasquale into the kitchen, thinking he really needed to do something about his fear of the dark.

Well, the mistake had been made, and there was nothing he could do about it now. He quickly forgot about the ticket, leaving Sam and Pasquale to scamper for cover. You had to have priorities. Bullets could kill. Quickly, he scanned the snow and found the gaping hole where his gun had punched through and dropped to the asphalt below.

With the gun in hand, he sank into the snow, using it as cover, and letting the cold numb the wound to his leg. A moment later, he peered over the top of the snowpack toward the back porch. What he saw amazed him. Jamal was leaning against the porch railing, his arm propped against the top of the old, splintered wood, his gun sweeping the area for a target. He was mortally wounded, blood trickling from the corners of his mouth. His face had paled to a dusky white, made all the starker given his naturally dark complexion. Dark red patches stained his clothes like he'd been busy making tomato sauce.

Flagg drew a bead on Jamal's head and slid his finger

around to the trigger guard. As he did so, Jamal's gun rotated back toward Flagg's position. Flagg could tell that he didn't have much left in him, but he did have something.

They both opened fire at the same time.

Jamal's final bullet flew wide and pinged off the cinderblock wall, spraying debris across the alley. Hot chunks of concrete splashed into the snow, causing it to sizzle. Not nearly as weak as Jamal, Flagg fired three times. Each bullet pierced Jamal's chest and finished the job Flagg had started back in Jamal's living room.

SILENTLY, Sam and Pasquale slipped through the courtyard, the sound of the last gunshot still ringing in Samantha's ears. A quick glance over her shoulder revealed a blanket of white behind them and nothing else. Ravenwood's denizens knew the drill, and so they would stay inside until the police cruisers surrounded the complex and they could walk and gossip among the safety of the blue uniforms.

The breezeway led them back out to Allen Avenue, where they turned north, across the expressway and back toward Samantha's Audi. It seemed to take an eternity, but when they clomped up alongside her car like a pair of Clydesdales, Sam noted that they'd only been gone for an hour. She leaned against the side of the car, exhaling slowly.

"Are you hurt?" Pasquale asked.

"No more than you," she answered.

"We need to get moving," Pasquale said, touching her back.

"Right," she said. "I have an idea."

After tucking the ticket into her jeans, she peeled off her coat and jammed it under the rear left tire of the car.

"Let's get out of here," she said.

Pasquale rocked his eyebrows upward. "You smart lady!"

They piled into the car, Samantha taking the wheel. She wrapped her fingers around the gearshift and gave it a little gas, praying that the tire would catch the coat. It spun briefly, sending her heart into her throat, before the radials latched onto the fabric and shot the car forward. The car rolled south one block to Grove Avenue, where Samantha turned west, away from the city.

"He's never going to leave us alone," she said as they puttered along, past the Victorian-style homes, Tudors, and Spanish-style haciendas that dotted the landscape. The further west they got, the fresher the snow was, the less disturbed. They were in the Fan, a neighborhood just west of downtown Richmond, so named because of its appearance on a map. A half-dozen streets threaded west through the neighborhood, fanning out from Belvidere near Virginia Commonwealth University.

Pasquale did not reply.

"We have to cash the ticket ourselves," she said. "After we cash it, he'll have no reason to chase us anymore."

"Except to kill us out of spite," Pasquale said.

She curled a bolt of her dark hair around her finger, silent.

"Yeah," she said. "I guess that's true."

"What are you going to do with the money?"

"I don't know. Maybe I'll buy the Dodgers. Maybe I'll buy this block of the Fan. I'll buy you the next one. There's a good burger place on it."

"Seriously."

"I could spend time tracking down Julius' other heirs."

"I thought he told you he didn't have any," Pasquale said.

"That doesn't mean there aren't any."

"Samantha."

"What? It's possible."

"I know that it's possible. But you'll be taking saliva samples until the end of time."

"I could donate it to charity," she said.

"That's one way to go," he said.

"You have a better idea?"

"I think you should keep it."

"What?"

"Look what you've gone through for it," he said. "Think about what you could do with it. Why not you? Consider it your severance package from Willett & Hall. Start a foundation. Make it your life's work. Pay yourself a salary, and put the rest to good work. You'd do a better job managing the money than any two-bit charity where people already are skimming off the top. Don't die for this ticket."

The idea ran through her like a well-strummed guitar note. What else could she do? The only two people with a legitimate claim to the ticket were dead. She didn't even know where to begin looking for any of Julius' other heirs. And she was tired. She was so tired. It seemed like every time she had blinked for the last three days, someone had died in front of her.

Would she ever get the ticket to its rightful owner, whoever that happened to be at this moment? Would she get killed before she could ever get it there? Was Pasquale's idea really that ridiculous? She could do a lot of good work with that money. She didn't need to get rich, did she? Sure, maybe bail out the folks, set them up for life. Balance the cosmic scales after the damage that her idiot brother had done. Give herself a comfortable living. Do good work. Never practice law again. These were not bad things. She was not a bad person. These thoughts cycled through her

mind like a hamster on a wheel as they continued west on
Grove Avenue.

"I'm really sorry you got caught up in all this," she said.
From the corner of her eye, she noticed him wince as he
shifted in his seat. "How're the ribs?"

"To be honest, they could use a little more sauce."

AS THE RUSH of adrenaline dissipated, like a quickly
dissolving thunderstorm, Flagg became acutely aware of the
pain in his leg. He examined the wound and was pleased to
discover that the bullet had flown clear through his leg,
exiting just above the knee. The one in his shoulder was a
bigger problem. It would require advanced attention and
would take weeks to heal. Fortunately, the snow had largely
stanched the bleeding from the wound, although that likely
would start up again when he was back indoors. He needed
to get first-aid supplies and some rest.

He pulled himself up, using the wall for support, and
began limping down Ravenwood's back alley. Above him,
Jamal's lifeless body dangled over the railing, but Flagg
never even looked up. He was too disgusted with himself.
This gangbanger had nearly been the end of him. Really
fantastic work, Charlie! Where's your head, man? Plus, he
really had to address this fear of the dark. It was getting a
little embarrassing. Really, Flagg? he thought to himself,
laboring through the snow. The dark?

An hour later, he found a home along Grove Avenue
that had been vacated for the holidays. Maybe he should
just switch careers. Breaking into homes was such child's
play, and they didn't get much easier than this. Four news-
papers, rolled tightly, were scattered across the porch. The

porch light was burning, and the driveway was knee-deep in snow, meaning no one had parked there in days. He found a spare key under a flowerpot, still sporting a long-since blackened husk of basil. The door swung open to reveal a pile of mail scattered haphazardly under the mail slot.

Once inside, he found a well-stocked bathroom just off the main hall. He gathered the necessary supplies, stripped down, got in the claw tub and went to work. First, he poured half a bottle of hydrogen peroxide on the entry wound and the rest on the exit wound, which was slightly larger as a result of the bullet expanding in flight. The wounds were clean, and he knew he was lucky. Guy like that might have been using cop-killers, which could have shredded his femoral artery. As it was, plenty of blood had spilled from the wound, coating the ceramic tub with a crimson sheen.

He cringed and groaned as the weak acid cleaned out the wound, but he knew that was nothing compared to the pain that lay ahead. Once that was done, he opened the bottle of rubbing alcohol. Without giving himself time to think about it, he sluiced it through the hole. It was a bit like dipping his leg into a roaring campfire. Screams of agony were piling up in the back of his throat like airliners waiting on a runway, but he managed to hold them back. Shiny tears rolled down his face, and he kept repeating his mantra in his head.

Survival of the fittest. Survival of the fittest. Survival of the fittest.

When he was done disinfecting the leg wounds, he threaded a long piece of dental floss, which he soaked with rubbing alcohol, through a disinfected sewing needle and stitched them closed. Afterwards, he dressed them with two large bandages and white medical tape. Then he turned his attention to the bullet in his shoulder. It had sliced through his shoulder blade but had not blown out the other side. He could feel it pressing just above his collarbone. Although it was not bleeding nearly as profusely, this one would be a bit more complicated than the clean leg wound.

He toddled down to the kitchen and found a large kitchen knife, which he disinfected with the rubbing alcohol. Back in the tub, he carved a small cylinder of tissue out of his shoulder around the bullet, as if he were coring a tomato. With the tip of the knife, he popped out the spent bullet, which clattered into the tub and traced a bloody semi-circle against the ceramic. He repeated the disinfection treatment with the gaping wound and dressed it in the same way as the leg wound. The pain was nothing short of apocalyptic, somewhere beyond what was normally possible to endure without losing consciousness. But Charles Flagg was not normal. He knew that. He had evolved.

His battlefield medical treatment was complete. As an added bonus, he found a nearly full bottle of cephalexin tablets in the medicine cabinet. He swallowed one right away, hoping that the antibiotics would help prevent any infection from setting in. It looked like there was enough for about a two-week course of treatment. Examining his dressings, he decided that he couldn't have done better had he gone to the emergency room. Professor Darwin would have been proud.

The idea of taking medication didn't thrill him, but evolution meant adapting to the world around you. Humanity, through its constant desire to overmedicate, had made bacteria infinitely stronger than they had been just a decade ago. Bacteria that humanity once may have fought off on its own had spawned generation after generation of superbugs. It gave him the willies just thinking about it.

A badly wounded but still-courteous houseguest, Flagg

rinsed his blood down the drain and pocketed the bullet. Really, it was the least he could do. He dressed quickly, but he felt listless, uneasy. Curiosity got the better of him, and he began exploring the various rooms of the house. In the dining room, he found a family portrait, professionally done, hanging on the wall. The patriarch was a heavyset suit type. The mother was not quite as rotund, but she looked like she could skip a meal or two. Her face was heavily made up, and she had a look of superiority on her face that Flagg wanted to slap away. The twin sons were tall and handsome.

Flagg didn't know quite what to make of this family. Darwinian success? Evolutionary kryptonite? The events of the last few days, starting with the disastrous telephone conversation with Olivia, weighed heavily on him. In this quest to find the ticket, he had encountered quite a range of humanity, as varied as any as he had ever faced in his career. His discoveries had surprised him.

Twice in the last three days, he had nearly died at the hands of people he had clearly underestimated. That business on the bridge – the kid had really shown some balls to try and save himself, or at least die on his own terms. He'd shown no hesitation at all. He knew that Flagg was going to kill him, and so he had done the only thing he could. And then this black kid, who could've just called 911 in an attempt to save himself, used his last dying breath to nearly turn Flagg into a historical footnote.

Was it possible that both would have made Professor Darwin proud? That they both had evolved into something worthwhile? That he had misinterpreted the great man's work? What if evolution took many forms? What if the human race was at the top of the evolutionary ladder because it could adapt to so many different environments? He didn't like where these thought processes were leading him, as if he were headed down a road and had just passed a Bridge Out sign.

A wave of fatigue washed over him, exhaustion that he had never experienced before. In the den, he found a thick microfiber couch with deep pillows. Just a few minutes, he thought. Just a few minutes. He lay down gingerly, wincing as he did so, and fell asleep almost immediately.

32

MONDAY, DECEMBER 24 - 6:00 P.M.

Christmas Eve dinner was supposed to be served at six, but predictably, things were running behind. Zaina didn't even have her makeup on at six, and makeup was a tremendously important piece of a Lebanese hostess' pre-game. What Zaina was doing at six was far more pedestrian: checking the kibbe, soaking the bulgur.

With Pasquale trailing behind, Samantha found her father in the den, drinking Arabic coffee and chatting with Hisham. He smiled broadly at her, and she felt heartbreakingly torn between her love for her father and her devotion to her mother.

"Hi, sweetheart," he said, putting down his paper. "What are you doing here?" Then he noticed Pasquale behind her.

"Pasquale! *Marhaba, habibe!*"

Omar leaned in after the traditional greeting and gave Pasquale a bear hug and kisses on both cheeks. Pasquale returned the favor.

"*Keefak?*" said Pasquale. *How are you?* Good heavens, her parents ate this stuff up.

"So good to see you, my boy!"

Samantha wished that her dad was a little more pissed off at the guy, given the emotional state his departure had left her in. There weren't many people, though, who dazzled like Pasquale Paoli.

"So, what are you all doing here?"

"I can't come for Christmas dinner?"

"No, it's not that," he said. "It just that we weren't expecting you tonight."

"Well," Samantha said, "it's Christmas. And Pasquale wanted to say hi."

She and Pasquale sat on the edge of the couch closest to the kitchen, opposite her father. As she looked around the room, the various mementos of her life staring back at her, she made a decision. She knew it was the right decision because she felt like she had become instantly realigned with her soul. It was the oddest sensation of her life.

"There's something I need to tell you," she said. "Mama should hear this, too.

"Zaina!" he barked out. "*Bin-teek haun!*" *Your daughter is here.*

Zaina rushed in from the kitchen, drying her hands on a threadbare hand towel. She squealed like a little girl when she saw Pasquale Paoli. She was just as big a fan as her husband.

"Pasquale!"

Samantha stood up and kissed her mother on each cheek.

"You stay to eat."

It was not a question.

"Sit down, Mama. I need to tell you guys something."

Zaina Khouri did not so much as sit down as she collapsed against the couch, her hand pressed against her heart.

"What is it?" she asked. "Are you sick? Omar, is she sick? You look sick. I knew something was wrong the other night."

It was safe to say that Zaina Khouri did not handle illness in her children well, and she tended to overreact to symptoms. When Samantha and her siblings were young, an unexplained bruise meant leukemia ("you shouldn't bruise so easily!"), a headache meant brain cancer ("you're too young for headaches!"), a sprained ankle meant ankle cancer ("your ankle should be strong!"). Samantha, naturally, had had her share of childhood illnesses, many of which she had concealed from her mother so as to spare her unnecessary worrying.

"No, Mama, I'm not sick! It's just a cold!" Sam left out her nagging concern that she might be dead by the New Year, but that, much to her mother's relief, would likely not be related to any disease.

"So here it is," she said. "After the holidays, I'm leaving my law firm. I'm not going to be a lawyer anymore."

"Are you getting married?" her father asked.

"No."

"Is it because you're sick?" her mother asked.

"Mama!"

"You don't look too good."

"No! I just don't want to be a lawyer anymore."

She watched her parents' reactions carefully. Her mother cried, which Samantha attributed to the fact that she had been the one to break through and get the education, fulfill the dream that had fueled her parents' move to America all those decades ago. That Samantha still planned on doing something with her life did not seem to occur to Zaina Khouri at the moment. Samantha knew that her mother had decided that she'd failed as a mother. Omar Khouri continued to sip his coffee without a word.

Hisham said nothing, wisely deferring to the man of the house.

"Hisham, can I talk to my parents for a few minutes alone?" Samantha asked.

"What, I'm not family?" Hisham barked, standing up in a huff. "I don't have anything to add?"

Samantha said nothing, because there was no point. He was offended in that macho Lebanese man way, and there was no undoing it now, even if she agreed to let him stay. He'd been eviscerated by a woman; he might never forgive her. That, she decided, she could live with. He stomped out of the room and made a beeline for the bar, where he'd pour a tall glass of *arak*, a potent Arabic liquor, and pout like a four-year-old.

"How bad is business, really?" Samantha asked when they were alone. "And tell me the truth."

Omar thoughtfully scraped a fingernail against his chin.

"It's fine, sweetheart," he said.

"Papa," she said, "come on."

"Don't worry about it," he said.

"Look, the reason I'm asking is that I want to buy the store from you," she said. "It's time for you guys to retire. Let me do this."

She sat quietly while her father processed this information, wondering where the hell she had come up with this idea.

"You cannot afford this," he said. "Can you?"

"Yes, we can," Pasquale said suddenly. "I'm bankrolling your daughter, Omar."

Omar took another sip of his coffee. From the corner of her eye, Samantha saw Pasquale wink at her.

"I love the store," Samantha said. "I know how important it is to you. It's important to all of us. I want to keep it alive."

"*Ya Allah,*" her mother said. Technically, it meant, "Oh, my God," but a looser translation was "Holy shit!"

Omar took a deep breath and let it out slowly, his chest deflating like a balloon. Samantha could almost see the stress and worry sluicing off his body like water rushing through a downspout.

"Yes," he said. "I want to hear more about this."

He did not consult with Zaina before making this decision, but Samantha did not expect him to. Zaina herself did not expect him to. It was just that kind of thing. If he decided that it was time to sell the store, then it was time to sell the store. Still, it made her smile to see her mother nodding her head vigorously.

"OK," Samantha said. "We'll get things started after the holidays."

"THAT'S QUITE an idea you've got there," Pasquale said, dunking a piece of pita bread into his hummus. Pasquale had an almost unholy love of hummus. He ate it by the gallon.

"Mmm," Samantha said, picking at her food. She hadn't eaten much.

They had drifted into the dim hallway, somewhat removed from the chaos of the family room. Still, even from here, Samantha could hear her sister Emily arguing with their cousin Hala about whether the kibbe had too many onions, and so they spoke in guarded whispers.

"You really want to do this?" Samantha asked.

"Yeah," Pasquale said. "I really do. I'm ready to come home. And that's wherever you are. I love that store. I think we could do a good job. You're not worried, are you?"

"I'm more worried about our little friend."

"He took two bullets," he said. "I think he's got other concerns."

"He managed to find us after you took him for that little swim."

"True. Look, if he shows up, we can just give him the ticket," he said. "He's not going to kill thirty Arabs."

"You sure about that?"

"Definitely. He'll probably think they're all terrorists anyway."

"Hilarious."

"OK, I'm not a hundred percent sure," he said. "Call it ninety percent."

"I can't stay here," she said, looking around. "I can't take the chance that he finds me here. If he came here and I wasn't here, I feel like they'd be OK. He'd have no reason to hurt them."

"Then we'll duck out of here after dinner," he said.

"Where will we go?"

"Somewhere," he said. "Can I finish eating first?"

"Sure," she said. Then, after a pause, she added: "What are you still doing here?" she asked.

"What do you mean?" he asked. "By the way, these are some damn good grape leaves."

"You came back at the drop of a hat. No questions."

"What can I say? I'm a hell of a guy."

She knew he was covering, that her questions were making him uncomfortable. His chewing slowed, and his eyes began drifting around the room. She touched his knee.

"You could've died. It would've been my fault."

"No, it would've been what's his name's fault."

"You know what I mean."

"Yeah, I know," he said. "I know. Look, for whatever

reason, this ticket became your responsibility, your cross to bear. It's nearly gotten us killed. You insisted on doing the right thing. I didn't want you to do it. All I could do is to try to keep you from getting hurt."

"And now?"

"Now? We've done all we can," he said. "Tomorrow, we lay low, and Wednesday you cash in the ticket. You do what you can."

"It doesn't seem right," she said.

"Right?" he repeated. "Was it right for Carter and his brother to kill Julius? Was it right for us to be hunted down by the goddamn boogeyman for the last forty-eight hours? If it hadn't been for you, Carter would be blowing this money on crystal meth and hookers for the next fifty years. Right? Look, if you want to try to find Julius' heirs, by all means, we can try. But let's do it in a way that doesn't risk your life and the lives of everyone around you. Remember what I told you at your place? That I hoped it never got out that you had the ticket? Look how many people have died. We both almost died."

"OK," she said, holding her palms up in surrender. "I get it. I get it."

But deep down, she wasn't sure she did.

33

Samantha lucked into a first-level parking spot in a public deck at the corner of 9th and Cary Street in the middle of downtown. For this, she was thankful, because she was freaking exhausted. After wedging her little coupe into a spot just a few steps from the street, she and Pasquale, both armed with expensive cups of coffee, set out toward lottery headquarters two blocks north on Bank Street. It was a cloudy, frigid morning, the mercury in the twenties, but the bulk of the storm had finally pulled away from the area. Long, high embankments of dirty snow flanked the street like bunkers as the snowplows worked to clear the roads.

As they turned left onto 9th Street, she caught a glimpse of herself in a reflective glass building panel. Yikes, she thought. She looked like hell. She was wearing jeans and a thick Florida State University sweatshirt, which she had found in her laundry one day in college. Its origin remained a mystery, as she did not know anyone who had ever gone to FSU, nor had she ever seen the sweatshirt before that day. It was her favorite item of clothing. The cold air felt good on her eyes, puffy and red from fatigue.

"You doing OK?" asked Pasquale.

"Just glad this is going to be over soon."

"How'd you sleep?"

She cut her eyes toward him without answering. This was her way of telling him, "not well." Pasquale took a quick sip of his coffee and glanced around the quiet buildings.

It had been two days since they'd skipped out on Christmas Eve dinner. Sam had spent the last two nights pacing around the two different hotel rooms they had stayed in, awaiting the opening of SuperLotto's Virginia headquarters. The first night, at a Holiday Inn Express just north of town, she sat in the uncomfortable chair by the door, which they blockaded with the dresser. She had considered reconsummating her relationship with Pasquale in the hopes it might relax her enough to fall asleep, but she thought such a maneuver likely would create a whole new set of issues she wasn't quite ready to deal with just yet.

She spent much of the time trying to convince herself to simply turn the ticket over to the police or some lottery official and that would be that. The problem was that she was a lawyer, and she knew human nature. She had seen firsthand the devastation wrought by the three-inch-square playslip, and yet she was having a hard time not cashing it for herself. Some good had to come from this terrible weekend.

So, instead, she had watched half a dozen reruns of *The Cosby Show* on Nickelodeon. At five, she watched the morning news on CNN, which had a brief bit about the SuperLotto ticket. The graphic banner striped across the bottom of the screen stunned her out of the chair and onto the floor, where she sat Indian-style and watched with rapt interest.

CLERK WHO SOLD $415 MILLION WINNING TICKET GUNNED DOWN

The same television reporter who had been so unhappy to report on the lottery mania three nights ago was really getting after it now. This was her star turn for the network, and she wasn't going to screw it up. Had Samantha seen her mailing it in a few nights earlier, she would have been amazed by the dramatic change. She used a snappy lead with strong verbs and scary adjectives.

"Police in Richmond, Virginia are hunting for a brutal killer this morning and asking whether the senseless murder of store clerk Carly Madison is connected to the winning $415 million ticket that she sold just two days earlier. There has been some speculation that the killer may have been looking for the ticket itself."

Gee, ya think?

They spent Christmas in a Red Roof Inn just south of town, the holiday meal consisting of fried chicken, mashed potatoes and cole slaw from a nearby grocery store. They ate on one of the two double beds in the room. She called her parents and wished them a Merry Christmas. They were not happy about her sudden and unexplained departure from Christmas Eve dinner, but there were no reports of a strange man looking for her.

That night, Pasquale took six more ibuprofen and was out within seconds of his head hitting the pillow. Sam drifted in and out of sleep. Her tidbits of slumber were punctuated by extremely bad dreams that involved an army of howler monkeys smoking cigars wrapped with thousand-dollar bills. By six, they were both showered and dressed and ready to go.

~

"HERE IT IS," Pasquale said, nudging Samantha with an elbow. The SuperLotto office was housed in a concrete-and-glass block between 9th and 10th Streets, just south of the Virginia Capitol.

"Here it is," Samantha repeated.

"So, do we need some kind of plan?" Pasquale asked.

"You mean, do we need to get our stories straight?"

Pasquale nodded.

"I've thought about that," she said. "They obviously know when and where the ticket was purchased. You know, it just occurred to me that we, on the other hand, don't know where Julius got it. If it comes up, I'll just say I asked a friend to buy me a ticket."

"Boy, you've got this all figured out for someone who doesn't want to cash the ticket."

"Please don't start with me," she said.

"Sorry."

"Here we go," she said.

Samantha took a deep breath and stepped into the rotating carousel door.

SUPERLOTTO OFFICES WERE like the wild teenagers of a family of banks. Sure, they looked like the other family members, with their crisp marble floors, cashiers working behind wood-paneled work stations and vaults full of cash. But instead of moodily taking money from quiet, well-behaved customers for safekeeping in low-interest-bearing accounts, this place shoveled cash out the door. Every day was like a fraternity kegger. The cashiers wore bright blue button-down shirts emblazoned with the SuperLotto logo, and classic rock thumped from hidden loudspeakers. A pair of wildly under-

trained armed guards patrolled the lobby, looking very official
with their uniforms and guns. A large electronic marquee
hung from the ceiling, displaying a series of rotating messages.

JACKPOT FOR THURSDAY'S DRAWING – $23 MILLION!

This one amused Samantha. The show must go on.

SUPERLOTTO – YOU'VE GOT TO BE IN IT TO WIN IT!

And you might get your head blown off to boot!

WINNERS – CHECK IN WITH CASHIER

Samantha threaded her way through the velvet ropes to
the front of the line. They were the first ones here. Behind
the counter, the cashiers were chitchatting and getting their
stations ready for the day. Samantha could hear some grum-
bling, and who could blame them? Who wanted to work the
day after Christmas?

Relax, you sad little elves, Samantha thought. This day is
about to get very exciting.

LAUREN WALSH WASN'T happy to be at work today. She had
put in a leave request a month ago, which had been
approved, but her bitch of a supervisor, Natalie, decided at
the last minute that she and the family were spending
Christmas at Vail. Suddenly, her approved leave request
went from Approved to "Sorry, you gotta haul your ass in
here." So this morning, she had pushed her way out the
door while her little boy clutched his new Thomas the Tank
Engine toys in his hands, giant crocodile tears streaming
down his little face. She hoped Natalie skied into a tree.
God, she hated this job.

As the first winners of the day approached her window,
she squeezed in a sip of Mountain Dew, the can hidden

under her work counter. The SuperLotto Policies and Procedures manual strictly prohibited cashiers from consuming food or beverage while manning their stations. She didn't care.

"Good morning," Lauren said, tucking the can below her desk.

"Hi," Samantha said. "I'm not really sure how this works." She held up the ticket.

"Let me take care of that," she said. "Got yourself a little Christmas bonus?"

"You could say that," Samantha said.

Mindlessly, Lauren took the ticket and waved her scanning wand over the bar code, which would verify the ticket's authenticity. Her computer responded strangely, drawing her gaze to the suddenly excitable monitor. A series of messages blinked angrily at her.

Ticket Authenticated: Notify Supervisor Immediately

Her heart pounding crazily in her chest, Lauren picked up her phone and dialed the on-duty supervisor. She couldn't believe it. This chick had won the whole goddamn jackpot. A tickle of envy crawled up her back like a bug.

"This is Lauren Walsh, Station 3."

SAMANTHA SAW the surprise in the cashier's face and wondered who she was calling. Probably the SWAT team. That's it, she was spending the next three years in federal prison. Defrauding the national lottery had to be a federal crime, right?

After a hushed discussion, Lauren hung up the phone and set a small SEE NEXT WINDOW placard on her desk.

"I need to take you upstairs," she said. "Hang on a minute."

Lauren came out from behind the counter and led them to a bank of elevators at the back of the lobby. Samantha could feel the woman's eyes boring in on her like a drill.

"Congratulations," Lauren said, while she waited for the elevator.

"Where are we going?" Pasquale asked.

"Upstairs," she said. "You'll meet with the regional manager, media relations, marketing, some other folks. Need to get you ready for the press conference. You know, the one with the oversized check? That sort of thing. It's going to be a big day."

The elevator doors whooshed open, and the trio stepped on board. They were silent during the fifteen-second trip to the third floor. When the doors slid open again, Samantha saw a nervous-looking man in a suit that was about two sizes too large waiting for them. A heavy-set woman stood by him.

"Hi, I'm Aaron Daggett," he said, strutting toward her with his hand extended. "Mid-Atlantic regional manager for SuperLotto. Congratulations!"

"Uh, thanks," Samantha said, taking his small, sweaty hand in her own. "Samantha Khouri. This is my friend Pasquale."

"Ms. Khouri, you are one lucky woman!"

If only you knew, she thought.

"I guess," she agreed. "A real long shot."

"You can say that again! Do you know the odds of winning the SuperLotto jackpot?"

Sam and Pasquale shook their heads.

"Well, believe me when I tell you they are pretty crappy."

"I bet they are."

"Hey, I'll take any bet you're taking! You're a lucky lady! I'm not washing this hand until I make it to Vegas!"

A few moments of awkward silence followed. Samantha cleared her throat.

"So what happens now?" she asked.

"Well," he said, coughing into his hand, "first things first. You need to put on this identification bracelet," he said. He looped a plastic bracelet stamped with a bar code onto her wrist.

"We're also going to fingerprint you and take your photograph. That way we'll always know you are who you say you are. Later this morning, we're going to fly you down to Atlanta. SuperLotto headquarters. That's where all the magic will happen."

"Magic?"

"Well, for one, it's where you will fill out all the necessary paperwork, decide whether you're taking the annual payout or the lump sum. Wait, wait, wait. I'm getting ahead of myself. Can I get you folks some coffee?"

Sam and Pasquale held up their cups.

"Right. You've got coffee. How silly of me. You have to understand, this is an exciting moment for our office. Biggest jackpot ever. And you won it!"

"Look," Samantha said. "I don't want a lot of hoopla."

"No hoopla?" he said, his face falling. "There's a news conference."

"I'm not really into that sort of thing," she said. "I really just played this on a whim. Asked someone to pick up a ticket for me. That's why I came in so early. I wanted to get it over with."

Aaron Daggett clicked his teeth together. He was obviously disappointed. Samantha didn't know why. Maybe he was planning to appear at the news conference with her.

"Do I have to do the news conference?" she asked.

"Well, we strongly encourage our players to appear at the news conference," he said. "You know, the whole oversize check and everything. It makes for quite a show."

"But I don't have to."

"No," said Daggett. "You don't. But we really think it's a lot of fun."

"Then I'll pass," she said. "Whatever the absolute minimum is to get my money. Please."

"Fine," he said. "Deb here will get you printed and photographed. I'll alert headquarters. The SuperLotto jet will be here soon."

"Jet?"

This seemed to get Daggett energized again.

"Yeah, a Gulfstream," he said. "They pick up all the jackpot winners in it. It's a really nice ride. You're going to love it."

An invisible cell phone began to ring.

Daggett held up an index finger. "Excuse me for a moment," he said, fishing the phone from his jacket pocket. He eased away from the group, but he remained within earshot.

"Aaron Daggett," he said. "Good morning, sir." A pause. "Yes, they're here now." Another pause. "I'll let them know."

Pasquale glanced over at Samantha, who shrugged her shoulders.

"Yes, sir, I will let them know," said Daggett.

He sauntered back to them, lightly tapping his palms together.

"Looks like you're getting a special visitor," said Daggett.

"Who's that?" Samantha asked, her mind flashing to Charles Flagg, back to finish his quest.

"The CEO."

"The CEO of what?"

"The CEO of Fool's Gold Trading Partners, LLC."

"What the hell is that?" asked Pasquale.

"Fool's Gold is the company that operates SuperLotto for the federal government."

"Why?" Sam asked.

"He didn't share that with me," Daggett said. "He just asked to meet you in the conference room in two hours. In the meantime, we can take care of the prints and the photograph."

"Fine with me," said Samantha.

TWO HOURS LATER, Samantha and Pasquale were in the conference room, sipping coffee from SuperLotto mugs. Theirs to keep. Samantha was pacing the room.

"Something weird is going on," she said. "They know we didn't buy the ticket."

"So? We didn't have to buy the ticket. It doesn't matter to them how we ended up with the ticket. All they care about is that we have the ticket. Besides, they wouldn't send the CEO. They'd send the police."

Pasquale had a point.

A knock on the door.

Samantha turned as the Chief Executive Officer of Fool's Gold Trading Partners, LLC, stepped into the room.

"Good morning," he said.

Samantha and Pasquale nodded toward him.

"I'm Arden McKinley."

34

Six years before Julius Wheeler bought his winning ticket at Lucky Lou's, a freshman Republican senator from Wyoming named Ted Dozier was looking to make a name for himself. He was a rising star in the party, and he had designs on a White House run in his future. First, though, he knew he needed to become a household name, lest he become one of these jokers in the primary debates that no one had ever heard of.

He read an article in The Economist about the popularity of national lottery games in Europe and decided that the U.S. government needed to horn in on some of the action. Why should the states have all the fun? A year into his term, he proposed Senate Bill 815, also known as the National Lottery Act, and almost immediately, the nation was transfixed by the prospect of a lottery jackpot growing exponentially each week.

Initially, members of Congress worried about muscling in on the state lotteries, which would, of course, be sacrificed at the altar of a national game. There were academic concerns about the Commerce Clause and the Fourteenth

Amendment, which most Americans neither understood nor gave a shit about. Early poll numbers indicated public support for the bill exceeded eighty percent nationwide. When the members of Congress realized that supporting the bill would grease their re-election campaigns, they quickly threw their full weight behind the Act. The bill was fast-tracked out of subcommittee, to the Appropriations Committee, and then to the Senate floor.

The bill quickly drew support from some heavy lobbies. The National Teachers' Council stepped up first when Senator Dozier announced that the bill would earmark seventy percent of the ticket sales for education. The Convenience Store and Gas Retailers Association just about fell over itself in support, as that lobby supported anything that got customers to drop more cash at the local quickie mart. The CSGRA was so excited it held two press conferences on the day that Senator Dozier introduced the bill.

Naturally, a handful of left-leaning Democrats argued passionately that the lottery was a regressive tax against poor people. Interestingly, the right-wing extremists had closed ranks with these same Democrats in opposition to the bill, but for a different reason. They believed that a national lottery was another step on the path toward a moral doomsday.

Despite this small but vocal minority, the National Lottery Act bill sailed through the Senate by an 86-14 vote. As public support for the bill swelled, the House over-whelmingly passed the bill, with only twenty-three votes against. The President signed the bill into law twenty-four hours later, creating the first nationwide lottery in American history. A rider to the bill provided that the government would not be responsible for the payment of any jackpot, nor would the government engage in any bailout of any lottery jackpot.

SuperLotto fever gripped the nation.

Before the first ticket could be punched, however, Congress needed someone to actually set up and run the lottery. A seven-member joint congressional committee was appointed to draft and issue an Invitation to Bid, a government procurement device designed to save taxpayers money by awarding government contracts to the lowest bidder, but which invariably cost them more when things went south and lawyers got involved. Four companies submitted bids, and Fool's Gold Trading Partners was awarded the contract when the committee declared it the only responsive bidder.

Four of the congressmen on the committee voted to declare the other three bidders as non-responsive. Not coincidentally, each of these public servants was treated to an all-expense paid trip to a destination of his choosing aboard Fool's Gold's corporate jet. This circumvention of the federal procurement and conflict of interest laws was made possible by the non-responsiveness loophole. You could drive a truck through it and no one would ever blink an eye. No one ever sought to close the loophole in the laws because there was too much graft at stake.

Fool's Gold, which had helped a dozen states get lotteries up and running, went to work immediately. It hired an advertising firm, which proposed three names for the lottery, including SuperLotto, MegaBucks and CashBomb. Focus groups responded least favorably to CashBomb, as it reminded them of Islamic terrorism, and most favorably to SuperLotto, especially the logo, which consisted of an anthropomorphic dollar bill, a big shit-eating grin on his face, decked out in a top hat and cane. His name was Bucky, and he was a colossal marketing coup. Within weeks, even before tickets went on sale, Bucky's image was slapped on the side of coffee mugs and lunchboxes, city buses and subways.

Upon the award of the contract, Fool's Gold Trading Partners, LLC moved into a sparkling new high-rise in downtown Atlanta and spared no expense in decorating and furnishing the place. Within two weeks, it had hired fifteen hundred new employees. Server farms and satellite offices were set up across the country, deals for the television and Internet broadcast of the weekly drawing were negotiated, playslips were designed, lottery machines were designed and tested. And most importantly, insurance policies were purchased. With seventy percent of ticket sales tagged for education and another twenty percent dedicated to payroll, overhead and operating expenses, these policies were critical, the game's life support system. Fool's Gold was self-insured for the first $10 million, but larger jackpots were insured through Meridian Risk Management Solutions.

Meridian happily guaranteed these jackpots through a complicated series of insurance and reinsurance plans that tempered its own exposure. Risk, after all, was just another commodity in a capitalist market. It was bought and sold like corn.

"WHY DON'T WE HAVE A SEAT?" McKinley said, taking one at the head of the long oak table. Samantha thought he may have stumbled a bit.

"Ohh-kay," Samantha said. She took a random seat about two-thirds of the way down the long edge of the table. Pasquale sat in between her and McKinley.

Sam noted McKinley was wearing an expensive suit, but

his tie was loosened, and his shirttail dangled over the front of his belt. It looked like it hadn't been tucked in for a while. It looked like it hadn't been changed in a while. Kind of a rough look for a big executive in the middle of the morning. She also thought she detected a hint of vodka in the air.

"So, congratulations, and all that," he said.

"Uh, thanks."

"That is a lot of money," he said, emphasizing the word 'lot.'

Samantha nodded.

"So," he said, "do tell me how you ended up with this little gem!"

"I was at work," she said. "A guy was buying tickets, and I asked him to get one for me."

"Really!" he said loudly. "Marvelous. That's just marvelous."

Sweat was beading on his forehead.

"You know that this is the biggest jackpot in SuperLotto history, right?"

"Yes, I think they talked about it on the news."

"The news," he said. "I like the news."

"Mr. McKinley, is something wrong?" Pasquale said.

"Is something wrong?" he repeated.

With that, he drew out a flask from his inside pocket and took a very long swig.

"I'm guessing that's not orange juice," Samantha said.

McKinley slapped the table and laughed out loud.

"Wanna pull?"

Samantha shook her head.

"What about you, cowboy?" McKinley said, tipping the flask toward Pasquale. "You look like you enjoy a good drink."

"Look, Mr. McKinley, if we could just get this show on the road, that would be great."

He took another drink.

"There isn't going to be any show," he said. His mood darkened considerably.

Samantha put her hands on the table and started to open her mouth.

"If I may," McKinley said, holding up one palm to silence his grand prize winner. "If I may."

Hoping to get something out of this nutjob, she leaned back in her chair.

"Let me tell you a story," he said. "When Fool's Gold won the contract to operate SuperLotto, it had a lot to do. Can you guess what the most important thing it had to do was?"

He looked first at Pasquale, then at Samantha. Neither spoke. A dull cord of worry began to wrap itself around her like a python squeezing its prey.

"I'm talking too fast for you," he said. "Let me axe you a question, as the blacks say. Where do you think the money comes from to pay out these jackpots?"

Again, Pasquale and Sam remained silent.

"You probably think ticket sales, right?"

"I guess that's part of it," Samantha said. She said it just to say something. He was worried that if he didn't say anything, McKinley might start to think he was hallucinating.

"Well, you'd be wrong," he said.

He took one final pull from the flask, draining the last bit of vodka. When it was empty, he tossed it onto the table.

"You'd be wrong," he repeated softly.

That was when everything fell into place for Samantha. McKinley's appearance, the strange tale he was telling.

"What the hell is going on here?" Pasquale asked.

"The insurance," Samantha said. "He's telling us the jackpot wasn't insured. There's no money to pay the jackpot."

"Tell her what she's won, Gene!" he barked, thinking back to that horrible phone call he'd received while Krista danced her beautiful dance on the macaroni and cheese three nights ago.

"IT WAS SUPPOSED to go out Wednesday," Bernard Shelton, SuperLotto's chief financial officer, had said.

"What are you talking about?" McKinley had asked angrily. Then: "Jesus. Don't say it."

"I'm sorry, sir."

He felt lightheaded.

"Did you hear me, sir?"

"No. Tell me again, because I can't fucking believe my ears."

Arden felt his insides drop, as if the scaffolding holding up his guts had failed. He had to go to the bathroom very badly all of a sudden, but his legs refused to respond to his commands. He became quite certain that if he didn't get to the bathroom quickly, he was going to soil himself. And yet, there he stood, the wireless phone glued to his ear, unable to move. Stark terror filled him like wet concrete. For a moment, he considered asking Krista to hold his face in the macaroni until he stopped breathing. That would be a fate preferable to the one he now likely faced.

"Bernie, would you please care to tell me how this could have happened?"

He was shouting now, his legs firing again, carrying him around the room. The urge to eliminate had passed, but that was because Arden McKinley had pissed his pants. He didn't even notice, as his energies were focused on the apocalypse that now faced his company.

"It was supposed to go out Wednesday," Bernie said in a small voice, referring to the monthly premium that kept the insurance policy alive. The insurance policy that protected Fool's Gold from being on the hook for the tens of millions of dollars it awarded each month.

"Yes, I know that it was supposed to go out Wednesday, Bernie," said Arden, totally oblivious to Krista and the macaroni and cheese congealing around her ankles and feet. "The goddamn janitors know that it's supposed to go out Wednesday. What I am trying to figure out is why it did not go out. See the difference, you idiot?"

"It was supposed to go out on Wednesday," repeated Bernie. McKinley let it go. There was nothing else to say. Short of building a time machine and traveling back two days, there wasn't a whole hell of a lot they could do. Who cared why it didn't go out? It wouldn't change anything.

"My office," Arden said. "Thirty minutes."

Thirty minutes later, Arden McKinley was sipping scotch and water (mostly scotch) while pacing the perimeter of the Fool's Gold executive conference room. He had completed about two dozen laps around the giant conference table while Bernard Shelton and Victoria Dean, Super-Lotto's chief operating officer, leafed nervously through the Meridian insurance policy. McKinley knew that nothing was going to change the fact that Thursday night's jackpot had been uninsured. He told them to keep reading, however, because to stop meant to admit that they were one hundred percent screwed.

"Here's a question!" Arden suddenly barked out.

He cleared his throat and fired the empty tumbler

against the wall, where the lead crystal exploded like a
bomb. Tiny shards of glass cut his face, but he didn't seem
to notice. Thin trails of blood streamed down his cheeks
like crimson tears, and the image bothered Bernard
Shelton for the rest of his days. The two underlings sat
silently, both expecting the same exact question, both
knowing the same answer, both knowing that they
wouldn't even have to answer, that their silence would be
enough.

"Does the company even have that much cash on hand? I
mean, let's say our lucky winner shows up on Wednesday
morning – and thank God for Christmas, it's the only lucky
break we caught – is our big check going to bounce?"

Victoria turned her attention to the SuperLotto Operations Manual, as if the answer was tucked inside. Shelton
continued leafing through the insurance policy while he
debated the pros and cons of informing his boss that at the
moment, Fool's Gold Trading Partners, LLC currently had
$21 million in cash on hand, spread across a number of
different accounts.

"Yeah, I didn't think so," he said softly. "I didn't think so."

Arden McKinley, his face bleeding, took the seat at the
far end of the table and grabbed a coaster. He slid it like a
hockey puck between his two palms, leaving a trail of
condensation underneath. A jackpot that his company
couldn't pay. The one goddamn thing the company was
supposed to do. This would be his life's legacy.

He tried to picture what would happen when the winner
came forward with the ticket. For prizes between fifty
dollars and $5,000, winners visited a local SuperLotto satel-
lite office, where their winning tickets were verified, certified
and paid by cashier's check. The jackpot winners also
visited the satellite offices, but, after their tickets were veri-

fied, were flown to Atlanta, where a press conference was held, and the oversized check was handed to the winner.

In this case, however, things were likely to unfold a little differently.

Well, congrats on the big win. Here's the thing. We're coming up just a little short on cash here. And oh, by the way, the company filed for bankruptcy protection this morning in a federal district court in Atlanta. You probably won't see a dime. Thanks for playing.

SuperLotto! You've got to be in it to win it!

Undoubtedly, Arden would have to appear before a congressional subcommittee to answer many, many uncomfortable questions. Hundreds of people would be out of work. The winner would sue Fool's Gold, tying it up in litigation for the next five years. He wondered briefly, the thought draped in terror, if he could be indicted for something like this.

"Can someone please turn on the television?" Arden asked quietly.

Shelton got up and turned on the small LCD television mounted in the corner of the room. The TV was tuned to the local Fox affiliate, currently broadcasting a *Seinfeld* rerun. Arden stared blankly at the screen.

"We can always hope the winner doesn't cash it in," Victoria said.

"What?" said Arden, morbidly depressed. He had been estimating the odds of a giant asteroid striking Earth between now and Wednesday. That would probably get him off the hook. Probably pretty slim. There was always a chance, though. The Discovery Channel made it seem like there was a goddamn assembly line of asteroids lining up to punch a hole in the planet.

"You know, if the ticket isn't cashed in six months, it's

void," Victoria said. "Maybe we'll get lucky, and the winner never steps forward. Loses the ticket or something."

"I don't think that's a very realistic thing to think about," said Shelton. "And we certainly shouldn't put any faith in such an outcome."

Arden ignored Shelton's retort, focusing instead on what Victoria had said. In particular, he zeroed in on the part about "if the ticket isn't cashed." Suddenly, it became clear. If the ticket wasn't cashed, then the jackpot prize wasn't paid out. It happened from time to time, especially on the tickets winning smaller prizes, those that hit on three, four or even five of the winning numbers. Shit, it was something!

"Where was the winning ticket sold again?" Arden asked.

"A little convenience store in downtown Richmond, Virginia."

Right, thought McKinley. It was sort of appropriate, almost poetic. Richmond was like Atlanta's goddamn spiritual brother! Both cities burned to the ground during the Civil War, and both were populated with families who longed to pack the towns up into time machines and zip on back to the mid-nineteenth century. This was a sign, McKinley thought. Of what, exactly, he was not sure.

The edges of a plan began to form in Arden McKinley's head. If the way out of this mess was ensuring that the winning ticket never saw the light of day, then he had to find the ticket. Find it and destroy it. How to find it, though? And who would find it? Who could be trusted to find it and not try to cash it in for himself? He couldn't think of anyone who wouldn't do just that.

The ticket, while virtually worthless to the winner, was now a fatal disease that had infected the company. If he could find someone to track it down, it would be a simple matter of convincing him that the ticket was a cancer metastasizing in the company's body and, like a tumor, it needed to be cut out. Although McKinley could promise a hefty bounty for the ticket's return, or proof of its destruction, any attempt to cash the ticket would void the reward.

Finally, one name bubbled to the surface. A name he'd heard bandied about by other businessmen he golfed with, went to strip clubs with, did deals with. Yup, McKinley had remembered thinking, this just might work.

Apparently, it had not.

"As SOON AS your ticket was authenticated this morning," he said, "Fool's Gold Trading Partners, LLC, filed for bankruptcy in the U.S. Bankruptcy Court in Atlanta. We've been waiting for you all weekend."

"This is unbelievable," Samantha said. "I cannot believe I am hearing this."

There was a remote control sitting on the table, which McKinley used to power up a flat-screen television mounted in the corner. He changed it to CNBC, where yet again, Samantha saw a Breaking News graphic that affected her directly.

COMPANY OPERATING SUPERLOTTO FILES FOR BANKRUPTCY PROTECTION

The graphic cycled to another equally ominous message.

JACKPOT UNINSURED: NO ADDITIONAL PRIZES FROM DECEMBER 20 DRAWING TO BE PAID

"Wait a minute," Pasquale said, getting up from his chair, still wincing from the broken ribs, and striding toward McKinley. "Did you send that psychopath after us to steal the ticket back?"

"What are you talking about?" he asked, half-heartedly. He was so drunk, he actually started to giggle.

"You did, didn't you, you asshole? You thought if you stole the ticket back, you'd get away with it. You could keep living the good life, flying around in your fucking Gulfstream."

"Sorry about that," McKinley said. "Can you blame me for trying?"

"That psychopath has been trying to kill us for three days!"

Pasquale grabbed McKinley by the collar. Samantha hustled up behind him and pulled him off the inebriated CEO.

"Do you have any idea how many people he's killed?" he said after he'd collected himself.

"Hey, I just told him to get the ticket back!" he said. "I didn't tell him to kill anyone."

"You're a worthless piece of shit," he said.

"Let's get out of here," Samantha said, laying a hand on Pasquale's shoulder. "It's over."

MCKINLEY WAITED until they were gone and then smoked a cigarette in the peaceful silence of the conference room. That had been really uncomfortable, but hey, he'd gotten through it. He'd get through this. He checked his watch; it was almost lunchtime. He was in the mood for cheesy pasta, a craving he attributed to his fond memories of Krista. He'd have a drink in the car on the way to Mamma Zu's, a well-known Italian restaurant in a section of town called Oregon Hill.

On his way to the elevator, he passed a smaller conference room, where Daggett was delivering the bad news to Lauren Walsh and her co-workers. Through the glass, he could see some of them crying. A few were holding hands.

Time to make himself scarce.

He rushed out the door onto Bank Street, where his limousine was waiting. He had to get out of here before the FBI impounded his car or arrested him or did whatever it was they did to a CEO when a giant company went belly up. He noticed a handwritten sign reading CLOSED UNTIL FURTHER NOTICE had been posted to the front door of SuperLotto headquarters.

"Yikes," he said softly, climbing into the plush rear of the limousine. When shit went bad, it went bad in a hurry.

Immediately, he tapped on the glass divider to signal the driver, Gus Victorino, to get a move on and turned his attention to the bar. McKinley was annoyed that Victorino couldn't even be bothered to open the door for him. What the hell was the point of having a driver if he couldn't handle such a basic task? That most certainly would be reflected in his tip.

"Can you pour me one?" a voice behind him asked. It startled him so badly, he dropped his crystal tumbler on the floor. He turned to see a ghastly looking figure sitting in the corner, shaded by the dim light.

"Hey, who the hell are you?"

"I'm Charles Flagg."

Flagg switched on the light above him, revealing every bit of the battle he'd been waging for the last three days.

"Flagg? Jesus, you look like hell! What are you doing here?"

"I'm here to see you," Flagg said.

"How the hell did you find me? I never even told you who I was!"

"Do you think I just got in this business?"

"Fine. Whatever. Actually, I'm glad you're here," McKinley said. "I want to tell you to your face that I'm not paying you another dime. She cashed the ticket! You know what that means?"

"I'm not asking for any payment."

"Good," replied McKinley. "You know, you really cocked things up. You let that bitch outsmart you? I can't fucking believe it! You're done in this business. Trust me. You'll never work again."

"What can I say? She beat me fair and square. She has evolved."

"Evolved? What the hell are you talking about?"

"Unlike you, she would make Professor Darwin proud."

McKinley was apoplectic now, his neck veins rippling like eels. "I hired you to do a job, a simple job, and you failed in every way, shape and form."

"My understanding of evolution has grown exponentially," Flagg said. "I don't call that a failure."

"Well, Congress would beg to differ."

"Your legal and financial issues do not concern me."

"Well, they concern me. I'll probably have to sell the condo at Vail now."

"You're pathetic."

"And you're a total loser."

"I have to ask," Flagg said. "What was the insurance policy? The one that would prevent me from cashing the ticket myself?"

"I made a digital recording of your voice when I hired you," McKinley said. "I then had it loaded into the company database. The voiceprint analysis would have identified you as an employee of the company, ineligible to win any prizes."

"Not that it would have mattered," Flagg said.

"What makes you say that?"

"Well, for one, the ticket, was, and always has been, worthless."

"Yeah, but as long as no one tried to cash the ticket, then the company wouldn't have gone belly up."

"That doesn't make any sense," Flagg said. "You didn't need the insurance policy." He was dealing with a real idiot here.

"Just get out of here," McKinley said, waving his hand over his shoulder. He turned to pour himself a scotch.

"That's the first intelligent thing I've ever heard you say," Flagg said. "A good one to end things on."

It was then, too late for it to make any difference, that McKinley realized that the car was still idling at the curb.

"Hey–" he said, turning back toward his visitor.

Flagg drew his pistol and fired a single shot into McKinley's head. Shaking his head at the man's shocking arrogance, Flagg stepped out onto the street and slipped into the empty driver's seat. The driver's body was slouched in the passenger seat.

Flagg shifted the car into drive and eased away from the curb. He turned west onto Main Street and disappeared into the city.

EPILOGUE

Samantha Khouri and Pasquale Paoli were questioned for hours by the Richmond City Police Department, the Henrico County Division of Police and the Federal Bureau of Investigation. With the exception of a few minor details, each gave remarkably similar accounts of the events leading up to Fool's Gold's bankruptcy filing, and both were cleared of any wrongdoing.

After a thorough investigation, Detective Douglas Byrd concluded that Carter Pierce was responsible for the murders of Todd Matheson and Julius Wheeler, and the cases were closed.

On extremely short notice, Meridian Risk Management Solutions, the company that would have insured Julius' jackpot, gave each of its employees a $1,000 bonus and threw an extremely large and extravagant New Year's Eve party.

Pasquale proposed marriage to Samantha on New Year's Day, exactly one year after her brother's suicide bomb attack. After careful consideration, she accepted his offer, and they were married eight months later. Shortly after she and Pasquale returned from their honeymoon, Samantha received a package with no return address. Inside the envelope was a dog-eared copy of Charles Darwin's *On the Origin of Species*.

Samantha and Pasquale purchased the grocery store from her parents, who retired. The store's new owners kept it afloat until the day the vice president of acquisitions of a large grocery store chain stopped in and tried Samantha's hummus. He loved it and began ordering it in bulk. Within a few months, it became the chain's best-selling international item. Samantha began adding more ready-made food items to the store's lineup, and a year later, she spun that division off the store and sold it for $3.5 million.

Senator Ted Dozier (R-Wyoming) convened congressional hearings to investigate the stunning collapse of Fool's Gold Trading Partners, LLC. The hearings lasted three days and were hastily adjourned when CNN broadcast grainy video it had received of Dozier accepting a bribe from the late Arden McKinley. SuperLotto was suspended, and the National Lottery Act was quickly repealed by a piece of hastily drafted emergency legislation.

Stunned by the shocking and violent deaths of her parents, Madison Pierce buckled down, graduated from medical school with honors and became a successful psychiatrist in Coral Gables, Florida.

Cameron Pierce, who reacted differently, died three years later after a botched robbery attempt of, coincidentally, the same bank where Jamal Wheeler's mother met her end. She was buried next to her parents.

Seven months after Carter's death, Dawn Robertson gave birth to a healthy baby boy, whom she named Carter. Twelve years later, after attending law school, she became a partner at Willett & Hall.

The Richmond Commonwealth's Attorney declined to

prosecute Monk for the deaths of Leroy Marshall and his brother Tommy, finding sufficient evidence of justifiable homicide.

The bankruptcy trustee appointed to handle the Fool's Gold bankruptcy retained the Atlanta office of Willett & Hall as counsel for the plaintiffs in the matter of *Unknown Heirs of Julius D. Wheeler vs. Fool's Gold Trading Partners, LLC*. Despite an exhaustive search, the firm was unable to positively identify a single living blood relative of either Jamal or Julius Wheeler. The case remains under an Order of Stay in a federal district court in Atlanta.

Fool's Gold Trading Partners, LLC, never emerged from bankruptcy and was quietly liquidated.

The murders of Jimmy Burrell, Bryan Stewart, Carly Madison, Mark Jenks, Carter Pierce, Ashley Matheson Pierce, Dr. Roger Bouzein, Piggy, Scotty Mitchell, Jamal Wheeler, Gus Victorino, and Arden McKinley remain unsolved.

Charles Flagg's whereabouts are unknown.

ABOUT THE AUTHOR

David lives in Virginia, where he works as a novelist. *The Jackpot* was his first book and was a No. 1 Legal Thriller on Amazon.

He is the author of *The Immune*, *The Living*, *Anomaly*, and *The Nothing Men*.

He is also the creator of a viral series of animated comedy films about law and publishing. They were featured on CNN, in the *Washington Post*, the *Huffington Post*, and the *Wall Street Journal*.

ALSO BY DAVID KAZZIE

THE IMMUNE (2015)

THE LIVING (2017)

ANOMALY (2018)

THE NOTHING MEN (2019)

Printed in Great Britain
by Amazon